Kanthapura

Kanthapura

by Raja Rao

New Directions

COPYRIGHT © 1963 BY RAJA RAO.

LIBRARY OF CONGRESS CATALOG CARD NUMBER: 63-18637

ISBN: 0-8112-0168-6

PUBLISHED BY ARRANGEMENT WITH
OXFORD UNIVERSITY PRESS BOMBAY.

FIRST PUBLISHED BY GEORGE ALLEN & UNWIN, LTD., LONDON, 1938.

REPRINTED BY OXFORD UNIVERSITY PRESS, BOMBAY, 1947.

FIRST PUBLISHED AS NEW DIRECTIONS PAPERBOOK 224 IN 1967.

PUBLISHED IN CANADA BY MC CLELLAND & STEWART, LTD.

COVER PHOTOGRAPH COURTESY INFORMATION SERVICE OF INDIA,
NEW YORK.

MANUFACTURED IN THE UNITED STATES OF AMERICA.

NEW DIRECTIONS BOOKS ARE PUBLISHED FOR JAMES LAUGHLIN
BY NEW DIRECTIONS PUBLISHING CORPORATION,
333 SIXTH AVENUE, NEW YORK 10014.

FIFTH PRINTING

CONTENTS

AUTHOR'S FOREWORD

There is no village in India, however mean, that has not a rich
sthala-purana, or legendary history, of its own. Some god or godlike
hero has passed by the village—Rama might have rested under this
pipal-tree, Sita might have dried her clothes, after her bath, on this
yellow stone, or the Mahatma himself, on one of his many pilgrimages through the country, might have slept in this hut, the low one,
by the village gate. In this way the past mingles with the present,
and the gods mingle with men to make the repertory of your grandmother always bright. One such story from the contemporary annals
of a village I have tried to tell.

The telling has not been easy. One has to convey in a language
that is not one's own the spirit that is one's own. One has to convey the various shades and omissions of a certain thought-movement
that looks maltreated in an alien language. I use the word "alien,"
yet English is not really an alien language to us. It is the language
of our intellectual make-up—like Sanskrit or Persian was before—
but not of our emotional make-up. We are all instinctively bilingual, many of us writing in our own language and in English. We
cannot write like the English. We should not. We cannot write
only as Indians. We have grown to look at the large world as part
of us. Our method of expression therefore has to be a dialect which
will some day prove to be as distinctive and colorful as the Irish or
the American. Time alone will justify it.

After language the next problem is that of style. The tempo of
Indian life must be infused into our English expression, even as the
tempo of American or Irish life has gone into the making of theirs.
We, in India, think quickly, we talk quickly, and when we move
we move quickly. There must be something in the sun of India
that makes us rush and tumble and run on. And our paths are paths
interminable. The *Mahabharata* has 214,778 verses and the *Rama-*

vii

yana 48,000. The *Puranas* are endless and innumerable. We have neither punctuation nor the treacherous "ats" and "ons" to bother us—we tell one interminable tale. Episode follows episode, and when our thoughts stop our breath stops, and we move on to another thought. This was and still is the ordinary style of our story-telling. I have tried to follow it myself in this story.

It may have been told of an evening, when as the dusk falls, and through the sudden quiet, lights leap up in house after house, and stretching her bedding on the veranda, a grandmother might have told you, newcomer, the sad tale of her village.

RAJA RAO
1937

NOTES

A note on the Indian pronunciation and English transliteration of Sanskrit names.

Certain letters in Sanskrit, from which modern Indian languages are derived, are pronounced differently in different parts of the country, and the system of transliteration into English often varies. This is particularly true of the three Sanskrit "s" sounds and the soft "t." Thus the name of the god Shiva is sometimes written Siva, though always pronounced Shiva; the heroine of Kalidasa's play is pronounced Shakuntala, but sometimes written Sakunthala; and the princess Damayanti (in Sanskrit) would be written and pronounced Damayanthi in parts of South India. The spellings in this edition of *Kanthapura* follow those of the Oxford University Press (Bombay) edition of 1947.

The author's notes on Indian terms and references which may be unfamiliar to American readers will be found at the back of the book. They are grouped by chapters and arranged in the sequence in which the words appear in the text.

Kanthapura

1

OUR VILLAGE—I don't think you have ever heard about it—
Kanthapura is its name, and it is in the province of Kara.
High on the Ghats is it, high up the steep mountains that face
the cool Arabian seas, up the Malabar coast is it, up Mangalore and
Puttur and many a centre of cardamom and coffee, rice and sugar
cane. Roads, narrow, dusty, rut-covered roads, wind through the
forest of teak and of jack, of sandal and of sal, and hanging over
bellowing gorges and leaping over elephant-haunted valleys, they
turn now to the left and now to the right and bring you through
the Alambè and Champa and Mena and Kola passes into the great
granaries of trade. There, on the blue waters, they say, our carted
cardamoms and coffee get into the ships the Red-men bring, and,
so they say, they go across the seven oceans into the countries where
our rulers live.

Cart after cart groans through the roads of Kanthapura, and on
many a night, before the eyes are shut, the last lights we see are
those of the train of carts, and the last voice we hear is that of the
cartman who sings through the hollows of the night. The carts pass
through the main street and through the Potters' lane, and then
they turn by Chennayya's pond, and up they go, up the passes
into the morning that will rise over the sea. Sometimes when Rama
Chetty or Subba Chetty has merchandise, the carts stop and there
are greetings, and in every house we can hear Subba Chetty's
350-rupee bulls ringing their bells as they get under the yoke.
"Ho," says Subba Chetty, "hé-ho," and the bulls shiver and start.
The slow-moving carts begin to grind and to rumble, and then we
hear the long harsh monotony of the carts' axles through the darkness. And once they are on the other side of the Tippur hill the
noise dies into the night and the soft hiss of the Himavathy rises
into the air. Sometimes people say to themselves, the Goddess of

the river plays through the night with the Goddess of the hill. Kenchamma is the mother of Himavathy. May the goddess bless us!

Kenchamma is our goddess. Great and bounteous is she. She killed a demon ages, ages ago, a demon that had come to demand our young sons as food and our young women as wives. Kenchamma came from the Heavens—it was the sage Tripura who had made penances to bring her down—and she waged such a battle and she fought so many a night that the blood soaked and soaked into the earth, and that is why the Kenchamma Hill is all red. If not, tell me, sister, why should it be red only from the Tippur stream upwards, for a foot down on the other side of the stream you have mud, black and brown, but never red. Tell me, how could this happen, if it were not for Kenchamma and her battle? Thank heaven, not only did she slay the demon, but she even settled down among us, and this much I shall say, never has she failed us in our grief. If rains come not, you fall at her feet and say "Kenchamma, goddess, you are not kind to us. Our fields are full of younglings and you have given us no water. Tell us, Kenchamma, why do you seek to make our stomachs burn?" And Kenchamma, through the darkness of the temple sanctum, opens her eyes wide— oh! if only you could see her eyelids quicken and shiver!—and she smiles on you a smile such as you have never before beheld. You know what that means—that every night, when the doors are closed and the lights are put out, pat-pat-pat, the rain patters on the tiles, and many a peasant is heard to go into the fields, squelching through the gutter and mire. She has never failed us, I assure you, our Kenchamma.

Then there is the smallpox, and we vow that we shall walk the holy fire on the annual fair, and child after child gets better and better—and, but for that widow of a Satamma's child, and the drunkard Dhirappa's brother's son, tell me, who ever has been taken away by smallpox? Then there was cholera. We gave a sari and a gold trinket to the goddess, and the goddess never touched those that are to live—as for the old ones, they would have died one way or the other anyway. Of course you will tell me that young Sankamma, Barber Channav's wife, died of it. But then it was not for nothing her child was born ten months and four days after he

2

was dead. Ten months and four days, I tell you! Such whores always die untimely. Ramappa and Subbanna, you see, they got it in town and our goddess could do nothing. She is the Goddess of Kanthapura, not of Talassana. They ought to have stayed in Talassana and gone to Goddess Talassanamma to offer their prayers.

"O Kenchamma! Protect us always like this through famine and disease, death and despair. O most high and bounteous! We shall offer you our first rice and our first fruit, and we shall offer you saris and bodice-cloth for every birth and marriage, we shall wake thinking of you, sleep prostrating before you, Kenchamma, and through the harvest night shall we dance before you, the fire in the middle and the horns about us, we shall sing and sing and sing, clap our hands and sing:

> Kenchamma, Kenchamma,
> Goddess benign and bounteous,
> Mother of earth, blood of life,
> Harvest-queen, rain-crowned,
> Kenchamma, Kenchamma,
> Goddess benign and bounteous.

And when the night is over, and the sun rises over the Bebbur mound, people will come from Santur and Kuppur, people will come from the Santur Coffee Estate and the Kuppur Cardamom Estate, from coconut gardens and sugar cane fields, and they will bring flowers and fruit and rice and dal and sugar candy and perfumed sweetmeats, and we shall offer you all, dancing and singing —the bells will ring, the trumpets tear through the groves, and as the camphor rises before you, we shall close our eyes and hymn your praise. Kenchamma, Great Goddess, protect us! O Benign One!"

Our village had four-and-twenty houses. Not all were big like Postmaster Suryanarayana's double-storied house by the temple corner. But some were really not bad to look at. Our Patwari Nanjundia had a veranda with two rooms built on to the old house. He had even put glass panes to the windows, which even Postmaster Suryanarayana could not boast of. Then there were the Kannayya-house people, who had a high veranda, and though the house was I know not how many generations old, it was still fresh

3

and new as though it had been built only yesterday. No wonder that Waterfall Venkamma roared day and night against Rangamma. "Why should a widow, and a childlesss widow too, have a big house like that? And it is not her father that built it," said she. "It's my husband's ancestors that built it. I've two sons and five daughters, and that shaven widow hadn't even the luck of having a bandicoot to call her own. And you have only too look at her gold belt and her Dharmawar sari. Whore!" And so, night and day did she howl, whenever she met Temple Lakshamma or Bhatta's wife Chinnamma coming back from the river. To tell you the truth, Venkamma's own house was as big and well-built as her sister-in-law's. But she said it was not large enough for her family. Besides, she could not bear the idea that it was occupied by Rangamma's father and mother, and when the vacations came Rangamma had all her younger brothers, and the children of the elder one from Bombay—"all those city-bred fashionable idiots"— to spend the summer. "Tell me," said Venkamma one day to Akkamma, bringing forward her falling sari over her shaven head, "why should our family feed theirs? If her parents are poor, let them set fire to their dhoti and sari and die. Oh, if only I could have had the courage to put lizard-poison into their food! Well that will come too." She would clap her hands and go into her house leaving Front-house Akkamma to hurry up her steps.

Akkamma had people come to visit them. You know, Coffee-planter Ramayya is a cousin of her sister-in-law, and when he is on his way to Karwar he sometimes drops in to see them—and even spends a night there. He left his Ford on the other side of the river, for the ferry did not ply at night, and he came along. Today he is there and people are all busy trying to see him. For midday meal he will have a vermicelli *paysam* and Patwari Nanjundia and his son-in-law are both invited there. There are others coming too. The Temple people and the Figtree-house people, and Dorè, the "university graduate" as they call him. He had lost his father when still young and his mother died soon after, and as his two sisters were already married and had gone to their mothers-in-law, he was left all alone with fifteen acres of wet land and twenty acres of dry land. And he said he would go to the city for "higher studies" and went to a university. Of course, he never got through the Inter even—but he had city ways, read city books, and even called himself a Gandhi-man. Some two years ago, when he had come back from Poona, he had given up his boots and hat and suit and had taken to dhoti and khadi, and it was said he had even given up his city habit of smoking. Well, so much the better. But, to tell you the truth, we never liked him. He had always been such a braggart. He was not like Corner-house Moorthy, who had gone through life like a noble cow, quiet, generous, serene, deferent and brahmanic, a very prince, I tell you. We loved him, of course, as you will see, and if only I had not been a daughterless widow, I should have offered him a granddaughter, if I had one. And I know he would have said: "Achakka, you are of the Veda Sastra Pravina Krishna Sastri's family, and is it greater for you to ask something of me, or for me to answer 'Yea'?" He's the age my Seenu is, and he and Seenu were as, one would say, our Rama and brother Lakshamana. They only needed a Sita to make it complete. In fact, on that day, as everybody knew, Coffee-planter Ramayya had come to offer his own daughter to Moorthy. But the horoscopes did not agree. And we were all so satisfied. . . .

Till now I've spoken only of the Brahmin quarter. Our village had a Pariah quarter too, a Potters' quarter, a Weavers' quarter, and a Sudra quarter. How many huts had we there? I do not know. There may have been ninety or a hundred—though a hundred may be the right number. Of course you wouldn't expect me to go to the Pariah quarter, but I have seen from the streetcorner Beadle Timmayya's hut. It was in the middle, so—let me see—if there were four on this side and about six, seven, eight that side, that makes some fifteen or twenty huts in all. Pockmarked Sidda had a real *thothi* house, with a big veranda and a large roof, and there must have been a big granary somewhere inside, for he owned as much land as Patwari Nanjundia or Shopkeeper Subba Chetty, though he hadn't half Kanthapura as Bhatta had. But lately, Sidda's wife went mad, you know, and he took her to Poona and he spent much money on her. Bhatta of course profited by the occasion and added a few acres more to his own domain. Clever fellow this Bhatta! One day he was sure to become the zamindar of the whole village

—though we all knew him walking about the streets with only a loincloth about him.

The Potters' street was the smallest of our streets. It had only five houses. Lingayya and Ramayya and Subbayya and Chandrayya owned the four big houses, and old Kamalamma had a little broken house at the end of the street where she spent her last days with her only son. Formerly, they say, the Potters' street was very flourishing, but now, with all these modern Mangalore tiles, they've had to turn to land. But Chandrayya still made festival-pots, and for Gauri's festival we've always had our pots done by him. He makes our images too and he even sold them at the Manjarpur fair. The rest of the Potters were rather a simple, quiet lot, who tilled their lands and now and again went out to the neighbouring villages to help people to make bricks.

Now, when you turned round the Potters' street and walked across the temple square, the first house you saw was the nine-beamed house of Patel Rangè Gowda. He was a fat, sturdy fellow, a veritable tiger amongst us, and what with his tongue and his hand and his brain, he had amassed solid gold in his coffers and solid bangles on his arms. His daughters, all three of them, lived with him and his sons-in-law worked with him like slaves, though they owned as much land as he did. But then, you know, the Tiger, his words were law in our village. "If the Patel says it," we used to say, "even a coconut-leaf roof will become a gold roof." He is an honest man, and he has helped many a poor peasant. And heavens! What a terror he was to the authorities!

The other Sudras were not badly fed householders and they had as usual two or three sons and a few daughters, and one could not say whether they were rich or poor. They were always badly dressed and always paid taxes and debts after several notices. But as long as Rangè Gowda was there, there was no fear. He would see them through the difficulties. And they were of his community.

The Brahmin street started just on the opposite side, and my own house was the first on the right.

Between my house and Subba Chetty's shop on the Karwar road was the little Kanthapurishwari's temple. It was on the Main street promontory, as we called it, and became the centre of our life. In fact it did not exist more than three years ago, and to tell you the truth, that's where all the trouble began. Cornerhouse Narsamma's son, Moorthy—our Moorthy as we always called him—was going through our backyard one day and, seeing a half-sunk linga, said, "Why not unearth it and wash it and consecrate it?" "Why not!" said we all, and as it was the holidays and all the city boys were in the village, they began to put up a little mud wall and a tile roof to protect the god. He was so big and fine and brilliant, I tell you, and our Bhatta duly performed the consecration ceremony. And as Rangamma said she would pay for a milk and banana libation and a dinner, we had a grand feast. Then came Postmaster Suryanarayana and said, "Brother, why not start a *Sankara-jayanthi?* I have the texts. We shall read the *Sankara-Vijaya* every day and somebody will offer a dinner for each day of the month." "Let the first be mine," said Bhatta. "The second mine," said Agent Nanjundia. "The third must be mine," insisted Pandit Venkateshia. "And the fourth and the fifth are mine," said Rangamma. "And if there is no one coming forward for the other days, let it always be mine," she said. Good, dear Rangamma! She had enough money to do it, and she was alone. And so the *Sankara-jayanthi* was started that very day.

It was old Ramakrishnayya, the very learned father of Rangamma, that said he would read out the *Sankara-Vijaya* day after day. And we all cried out, "May the Goddess bless him," for there was none more serene and deep-voiced than he. We always went to discuss Vedanta with him in the afternoons after the vessels were washed and the children had gone to school. And now we gathered at the Iswara's temple on the promontory, instead of on Rangamma's veranda. How grand the *Sankara-jayanthi* was! Old Ramakrishnayya read chapter after chapter with such a calm, bell-metal voice, and we all listened with our sari fringes wet with tears. Then they began to lay leaves for dinner. And one boy came and said, "I shall serve, aunt!" And another came and said, "Can I serve *paysam*, aunt?" And another came and said, "I shall serve rice, aunt," and this way and that we had quite a marriage army and they served like veritable princes. Then, when we had eaten and had washed our hands, the younger women sang, and we discussed the *maya-*

7

vada, and after that we went home. We hastily pushed rice onto the leaves of the young and came back for the evening prayers. There used to be bhajan. Trumpet Lingayya with his silver trumpet was always there, and once the music was over, we stayed till the camphor was lit, and throwing a last glance at the god, we went home to sleep, with the god's face framed within our eyes. It was beautiful, I tell you—day after day we spent as though the whole village was having a marriage party.

Then sometimes there used to be *Harikathas*. Our Sastri is also a poet. You know, the Maharaja of Mysore had already honoured him with a palace shawl, and Sastri had just sent His Highness an epic on the sojourn of Rama and Sita in the hill country. They said he would soon be honoured with a permanent place in the court. And he is a fine singer, too. But he is an even grander *Harikatha*-man. When he stood up with the bells at his ankles and the cymbals in his hands, how true and near and brilliant the god-world seemed to us. And never has anyone made a grander *Harikatha* on Parvati's winning of Siva. He had poetry on his tongue, sister. And he could keep us sitting for hours together. And how we regretted the evening the *Sankara-jayanthi* was over. The air looked empty.

But by Kenchamma's grace it did not end there. The next morning Moorthy comes to us and says, "Aunt, what do you think of having the Rama festival, the Krishna festival, the Ganesh festival? We shall have a month's bhajan every time and we shall keep the party going."

"Of course, my son," say we, "and we shall always manage each to give a banana libation if nothing else."

"But," says he, "to have everything performed regularly we need some money, aunt."

"Money!"

It made us think twice before we answered, "And how much money would you need, my son? But, if it's camphor, I'll give it. If it's coconut, I'll give it. If it's sugar candy . . ."

"No, aunt," says Moorthy, "it's not like that. You see, aunt, while I was in Karwar we had Rama's festival and Ganapati's festival, and we had evening after evening of finest music and *Harikatha* and gas-light processions. Everybody paid a four-anna bit and we had so much money that we could get the best *Harikatha*-men like Belur Narahari Sastri, Vidwan Chandrasekharayya . . ."

"Do you think they'll come here?" say I.

"Of course, aunt. And what do you think: pay them ten rupees and give them their cart fare and railway fare and that'll do. They don't ask for palanquins and howdahs. And we shall have *Harikathas* such as no one has ever heard or seen in Kanthapura."

"All right, my son. And how should we pay?"

We know Moorthy had been to the city and he knew of things we did not know. And yet he was as honest as an elephant. "One rupee, aunt. Just one rupee. And if there is some money left, we shall always use it for holy work. You understand, aunt? That is what we did in Karwar."

"Yes," say I, though a rupee was a lot to me. I have seven acres of wet land and twelve acres of dry land and they yield just enough for my Seenu and me to have our three meals a day. A rupee! It was a twenty-fifth of my revenue, and tell me, when did we ever pay it in time? But the rupee is for the gods. And it is Moorthy that asks for it. We always bless him.

So Moorthy goes from house to house, and from younger brother to elder brother, and from elder brother to the grandfather himself, and—what do you think?—he even goes to the Potters' quarter and the Weavers' quarter and the Sudra quarter, and I closed my ears when I heard he went to the Pariah quarter. We said to ourselves, he is one of these Gandhi-men, who say there is neither caste nor clan nor family, and yet they pray like us and they live like us. Only they say, too, one should not marry early, one should allow widows to take husbands and a brahmin might marry a pariah and a pariah a brahmin. Well, well, let them say it, how does it affect us? We shall be dead before the world is polluted. We shall have closed our eyes.

So, he goes, Moorthy, from house to house, from householder to householder, and—what do you think?—he gathers a hundred and forty-seven rupees. Everybody says, "Take it, my son." And Rangamma gives him a ten-rupee note and says, "Last harvest, when Ramayya's Chennayya had paid back his mortgage loan, I asked,

9

'What shall I do with this money?' and I sent a hundred rupees to a brahmin orphanage in Karwar. Well, money spent there or here, it is all the same to me." And then Agent Nanjundia pays two rupees, his son the teacher pays one, and his sister's husband pays two, three, or four, I don't quite remember, and so goes Moorthy gathering money in his ascetic's bowl. And what a grand festival we had the following *Ganesh-jayanthi*. There were reading parties and camphor ceremonies every evening, and our young men even performed a drum and sitar bhajan. And it was on one of those evenings that they had invited Jayaramachar—you know Jayaramachar, the famous *Harikatha*-man? They say he had done *Harikatha* even before the Mahatma. And a funny *Harikatha*-man he is too, sister.

"Today," he says, "it will be the story of Siva and Parvati." And Parvati in penance becomes the country and Siva becomes heaven knows what! "Siva is the three-eyed," he says, "and Swaraj too is three-eyed: Self-purification, Hindu-Moslem unity, Khaddar." And then he talks of Damayanthi and Sakunthala and Yasodha and everywhere there is something about our country and something about Swaraj. Never had we heard *Harikathas* like this. And he can sing too, can Jayaramachar. He can keep us in tears for hours together. But the *Harikatha* he did, which I can never forget in this life and in all lives to come, is about the birth of Gandhiji. "What a title for a *Harikatha!*" cried out old Venkatalakshamma, the mother of the Postmaster. "It is neither about Rama nor Krishna."—"But," said her son, who too has been to the city, "but, Mother, the Mahatma is a saint, a holy man."—"Holy man or lover of a widow, what does it matter to me? When I go to the temple I want to hear about Rama and Krishna and Mahadeva and not all this city nonsense," said she. And being an obedient son, he was silent. But the old woman came along that evening. She could never stay away from a *Harikatha*. And sitting beside us, how she wept! . . .

This is the story Jayaramachar told us.

In the great heavens, Brahma, the self-created one, was lying on his serpent, when the sage Valmiki entered, announced by the two doorkeepers. "Oh, learned sire, what brings you into this distant world?" asked Brahma, and, offering the sage a seat beside him,

10

fell at his feet. "Rise up, O God of Gods! I have come to bring you sinister news. Far down on the earth you chose as your chief daughter Bharatha, the goddess of wisdom and well-being. You gave her the sage-loved Himalayas on the north and the seven surging seas to the south, and you gave her the Ganges to meditate on, the Godavery to live by, and the pure Cauvery to drink in. You gave her the riches of gold and of diamonds, and you gave her kings such as the world has never seen! Asoka, who loved his enemies and killed no animal; Chandragupta, who had the nine jewels of wisdom at his court; and Dharmaraya and Vikramaditya and Akbar, and many a noble king. And you gave her, too, sages radiating wisdom to the eight cardinal points of the earth, Krishna and Buddha, Sankara and Ramanuja. But, O Brahma, you who sent us the prince propagators of the holy law and sages that smote the darkness of ignorance, you have forgotten us so long that men have come from across the seas and the oceans to trample on our wisdom and to spit on virtue itself. They have come to bind us and to whip us, to make our women die milkless and our men die ignorant. O Brahma, deign to send us one of your gods so that he may incarnate himself on earth and bring back light and plenty to your enslaved daughter . . ."—"O sage," pronounced Brahma, "is it greater for you to ask or for me to say 'Yea'? Siva himself will forthwith go and incarnate himself on the earth and free my beloved daughter from her enforced slavery. Pray seat yourself; the messengers of heaven shall fly to Kailas and Siva be informed of it."

And lo, when the Sage was still partaking of the pleasures Brahma offered him in hospitality, there was born in a family in Gujerat a son such as the world has never beheld! As soon as he came forth, the four wide walls began to shine like the kingdom of the sun, and hardly was he in the cradle than he began to lisp the language of wisdom. You remember how Krishna, when he was but a babe of four, had begun to fight against demons and had killed the serpent Kali. So too our Mohandas began to fight against the enemies of the country. And as he grew up, and after he was duly shaven for the hair ceremony, he began to go out into the villages and assemble people and talk to them, and his voice was so pure, his forehead so brilliant with wisdom, that men followed him, more and more men followed him as they did Krishna

11

the flute-player; and so he goes from village to village to slay the serpent of the foreign rule. Fight, says he, but harm no soul. Love all, says he, Hindu, Mohammedan, Christian or Pariah, for all are equal before God. Don't be attached to riches, says he, for riches create passions, and passions create attachment, and attachment hides the face of truth. Truth must you tell, he says, for truth is God, and verily, it is the only God I know. And he says too, spin every day. Spin and weave every day, for our Mother is in tattered weeds and a poor mother needs clothes to cover her sores. If you spin, he says, the money that goes to the Red-man will stay within your country and the Mother can feed the foodless and the milkless and the clothless. He is a saint, the Mahatma, a wise man and a soft man, and a saint. You know how he fasts and prays. And even his enemies fall at his feet. You know once there was an ignorant Pathan who thought the Mahatma was a covetous man and wanted to kill him. He had a sword beneath his shirt as he stood waiting in the dark for the Mahatma to come out of a lecture hall. The Mahatma comes and the man lifts up his sword. But the Mahatma puts his hands on the wicked man's shoulders and says, "Brother, what do you want of me?" And the man falls at the feet of the Mahatma and kisses them, and from that day onwards there was never a soul more devoted than he. And the serpent that crossed the thighs of the Mahatma, a huge serpent too. . . .

And there were other stories, he told us, Jayaramachar. But hardly had he finished the *Harikatha* and was just about to light the camphor to the god, than the Sankur police jemadar is there. Moorthy goes to him and they talk between themselves, and then they talk to Jayaramachar, and Jayaramachar looks just as though he was going to spit out, and we never saw him again. Our Moorthy performed the camphor ceremony and from that day onwards Moorthy looked sorrowful and calm. He went to Dorè and Sastri's son, Puttu, and Puttu went to Postmaster Suryanarayana's sons, Chandru and Ramu, and then came Pandit Venkateshia and Front-house Sami's son, Srinivas, and Kittu, and so Kittu and Srinivas and Puttu and Ramu and Chandru and Seenu, threw away their foreign clothes and became Gandhi's men.

Two days later, Policeman Badè Khan came to live with us in Kanthapura.

12

2

To tell you the truth, Badè Khan did not stay in Kanthapura. Being a Mohammedan he could stay neither in the Potters' street nor in the Sudra street, and you wouldn't of course expect him to live in the Brahmin street. So he went to Patwari Nanjundia and growled at him, and the Patwari trembled and lisped and said he could do nothing. "Only the Patel can do something." Then, straight went Badè Khan to the Patel and said, "Hè, Patel. The Government has sent me here, and I need a house to live in."

"Hm," said Patel Rangè Gowda, crossing the threshold onto the veranda, "a house. Well, you can look round and see. I can't think of one for the moment." He opened his betel-bag and carefully taking a tobacco leaf, he seated himself, and wiping the tobacco leaf against his dhoti, he put it into his mouth, then put an areca nut with it and began to munch.

Badè Khan was getting restless. Not only did the Patel look indifferent but he hadn't even asked Badè Khan to seat himself. So, he went up the three steps and sat by a pillar, his feet hanging down the veranda and his stick between his legs. They were silent for a moment. Then, "Hè, Chenna," cried Rangè Gowda, turning toward the inner courtyard, "you had better go to the big field and see whether those sons of concubines are planting well. And tell Mada to hurry back before midday and fill the carts with sacks. Tomorrow is the fair."

Meanwhile the cattle were coming out of the main door, the whitey, the blotchy, and the one-horned one and Lakshmi and Gauri, and then the bulls and buffaloes, and they hurried down the steps ringing their bells and banging their clogs, and young Sidda was behind them, his stick in his hand and the dung-basket on his head. Badè Khan could not see Rangè Gowda, and he spat nervously into the gutter and sat dropping the lathi-ring on the

13

steps. Rangè Gowda looked up, then put a lime-smeared betel-leaf into his mouth and said, "So you want a house, police sahib? I am sorry I have none to offer you."

"You are the representative of the Government and I have a right to ask you to offer me a house."

"Representative of the Government," repeated the Patel. "Yes, I am. But the Government does not pay me to find houses for the police. I am here to collect revenue."

"So you are a traitor to your salt-givers!"

"I am not a traitor. I am telling you what is the law!"

"I didn't know you were such a learned lawyer too," laughed Badè Khan. "But a final word. Will you oblige me by procuring me a house or not?"

"No, police sahib. I tell you humbly I cannot. I am not the owner of the whole village. But if there is anyone who is ready to offer you a house, please take it and turn it into a palace. I can see no objection to that." He still munched his tobacco, and pasting the betel-leaves with lime, he put them into his mouth and munched on.

"You don't know who you're speaking to," Badè Khan grunted between his teeth as he rose.

"I know I have the honour of speaking to a policeman," the Patel answered in a singsong way. Meanwhile his grandson, the little Puttu, came out, and he took the child in his arms and laid him on his lap and tickled him under the armpits to make him laugh. Badè Khan went down one step, two steps, three steps, and standing on the gutter-slab, growled at the Patel, "The first time I corner you, I shall squash you like a bug."

"Enough! Enough of that," answered the Patel indifferently. "You'd better take care not to warm your hands with other's money. For that would take you straight to the pipal tree. . . ."

"Oh, you—!" spat Badè Khan, trying not to swear, and once he was by Sampanna's courtyard he began to grumble and growl, and he marched on, thumping over the heavy boulders of the street. At the temple square he gave such a reeling kick to the one-eared cur that it went groaning through the Potters' street, groaning and barking through the Potters' street and the Pariah street, till all the

14

dogs began to bark, and all the cocks began to crow, and a donkey somewhere raised a fine welcoming bray.

So Badè Khan went straight to the Skeffington Coffee Estate and he said, "Your Excellency, a house to live in?" And Mr. Skeffington turned to his butler and said, "Give him a hut," and the butler went to the maistris' quarters and opened a tin shed and Badè Khan went in and looked at the plastered floor and the barred windows and the well near by, and he said, "This will do," and going this way and that, he chose a Pariah woman among the lonely ones, and she brought along her clay pots and her mats and her brooms, and he gave her a very warmful bed.

The next day, and the day after and the day after that, we saw nothing more of Badè Khan. Some said he went to bring the Police Inspector. Others said he was only a passing policeman who had come to squeeze money out of people. But on the fourth or fifth day, Postman Surappa went up the Front-house steps, and seating himself by grandfather Ramanna, asked for a pinch of snuff and told him, just in passing, that there was a policeman of some sort in the Skeffington Estate. And they all cried out and said: "Oh, Surappa, you had better tell those tales to whitewashed walls. Nobody who has eyes to see and ears to hear will believe in such a crow-and-sparrow story. It was a passing policeman. And he wanted to make money by terrorizing the ignorant. One has seen so many of these fellows. And once they have a rupee in their hand or a dozen coconuts or a measure of rice, they walk away and are never heard of again."

But Waterfall Venkamma would have none of this. "Policemen do not come along like that in these civilized days," she mocked. "I know why they've come. They've come because of Moorthy and all this Gandhi affair. He with his kitchen she-friends and all this bragging city-talk!" and she spat into the street. And, as everybody knew, she had no particular love for Moorthy. He had refused her second daughter, for whom bridegroom after bridegroom was being sought—and she was nearing *the* age. And then there was that other affair. Moorthy was so often at the "next-house-woman's kitchen," as she used to say. Since that *Sankara-jayanthi* Moorthy

15

was always to be seen going up the Kannayya-house steps and then he would come out sometimes in one hour, sometimes in two hours, and sometimes in three hours, and he even took others of his gang with him too. They said Rangamma's house was now becoming something of a Congress House, and there they were always piling books and books, and they had even brought spinning wheels from the city. The expulsion of Jayaramachar from Kanthapura had made a big noise in the city, and the Karwar Congress Committee had written to Moorthy to go and see them. And when he had gone to see them, they had given him books and papers and spinning wheels, and all this for nothing, it was said! And that was why our boys were so busy now. They went to the Sudra quarters and the Potters' quarters and the Weavers' quarters and they cried, "Free spinning wheels in the name of the Mahatma!" And it was Moorthy who came to the Brahmin street. "Sister," says he to Nose-scratching Nanjamma, "sister, the Congress is giving away free spinning wheels. Will you spin, sister? You see, you have nothing to do in the afternoons after the vessels are washed and the water drawn, and if you spin just one hour a day, you can have a bodice-cloth of any colour or breadth you like, one bodice-cloth per month, and a sari every six months. And, during the first month, the cotton is given free."

"May I ask one thing, Moorthy? How much has one to pay?"

"Nothing, sister. I tell you the Congress gives it free."

"And why should the Congress give it free?"

"Because millions and millions of yards of foreign cloth come to this country, and everything foreign makes us poor and pollutes us. To wear cloth spun and woven with your own God-given hands is sacred, says the Mahatma. And it gives work to the workless, and work to the lazy. And if you don't need the cloth, sister—well, you can say, 'Give it away to the poor,' and we will give it to the poor. Our country is being bled to death by foreigners. We have to protect our Mother."

Nanjamma does not know what all this is about. Brahmins do not spin, do they? "My son, we have weavers in the village. There is Chennayya and Rangayya. . . ."

"Yes, sister. But they buy foreign yarn, and foreign yarn is bought with our money, and all this money goes across the oceans.

16

Our gold should be in our country. And our cotton should be in our country. Imagine, sister," says he, seating himself, "you grow rice in the fields. Then you have mill agents that come from Shola-pur and Bombay and offer you very tempting rates. They pay you nineteen rupees a khanda of paddy instead of eighteen rupees eight annas, as Gold-bangle Somanna or Mota Madanna would pay. They will even pay you nineteen rupees and two annas, if you will sell more than twenty khandas. Then they take it away and put it into huge mills brought from their own country and run by their own men—and when the rice is husked and washed and is nothing but pulp, they sell it to Banya Ramanlal or Chotalal, who send it by train to Banya Bapanlal and Motilal, and Bapanlal and Motilal send it to the Tippur Fair, and Subba Chetty and Rama Chetty will cart twenty sacks of it home. And then you have no rice before harvest, and there's your granddaughter's marriage, for example, or your second daughter is pregnant and the whole village is to be invited for the seventh-month ceremony. You go to Subba Chetty and say, 'Hè Chetty, have you fine rice?'—'Why, I have fine white rice,' says he, and shows you rice white and small as pearls, all husked and washed in the city. And you say, 'This looks like beautiful rice,' and you pay one rupee for every three and a half seers. Now tell me, Nanjamma, how much does Husking-Rangi ask from you for every twenty measures of paddy?"

"Why it all depends. Sometimes it is six and a half and some-times it is seven, with seven measures of fodder-husk."

"Now, sister, calculate and you will see. You get six seers to the rupee, not to speak of the fodder-husk, instead of seven, and your rice does not go into the stomach of Rangi or Madi, but goes to fatten some dissipated Red-man in his own country. Now, do you understand, sister?"

"Well, if I say 'Yes,' what then?"

"And then—you sow, and your harvest is grand this year. And more people come from Bombay and Sholapur. And they bring bigger carts and larger money-sacks. Then you say, 'They pay twenty rupees a khanda this year. If I keep my rice it is all such a bother measuring it out to Rangi and measuring it back from her and quarreling over her measures.' And there are the rats and the worms and the cattle, and then you have to pay revenue, and

17

Bhatta's interest. And, who knows, rice may go down in price, as it did two years ago. So you go to the agent and say, 'All right. I can give you forty-four khandas.' And, as he opens his bag and counts out rupee after rupee, in the backyard they are already saying, 'Three. Hm—Four. Hm—Five, and the God's extra. Hm,' their gaping sacks before them. Night comes and our granary is empty as a mourning-house. Then, the next morning, Husking-Rangi meets you on your way to the river, and says, 'And when shall I come for the paddy, mother?'—'Let Dasara come, Rangi. We've still last year's rice. We haven't swallowed it all,' you say. But Rangi knows the truth, and when the rainy season comes and there's little rice to eat, she will pass by your door and spit three times at you in the name of her children. Then she too will go to work on the fields with her husband. And so two work on a field that hardly needed one, and the children will go foodless. And the next harvest's agents will come and bring veritable motor lorries, such as they have in the Skeffington Coffee Estate, and they will take away all your rice and you will have to go to Subba Chetty and buy perhaps the very rice that grew in your field, and at four seers a rupee too. The city people bring with them clothes and sugar and bangles that they manufacture in their own country, and you will buy clothes and sugar and bangles. You will give away this money and that money and you will even go to Bhatta for a loan, for the peacock-blue sari they bring just suits Lakshmi, and Lakshmi is to be married soon. They bring soaps and perfumes and thus they buy your rice and sell their wares. You get poorer and poorer, and the Pariahs begin to starve, and one day all but Bhatta and Subba Chetty will have nothing else to eat but the pebbles of the Himavathy, and drink her waters saying, 'Rama-Krishna, Rama-Krishna!' Sister, that is how it is. . . ."

"Oh, I am no learned person," explains Nanjamma. "You have been to the city and you should know more than me. But tell me, my son, does the Mahatma spin?"

"The Mahatma, sister? Why, every morning he spins for two hours immediately after his prayers. He says spinning is as purifying as praying."

"Then, my son, I'll have a charka. But I can pay nothing for it."

"You need pay nothing, sister. I tell you the Congress gives it free."

"Really, you mean it will cost me nothing. For, you see, I'm so occupied at home, and maybe I'd never find time to spin. . . ."

"It's yours, sister. And every month I shall come to ask you how many yards you have spun. And every month I shall gather your yarn and send it to the city. And the city people will give you a reduction on the cotton, and for the rest you have your cloth."

"You are a clever fellow to know all these tricks!" says Nanjamma, beaming. "Have a cup of coffee, Moorthy." And she goes in and brings out a warm cup of coffee, and in a silver cup too, and when he has finished drinking, he goes down the street to see Post-office Suryanarayana.

Post-office Suryanarayana is already a Gandhist. He asks for two charkas. Then he goes, Moorthy, to Pandit Venkateshia and Snuff Sastri and Rangamma's widowed sister, Seethamma, and her daughter, Ratna, and Cardamon-field Ramachandra, and they all say, "Oh yes, my son. Oh yes!" And so he leaves the Brahmin quarter and goes to the Pariah quarters, and the Pariahs are so happy to see a Brahmin among them that they say, "Yes, yes, learned one"; and Left-handed Madanna's son, Chenna, and Beadle Timmayya's son, Bhima, and old Mota and One-eyed Linga and Jacktree Tippa, all of them follow him home, and to each one of them he gives a spinning wheel and a seer of cotton hemp, and they go back with their spinning wheels upon their shoulders, their mouths touching their ears with delight. Not a pie for this! . . . They would spin and spin and spin, and if that Brahmin boy was to be believed they would have clothes to wear, blankets and shirts and loincloths. They said it was all from the Mahatma!

When they were just by the village gate, they saw a hefty, bearded man, sitting on the village platform, distractedly smoking a cigarette.

"The policeman," whispered Mota to Bhima. "The same who was seen the other day."

"But he has no uniform."

"They sometimes prowl about like this."

They grew silent as they neared the platform. And when they had passed into the Pariah street they looked back and saw him jump down from the platform, and thump past the temple corner on to the Brahmin street. Oh, the rogue!

3

B HATTA was the only one who would have nothing to do with these Gandhi-bhajans. "What is all this city chatter about?" he would say; "we've had enough trouble in the city. And we do not want any such annoyances here. . . ." To tell you the truth, Bhatta began all this after his last visit to the city. Before that he used to sit with us and sing with us, and sometimes, when Moorthy was late in coming, he would go and get the white khadi-bound *My Experiments with Truth* and ask Seenu to read it and explain it himself. Then suddenly he went to the city. Business took him there, he said. You see, he always had papers to get registered—a mortgage bond, a bill of sale, a promissory bond—and for this reason and that reason he was always going to the city. After all, when it was the other party that paid the cart fare, what did it matter to him to go to the city? A day in the city is always a pleasant thing. And nowadays, they said, he had even begun to lend out money there. Advocate Seenappa, you know, had appointed him manager of the haunted-tamarind-tree field, and we all knew in what straits that debauchee was now. So Bhatta began to loan out one hundred and two hundred and three hundred rupees. Then came the district elections, and Chandrasekharayya said "Two thousand for it" and so he had it, and that is how Chandrasekharayya is now President of the Tamlapur Taluk. And then there was the Kotyahalli widow, who lived with her widowed mother. It was Bhatta that managed her lands, and she was involved with her husband's brother. That meant money. Money meant Bhatta—always smiling, always ready, always friendly. Bhatta was a fine fellow for all that. With his smiles and his holy ashes, we said he would one day own the whole village. I swear he would have too had not the stream run the way it did.

So for many a year he was always going to the city. That was why it was so difficult to get him for an obsequial dinner or a marriage ceremony. He would say, "Why not ask Temple Rangappa or Post-office-house Suryanarayana?" And yet Bhatta began life with a loincloth at his waist, and a copper pot in his hand. You should have heard young Bhatta say, "Today is the eleventh day of the bright fortnight of Sravan. Tomorrow, twenty seconds after the sixteenth hour, Mercury enters the seventh house, and Eka-dashiday begins."—"When is the Dasara, Bhattarè?" you would ask, and he would open his oily calendar and lay it carefully on his bulging lap, and deeply thoughtful, and with many learned calculations on his agile fingers, he would say, "In one month and four days, aunt. In just one month and four days." And then you asked him for an obsequial dinner for the ninth day of the next moon-month, and he would smile and say, "Of course, aunt. Of course." After that he would take his coconut and money offerings and hurry down to Pandit Venkateshia's house, for the anniversary of his father's death. Bhatta is the First Brahmin. He would be there before it is hardly eleven—his fresh clothes, his magnificent ashes and all—and seated on the veranda he would begin to make the obsequial grass-rings. Such grass-rings and such leaf-cups too! Never has anything better been seen. And it was so pleasant to hear him hum away at the Gita. The very walls could have repeated it all.

Ramanna is the Second Brahmin. He would come along before noon. The ceremony would begin. Bhatta is very learned in his art. It would be all over within the winking of an eye. Then the real obsequial dinner begins, with fresh honey and solid curds, and Bhatta's beloved Bengal-gram *khir*. "Take it, Bhattarè, only one cup more, just one? Let us not dissatisfy our manes." The children are playing in the shadow, by the byre, and the elderly people are all in the side room, waiting for the holy brahmins to finish their meal. But Bhatta goes on munching and belching, drinking water and then munching again. "Rama-Rama. Rama-Rama." One does not have an obsequial dinner every day. And then, once the holy meal is over, there is the coconut and the two rupees, and if it is the That-house people it is five, and the Post-office-house people two-eight. That is the rule.

Bhatta comes home. Savithri has eaten only a dal-soup and rice.

When the master of the house is out, better not bother about the meal. He will bring some *odès* in his glass, and for the evening meal a good coconut chutney and soup will do. On the nights of obsequial dinners he eats so little. The child will get a morsel of rice.

"Did they pay you the two rupees?" asks Savithramma, waking up on her mat.

"What else would they do?" Bhatta goes straight into his room, opens his casket and the two rupees have gone in.

He knows how much there is in it. Something around three hundred and fifty rupees. Already a little had been loaned out; just ten rupees to Rampur Mada. For a nuptial ceremony of some sort. Six per cent interest, and payable in two months. Fine thing. Then Mada sends Lingayya. Lingayya's revenue is not fully paid. The revenue inspector is brandishing a search warrant. It has to be paid before the coming week. Just twenty-one rupees and eight annas. Payable soon after harvest. For six months it shall be ten per cent interest—"Learned Maharaja, anything you deem just!"—"All right, you are a father of many children, let it be nine and a half."—"Your slave, Maharaja. You are like a great father." And Lingayya gets the money. Next Lingayya and Mada send Kanthamma, our Potters' street Kanthamma. This time it is her son's marriage. She will not die without her son having a wife. And it shall be grand. One hundred and twenty rupees, she needs. Her two and a half acres of wet land to be mortgaged for three years.—"It means a bond, Kanthamma"—"Learned Bhattarè, whatever you like. Do I know how to decipher your books or your papers? You will say 'This is the paper, Kanthamma.' And I shall put my thumb-mark on it."—In a week's time the papers are ready. Kanthamma gets the money. Just seven per cent interest.

Meanwhile, alas! Savithramma dies. An accident. She went to fetch water from the champak well, slipped, fell, and died. Offers for marriage came to Bhatta from here and there. From Kupper Suryanarayana, from Four-beamed-house Chandrasekharayya, and from Alur Purnayya. Purnayya has a grown-up daughter, who will "come home soon." She is twelve and a half years old, and in a year's time Bhatta can have someone to light his bath fire at least. A thousand rupees cash, and five acres of wet land beneath the

22

Settur canal. And a real seven-days marriage. The horoscopes agree marvellously. "Well, if the heavens will it, and the elders bless it, let our family creepers link with each other!" Laced bodice-cloth for each visitor, and a regular sari for the heads of the family. Cart after cart went to Alur, cart after cart with the Front-house people, and the Temple people and the Post-office-house people, and when they returned eight days later they looked as though much ghee had gone into them and much laughter. Only the other day Puttur Satamma was saying, "Never have we seen a marriage like Bhatta's. Such *pheni*. After all, a zamindar's house, my sister!"

Bhatta became richer and richer. He could lend out more money. And now he was no more a pontifical Brahmin. He was a land-owner. To crown it all, the girl came of age in two month's time, and so the house was bright as ever. But life around him had changed. Temple Rangappa and Front-house Suranna did not go to the river as they did before. Every early morning they stood before Bhatta's house and said, "Hè, Bhattarè, are you up? Time to go to the river, hè!" And if Bhatta was asleep, they knocked at the door and woke him up and took him along with them. Then this man came for a hundred rupees, and that other for three hundred, and Patwari and Patel, Pariahs and plantation coolies were at the door for loans. "Just for a month, learned one? The rains have played foul with us." Or, "That rogue has gone to get the best lawyer in Karwar. And I am no son of a prostitute that I cannot get a better one than he. Oh, just three hundred for the moment, maharaja. My coconut field in mortgage." Five hundred becomes four hundred and fifty, the four hundred and fifty becomes four hundred, then three eighty and three seventy-five—but Bhatta will have the last word. That field is not worth more than two hundred and fifty rupees. Let us say two hundred and seventy-five. Two hundred and seventy-five it shall be. Stamp charges three rupees, registration bribes two-eight, and eight annas for the head peon and four annas for the doorkeeper.

"And what advocate are you having, Timma?"

"Why? What do I know, learned one?"

"Why not have Advocate Seenappa? He's the best criminal law-yer in the district."

"As you like, says the licker of your feet."

23

Advocate Seenappa alone will be chosen. The next day when the registration is going on, Timma and Bhatta go to see Seenappa.

"Ah, come in, Bhattarè. How are the rains in your parts?"

"Oh! fine, fine! I've come to bring you Timma, a man with a family and children, and I said to him, I'll drop a word in your ear. He and his ancestors have cultivated our fields for generations. . . ."

"Your Bhatta is like a brother to me," said Advocate Seenappa. "Timma, we'll win the case." And he won the case.

Then there was Chennayya's civil case about the field boundaries; Pariah Sidda's canal-water case, and this case and that case, and Bhatta would say "I'll take you to Advocate Seenappa" or "I'll take you to Advocate Ramachandrayya," and we all said, "Now Bhatta himself is becoming a lawyer." For, when concubine Chowdy and her neighbour Madanna quarrelled over the jasmine plant, Bhatta said, "Let them come and we'll settle it." And he did settle it— and for ten rupees too. Then there was the case between Sampanna and Siddayya, and Chenna and her daughter-in-law, Sati, over the adoption, and Siddi and Venki about the poisoning of little Bora, and Seetharam and Subbayya over the night-grazings—he settled them all. And we said, "There's no use going to the city for a lawyer. We've got one in Kanthapura." But Bhatta always said, "Your humble servant. I lick your feet." And when it was not he that settled a dispute, he took it to Seenappa or Ramanna, or when it was a small case of giving a notice or making an appeal, he went sometimes to Advocate Ramaswamy, "the three-pice advocate" as they used to call him, and he was as good as any other. The notice would go, or the appeal would be drafted, and Bhatta would get just two rupees for his trouble. Just two rupees, you know. Three if it was an appeal!

Bhatta now owned thirty-seven acres of wet land and ninety acres of dry land in all the villages—in Kanthapura and Santur and Puttur and Honnalli. And there was not a Pariah or a Brahmin that did not owe him something. He was so smiling and so good. Never had he charged us more interest than Subba Chetty or Rama Chetty. Those two brothers were the ruin of our village.

They said, too, that it was Bhatta who had sent our Fig-tree-house Ramu to the city for studies. Why should he have done that?

Ramu was not his son or nephew, but just a distant relation. "If you will bring a name to Kanthapura—that is my only recompense. And if by Kenchamma's grace you get rich and become a collector, you will think of this poor Bhatta and send him the money—with no interest, of course, my son, for I have given it in the name of God. If not, may the gods keep you safe and fit. . . ."

I tell you, he was not a bad man, was Bhatta. But this dislike of the Gandhi-bhajan surprised us. After all there was no money in it, sister! But don't they say, "Less strange are the ways of the gods than are the ways of men."

One day, when Bhatta was returning from the river after his evening ablutions, he did not turn at the Mari-temple corner, but went straight along the Lantana lane and hurried up the steps of the Kannayya house. Old Ramakrishnayya was sitting on the veranda, his hand upon his nose, deep-breathful in meditation. Satamma was lying by the door, her head upon her arms, resting. And from the byre came the sound of milking—Rangamma was there.

As soon as Satamma saw Bhatta, she rose up quickly and asked why he had deigned to honour them so, and what happy news brought him there and how his wife and children were; and Bhatta answered it all by saying how very busy he had been, what with the bad rains and the sick cattle, and the manuring work and the hoeing work and the weeding work, and to top it all, those bonds and bonds and bonds to sign—really, if the very devils wanted to take his place, he would say, Take it! and bless those generous souls. "Really, aunt, this business is terrible. One cannot even go and see if one's relations are dead or alive. How are you all, aunt?"

"Like this. As usual."

Then the byre door creaked and Rangamma came out with a sobbing lantern in one hand and the bright frothing milk pot in the other, and when she hears a stranger's voice, she says, "Is it Bhattarè? What an honour!" And Bhatta speaks again of the rains and the cattle and the peasants, and Rangamma goes in and comes out again and sits with the others. Ramakrishnayya has finished his meditation, and leaning against the wall he sits quietly in the dark. He was a silent, soft-voiced, few-worded man, our Ramakrishnayya.

"Has your son found a good horoscope to go with his daughter's?" Bhatta begins again. "It is so difficult to find bridegrooms these days. When I was in town the other day, I went to see old Subrama Pandita. And he was telling me how he could find no one for his last granddaughter. No one. Every fellow with a Matric or an Inter asks, 'What dowry do you offer? How far will you finance my studies?—I want to have this degree and that degree.' Degrees. Degrees. Nothing but degrees or this Gandhi vagabondage. When there are boys like Moorthy, who should get safely married and settle down, they begin this Gandhi business. What is this Gandhi business? Nothing but weaving coarse handmade cloth, not fit for a mop, and bellowing out bhajans and bhajans, and mixing with the Pariahs. Pariahs now come to the temple door and tomorrow they would like to be in the heart of it. They will one day put themselves in the place of the Brahmins and begin to teach the Vedas. I heard only the other day that in the Mysore Sanscrit College some Pariahs sought admission. Why, our Beadle Timmayya will come one of these days to ask my daughter in marriage! Why shouldn't he?"

Rangamma lifts her head a little and whispers respectfully, "I don't think we need fear that, Bhattarè. The Pariahs could always come as far as the temple door, couldn't they? And across the Mysore border, in Belur, they can even enter the temple once a year. . . ."

"That is what you think, Rangamma. But I, who so often go to the city, I see it more clearly. Listen! Do you know Advocate Rama Sastri, the son of the old, orthodox Ranga Sastri, has now been talking of throwing open his temple to the Pariahs? 'The public temples are under the Government,' he says, 'but this one was built by my ancestors and I shall let the Pariahs in, and which bastard of his father will say no?' I hope, however, the father will have croaked before that. But really, aunt, we live in a strange age. What with their modern education and their modern women. Do you know, in the city they already have grown-up girls, fit enough to be mothers of two or three children, going to the universities? And they talk to this boy and that boy; and what they do amongst themselves, heaven alone knows. And one, too, I heard, went and married a Mohammedan. Really, aunt, that is horrible!"

"That is horrible," repeats Satamma. "After all, my son, it is the Kaliyuga-floods, and as the sastras say, there will be the confusion of castes and the pollution of progeny. We can't help it, perhaps. . . ."

But Rangamma whispers again from the corner: "Has the Mahatma approved it? I don't think so. He always says let the castes exist, let the separate-eating exist, let not one community marry with the other—no, no, Bhattarè, the Mahatma is not for all this pollution."

"Is that why, Rangamma," interrupts Bhatta angrily, 'is that why the Mahatma has adopted a Pariah girl as a daughter? He is a Vaisya and he may do what he likes. That does not pollute me. But, Rama-Rama, really if we have to hang the sacred thread over the shoulders of every Pariah . . . it's impossible, impossible. . . . In fact that's what I was saying to the Swami the other day."

"Why, have you been to the Swami?" asks Satamma, eagerly.

"When I was last in the city, yes. He had come back from his tour in Mysore. And I, good Brahmin that I am, I went to touch his feet and ask for the *tirtham*. You know our Seetharamu, Maddur Seetharamu, is his master of the household. And he is my wife's elder brother's wife's brother-in-law. And after I have seen the Swami, I go to see Seetharamu and we speak of this and that, of Hariharapura, of Kanthapura and Talassana, and then suddenly he turns to me and says, 'I want your help, Bhattarè'—And I say, 'What can I do for you, Seetharamu? Anything you like!'—He says, 'The Swami is worried over this Pariah movement, and he wants to crush it in its seed, before its cactus roots have spread far and wide. You are a Bhatta and your voice is not a sparrow voice in your village, and you should speak to your people and organize a Brahmin party. Otherwise Brahminism is as good as kitchen ashes. The Mahatma is a good man and a simple man. But he is making too much of these carcass-eating Pariahs. Today it will be the Pariahs, tomorrow it will be the Mohammedans, and the day after the Europeans. . . . We must stop this. The Swami says he will outcaste every Brahmin who has touched a Pariah. That is the right way to begin. Bhattarè, we need your help.'—'Well, Seetharamu,' say I, 'this Bhatta who has been a pontifical Brahmin cannot be on the side of the Pariahs. And I know that in our good village there is no Brahmin who has drunk of our holy Himavathy's water and wants caste pollutions. I shall speak to our people,' say I. And that is why I have come to see you."

Rangamma and Satamma and Ramakrishnayya are troubled and silent. From the lit Front-house comes the

Rock, Rock,
  Rock the cradle of the Dancer,
  Rock the cradle of the Blue God,
  Rock the cradle of the Blissful,
  Rock the cradle of the One,
Rock, Rock, Rock,

and from the byre comes the noise of the calves sucking and the spitting sounds of the wall-lizards, and from the temple square tamarind comes the evening clamour of the hanging bats. Suddenly a shooting star sweeps across the sky between the house-roof and the byre-roof, and Ramakrishnayya says, "Some good soul has left the earth."

This cools Bhatta, and wiping his forehead, he says: "Rangamma, you are as a sister to me, and I am no butcher's son to hurt you. I know you are not a soul to believe in all this Pariah business. But I only want to put you on your guard against Moorthy and these city boys. I see no fault in khadi and all that. But it is this Pariah business that has been heavy on my soul. . . ."

Our Rangamma is no village kid. It is not for nothing she got papers from the city, *Tai-nadu, Vishwakarnataka, Deshabhandu,* and *Jayabharatha,* and she knows so many, many things, too, of the plants that weep, of the monkeys that were the men we have become, of the worms, thin-as-dust worms that get into your blood and give you dysentery and plague and cholera. She told us, too, about the stars that are so far that some have poured their light into the blue space long before you were born, long before you were born or your father was born or your grandfather was born; and just as a day of Brahma is a million million years of ours, the day of the stars is a million million times our day, and each star has a sun and each sun has a moon, and each moon has an earth, and some there are that have two moons, and some three, and out

28

there between the folds of the Milky Way, she told us, out there, there is just a chink, and you put your eyes to a great tube and see another world with sun and moon and stars, all bright and floating in the diamond dust of God. And that gave us such a shiver, I tell you, that we would not sit alone in the kitchen that night or the night after. And she told us, too, how in the far-off countries there were air vehicles that move, that veritably move in the air, and how men sit in them and go from town to town; and she spoke to us, too, of the speech that goes across the air; and she told us, mind you, she assured us—you could sit here and listen to what they are saying in every house in London and Bombay and Burma. But there was one thing she spoke of again and again—and, to tell you the truth, it was after the day the sandal merchant of the North came to sell us his wares and had slept on her veranda and had told her of the great country across the mountains, the country beyond Kabul and Bukhara and Lahore, the country of the hammer and sickle and electricity—it was then onwards that she began to speak of this country, far, far away; a great country, ten times as big as, say, Mysore, and there in that country there were women who worked like men, night and day; men and women who worked night and day, and when they felt tired, they went and spent their holiday in a palace—no money for the railway, no money for the palace—and when the women were going to have a child, they had two months' and three months' holiday, and when the children were still young they were given milk by the Government, and when they were grown up they were sent free to school, and when they grew older still they went to the universities free, too, and when they were still more grown-up, they got a job and they got a home to live in and they took a wife to live with and they had many children and they lived on happily ever after. And she told us so many marvellous things about that country; and mind you, she said that there all men are equal—every one equal to every other—and there were neither the rich nor the poor. . . . Pariah Ramakka, who heard of it one day, said, "So in that country Pariahs and Brahmins are the same, and there are no people to give paddy to be husked and no people to do it—strange country, Mother." But Rangamma simply said, "My paper says nothing about that," and continued measuring the unhusked rice. Oh, she told us so many, many interesting things—and all came from these white and blue papers, sister!

So, as I was saying, Rangamma was no village kid like us, and she could hold a word-for-word fight with Bhatta. But you know what a deferent, soft-voiced, gentle-gestured woman she is. She simply said something about Gandhiji's *Life,* and how she would look into it, and how she would ask Moorthy—and at the name of Moorthy, Bhatta again went into a rage and said that the first time he saw Moorthy in the Pariah street he would have him out-casted and old Ramakrishnayya said, with his usual goodness, that it was no use harming a young man, and that young men were always fervent till they touched the bitter leaves of life, and that Moorthy, particularly, was a nice Brahminic boy—he neither smoked nor grew city-hair, nor put on suits and hats and shoes. And at this Bhatta grew suddenly calm and respectful and he said it was all a passing anger, and that Moorthy was a good fellow and if only he would ge married and settle down, nobody would be happier "than this poor Bhatta, well-wisher of cows and men. . . ."

Then Rangamma's sister, Kamalamma, came along with her widowed daughter, Ratna, and Bhatta rose up to go, for he could never utter a kind word to that young widow, who not only went about the streets alone like a boy, but even wore her hair to the left like a concubine, and she still kept her bangles and her nose rings and earrings, and when she was asked why she behaved as though she hadn't lost her husband, she said that that was nobody's business, and that if these sniffing old country hens thought that seeing a man for a day, and this when she was ten years of age, could be called a marriage, they had better eat mud and drown themselves in the river. Kamalamma silenced her and called her a shameless and wicked-tongued creature and said that she ought never to have been sent to school, and that she would bring dishonour to the house. Ratna would beat her clothes on the riverstones, beat them and wet them and squeeze them, and packing them up, she would hurry back from the river alone—all alone across the fields and the lantana growth. The other women would speak of the coming Rampur Temple festival or of the Dharmawar sari which young Suramma had bought for her son's haircutting ceremony, and when Kamalamma was gone they would spit behind her and make this face and that, and throwing a handful of dust in her direction, pray for the destruction of the house. Kenchamma protected virtue and destroyed evil. She would work the way of Dharma. . . .

Bhatta, however, would not say all this. After all, he was not a woman, and Ratna's father was, moreover, his second cousin. And Ratna had lain in his lap as a child, and had played with him in his courtyard, and if she was rough of tongue, she was of the Chanderhalli family and she would bring shame to none. And as for all these fools who were saying she was found openly talking to Moorthy in the temple, and alone too—well, let them say what they liked. You cannot put wooden tongues to men.

But somehow Bhatta could not bear the sight of these "modern ways" of Kamalamma's daughter, particularly since she came of age, and when her sari fell over her shoulders and bared her bodice, it always made him feel uncomfortable. So he rose up and, saying "I'll go," went down the steps and disappeared into the night.

At Agent Nanjudia's house they were haggling with some peasants, and in the Post-office-house there was a lamp on the wall, and they were seated at their eating-leaves, and when Bhatta turned round the promontory corner and passed Rama Chetty's shop, he saw in front of him a figure moving with slow, heavy steps. And as the sky was all black now and not a star stood to the summit of the mountains, he thought it was Pandit Venkateshia going to see his daughter. But he could not make sure and something stopped him from saying, "Who's there?" and the nearer Bhatta came the slower moved the person, and at last, when Bhatta was by Dorè's cardamom gardens, something in him trembled and he said, "Who's there, brother?" And there was no answer but a cough and a sneeze and the beating of a stick against the quiet branches of the pipal; and when Bhatta repeated, "Who's there, brother!" this time, firm and sharp, came the answer, "What does that matter to you?" and as Bhatta entered his courtyard, there fell on the figure a pale, powdery light from the veranda lantern, showing a beard, a lathi, and a row of metal buttons. Then suddenly the figure turned to Bhatta and said:

"Oh, is it Bhattarè? Pardon me. . . . I'm Badè Khan the police-man. I'd just gone to Rama Chetty for some provisions. . . ."

"It does not matter, sahib," says Bhatta.

31

"Oh, it does matter, maharaja. I fall at your feet."

Now what Bhatta had said was at the river the next morning, and Waterfall Venkamma said, "Well done, well done! That's how it should be—this Moorthy and his city talk." And Temple Lakshamma said that Moorthy could do what he liked in his own house but in this village there should be none of this Pariah business, and Venkamma and Timmamma looked approvingly at Post-office-house young Chinnamma, who said it was all untrue, for Moorthy was such a deep-voiced, God-loving person, and would do no mixing of castes. But when they saw old Narsamma, Moorthy's mother, they fell to talking of this and that, and they did not even answer her "How are you all, sisters?" Old Narsamma went and placed the clothesbasket beneath the serpent pipal, and sat over the platform for a moment to rest. She was a pious old woman, Narsamma, tall and thin, and her big, broad ash-marks gave her such an air of asectic holiness. She was nearing sixty-five years of age, and it was not for nothing she had borne eleven children, five of them dead; and of the remaining six, Moorthy was the only son; the rest were daughters, married here and there, one to a *shanbhog* across the Mysore border, another to a priest, and another to a landowner, another to a revenue inspector, and the last one to a court clerk— all well married, with large families of brothers-in-law and sisters-in-law, and all of them blessed with children except Sata, the second daughter who never had a child in spite of all her money and pilgrimages. But it was Moorthy, the youngest, whom Narsamma loved the most—the youngest is always the holy bull, they say, don't they?—and she thought that he, with his looks and his intelligence, should one day be a sub-collector at least. And why not? He was so brilliant in school, and he was so deferential in his ways. And they began to ask for his horoscope when he was hardly sixteen.

But Moorthy would have none of this. For, as everybody knew, one day he had seen a vision, a vision of the Mahatma, mighty and God-beaming, and stealing between the Volunteers. Moorthy had got onto the platform, and he stood by the Mahatma, and the very skin of the Mahatma seemed to send out a mellowed force and love, and he stood by one of the fanners and whispered, "Brother, the next is me." And the fanner fanned on and the Mahatma

32

spoke on, and Moorthy looked from the audience to the Mahatma and from the Mahatma to the audience, and he said to himself, "There is in it something of the silent communion of the ancient books," and he turned again to the fanner and said, "Brother, only when you are tired?" And the fanner said, "Take it, brother," and Moorthy stood by the Mahatma and the fan went once this side and once that, and beneath the fan came a voice deep and stirring that went out to the hearts of those men and women and came streaming back through the thrumming air, and went through the fan and the hair and the nails of Moorthy into the very limbs, and Moorthy shivered, and then there came flooding up in rings and ripples, *"Gandhi Mahatma ki jai!"—"Jai Mahatma!"* and as it broke against Moorthy, the fan went faster and faster over the head of the Mahatma, and perspiration flowed down the forehead of Moorthy. Then came a dulled silence of his blood and he said to himself, "Let me listen," and he listened, and in listening heard, "There is but one force in life and that is truth, and there is but one love in life and that is the love of mankind, and there is but one God in life and that is the God of all," and then came a shiver and he turned to the one behind him and said "Brother," and the man took the fan from Moorthy and Moorthy trembled back and sought his way out to the open, but there were men all about him and behind the men, women, and behind them carts and bullocks and behind them the river, and Moorthy said to himself, "No, I cannot go." And he sat beside the platform, his head in his hands, and tears came to his eyes, and he wept softly, and with weeping came peace. He stood up, and he saw there, by the legs of the chair, the sandal and the foot of the Mahatma, and he said to himself, "That is my place." And suddenly there was a clapping of hands and shoutings of *"Vandè Mataram, Gandhi Mahatma ki jai!"* and he put forth his hands and cried, *"Mahatma Gandhi ki jai!"* And as there was fever and confusion about the Mahatma, he jumped onto the platform, slipped between this person and that and fell at the feet of the Mahatma, saying, "I am your slave." The Mahatma lifted him up and, before them all, he said, "What can I do for you, my son?" and Moorthy said, like Hanuman to Rama, "Any command," and the Mahatma said, "I give no command save to seek truth," and Moorthy said, "I am ignorant, how

33

can I seek Truth," and the people around him were trying to hush him and to take him away, but the Mahatma said, "You wear foreign cloth, my son."—"It will go Mahatmaji."—"You perhaps go to a foreign university."—"It will go, Mahatmaji."—"You can help your country by going and working among the dumb millions of the villages."—"So be it, Mahatmaji," and the Mahatma patted him on the back, and through that touch was revealed to him as the day is revealed to the night the sheathless being of his soul; and Moorthy drew away, and as it were with shut eyes groped his way through the crowd to the bank of the river. And he wandered about the fields and the lanes and the canals and when he came back to the college that evening, he threw his foreign clothes and his foreign books into the bonfire, and walked out, a Gandhi's man.

That's how it was that he returned to our village in the middle of the last harvest, and when Narsamma saw him coming down the Karwar road, his bundle in his hand, she cried out, "What is it, my son, that brings you here?" and he told her of the Mahatma he had seen and of the schools that were corrupt, and Narsamma fell upon the floor and began to weep and to cry, saying that she would never look upon his face again. But, after all, she let him stay and she was glad to have him at home. She said, "You need not be a sub-collector or an assistant commissioner. You can look after your hereditary lands and have your two meals a day. . . ." And the very next week there turned up Santapur Patwari Venkataramayya to offer his third daughter in marriage; but Waterfall Venkamma said that her daughter's horoscope went incomparably better, and Nose-scratching Nanjamma said her granddaughter Sita was only seven years old but she should be married soon, if Moorthy would only say, "Yes, aunt!" But Moorthy simply said he did not wish to marry, and when Narsamma said, "You are a grown-up boy, Moorthy, and if you don't marry now, you will take to evil ways," Moorthy, deferential as ever, said, "No, mother. I swear upon my holy thread I shall keep pure and noble and will bring no evil to my ancestors." But every time there was a horoscope moving about, Narsamma always had it compared with Moorthy's, for one day he would surely marry. He was the only son and she would have liked to close her eyes with an ever-lit house and sons and grandsons that would offer unfailing oblations to the manes. And when Moorthy began this

Gandhi affair she was glad everybody talked to him and came to see him, and she hoped this way Maddur Coffee-planter Venkatanarayana himself would offer his daughter in marriage. After all Moorthy, too, had twenty-seven acres of wet land and fifty-four acres of dry land, and a cardamom garden, and a twenty-five-tree mango grove, and a small coffee plantation. Surely Venkatanarayana would offer his daughter in marriage! And there would be such a grand marriage, with a city band and motorcars and such an army of cooks, and there would be such a royal procession in the very heart of the city, with fire display and all. A real grand marriage, I tell you!

And from the day she saw this, as if in a vision, she would neither sleep nor sit, and she spoke secretly of it to Post-office-house Chinnamma, who was Maddur Coffee-planter Venkatanarayana's cousin and Post-office Chinnamma said, "Of course I shall speak to Venku when he comes here next," and she spoke of it to Puttamma whose sister was Coffee-planter Venkatanarayana's second wife. And the whisper went from house to house that Moorthy was to be married to the second daughter of Venkatanarayana. "Why," said Temple Lakshamma, "why, even the marriage day has been fixed—it will be in the dark half of the Sravan month," and they all said that soon the village would begin to prepare vermicelli and rice-cakes and *happalams,* and they all said, "This will be a fine marriage and we shall feast as we have never done—think of it, a coffee planter!"

But Waterfall Venkamma knew better. This good-for-nothing fellow, who could not even pass an examination and who had now taken to this Pariah business—why, he could beg, cringe, and prostrate himself before the coffee planter but he would not even have the dirt out the body of his second daughter.

"Ah, well," she said, "if you want to know, I shall go straight to Narsamma herself and find it out"; and straight she went, her sari falling down her shaven head, and she walked fast, and when she came to Moorthy's house she planted herself straight before his mother and cried, "Narsamma, I have come to ask you something. You know you said you did not want my daughter for your son. I am glad of it now and I say to myself, thank heaven I didn't tie my daughter to the neck of a Pariah-mixer. Ah, well! I have horo-

35

scopes now from Bangalore and Mysore—with real B.A.s and M.A.s, and you will see a decent assistant commissioner take my daughter in marriage. But what I have come for is this: Tell me, Narsamma, it seems your son wants to marry Coffee-planter Venkatanarayana's daughter. He will do nothing of the kind. God has not given me a tongue for nothing. And the first time your honoured guests come out after the marriage papers are drawn, here shall I be in this corner, and I shall tumble upon them, I a shaven widow, and I shall offer them a jolly good blessing ceremony in the choicest of words. Do you hear that, Narsamma? Well, let him take care, Moorthy. And our community will not be corrupted by such dirt-gobbling curs. Pariah! Pariah!" She spat at the door and walked away, to the consternation of Narsamma, and the whole village said Venkamma was not Waterfall Venkamma for nothing, and that Narsamma should not take it to heart. And when Narsamma saw her at the river the next day, Venkamma was as jolly as ever and she said she had a bad tongue and that one day she would ask Carpenter Kenchayya to saw it out, and Narsamma said, "Oh, it does not matter, sister," and they all talked together happily and they came back home, their baskets on their heads, content.

But on this particular morning Venkamma was beginning to boil again. As Narsamma came forward, and, placing her basket on the sands, began to unroll her bundle, Venkamma plants herself like a banana-trunk in front of her and cries out:

"Hè, Narsamma. Do you know what your son is bringing to this village?"

"What?" trembles Narsamma.

"What? It's for nothing you put forth into the world eleven children, if you do not even know what your very beloved son is always doing. I will tell you what he is doing: he is mixing with the Pariahs like a veritable Mohammedan, and the Swami has sent word through Bhatta to say that the whole of Kanthapura will be excommunicated. Do you hear that? A fine thing, too, it is, you with your broad ash-marks and your queer son and his ways. If he does not stop mixing with the Pariahs, this very hand—do you hear?—this very hand will give him two slaps on his cheeks and one on the buttocks and send him screaming to his friends, the Pariahs. Do you hear? And I have daughters to marry, and so has

36

everybody else. If you have none, so much the worse for you. And we shall stand none of this Pariah affair. If he wants to go and sleep with those Pariah whores, he can do so by all means. But let him not call himself a Brahmin, do you hear? And tell him, the next time I see him in the Brahmin street, he will get a jolly fine marriage-welcome with my broomstick."

"Oh, calm yourself, Venkamma!" says Post-office-house Chinnamma, the second daughter-in-law of the house. "After all, it is not for a woman to hold out in such speech. And Bhatta has not said the village is to be excommunicated. It shall be only if we mix with the Pariahs. . . ."

"Oh, go away! What do you know of the outside world, you kitchen queen? I know. Bhatta met me yesterday and he told me all about it. The Swami has said that if this Pariah business is not stopped immediately the village will be excommunicated."

"When, Venkamma, when?" trembled Narsamma. "Ex-com-mu-ni-cation!"

"I told you, it was yesterday. I saw Bhatta. And he told me this. If not, how should I know?"

"Why, Venkamma," says Chinnamma, "it was I who told it to you this morning!"

"Ah, my daughter of daughters, you think the cock only crows because of you, young woman. I listened to you as though I didn't know of it. But to tell you the truth I knew it long ago. . . ."

"Truly, excommunication?" asks Narsamma. "Truly?" and a tear big as a thumb ran down her pouchy cheeks. "No, not my son. No. Never will my son bring dishonour to his family. He has promised me. No dishonour to his family. Never. Never." And as she began to unroll her bundle, something came up from her stomach to her throat, and she burst out sobbing. She sat herself down and she began to sob. Meanwhile Rangamma and her mother came along to the river. And they tried to console her. But no. Narsamma went on shivering and sobbing. "Oh, Moorthy, you must never do that! Never!" And Rangamma and young Chinnamma said Moorthy was a fine fellow and he did nothing wrong, and if the Swami wanted to excommunicate him they would go to the city themselves and have the excommunication taken away. But Narsamma would not listen. "Oh, Moorthy, if your departed father were alive what

37

would he think of you, my son, my son, my son? . . ." And she hastily entered the river and took a hurried bath, and just wetting her washing, she said she was going home. But Rangamma said, "Wait, aunt, I'm coming with you," and they walked by the river-path and over the field-bunds and by the mango grove, and at every step Narsamma cried out that this was a sin and that was a sin, and she began to weep and to beat her breasts; but Rangamma said nothing was the matter and that, when Moorthy came from town, everything would be settled; but Narsamma would have nothing of it. "Oh, they'll excommunicate us—they'll excommunicate us, the Swami will excommunicate us," she said, and she rolled on the floor of her house while Rangamma stood by the door, helpless as a calf.

4

THE DAY DAWNED over the Ghats, the day rose over the Blue Mountain, and churning through the grey, rapt valleys, swirled up and swam across the whole air. The day rose into the air and with it rose the dust of the morning, and the carts began to creak round the bulging rocks and the coppery peaks, and the sun fell into the river and pierced it to the pebbles, while the carts rolled on and on, fair carts of the Kanthapura fair—fair carts that came from Maddur and Tippur and Santur and Kuppur, with chillies and coconut, rice and ragi, cloth, tamarind, butter and oil, bangles and kumkum, little pictures of Rama and Krishna and Sankara and the Mahatma, little dolls for the youngest, little kites for the elder, and little chess pieces for the old—carts rolled by the Sampur knoll and down into the valley of the Tippur stream, then rose again and groaned round the Kenchamma hill, and going straight into the temple grove, one by one, with lolling bells and muffled bells, with horn-protectors in copper and back-protectors in lace, they all stood there in one moment of fitful peace; "Salutations to thee, Kenchamma, goddess supreme,"—and then the yokes began to shake and the bulls began to shiver and move, and when the yokes touched the earth, men came out one by one, travellers that had paid a four-anna bit or an eight-anna bit to sleep upon pungent tamarind and suffocating chillies, travellers who would take the Pappur carts to go to the Pappur mountains, the Sampur carts to go to the Sampur mountains, and some too that would tramp down the passes into the villages by the sea, or hurry on to Kanthapura as our Moorthy did this summer morning, Moorthy with a bundle of khadi on his back and a bundle of books in his arms.

He skirted the temple flower garden and, hurrying round Boranna's toddy booth and crossing the highway, he rushed up the village road to the panchayat mound, turned to the left, followed

39

Bhatta's Devil's field, where Pariah Tippa was weeding, jumped across Seethamma's stile and went straight through the backyard. Maybe Ratna would be at the well, he thought. But Ratna was not there and the rope hung over the pulley, solemn and covered with flies; so he ran over the temple promontory and straight across the Brahmin street corner to Rangamma's house, but, seeing that Rangamma had not yet returned from the river, he threw the bundles into the Congress-room and walked back to see his mother, who sat by the threshold, her bundle of dirty clothes beside her, herself unwashed and morose.

"O Mother, you are here to give warm coffee to your son," cried Moorthy, as he went over the steps and moved forward to fall at her feet. But she pushed him away and told him he should never show himself again, not until he had sought *prayaschitta* from the Swami himself.

"Oh! to have a son excommunicated! Oh! to have gone to Benares and Rameshwaram and to Gaya and to Gokurna, and to have a son excommunicated! I wish I had closed my eyes with your father instead of living to see you polluted. Polluted! Go away, you Pariah!"

"But what is all this about, Mother?"

"What? Don't talk like an innocent. Go and stand on the steps like a Pariah. Let not your shadow fall on me—enough of it."

"But why, Mother?"

"Why? Go and ask the squirrel on the fence! I don't know. Go away, and don't you ever show your face to me again till you have been purified by the Swami." And she rose up and rushed down the steps, running through the Brahmin street and the Potters' street, and when she was by the Aloe lane she grew so violent with Pariah Bedayya, because he would not stand aside to let her pass by, that she spat on him and shouted at him and said it was all her son's fault, that he had brought shame on her family and on the community and on the village, and she decided there and then that she would go to Benares and die there a holy death lest the evil follow her. But when she came to the river, they were all so occupied with their washing that she too began to bang her clothes on the stones, and in banging she grew calmer. And when she had taken her bath and came back home telling her beads, she felt the sands and the grass and the shadows so familiar that she went straight to the kitchen and began to cook as usual. But where was Moorthy? He would come. He was only at Rangamma's house. Oh, he was no wicked child to leave the village without telling her. Oh, the fool that she was to have been so angry with him! Age brings anger. It is just a passing rage. And she sat herself down to meditate, but the *gayathri* muttered itself out soft and fast, and now and again when she opened her eyes and looked toward the main entrance through the kitchen door, her eyes fell on the royal sacred flame and the breathful flowers and the gods, and the walls looked angry and empty. Yes, Moorthy would come! And when the prayer was said and the rice water was on the hearth, she walked up to the veranda to see if he was on Rangamma's veranda, but he was not. And as Seenu was passing by the door, she asked him, if he went by Rangamma's house, to tell Moorthy that the coffee was ready—"Poor boy, he must be so hungry after a night in the cart!"—and she went in crying, "Rama-Rama," and a tear ran down her cheeks.

Then there were footsteps at the door and they were heavy and odd and they were not Moorthy's but Bhatta's, and Bhatta told her that Moorthy had been very angry with him for having said the Swami was going to excommunicate him, that it was not true, that the Swami had only said he would excommunicate Moorthy if he continued with this Pariah business. "And Moorthy says, 'Let the Swami do what he likes. I will go and do more and more Pariah work. I will go and eat with them if necessary. Why not? Are they not men like us. And the Swami, who is he? A self-chosen fool. He may be learned in the Vedas and all that. But he has no heart. He has no thinking power.' And what shall I say to that, Narsamma?"

"He says that, learned Bhattarè?"

"Yes, that is what he just told me. I was passing by Rangamma's house after a peep into the temple, and Rangamma says, 'Moorthy is here, and he wants to see you, Bhattarè,' and I go and I see Moorthy angry and disrespectful. O these unholy days, Narsamma! I pity you. . . ."

"Is there nothing that can be done now, Bhattarè?" asks Narsamma, her voice trembling.

"Nothing, Narsamma. If he goes on at this rate I will have to tell the Swami about it. I do not want our community polluted and the manes of our ancestors insatiate. Never, Narsamma, never. . . ."

"But he is so reasonable, Bhattarè. I cannot imagine our Moorthy saying these things, Rama-Rama. . . ."

"Poor Narsamma. You have never been to the city. You cannot even imagine the pollutions that go on there. It was not for nothing that Moorthy went to the university. Well, well, one has to close one's eyes and ears, or else the food will not go down one's throat these days. . . ."

Then Moorthy comes in, and Narsamma begins to weep and Bhatta grows silent, and when Moorthy has gone to wash his feet in the bathroom, Bhatta goes away, leaving Narsamma shaking with sobs. Moorthy does not go to her, says not even a kind word. Then Narsamma rises, wipes her face and goes into the kitchen, and when the food is cooked, she lays a leaf in the main hall, and does not even put a glass of water for the libations. And she goes to the veranda, where Moorthy is reading and says:

"The leaf is laid."

"I'm coming." And Moorthy sits by the kitchen threshold and eats like a servant, in mouthfuls, slowly and without a word. And when he has eaten his meal, he goes and washes himself at the well, and Narsamma munches her food alone in the kitchen, while tears run down her cheeks. "Oh, this Gandhi! Would he were destroyed!"

From that day on they never spoke to each other, Narsamma and Moorthy. He sat and ate his food by the kitchen threshold and she in the kitchen, and everybody saw that Narsamma was growing thin as a bamboo and shrivelled like banana bark. But Moorthy went more and more into the Pariah quarters, and now he was seen walking side by side with them, and then one day when Beadle Timmayya's son, Puttayya, lost his wife, he even carried the body for a while, and when everybody saw him doing this openly—for it was on the river path, mind you—they all cried, "Oh, he's lost!" And Bhatta ran down to the city that very morning and came back two days later with the word of the Swami that Moorthy was excommunicated, he, his family, and all the generations to come. "What! Never to go to the temple or to an obsequial dinner? Never to a marriage party, or a haircutting ceremony? . . . Oh!" moaned

42

Narsamma, and that very night, when the doors were closed and the voices had died away, she ran through the Brahmin street and the Potters' street, and standing at the village gate, she spat once toward the east and once toward the west, once toward the south and once toward the north, and then, spitting again thrice at the Pariah huts, where the dogs began to raise a howl, she ran over the Fig-tree field bund, and she had such a shiver at the thought of all the ghosts and the spirits and the evil ones of flame, that she trembled and coughed. But there was something deep and desperate that hurried her on, and she passed by Rangamma's sugar cane field and by the mango grove to the river, just where the whirlpool gropes and gurgles, and she looked up at the moonlit sky, and the winds of the night and the shadows of the night and the jackals of the night so pierced her breast that she shuddered and sank unconscious upon the sands, and the cold so pierced her that the next morning she was dead.

They burnt her where she lay, and when the ashes were thrown into the river, Rangamma turns to Bhatta and says:

"He's alone. The obsequial ceremonies will be held in our house."

"What obsequies?"

"Why, Narsamma's."

"But who will officiate?"

"You."

"You can offer me a king's daughter, but never will I sell my soul to a Pariah."

But Moorthy left us that very night, and some said he went to Seringapatam, and some said to the Tungabhadra, and some said he went over to his brother-in-law of Harihar and there they did it all, but nobody thinks of it now and nobody talks of it, and when Moorthy came back he lived on in Rangamma's house. They gave him food by the kitchen door as Narsamma did, and he still went to the Pariahs, and he still gave them cotton to spin and yarn to weave, and he taught them alphabets and grammar and arithmetic and Hindi, and now my Seenu, too, was going to go with him. When Seenu would begin to teach them, Moorthy would go up to the Skeffington Coffee Estate, for there, too, were Pariahs and they, too, wanted to read and to write. Moorthy would go there tomorrow.

5

THE SKEFFINGTON Coffee Estate rises beyond the Bebbur mound over the Bear's hill, and hanging over Tippur and Subbur and Kantur, it swings round the Elephant valley, and rising to shoulder the Snow Mountains and the Beda Ghats, it dips sheer into the Himavathy, and follows on from the Balèpur tollgate corner to the Kenchamma hill, where it turns again and skirts Bhatta's Devil's fields and Rangè Gowda's coconut garden, and at the Tippur stream it rises again and is lost amidst the jungle growths of the Horse-head hill. Nobody knows how large it is or when it was founded; but they all say it is at least ten thousand acres wide, and some people in Kanthapura can still remember having heard of the hunter sahib who used his hunter and his hand to reap the first fruits of his plantation; and then it began to grow from the Bear's hill to Kantur hill, and more and more coolies came from beneath the Ghats, and from the Bear's hill and Kantur it touched the Snow Mountains, and more and more coolies came; and then it became bigger and bigger, till it touched all the hills around our village, and still more and more coolies came—coolies from below the Ghats that talked Tamil or Telugu and who brought with them their old men and their children and their widowed women—armies of coolies marched past the Kenchamma temple, half-naked, starving, spitting, weeping, vomiting, coughing, shivering, squeaking, shouting, moaning coolies—coolie after coolie passed by the Kenchamma temple, the maistri before them, while the children clung to their mothers' breasts, the old men to their sons' arms, and bundles hung over shoulder and arm and arm and shoulder and head; and they marched on past the Kenchamma temple and up to the Skeffington Coffee Estate—coolies from below the Ghats, coolies, young men, old men, old women, children, baskets, bundles, pots, coolies passed on—and winding through the twists of the Estate path—by the

44

Buxom-pipal bend, over the Devil's Ravine bridge, by the Parvati-well corner—they marched up, the maistri before them, the maistri that had gone to their village, and to the village next to their village, and to the village next to that, and that is far away, a day's journey by road and a night's journey by train and a day again in it, and then along the Godavery's banks, by road and by lane and by foot-path, there he came and offered a four-anna bit for a man and a two-anna bit for a woman, and they all said, "Is there rice there?" and he said, "There is nothing but rice around us"; and they all said, "That is a fine country, for here, year after year, we have had neither rain nor canal-water, and our masters have left for the city"; and so he gave them a white rupee for each and they said, "This is a very fine man," and they all assembled at night, and Ramanna the elder said, "Now we will go, a four-anna bit for a man and a two-anna bit for a woman," and they all said, "There, there's rice"; and the pots became empty of water and the sacks began to grow fat with clothes, and the pots on their heads and the clothes in their arms, they marched on and on by the Godavery, by path and by lane and by road; and the trains came and they got into them, and the maistri bought them a handful of popped rice for each and a little salted gram for each, and he smiled so that they all said, "It will be fine there, a four-anna bit for a man and a two-anna bit for a woman," and the maistri said, "You will just pick up coffee seeds, just pick them up as you pick up pebbles by the river."—"Is that all, maistri?"—"Of course, what else? And the sahib there, he is a fine man, a generous man—you will see . . ."; and the trains moved on with the coolies, men, women, children; then plains came with dust and desert and then mountains rose before them, blue mountains, and the trains sneezed and wheezed and snorted and moved on; and the coolies all came out at Karwar and marched on, by the road and street and footpath, and they passed this way beneath hanging mountains, and that way over towering peaks, and the streamlets hissed over their shoulders and purred beneath their feet, and they said there were tigers and elephants and bears in the jungles, and when the children cried, the mothers said, "I'll leave you here with the tigers; but if you don't cry, I'll take you over the mountains where you can have milk like water—just like water," and the child stopped crying; and the nearer they came, the

45

harder became the road and the stiffer the maistri, and when they had all passed by the Kenchamma hill, the young men, old men, old women, children and mothers, the maistri stood at the back, and when they had all passed by the Estate entrance, one by one, he banged the gate behind him and they all walked up, coolie after coolie walked up, they walked up to the Skeffington bungalow.

And when they had sat themselves down beneath the hanging banyan roots beside the porch, men, women, and children, the bundles and baskets beside them, the maistri went in, and came out with the sahib, a tall, fat man with golden hair, and he had spectacles large as your palm, and he looked this side at the men and that side at the women, now at the arms of Pariah Chennayya and now at the legs of Pariah Siddayya, and he touched Madhavanna's son, Chenna, then but a brat of seven, with the butt of his whip, and he laughed and he wanted everyone to laugh with him, and when the child began to cry, he looked at the child's face and began to laugh at him, but the child cried more and more, and the sahib rose up suddenly and went in, and came out with a round white peppermint and said he was not a bad man and that everybody would get a beating when they deserved one and sweets when they worked well. "Tell them that—repeat them that," he said to the maistri who was standing behind him, and the maistri repeated, "The sahib says that if you work well you will get sweets and if you work badly you will get beaten—that is the law of the place." And they all rose up like one rock and fell on the ground saying, "You are a dispenser of good, O maharaja, we are the lickers of your feet . . ."; and the women rose behind the men, and they stood fleshy with joy, and turning to the sahib, Madanna's widow Sankamma says, "Sahib—we shall have a two-anna bit for each womanhand and a four-anna bit for each man-hand?" And the maistri grew so fierce at this that he howled and spat at her and said his word was the word, and that he hadn't a hundred and eight tongues, and Sankamma simply put her hand upon her stomach and gaped at him, while the sahib said, "What is all this, Anthony?" and Anthony said something to the sahib in the Christian tongue, and the sahib said, "You all go and settle down in your huts—and tomorrow be ready for work at five!" And they all fell down to kiss the feet of the sahib, and the sahib fetched a few more peppermints

46

and the children all ran to him and the women came running behind them, and the men put their hands shyly between the hands
of the women, and at this the maistri grew so furious again that he
beat them on the back and drove them to their huts by the foot of
the hill. And each one took a hut to himself and each one began
to put up a thatch for the one that had no thatch, a wall for the one
that had no wall, a floor for the one that had no floor, and they
spent the whole afternoon thatching and patching and plastering;
and when the evening came they all said, "This will be a fine place
to live in," and they slept the sleep of princes.

And the next morning they rise with the sun, and the men begin
to dig pits and to hew wood and the women to pluck weeds and to
kill vermin; and when the sun rises high, and one rests his axe for
a while to open the tobacco pouch, or one rests his basket to open
the betel bag, there he is, the maistri, there behind some jack, and
he says, "Hè, there! What are you waiting for? Nobody's marriage
procession is passing. Do you hear?" and when you do not pick up
your axe or put your hand to a coffee plant, he rushes down the
hill, crunching the autumn leaves beneath him, and up there by
the bamboo cluster the red face of the sahib peeps out, and they
all swing their arms this way and that and the axes squeak on the tree
and the scissors on the leaves. But when the talkative Papamma
opens her *Ramayana* and speaks of the leaks in the roofs and leaks
in the measures and leaks in the morals, there's a crunch of feet
again, but it dies away into the silence only to rise on the top of
the other shoulder of the hill. And they have hardly begun to
work again when Lakkamma cries out, "Hè, hè, hè, a snake! a huge
snake! a cobra!" and rushes away to hide behind a tree. And they
all leave their work and come to see if there is a snake and what
he looks like. But he has disappeared into the bamboo bush; and
Pariah Siddayya, who has been in these estates for ten years and
more, says never mind, and explains that cobras never harm anyone
unless you poke your fuel chip at them; and seating himself on a
fallen log, he tells you about the *dasara havu* that is so clever that he
got into the sahib's drawer and lay there curled up, and how, the
other day, when the sahib goes to the bathroom, a lamp in his

hand, and opens the drawer to take out some soap, what does he see but our maharaja, nice and clean and shining with his eyes glittering in the lamplight, and the sahib, he closes the drawer as calmly as a prince; but by the time he is back with his pistol, our maharaja has given him the slip. And the sahib opens towel after towel to greet the maharaja, but the maharaja has gone on his nuptial ceremony and he will never be found.

"Now," continues Pariah Siddayya, mopping his face, "now as for water snakes, take my word, they are as long as they are silly, like the tongues of our village hussies. They just hang over a streamlet or pond, as thought the whole world has closed its eyes. You can pick them up by their tails and swing them round and round, once, twice, thrice, and throw them on the nearest rock you find. If they don't die, they'll at least leave basket and bundle for ages to come. But the snake that is as short as he is wicked is the green snake. You would think it was a rope, but when it is beside a bamboo, you would say, 'Why! it is a bamboo leaf!' That's how our Sankamma, gathering cow dung, put her hand out to remove a bamboo leaf, and what should the bamboo leaf do but hiss and fall upon her arm, where by Kenchamma's grace she had her dung basket, and he, furious, ran back into the thicket like a barking puppy and left a palm's width of poison on the ground.

"He is bad enough, the green snake, but you haven't seen the flying snakes of this country. Now you know the cobra, the python, the green snake, the water snake, the krait, and the rattlesnake, and you know how they move. They move like this—on the earth, like all living creatures. But here there's another monster; he flies from tree to tree, and when your turban is just a little loose, and say your pate uncovered, this fine gentleman merely hangs down and gives you a nice blessing. But thank heavens it is not with us here that he is often found. He likes the sumptuous smell of cardamoms and his home is amongst them. That's why all these cardamom-garden coolies wear, you know, a slab thin as a cloth on their heads. There was that fellow Mada who died leaving three children and a yelling wife. There was also that bent-legged Chandrayya. He died God knows how, but they found him in the garden, dead. This flying snake, I tell you, is a sly fellow. He is not like the cobra, frank in his attack and never aggressive. Why, the other day there was Ramayya pushing the maistri's bicycle up through the Wadawalè Ghats, for the maistri had come up in a passing lorry, and the bicycle was left down at the Sukkur police station, and the maistri says, 'Go and get it, Ramayya.' So Ramayya goes down that night, and the next morning he says to himself, 'Why go by the main road, there's daylight and I have the bicycle-bell to ring if there's anything coming.' And so he takes the Kalhapur tank-weir path, and crossing into the Siddapur jungles he is pushing the bicycle when he sees the flat footmarks of a tiger that must have feasted on a deer somewhere, and he says to himself, 'This might be difficult business,' and begins to ring the bell. Then, as he is just by a flowering aloe, what should rattle up but a huge cobra as long as this—that the bicycle-wheel had run down. Ramayya cried out, 'Ayyo . . . Ayyoo . . .' and ran away. And after a whiff of breath and a thousand and eight Rama-Ramas, he comes back and there is no cobra nor his dirt there, and he takes the bicycle, and looking this side and that side, he runs with it along the footpath and no cobra pursued him.

"Never, I tell you, has a cobra bitten an innocent man. It was only Chennayya's Dasappa who ever died of a cobra bite. But then he went and poked his stick into the hole, poked and poked, saying he had the eagle-mark on his hand and never a snake did harm him, but within six months Father Naga slips right into his hut, and, touching neither his grown-up daughter nor his second child, nor his suckling brat nor his wife who lay beside him, it gives him a good bite, right near his bloody throat, and slips away God knows how or where. Barber Ramachandra comes in and wails out this chant and that chant, but he was not a very learned man in his charms, and Dasappa bloody well croaked. . . ."

And so he goes on, Siddayya, telling story after story, looking to this side and that for signs of the maistri, and they all lime their betel leaves and twist the tobacco leaves and munch on, when suddenly there is neither crunch nor cough, but the maistri's cane has touched Vanamma and Siddamma and Puttayya, and everyone is at his axe or scissors and never a word is said. And they work on with axe and scissors till the sun's shadow is dead, and then they go back to their huts to gobble ragi paste and pickles, and when

49

the maistri's whistle pierces the air, they rise and go, each one to his pit and plant.

But the afternoon sun is heavy and piercing and as each axe splits the wood or as each pick tears the earth, from head and arm-pit and waist the perspiration flows down the body, and when the eyes are hot and the head dizzy, Rachanna and Chandranna and Madanna and Siddayya lean back against the trunks of the jacks, and the freckled, hard bark sweats out a whiff of moisture that brings out more perspiration and then the body grows dry and balmed; but when the eyes seek the livid skies across the leaves, there is something dark and heavy rising from the other side of the hill, something heavy and hard and black, and the trees begin sud-denly to tremble and hiss, and as Rachanna and Chandranna and Madanna and Siddayya strike their axes against the wood, there is a gurgle and grunt from behind the bamboo cluster—and the gurgle and grunt soar up and swallow the whole sky. The darkness grows thick as sugar in a cauldron, while the bamboos creak and sway and whine, and the crows begin to wheel round and flutter, and everywhere dogs bark and calves moo, and then the wind comes so swift and dashing that it takes the autumn leaves with it, and they rise into the juggling air, while the trees bleat and blub-ber. Then drops fall, big as the thumb, and as the thunder goes clashing like a temple cymbal through the heavens, the earth itself seems to heave up and cheep in the monsoon rains. It churns and splashes, beats against the treetops, reckless and wilful, and sud-denly floating forwards, it bucks back and spits forward and pours down upon the green, weak coffee leaves, thumping them down to the earth, and then playfully lounging up, the coffee leaves rising with it, and whorling and winnowing, spurting and rattling, it jerks and snorts this side and that; and as Rachanna and Madanna and Chandranna and Siddayya stand beside the jacks, the drops trickle down the peeling bark, then touch the head; then the back and the waist, and once when the trees have all groaned down as though whipped to a bow, there is such a swish of spray that it soaks their dhotis and their turbans, and they stand squeezing them out. Then somewhere there is a lightning again and suddenly the whole

50

Himavathy valley becomes as clear as under the moon, and in Kanthapura the smoke is seen to rise from every house and curl round the golden dome of the temple, and the streets look red and clear and flat, except for a returning cow or courtyard cart. Then the darkness again, and the trees bend and shiver and the bamboos creak.

"Hè, this wretch! What's all this noise about?" asks Madanna of Siddayya.

"Ah, in this country it's like this," says Siddayya. "And once it begins there is no end to her tricks. . . ."

"Hm!"

And from the bamboo cluster the voices of women are heard, and high up there, on the top of the hill, the sahib is seen with his cane and his pipe, and his big heavy coat, bending down to look at this gutter and that. The rain swishes round and pours, beating against the treetops, grinding by the tree trunks and racing down the waving paths. It swings and swishes, beats and patters, and then there is but one downpour, one steady, full, ungrudging pour. And somewhere is heard a whistle, the maistri's whistle, which whines and whines, and Siddayya says to Madanna, "That's for us to go home," and "Hè-ho, hè-ho," the husbands call to their wives, fathers to their daughters, mothers to their sons, and elder brother to younger brother, and through slush and stream they move on, men and women and children, squeezing their clothes and wiping their hair, and the rain pours on and on, a steady, full, ungrudging rain.

"It's like this in the mountains."

"How long?"

"One day, two days, three days. . . . And till then eat and sleep with your woman, sleep with your woman and eat. . . ."

"Fine thing . . . this rain. . . ."

It poured just three nights and four days—the southwest rain.

And when the days became broad and the sky became blue as a marriage shawl, men and women and children rose again with the whistle to go to work—but for Rachanna's child, Venki, seven years old, and Siddanna's wife, Sati, the same who had had the stomach-ache in the train, and Sampanna's sister-in-law, and Mada's two children. They all lay on their mats; for on the night before, they all had chills, and the chills rose and rose, while every dhoti, coat

51

and turban and blanket was heaped on them, and yet the chill was piercing as ever. And then came fever, leaping, flaming fever, and the whole night they grinned and grit their teeth, and they cried for water and water and water, but the elders said, "No, no one drinks water when he has fever," and with the morning the fever went down, but a weakness remained which made their heads dizzy and their stomachs nauseating.

"Oh, it's the fever of this country," Siddayya explained. "It's always like this. It harms no one. It comes every two days and goes away, and when you know it better, you can work with it as well as any."

But this morning they would not work. It simply made them vomit at every step. When the sahib heard of it he sent a new man, who looked just as tall and as city-bred as the maistri, and he gave them eight pills each, eight pills for two days, and said if they took them, well, the fevers would die away. But "Don't bother to swallow them," explained Siddayya. "They are as bitter as the neem-leaves and the fever will come just the same. The sahib says that in his country they are always used for fever. But he does not know our country, does he?" And the women said, "That is so —what does he know about us?" And Siddanna's wife, Sati, asked her neighbour Satamma, who had lived there for one year and more, what goddess sanctified the neighbouring region, and when Satamma said it was our Kenchamma, she tore a rag from her sari fringe, and put into it a three-pice bit and a little rice and an areca nut, and hung it securely to the roof. And, of course, she woke up the next morning to find no fever at all, though Madanna's second child still had it, hot, very hot. "Oh, it's the grace of Kenchamma," she said to Madanna; so Madanna did the same, but the fever would not go. And so he said he would try the sahib's pill, but his wife said, "If the gods are angry—they'll take away not only your children but yourself, oh, you man . . ." and he, frightened, beat his cheeks and asked pardon of Sri Kenchamma. But he had had a wicked thought. Kenchamma would not forgive him. Fever on fever came, and the poor child's ribs began to show and its belly to swell, and one day as he was just going to sleep, the child began to say this and that wildly and they all said, "Go and call the sahib," and when the sahib came, the child shivered and died in his arms.

52

And the sahib grew so fierce that he gave Madanna a whipping there and then, and ordered that everybody should by his command take six pills a day. Some took them but others threw them into the back yard, and the maistri-looking man who had brought them said, "If you don't take it, it does not matter. But never tell the sahib you don't, and let me use it for myself"; and the women said, "Of course! Of course!" But one by one in this house and that, in this line and that, fevers came, and when it was not fever it was stomach-ache and dysentery, and when it was not dysentery it was cough; and one thing or the other, such things as were never heard of in the plains.

"On the Godavery it's not like this, is it, Father Siddayya?"

"No, brother. But this wretch of a rain," and drawing away his hookah, he spat the southwest way.

But the southwest rain went flying away, and then came the northeast wind and it blew and blew until the thatches were torn away and the walls felled; and then it dripped, fine, endless, un-flooding rain, whilst the fevers still came and went. Then Madanna's second child died, too, and two days later Sidda's father Ramayya, and Venka's old mother—and just as children began to fall out of their mother's wombs, children, men, and women were going away and were buried or burnt on the banks of the Himavathy.

Then Pariah Rangayya said, "We'll make three hundred rupees in all—three hundred rupees each, and we shall take our money and scuttle down the passes like kitchen bandicoots; and once we are there we'll throw over a few clods of earth, and grass won't grow where the rice is thrown. . . ."

"Ah, you have much mind," laughed Siddayya quietly, sucking away at his hookah. "We all said that. . . ."

"Why not, uncle? We earn four annas a day for each man-hand and that makes one rupee twelve annas a week, and that makes seven rupees eight annas a month. That's what we make, and throwing in the three rupees or so that our women make, and the little that the brats make, and taking from all this our five rupees for ragi and rice water, the rest is all with the sahib. And what after all is the railway fare we owe to the maistri—we still can have our three hundred rupees to take back with us? Now, isn't that true, uncle?"

53

"Well, so be it!" said Siddayya, and walked away silently. He knew that when one came to the Blue Mountain one never left it. But for Satanna and Sundarayya, who had not brought their women with them, and had sworn before the goddess, "Goddess, break my legs if ever we seek the toddy booth." For once you get there, the white, frothy toddy rises to the eyes, and as Timmayya's Madayya beats the drum and everybody sings,

> Laugh, laugh, laugh away,
>   The King of Heaven is coming,
> Hè, the King of Heaven is coming,
>   Say, Bodhayya,
>   The King of Heaven is coming,

pot after pot of toddy is brought to you, and you drink and you sway your shoulders this way and that, and you cry out, "Well done! Well done for our Madayya!"

> . . . And the King of Heaven is coming.

And money goes this way and that, and there are marriages and deaths and festivals and caste-dinners, and a sheep costs five rupees now, and Rama Chetty sells fine rice at three seers and a half a rupee, and butter is twelve annas a seer; and then so much for the maistri for procuring an advance, and so much for Butler Sylvester for stolen fuel, and so much for Bhatta's interest charges, for if your woman has put forth a she-goat, a she-goat needs a he-goat, and a he-goat, well, you have to weigh it out in gold. And gold has wiles as a wanton woman has wiles. "Three hundred rupees! Well, if he'll have it, let him have it. This much I know, nobody who sets foot on the Blue Mountain ever leaves it. That is her law!"

For ten years deaths and births and marriages have taken place, and no one that came from the Godavery has ever gone back to it. And the old sahib is dead, and the new one, his nephew, has not only sent away many an old maistri and man, but he has bought this hill and that, and more and more coolies have flowed into the Skeffington Coffee Estate. He is not a bad man, the new sahib. He does not beat like his old uncle, nor does he refuse to advance money; but he will have this woman and that woman, this daughter and that wife, and every day a new one and never the same two

54

within a week. Sometimes when the weeds are being pulled or the vermin killed, he wanders into the plantation with his cane and pipe and puppy, and when he sees this wench of seventeen or that chit of nineteen, he goes to her, smiles at her, and pats her on her back and pats her on her breasts. And at this all the women know they have to go away, and when they have disappeared, he lies down there and then, while the puppy goes round and round them, and when the thing is over he takes her to his bungalow and gives her a five-rupee note or a basket of mangoes or plantains, and he sends her home to rest for two days. But when the girl says, "Nay," and begins to cry at his approach, he whistles, and the maistri is there, and he asks the maistri, "To whom does this wench belong?" and the maistri says, "She's Sampanna's granddaughter," or, "She's Kittayya's young wife," or, "She's to be married to Dasayya the one-eyed"; and that night Sampanna or Kittayya or Dasayya is informed of it, and if he doesn't send her, a week's salary is cut, and if he doesn't send her then, still more money is cut, and if he still doesn't send her, he'll get a whipping, and the maistri will entice the wench with this or that and bring her to the master. It's only when it is a Brahmin clerk that the master is timid, and that since the day Seetharam wouldn't send his daughter. The master got so furious that he came down with his revolver, and the father was in the back yard and the young son shouted out, "The sahib is there, the sahib," and as Seetharam hears that, he rushes to the door, and the sahib says, "I want your daughter Mira," and Seetharam says, "I am a Brahmin. I would rather die than sell my daughter."— "Impudent brute!" shouts the sahib, and bang! The pistol-shot tears through the belly of Seetharam, and then they all come one by one, this maistri and that butler, and they all say, "Master, this is not to be done." And he says, "Go to hell!" and he takes his car and goes straight to town to see the district superintendent of police and there is a case, and it drags on and on, and the sahib says he will pay one thousand five hundred rupees, two thousand rupees as damages to the widow and children. But he paid neither one thousand five hundred nor two thousand, for the Red-man's court forgave him. But everybody in the Skeffington Coffee Estate knows now he'll never touch a Brahmin girl. And when a Pariah says, "No," he hardly ever sends the maistri to drag her up at night.

That is why, when Badè Khan came, the sahib said to himself, "This will be a fine thing—a policeman on the spot is always useful." And so it is, for Badè Khan has just to sneeze or cough and everybody will say, "I lick your feet!" No, not exactly. Those Brahmin clerks Gangadhar and Vasudev go straight in front of him and do not care for the beard of Badè Khan. They are city boys, you see. And when they are there even Rachanna and Sampanna and other Pariahs say, "Let Badè Khan say what he likes, our learned ones are here. . . ." And it is they indeed, Gangadhar and Vasudev, that took the Pariahs down to Kanthapura for the bhajans, and it is they that asked our learned Moorthy to come up. They said the Pariahs must learn to read and to write, and when they can do this they can speak straight to the sahib and ask for this and that, money and material and many holidays. Why should not Pariah Rachanna and Sampanna learn to read and to write? They shall. And Badè Khan can wave his beard and twist his moustache. What is a policeman before a Gandhi's man? Tell me, does a boar stand before a lion or a jackal before an elephant?

6

MOORTHY IS COMING up tonight. In Rachanna's house and Madanna's house, in Sampanna's and Vaidyanna's, the vessels are already washed and the embers put out, and they all gather together by Vasudev's tin-shed in the Brahmin lines to meet Moorthy. Now and again there is a rustle of leaves and it is one-eyed Nanjayya or Chennayya's daughter, Madi, who is coming up from the lines, and once they are in the courtyard, they seat themselves on the earth and begin to whisper to their neighbours. Inside the house of Vasudev is seen a faint oil-light, and his widowed mother is seen to serve him his evening meal. The brass vessels shimmer and shake, and then there is only the long, moving shadow on the wall. There, in the streaming starlight, Kanthapura floats like a night procession of the gods over still waters, and up the Bebbur mound is seen a wavering lantern light. That's surely *he*. Yes, he's coming. He will be here soon.

"Learned one, he is coming," cries out Rachanna, looking towards Vasudev's shed. "Can't you shut your mouth, you Pariah!" shouts back Vasudev's mother. "You always want to pollute the food of Brahmins with your evil tongues."—Rachanna does not care. She's an old sour-milk, she is! Vasudevappa does not speak like that, does he? Then there is a rustle of leaves again and the heavy tread of Badè Khan's boots is heard. He skirts Vasudev's courtyard, and with his lathi in his hand and his mongrel before him, he passes on along the main path down the hill toward the gate. Between the creak of bamboos is heard the creak of the gate, and after that there is nothing but the creak of bamboos again and the whispered chatter of men.

The moving light is seen by the tortoise-rock and it dips now into the watery rice fields and now into the wake river, and sometimes it rises sheer across the plateau into the treetops of the Skeffington

57

Coffee Estate. Then it swings back again, and dies quickly into the Bebbur jungle growth.

Moorthy will soon be here.

But Moorthy will not come tonight. Vasudev has finished his meal, and has washed his hands, and as he comes out Gangadhar is there with his son and his brother-in-law, and they all look toward the valley, where there is nothing but a well-like silence and the scattered whiffs of fireflies. From behind the Bebbur jungle comes the mournful cry of jackals, and from somewhere beyond the Puppur mountains comes the grunt of a cheetah or tiger, and the carts are already seen to pull up the Mena Ghats. Everybody goes from this side to that, and Rachanna swears he has seen the light and Madanna says he has seen it, too, and they all rise up, and Rachanna says he will go and look near the gate, and Madanna says he will go, too, and young Venku and Ranga both say, "I'm coming with you, uncle," and when they are all at the gate they hear a grunt and a growl, and a soft whispering answer, and Rachanna cries out, "Who's there?"—"Why, your wife's lover, you son of my woman," spits back Badè Khan—and when they are near, they see the lantern light creeping up the banyan roots, and a white shadow beneath them, and Rachanna says that must be *he*.

"Learned master Moorthy?"

"Yes, Rachanna."

"Stitch up your mouth. Do you hear?"

"I am a free man, police sahib. I can speak," says Moorthy.

"Free man you may be in your palace. But this is the Skeffington Coffee Estate. And these are Skeffington Coffee Estate coolies. You'd better take care of your legs. I've orders."

"Coolies are men, police sahib. And according to the laws of your own Government and that of Mr. Skeffington no man can own another. I have every right to go in. They have every right to speak to me."

"You will not cross this gate."

"I shall!"

Meanwhile Vasudev has arrived, and behind him Gangadhar and the men and the women, and from behind the bamboo cluster the maistri too, and the butlers from the bungalow, and then there is such a battle of oaths: "son of concubine" . . . "son of a widow" . . . "I'll sleep with your wife" . . . "you donkey's husband" . . . "you ass" . . . "you pig" . . . "you devil" . . . and such a shower of spittle and shoes, and "Brother, stop there" . . . "No, not till I've poured my shoe-water through his throat" . . . "No, no, calm yourself" . . . "Oh, you bearded monkey" . . . "Oh, you Pariah-log," and as Moorthy forces himself up, Badè Khan swings round and —bang!—his lathi has hit Moorthy and his hands are on Moorthy's tuft, and Rachanna and Madanna cry out, "At him!" and they all fall on Badè Khan and tearing away the lathi, bang it on his head. And the maistri comes to pull them off and whips them, and the women fall on the maistri and tear his hair, while Moorthy cries out, "No beatings, sisters. No beatings, in the name of the Mahatma." But the women are fierce and they will tear the beard from Badè Khan's face. Gangadhar and Vasudev go up to the pillars of the gate and cry, "Calm! Calm!" Badè Khan, spitting and kicking, says he will have every one of them arrested, and as the maistri whips the coolies up the Estate path, Vasudev leads Moorthy away down to Kanthapura and spends the night there.

The next morning the maistri is there at Rachanna's door: "You will clear out of here, instantly!" and Rachanna's old wife falls at the feet of the maistri and begs him to let them stay on, and she falls again at his feet and wriggles before him, but Rachanna drags her away and tells her to pack the baskets and bundles, and turns to the mastri and says, "You owe me seventy-six rupees in cash," and the maistri laughs and answers, "You have the tongue to ask that too?" and Rachanna says he will not leave his hut till he's paid, and at this the maistri goes away and comes back with Badè Khan and the butlers, and with the whip on his back and kicks on the buttocks, they drive him and his wife and his two orphaned grandchildren to the gate and throw their clay pots after them. Neither Puttamma nor Papamma nor old Siddayya, who were working by the bamboo cluster, turn toward Rachanna. "Thoo! Thoo! Thoo!" spits Rachanna, looking toward them, and with his grumbling wife behind him and the little ones in his arms, he goes down the path over the Devil's ravine bridge and by the Parvati-well and beneath the buxom pipal tree, and turning by the

Kenchamma grove, they all fall flat in prostration before the goddess and say, "Goddess Kenchamma, oh, do not leave us to eat dust!" Then they rise up and tramp up the Ghat road to Kanthapura. They go to Moorthy and Moorthy takes them to Patel Rangè Gowda, and Rangè Gowda says, "We'll show our mountain tricks to the bearded goat," and he goes to Beadle Timmayya and says, "Give him shelter and water and fire, Timmayya!" and Timmayya gives him a place in the back yard, and as Rachanna builds his hut, the woman goes with the other women to pound rice, and that is how Rachanna came to live with us. And as everybody saw, from that time Moorthy grew more sorrowful and calm, and it was then, too, that he began his "Don't-touch-the-Government" campaign.

7

A ND THIS is how it all began. That evening Moorthy speaks to
Rangamma on the veranda and tells her he will fast for three
days in the temple, and Rangamma says, "What for, Moorthy?"
and Moorthy says that much violence had been done because of
him, and that were he full of the radiance of ahimsa such things
should never have happened, but Rangamma says, "That was not
your fault, Moorthy!" to which he replies, "The fault of others,
Rangamma, is the fruit of one's own disharmony," and silently he
walks down the steps, and walks up to the temple, where, seated
beside the central pillar of the mandap, he begins to meditate. And
when the evening meal is over Rangamma comes to find our Seenu,
and lantern in hand and with a few bananas in her sari fringe, she
goes to the temple, and Moorthy, when he sees the light, smiles
and asks what it is all about. Rangamma simply places the bananas
before him and stands waiting for a word from him. Moorthy lifts
up the bananas and says, "I will drink but three cups of salted
water each day, and that I shall procure myself. I shall go to the
river and get water, and tomorrow if you can get me a handful of
salt, that is all I ask."

At this Rangamma lets fall a tear, and Seenu, who has been
silent and has been looking away toward the sanctum and the idols
and the candelabras and the flowers, turns towards Moorthy and
says, "No, Moorthy, this is all very well for the Mahatma, but
not for us poor creatures," to which Moorthy answers calmly,
"Never mind—let me try. I will not die of it, will I?" And Rangamma
says this and Seenu says that, and there is no end to the song.
Then Ramakrishnayya himself comes to take Rangamma away and
he says, "Let the boy do what he likes, Ranga. If he wants to rise
lovingly to God and burn the dross of the flesh through vows, it is
not for us sinners to say 'Nay, nay',", and after a hurried circumam-

bulation of the temple, they go down the promontory and hurry back home.

Moorthy said his *gayatri* thrice a thousand and eight times, and when the sanctum lights began to flicker he spread out his upper cloth on the floor and laid himself down. Sleep slowly came over him, and so deep was his rest that people were already moving about in the streets when he awoke. He rose quickly and hurried down to the river and hurried back again and, seated by the central pillar, began once more to meditate. People came and people went; they banged the bell and touched the bull and took the flowers, and still did Moorthy enter deeper and deeper into meditation; and it was only Waterfall Venkamma who roused him with her loud laughter: "Ah, the cat has begun to take to asceticism," says she, "only to commit more sins. Hè, son! when did you begin to lie to your neighbours? As though it were not enough to have polluted our village with your Pariahs! Now you want to pollute us with your gilded purity! Wait! Wait! When you come out of this counting of beads, I shall give you a fine welcome with my broomstick!" But as Moorthy does not move, she puts her hand into her clothes-basket, and taking out a wet roll of sari, she holds it over his head and squeezes it. "This is an oblation to thee, Pariah!" says she, and as she sees Rangamma's sister, Seethamma, drawing near, she laughs at Moorthy and laughs again, and then she jabbers and shouts and goes away, still chattering to herself. Moorthy loosens his limbs and, holding his breath, says to himself, "I shall love even my enemies. The Mahatma says he would love even our enemies," and closing his eyes, tighter, he slips back into the foldless sheath of the soul, and sends out rays of love to the east, rays of love to the west, rays of love to the north, rays of love to the south, and love to the earth below and to the sky above, and he feels such exaltation creeping into his limbs and head that his heart begins to beat out a song, and the song of Kabir comes into his mind:

> The road to the City of Love is hard, brother,
> It's hard,
> Take care, take care, as you walk along it.

Singing this his exaltation grows and grows, and tears come to his eyes. And when he opens them to look round, a great blue radiance

62

seems to fill the whole earth, and, dazzled, he rises up and falls prostrate before the god, chanting Sankara's "Sivoham, Sivoham. I am Siva. I am Siva. Siva am I."

Then he sat himself down by the central pillar and slipped back into meditation. Why was it he could meditate so deeply? Thoughts seemed to ebb away to the darkened shores and leave the illumined consciousness to rise up into the back of the brain, he had explained to Seenu. Light seemed to rise from the far horizon, converge and creep over hills and fields and trees, and rising up the promontory, infuse itself through his very toes and finger tips and rise to the sun-centre of his heart. There was a vital softness about it he had hardly ever felt. Once, however, in childhood he had felt that vital softness—once, as he was seated by the river, while his mother was washing the clothes, and the soft leap of the waters over smooth boulders so lulled him to quiet that he closed his eyes, and his closed eyes led him to say his prayers, and he remembered the child Prahlada who had said Hari was everywhere, and he said to himself, "I shall see Hari, too," and he had held his breath hushed, and the beating of the clothes sank into his ears, and the sunshine sank away into his mind, and his limbs sank down into the earth, and then there was a dark burning light in the heart of the sanctum, and many men with beards and besmeared with holy ashes stood beside the idol, silent, their lips gently moving, and he, too, entered the temple like a sparrow, and he sat on a handle of the candelabra, and as he looked fearfully at the holy, floods suddenly swept in from all the doorways of the temple, beating, whirling floods, dark and bright, and he quietly sank into them and floated away like child Krishna on the pipal leaf. But it was so bright everywhere that he opened his eyes and he felt so light and airy that his mother looked near and small like one at the foot of a hill. And up there over the mountains there was nothing but light and that cool, blue-spreading light had entered his limbs. And that very evening he said to his mother, "Mother, now you can throw me down the mountains," and she asked, "Why, my son?" and he answered, "Why, mother, because Hari will fly down and hold me in his arms as I roll down the mountains. And if you send elephants to kill me, the elephants will stand by and say, 'This is Hari's child,' and lift me up with their trunks and seat me on their backs and throw a garland round my neck. And the poison you will give me in the cup of death will become the water of flowers, for, Mother, I have seen Hari. . . ."

The next time he felt like that was when he had those terrible floods, and he had, he told us later, seated himself by the river and said, "I may be drowned, but I shall not rise, Mother Himavathy, till thy waters are sunk down to thy daily shores." And who will say the waters did not sink back that very evening? But no other such vision of the holy had he till that holy vision of the Mahatma.

But this morning his soul sounded deeper still. Why?—he began to ask himself. No answer came, but he merged deeper into himself and radiance poured out of his body and he seemed to rise sheer into the air. He floated and floated in it, and he felt he could fly so far and so free that he felt a terror strike his being and, suddenly perspiring, he drew his soul back to the earth, and, opening his eyes, touched his limbs and felt his face and hit the floor to feel he was alive. But he had caught a little of that primordial radiance, and through every breath more and more love seemed to pour out of him.

That was why, when Ratna came to see him, he felt there was something different in his feelings toward her. Her smile did not seem to touch his heart with delicate satisfaction as it did before. She seemed something so feminine and soft and distant, and the idea that he could ever think of her other than as a sister shocked him and sent a shiver down his spine. But Ratna looked at him sadly and shyly, and whispered, "Is there anything I can do?" and Moorthy answered, "Pray with me that the sins of others may be purified with our prayers." She could hardly grasp his idea. She was but fifteen. Praying seemed merely to fall flat before the gods in worship. So she said she would make ten more prostrations before the gods, and when her mother came along, she stood silent, and once Seethamma had finished her circumambulations, they smiled to Moorthy and walked back home.

Rangamma came as the cattle were being driven to the fields, and she brought with her a handful of salt. Moorthy poured a little water into his tumbler, and throwing in a pinch of salt, swallowed it all, crying, "Rama-Krishna, Rama-Krishna." But the coolness in his empty stomach made him shiver. Then a warmth rose in his veins and he felt strength streaming into his limbs. Rangamma again tried to persuade him to eat a little—"just not to be too weak, for even the *dharma sastras* permit it," she said. But Moorthy had little strength to answer her, and he simply smiled back, saying, "Nay." And when she came back in the evening there were already around Moorthy, Pariah Rachanna and Beadle Timmayya and Patel Rangè Gowda, and Dorè, who had just come back from one of his tours. And Dorè laughed and mocked at Moorthy, saying it was not for a university fellow to play all these grandma's tricks. But they silenced him. And then there were also there the other boys Kittu and Ramu and Postmaster's Seetharamu and our Seenu and Devaru's son, Subbu, and Moorthy sat among them smiling and calm, saying a word now and again. But strength was going out of his breath and his face began to grow shiny and shrivelled, and when dusk fell they all left him, and it was only Rangamma that went to sit near him for one moment in silence. "The great enemy is in us, Rangamma," said Moorthy, slowly, "hatred is in us. If only we could not hate, if only we would show fearless, calm affection to-ward our fellow men, we would be stronger, and not only would the enemy yield, but he would be converted. If I, I alone, could love Badè Khan, I am sure our cause would win. Maybe—I shall love him—with your blessings!" Rangamma did not understand this, neither, to tell you the truth, did any of us. We would do harm to no living creature. But to love Badè Khan—no, that was another thing. We would not insult him. We would not hate him. But we could not love him. How could we? He was not my uncle's son, was he? And even if he were. . . .

The next day Moorthy was weaker still. But Bhatta, furious that Moorthy was pretending to be pious, tried to talk to him, and when Moorthy, smiling, just said, "Bhattarè, I am weak: I shall explain this to you another time," Bhatta insulted him and swore he would beat the drum and denounce this cat's conversion to ascetic-ism. But Moorthy simply smiled back again, for love was growing in him.

On the third day such exaltation came over him that he felt blanketed with the Pariah and the cur. He felt he could touch the stones and they would hang to his hands, he felt he could touch a snake and it would spread its sheltering hood above him. But as he rose he felt such a dizziness enter his head that he had to hold to the wall to move, and when he sat down after the morning prayers he felt his heart beating itself away. His eyes dimmed and the whole temple seemed to shake and sink, and the fields rose up with crops and canals and all stood in the air while the birds seemed to screech in desolation. And as he lay back on his mat, a languor filled his limbs and he felt the earth beneath him quaking and splitting. When he awoke he saw Rangamma and our Seenu and Ratna all in tears, and he moved his head and asked, "What's all this?" and Rangamma, so happy that he had at last awakened from his swoon, smiled back at him and said there was nothing the matter, and as he turned toward the courtyard he saw Pariah Rachanna and Lingayya standing with joined palms. Something was the matter, thought Moorthy, and holding to the pillar he slowly sat up, and he saw the sunshine flooding through the valley, while the bulls and buffaloes were husking paddy by the haystacks, and the canal water ran muddy as ever, and up the Bebbur mound the empty footpath, quivering in the heat, ran up into the Skeffington Coffee Estate. Then suddenly he broke into a fit of sobs, and they stood round him and asked, "What's the matter? What?" and Moorthy would not answer. For somewhere behind the dizzy blare was a shadow that seemed to wail like an ominous crow, and he broke into sobs in spite of himself. Then Rangamma took an orange from her sari-hem and offered it to Moorthy imploringly, and Moorthy looked at it distraught.

"An orange. This is an orange, Rangamma. And I cannot eat an orange," he said, and Rangamma thought, "Well, he has lost his reason." But Moorthy grew calmer, and he said, "Give me a little salted water. There is river water in this pot." And as they gave it to him, he held the tumbler long in his hands, and then slowly lifting it up to his lips, he drank one gulp, then another, and then another, and at each sip he seemed to feel light coming to his eyes, and such perspiration poured out from him that he laid himself down and covered himself gently, and sank back to sleep, and Rangamma said to Ratna, "Sit in the courtyard, my daughter, and watch when he wakes. I have to go and cook." At which Ratna was so happy and so proud that she sat by the bull and began to pray. "God, God," she said, "keep him strong and virtuous, and may he rise out of this holier and greater; God, I shall offer ten coconuts and a kumkum worship. God, keep him alive for me." Then she rose and fell prostrate before the gods in the sanctum.

By the evening, the critical period being over, Moorthy felt stronger and he said to Rangamma, "Rangamma, if we had a bhajan this evening?" and Rangamma said, "But Moorthy, you are weak" —to which Moorthy replied, "No, I'm weak no more. And if I am weak, Seenu will lead the bhajan." And as dusk fell, Seenu lighted the oil lamps of the sanctum, and going up the promontory he rang the bell and blew the conch, and men came from the Potters' street and the Brahmins' street and the Weavers' street and the Pariah street; but Vasudev and Gangadhar were the only ones to come from the Skeffington Coffee Estate.

But later, Badè Khan came, too, to join them.

When the bhajan was over and Seenu was taking round the camphor censer, Moorthy observed how poor the Brahmin corner was. Neither Patwari Nanjundia nor Temple Nanjappa nor Schoolmaster Devarayya were there, nor their wives nor their children. The short, round picture of Bhatta came to his mind, but he put it away and thought of God. He would send out love where there was hatred and compassion where there was misery. Victory to the Mahatma!

A peace so vital entered his soul that the radiance of the earth filled him till the soul shone like an oleander at dawn.

The next morning he broke the fast, and lighter in limb and lighter in soul, he walked out to preach the "Don't-touch-the-Government" campaign.

8

First he goes to see Rangè Gowda. Nothing can be done without Rangè Gowda. When Rangè Gowda says "Yes," you will have elephants and howdahs and music processions. If Rangè Gowda says "No," you can eat the bitter neem leaves and lie by the city gates, licked by the curs. That's how it is with our Rangè Gowda.

"Rangè Gowda, Rangè Gowda," says Moorthy, "there's something I want of you."

"Come in, learned one, and, seated like a son, explain to me what you need. If there's anything this fool can do, do but open your mouth and it shall be done."

And seated on the veranda, Moorthy explains to Rangè Gowda his program. Things are getting bad in the village. The Brahmins who were with him for the bhajans are now getting fewer and fewer. Some people have gone about threatening the community with the Swami's excommunication, and people are afraid. There is Waterfall Venkamma and Temple Rangappa and Patwari Nanjundia and Schoolmaster Devarayya—and then, of course, there's Bhatta. And when Bhatta's name is mentioned, Rangè Gowda's neck stiffens and spitting across the veranda to the gutter, he says, "Yes, he had come to see me too."

"To you, Rangè Gowda?"

"Yes, learned Moorthappa. He had, of course, come to see me. He wanted me to be his dog's tail. But I said to him, the Mahatma is a holy man, and I was not with the jackals but with the deer. At which Bhatta grew so furious that he cried out that this holy man was a tiger in a deer's skin, and said this about pollution and that about corruption, and I said to him, 'So it may be, but the Red-man's Government is no swan in a Himalayan lake.' Bhatta grew fierce again and said, 'We shall eat mud and nothing but

68

mud.' 'Yes,' says I, 'if every bloke eats mud, I, too, shall eat mud. The laws of God are not made one for Rangè Gowda and one for Puttè Gowda. Mud shall I eat, if mud I should eat'." And Rangè Gowda chuckles and spits, and munches on.

Then Moorthy says, "This is what is to be done. We shall start a Congress group in Kanthapura, and the Congress group of Kanthapura will join the Congress of All India. You just pay four annas or two thousands yards of yarn per year, and that is all you have to do, and then you become a Congress member. And you must vow to speak truth, and wear no cloth but the khadi cloth."

"Oh yes, Moorthappa! If you think there is no danger in it, I see no objection to joining it. Tell me only one thing: Will it bring us into trouble with the Government?"

This Moorthy thinks over and then he says, "This is how it is, Rangè Gowda. Today it will bring us into no trouble with the Government. But tomorrow when we shall be against the Red-man's Government it will bring us into trouble. You see Badè Khan is already here. . . ."

"Ah!" says Rangè Gowda. "And I shall not close my eyes till that dog has eaten filth," but Moorthy interrupts him and says such things are not to be said, and that hatred should be plucked out of our hearts, and that the Mahatma says you must love even your enemies.

"That's for the Mahatma and you, Moorthappa—not for us poor folk! When that cur Puttayya slipped through the night and plastered up the drain and let all the canal water into his fields and let mine get baked up in the sun, do you think kind words would go with him? Two slaps and he spits and he grunts, but he will never do that again."

"That must not be done, Rangè Gowda. Every enemy you create is like pulling out a lantana bush in your back yard. The more you pull out, the wider you spread the seeds, and the thicker becomes the lantana growth. But every friend you create is like a jasmine hedge. You plant it, and it is there and bears flowers and you offer them to the gods, and the gods give them back to you and your women put them into their hair. Now, you see, you hit Puttayya and Puttayya goes and speaks of it to Madanna, and Madanna to Timmanna, and Puttayya and Timmanna and Madanna will hold vengefulness against you and some day this vengefulness will break forth in fire. But had you reasoned it out with Puttayya, maybe you would have come to an agreement, and your canal water would go to your fields, and his canal water to his fields."

"Learned master, at this rate I should have to go and bow down to every Pariah and butcher and, instead of giving them a nice licking with my lantana switch, I should offer flowers and coconuts and betel leaves in respect and say, 'Pray plough this field this-wise, maharaja! Pray plough this field that-wise, maharaja!' And I should not howl at my wife and let my son-in-law go fooling with Concubine Siddi's daughter, Mohini, who's just come of age. No, learned master, that is not just."

"It's a long story, Rangè Gowda, and we shall speak of it another time. But you are a father of many children and an esteemed elder of your community and of the whole village, and if you should take to the ways of the Congress, then others will follow you."

"But, learned master, there's nothing in common between what you were saying and this."

"Most certainly, Rangè Gowda. One cannot become a member of the Congress if one will not promise to practice ahimsa, and to speak truth and to spin at least two thousand yards of yarn per year." At which Rangè Gowda bursts out laughing again and says, "Then I too will have one day to sit and meditate, taking three cups of salted water per day!" and Moorthy laughs with him, and once they have talked over rents and law courts and the sloth of the peasants, Rangè Gowda turns back to the subject and says, "Do what you like, learned master. You know things better than I do, and I, I know you are not a man to spit on our confidence in you. If you think I should become a member of the Congress, let me be a member of the Congress. If you want me to be a slave, I shall be your slave. All I know is that what you told me about the Mahatma is very fine, and the Mahatma is a holy man, and if the Mahatma says what you say, let the Mahatma's word be the word of God. And if this buffalo will trample on it, may my limbs get paralysed and my tongue dumb and my progeny be forever destroyed!" Then Moorthy stands up and says it is no light matter to be a member of the Congress and that every promise before the Congress is a promise before the Mahatma and God, and Rangè

Gowda interrupts him, saying, "Of course, of course. And this Rangè Gowda has a golden tongue and a leather tongue, and what is uttered by the golden tongue is golden and sure, and what is uttered by the leather one is for the thief and concubine," and Moorthy says, "May the Mahatma's blessings be with us," and hurrying down the steps, he slips round to the Weavers' street, goes straight to the Weavers' elder, Ramayya, and he says, "Ramayya, will you be a member of the panchayat of all India?"; and Ramayya asks, "And what's that, learned one?" and Moorthy sits down and explains it, and Ramayya says, "Oh, if the patel is with you, the panchayat is with him," and Moorthy says, "Then, I'll go. I've still to see Potters' elder, Siddayya." And Potters' elder, Siddayya, when he hears of the Mahatma and the patel, says, "Of course, I'm with the patel and the panchayat," and then Moorthy thinks, "Now, this is going well," and rushes down the Pariah quarter to see Rachanna. But Rachanna is out mowing at the river-eaten field, and Rachanna's wife is pounding rice, and she says, "Come and sit inside, learned one, since you are one of us, for the sun is hot outside," and Moorthy, who had never entered a Pariah house—he had always spoken to the Pariahs from the gutter-slab—Moorthy thinks this is something new, and with one foot to the back and one foot to the fore, he stands trembling and undecided, and then suddenly hurries up the steps and crosses the threshold and squats on the earthen floor. But Rachanna's wife quickly sweeps a corner, and spreads for him a wattle mat, but Moorthy, confused, blurts out, "No, no, no, no," and he looks this side and that and thinks surely there is a carcass in the back yard, and it's surely being skinned, and he smells the stench of hide and the stench of pickled pigs, and the room seems to shake, and all the gods and all the manes of heaven seem to cry out against him, and his hands steal mechanically to the holy thread, and holding it, he feels he would like to say, "Hari-Om, Hari-Om." But Rachanna's wife has come back with a little milk in a shining brass tumbler, and placing it on the floor with stretched hands, she says, "Accept this from this poor hussy!" and slips back behind the corn-bins; and Moorthy says, "I've just taken coffee, Lingamma . . ." but she interrupts him and says, "Touch it, Moorthappa, touch it only as though it were offered to the gods, and we shall be sanctified"; and Moorthy, with many a

71

trembling prayer, touches the tumbler and brings it to his lips, and taking one sip, lays it aside.

Meanwhile Rachanna's two grandchildren come in, and gazing at Moorthy, they run into the back yard, and then Madanna's children come, and then Madanna's wife, pestle in hand, and Madanna's wife's sister and her two-months-old brat in her arms, and then all the women and all the children of the Pariah quarter come and sit in Rachanna's central veranda and they all gaze silently at Moorthy, as though the sacred eagle had suddenly appeared in the heavens. Then Moorthy feels this is the right moment to talk, and straightening his back, he raises his head and says, "Sisters, from today onward I want your help. There is a huge panchayat of all India called the Congress, and that Congress belongs to the Mahatma, and the Mahatma says every village in this country must have a panchayat like that, and everybody who will become a member of that panchayat will spin and practice ahimsa and speak the truth." At this Rachanna's wife says, "And what will it give us, learned one?" and Moorthy says something about the foreign Government and the heavy taxations and the poverty of the peasants, and they all say, "Of course, of course," and then he says, "I ask you: will you spin a hundred yards of yarn per day?" But Madanna's wife says, "I'm going to have a child," and Satanna's wife says, "I'm going for my brother's marriage," and her sister says, "I'll spin if it will bring money. I don't want cloth like Timmayya and Madayya get with all their turning of the wheel," and Chennayya's daughter says, "I shall spin, learned master, I shall spin. But I shall offer my cloth to the Mahatma when he comes here," at which all the women laugh and say, "Yes, the Mahatma will come here to see your pretty face," and the children who had climbed on the rice-sacks cry out, "I too will turn the rattle, Master, I too." And Moorthy feels this is awful, and nothing could be done with these women; so, standing up, he asks, "Is there no one among you who can spin a hundred yards of yarn per day?" And from this corner and that voices rise and Moorthy says, "Then come forward and tell me if you can take an oath before the goddess that you will spin at least a hundred yards of yarn per day," and they all cry out, "No oath before the goddess! if we don't keep it, who will bear her anger?"

72

Then Moorthy feels so desperate that he says to Rachanna's wife, "And you, Rachanna's wife?" and Rachanna's wife says, "If my husband says 'Spin,' I shall spin, learned one." And Moorthy says he will come back again in the evening, and mopping his forehead, he goes down the steps and along the Pariah street, and going up the promontory, enters the temple, bangs the bell and, performing a circumambulation, asks blessings of the gods, and hurries back home to speak about it all to Rangamma.

But as he goes up the steps something in him says, "Nay," and his hair stands on end as he remembers the tumbler of milk and the Pariah home, and so he calls out, "Rangamma, Rangamma!" and Rangamma says, "I'm coming," and when she is at the threshold, he says he has for the first time entered a Pariah house and asks if he is permitted to enter; and Rangamma says, "Just come the other way round, Moorthy, and there's still hot water in the cauldron and fresh clothes for the meal." So Moorthy goes by the back yard, and when he has taken his bath and clothed himself, Rangamma says, "Maybe you'd better change your holy thread," but Moorthy says, "Now that I must go there every day, I cannot change my holy thread every day, can I?" and Rangamma says only, "I shall at least give you a little Ganges water, and you can take a spoonful of it each time you've touched them, can't you?" So Moorthy says, "As you will," and taking the Ganges water he feels a fresher breath flowing through him, and lest anyone should ask about his new adventure, he goes to the riverside after dinner to sit and think and pray. After all a Brahmin is a Brahmin, sister!

And when dusk fell over the river, Moorthy hastily finished his ablutions, and after he had sat at his evening meditations, he rushed back home, and after taking only a banana and a cup of milk, he rushed off again to the Pariah night school that Seenu held in the panchayat hall every evening. And when Seenu heard of the Congress committee to be founded, his mouth touched his ears in joy, and he said he would wake up Kittu and Subbu and Post-office-house Ramu from their inactivity. Moorthy said that would be fine and he went out to see Rachanna, who was sitting by the veranda, sharpening his sickle in the moonlight, and with him were Siddanna and Madanna and Lingayya, and when they heard about the Congress committee, they all said, "As you please,

73

learned master."—"And your women?" asked Moorthy.—"They will do as we do," said Rachanna, and Moorthy went again to the Potters' street and the Weavers' street, and they all said, "If the elder says 'Yes', and the patel says 'Yes', and the panchayat says 'Yes', what else have we to say?" And then he went home and told the whole thing to Rangamma and she too said, "Of course, of course." And Seethamma and Ratna said, "Splendid—a Congress committee here," and Moorthy said, "We shall begin work straight off."

The next morning he went and recounted the whole thing to Rangè Gowda, and Rangè Gowda said, "I am your slave." Then Moorthy said, "We shall hold a meeting today"—and Rangè Gowda said, "Of course."—"Then this evening," said Moorthy.—"As you please, learned one," answered Rangè Gowda—and Moorthy then said, "We shall hold a gods' procession and then a bhajan, and then we shall elect the committee." And as evening came, Moorthy and Seenu and Ramu and Kittu were all busy washing the gods and knitting the flowers and oiling the wicks and fixing the crowns, and as night fell the procession moved on and people came out with camphor and coconuts, and Seenu took them out and offered them to the gods, and Ramu shouted out, "This evening there's bhajan," and everybody was so happy that before the procession was back in the temple, Rangè Gowda was already seated in the mandap explaining to Elder Ramayya and to Elder Siddayya and to others around them about weaving and ahimsa and the great, great Congress. And they all listened to him with respect. When Moorthy entered they all stood up, but Moorthy said, "Oh, not this for me!" and Rangè Gowda said, "You are our Gandhi," and when everybody laughed he went on: "There is nothing to laugh at, brothers. He is our Gandhi. The state of Mysore has a maharaja, but that maharaja has another maharaja who is in London, and that one has another one in heaven, and so everybody has his own Mahatma, and this Moorthy, who has been caught in our knees playing as a child, is now grown up and great, and he has wisdom in him and he will be our Mahatma," and they all said, "So he is!" And Moorthy felt such a quiet exaltation rise to his throat that a tear escaped and ran down his cheek. Then he looked back toward the bright god in the sanctum, and closed his eyes and sent up a prayer, and, whispering to himself, *"Mahatma Gandhi ki jai!"* he rang the bell and spoke to them of spinning and ahimsa and truth. And then he asked, "Who among you will join the panchayat?" and voices came from the Sudra corner and the Pariah corner and the Brahmin corner and the Weavers' corner, and to each one of them he said, "Stand before the god and vow you will never break the law," and some said they asked nothing of the gods, and others said, "We don't know whether we have the strength to keep it up," and then Rangè Gowda grew wild and shouted, "If you are the sons of your fathers, stand up and do what this learned boy says," and Rangè Gowda's words were such a terror to them that one here and one there went up before the sanctum, rang the bell and said, "My master, I shall spin a hundred yards of yarn per day, and I shall practise ahimsa, and I shall seek truth," and they fell prostrate and asked for the blessings of the Mahatma and the gods, and they rose and crawled back to their seats. But when it comes to the Pariahs, Rachanna says, "We shall stand out here and take the vows," and at this Moorthy is so confused that he does not know what to do, but Rangè Gowda says, "Here in the temple or there in the courtyard, it is the same god you vow before, so go along!" And Rachanna and Rachanna's wife, and Madanna and Madanna's wife swear before the god from the courtyard steps.

And when it is all over, Rangè Gowda says, "Moorthappa will be our president," and everybody says, "Of course, of course." Then Seenu turns towards Rangè Gowda and says, "And Rangè Gowda our super-president and protector," and everybody laughs, and Rangè Gowda says, "Protector! yes, protector of the village fowl!" Then Seenu says, "Rangamma will be the third member," but Rangamma says, "No, no," and Moorthy says, "We need a woman in the committee for the Congress is for the weak and the lowly"; and then everybody says, "Rangamma, say yes!" and Rangamma says, "Yes." And Moorthy then turns toward the Pariahs and says, "One among you!" and then there is such a silence that a moving ant could be heard, and then Moorthy says, "Come, Rachanna, you have suffered much, and you shall be a member," and Rachanna says, "As you will, learned master!" And then Moorthy says, "Seenu is our fifth member," and Rangè Gowda says, "Every Rama needs an Anjanayya, and he's your fire-tailed Hanuman," and they all laugh, and so Moorthy and Rangè Gowda and Rangamma and

75

Rachanna and Seenu become the Congress panchayat committee of Kanthapura.

And two days later Moorthy made a list of members and twenty-three were named, and five rupees and twelve annas were sent to the provisional Congress committee. And one morning everybody was told that in Rangamma's blue paper was a picture of Moorthy. And everybody went to Rangamma and said, "Show it to me!" and when Ranagmma gave them the paper, they looked this side and that, and when they came to the picture, they all exclaimed, "Oh, here he is—and so much like him too!" And then they all said, "Our Moorthy is a great man, and they speak of him in the city and we shall work for him," and from then onward we all began to spin more and more, and more and more, and Moorthy sent bundles and bundles of yarn, and we got saris and bodice cloths and dhotis, and Moorthy said the Mahatma was very pleased. Maybe he would remember us!

9

WHEN BHATTA heard of the Congress committee, he said to
himself, "Now this is bad business," and seated on the
veranda, he began to think and think, and the fair carts rolled by
and the dust settled down, and the noise of the snoring cattle came
from the byre, and the bats began to screech and screech, and from
the Bebbur mound rose the wailings of the jackals, and even the
moon plumped up above the Kenchamma hill, and still Bhatta sat
on the veranda thinking. There must be an end to this chatter.
If not, the very walls of Kanthapura would crackle and fall before
the year was out. What with his fastings and his looks, Moorthy
was holding sway over the hearts of the people. And even the
Swami's excommunication did nothing to stop it. Well, well, he
said to himself, every squirrel has his day, and now for every
Congress member the interest will go up to 18 and 20 per cent.
And no kind words either—ah, my sons!—and no getting away from
law courts. Pariah Lingayya has his big-bund field in mortgage, and
if he does not pay up this harvesttime, he will have not a rag-wide
left. And there will be no accepting, "Just a week, master. Just a
week more, say ten days, and this gold-flower in guarantee. . . ."
None of that any more. Then there is Madanna's coconut garden,
and Pandit Venkateshia's Bebbur-field, though with the Brahmins
it's not such easy business.

"Well, well, every squirrel will have his day," repeated Bhatta
to himself. "But Temple Rangappa is still with me, and Patwari
Nanjundia and Schoolmaster Devarayya, and, of course, Rama
Chetty and Subba Chetty. And they are all with me and the
Swami, and against all this Pariah business. And there is Venkamma too." And at the thought of Venkamma an idea came into
his head like a cart-light in the dark, an auspicious, happy idea,
and he said, "I shall find a bridegroom for her daughter, and she

77

will be always with us, and what with her tongue and her tail, she will set fire where we want." And at this Bhatta felt so happy that he began to search in his mind for this bridegroom and that bridegroom, and he said, there was Shanbhog Ramanna of Channè-halli, and Astrologer Seetharamiah of Rampur, and then of course there was Advocate Seenappa.

"Seenappa," he repeated to himself, "he's just lost his wife. And very soon, when I have to go and speak about the new harvests, he will speak about marriage, and I shall say there is a fine girl in Kanthapura, and he will say, 'Is she ripe for marriage?' and I shall say, 'She will come home in a few weeks' time,' and that will do it, and Venkamma will be so happy to have an advocate for a son-in-law. 'After all, Venkamma, what does it matter whether it is first marriage or a second marriage? What we ask is that your daughter will have enough to eat, and be blessed with many children, and perform all the rites, isn't it? Seenappa is thirty-four, but you would say he is twenty-one if you saw him, and he has only three children, and one of them is soon to be married and will go away to her mother-in-law's, and your daughter will have the two godlike children to live with. What do you say to that, Venkamma?' And Venkamma will answer, 'Of course! Of course! Bhattarè, whatever you say will be done,' and Seenappa will be so happy; after all a mother-in-law in Kanthapura, and so near his wet lands too . . . and this Bhatta will himself perform the marriage, and the Swami will bless them."

"That is a fine idea," concluded Bhatta, and as he went in and groped for his bed, he felt such joy rise to his heart that he woke up his wife and said, "Come, don't sleep!", and when she muttered, "Oh, let me sleep," he said, "Oh, be a wife!" and she said she was tired; but Bhatta said he was very happy and Venkamma's daughter would be married to Advocate Seenappa, and she said, "And what does that matter to me?" Meanwhile the child woke up, and when she had rocked it to sleep again, she slipped into his bed, and chattering fool that she was, she said he had never loved her as on that night.

And when the morning came, he rushed to the river and back, and then to Venkamma's house; but there was no Venkamma yet, and he said he would come back, and he went home and was hardly

seated for meditation than Venkamma arrives, important as a buffalo, and she says, "What is it, Bhattarè, that you honour us with
your visit?" and Bhatta says, "Oh, nothing at all. It is only about
a horoscope I've in hand, and maybe it would go with Ranga's."
And Venkamma cries out, "Oh, Bhattarè, you will save my honour
and the honour of my family, if you manage it," and Bhatta says,
"Oh, never mind, Venkamma, after all every pious member of the
community has duties toward every other, and if your daughter is
not married in time, maybe nobody will marry my daughter either,"
and Venkamma is so happy that she begins to weep, and Bhatta's
wife comes and says, "Oh, don't weep, aunt. The will of the gods
shall be done," and Venkamma rises up and says, "May Kenchamma
bless you!"

And on her way back home she meets Rangamma, and looking
away she spits behind her, and then she sees Temple Rangappa's
wife Lakshamma, and she says the marriage is for Sravan, and
Lakshamma says, "Then we shall have *laddu* this year?" and Venkamma says, "*Laddu* and *pheni*," and by the evening everybody in
the village is saying, "Venkamma's daughter, Ranga has *at last*
found a husband, sister!"—"Where does he come from?" asks nose-
scratching Nanjamma of Satamma.—"Oh, it seems he is from a
well-to-do family. May the goddess bless the girl. If not, what
should we have seen before we closed our eyes?"—And people say,
"Well, Venkamma is going to have a rich son-in-law,"—and Postmaster Suryanarayana's wife Akkamma says, "My Putta will sing:
'For what deed in my past life have you sought me in this, my
lord?' "—and Satamma says, "Your Putta sings it so well, sister"—
and Putta feels so pleased that she begins to hum the song to herself, twisting the wet sari, and everybody says, "Go on, Putta, go
on!" and she begins it, and they all leave the clothes on the stones
and follow her, and when she stops, Ratna, who never could sing
these songs, says as though only to her mother, "I shall sing them
an English song," at which Satamma says, "Enough of this. Let
our marriages at least be according to the ancient ways," and
Subbamma and Chinnamma say they will put on the blue and
broad-filagree Benares sari, and young Kamalamma says she will
wear the Dharmawar sari in peacock blue, and Venkamma feels
such esteem around her that she says to herself, "Ah, you widows,

you will not even lick the remnant leaves in the dust-bin, you polluted widows. . . ."

But when the marriage day draws near, she sends her elder daughter to every house, saying, "Tell them you shall not light your kitchen fires for one whole week, and, if you like, for ten whole days. I am not marrying my daughter to Advocate Seenappa for nothing." And everybody asks, "I think it's an advocate your sister is marrying?" and Venkamma's elder daughter says, "Yes, our Ranga is the most fortunate of us all; his father owns three villages and a coconut garden, and a small coffee plantation in Mysore, and their family is called the 'bell-people,' as his grandfather distributed holy bells to every guest that stayed with them." And Satamma says, "My daughter had not that luck," and Nanjamma says, "My daughter hadn't that luck either." But on the first day, as the bridegrooms' procession came along, and we all stood by the village gate, with coconuts and kumkum water to welcome him, what should we see but a middle-aged man, with two fallen teeth and a big twisted moustache. But Venkamma said he was only twenty-five, and he had married at seventeen, and his elder daughter was only seven years old, but we all knew that it came out of Venkamma's head. But Bhatta said he was only about thirty, and that he earned at least three hundred rupees a month; that he had sixty acres of wet land and two hundred acres of dry land, and that his sisters wore half-seer gold belts and diamond earrings and Dharmawar saris, and that they gave the bride a full-seer gold belt; and it was said they would give us a French sovereign each, and indeed every woman of Kanthapura was given a French sovereign. And what a party the marriage was, with jokes and feasts and festive lights, and we all said, "This Bhatta and Venkamma are not so wicked after all," and Bhatta said to Venkamma, "Let everybody be well satisfied," and Venkamma said, "So they shall be!" and every Pariah and cur in Kanthapura was satisfied. Only Moorthy wandered by the river all day long, and when dusk fell and evening came he stole back home, hurried over the meal that Rangamma served, spread his bedding and laid himself down, thinking, how, how is one an outcaste?

10

KARTIK has come to Kanthapura, sisters—Kartik has come with the glow of lights and the unpressed footstep of the wandering gods; white lights from clay trays and red lights from copper stands, and diamond lights that glow from the bowers of entrance leaves; lights that glow from banana trunks and mango twigs, yellow light behind white leaves, and green light behind yellow leaves, and white light behind green leaves; and night curls through the shadowed streets, and hissing over bellied boulders and hurrying through dallying drains, night curls through the Brahmin street and the Pariah street and the Potters' street and the Weavers' street and flapping through the mango grove, hangs clawed for one moment to the giant pipal, and then shooting across the broken fields, dies quietly into the river—and gods walk by lighted streets, blue gods and quiet gods and bright-eyed gods, and even as they walk in transparent flesh the dust gently sinks back to the earth, and many a child in Kanthapura sits late into the night to see the crown of this god and that god, and how many a god has chariots with steeds white as foam and queens so bright that the eyes shut themselves in fear lest they be blinded. Kartik is a month of the gods, and as the gods pass by the Potters' street and the Weavers' street, lights are lit to see them pass by. Kartik is a month of lights, sisters, and in Kanthapura when the dusk falls, children rush to the sanctum flame and the kitchen fire, and with broom grass and fuel chips and coconut rind they peel out fire and light clay pots and copper candelabras and glass lamps. Children light them all, so that when darkness hangs drooping down the eaves, gods may be seen passing by, blue gods and quiet gods and bright-eyed gods. And as they pass by, the dust sinks back into the earth, and night curls again through the shadows of the streets. Oh! have you seen the gods, sister?

81

Then when the night is on this side of the day, and the Kartik lights have died down, a child wakes up here and begins to cry and a cough is heard there, and in Suryanarayana's house a lantern is seen in the courtyard, and the beat of feet is heard here and the hushed voices of men and women are heard there. Then there is a fuss and a flutter in Rangamma's house, and everyone rubs his eyes and asks, "Sister, who is dying? Sister, who is dying?" and Nanjamma says to her neighbour Ratnamma, "And old Ramakrishnayya? We saw him only yesterday evening at the river, and he looked so hale and healthy," and Postmaster Suryanarayana's wife Satamma says, "No, surely it is the heart trouble of Rangamma," and then comes the roar of Waterfall Venkamma, "Ah, you will eat blood and mud I said, you widow, and here you are!"; and Pandit Venkateshia's daughter-in-law Lakshmi takes her lantern and rushes to Venkamma and says, "And what is it, Venkamma?"—"Oh, daughter of the mother-in-law, what is it but that this Pariah-polluter has had royal visits?"—"But what is it, Venkamma, what?" —"Ah, you are a nice one, too, and three legs of a bedstead plus one makes four, does it or does it not, my daughter?" And seeing Timmamma and Satamma she says, "Oh, don't you see the police-man at the steps?" and Timmamma swings the lantern, and beneath the bulging veranda stones is seen the gaunt figure of a policeman, and one by one as the men rise up and gather in the Post-office-house courtyard, the children wake up and rush to the hanging lanterns, broom grass and cattle grass in hand, and our Seenu says, "I'll go," and as he gathers his shawl and goes to Rangamma's door the policeman says he has no permission to let anyone in, and Seetharam comes along and Dorè and Ramanna and the elders, and everybody gathers in the courtyard half covered and half awake, while from this lane and that lane rises the thin dust of Kartik lights re-lit.

And there is noise in this part of Rangamma's house and that, and there comes the regular cry of Rangamma's mother: "Oh, sinners, sinners, to have this in our old age!" and Ramakrishnayya comes and spits across the courtyard and behind him comes Rangamma, a shawl thrown over her shoulders, and then there is seen a light in the front room and Surappa says, "We cannot see anything from here—come let us go up to Sami's," and we all rush up there and standing on the veranda we see what is happening in Moorthy's room. Over against the cracked wall Moorthy is standing, a bright light falling on his tight-lipped face, and the police inspector, a short, round man, is standing beside him, a notebook in his hand. In the middle of the room is a heap of books and charkas and cotton and folded cloth, and policemen in uniform are turning them this side and that, and trunks are laid open and boxes are slit through, and sometimes there is laughter. The voice of the police inspector is not heard. But now and again we see Moorthy's head nodding—he merely nods and nods and seems to smile at nothing.

The police inspector then turns toward Badè Khan, who is now seen clearly in the lantern light, and shouts, "Bind this man!" and when they are beginning to pull out ropes from their belts, there is noise in the street below, and there comes Rangè Gowda, Mada and a lantern with him, and when he sees the policemen, he says something to Mada, and Mada goes away, and before the cock has time to crow three times, there is Pariah Rachanna and Madanna and Lingayya and Lingayya's woman, and they all gather at Rangamma's door and cry out, "Hèlè! Hèlè! What are you doing with our master?" and the policeman shouts, "Hè, shut up, you sons of my woman!"—"Hè, hè, do you think we are going to be silent because of your beards and batons . . ."—"If you are not silent, you will get a marriage greeting today!"—and Rachanna says, "Ah, I've seen your elders, you son of my concubine, and I shall see . . ."—And at this the policeman grows so wild that he waves his lathi and Rachanna comes forward and says, "Hè, beat me if you have the courage!" and Rangamma leans out of the veranda darkness into the starlight and says, "Hè, Rachanna, this must not be done!" and Rachanna says, "And what is to be done, mother? They are going to take away our master!" And Rangè Gowda says something to Mada and Mada says something to Rachanna and Rachanna says something in the ear of everyone, and when Moorthy is seen on the threshold, the bright light of the police lantern falling on his knit face, Rachanna cries out, *"Mahatma Gandi ki jai!"* and the policeman rushes at them and bangs them with his lathi and Rachanna quavers out the louder, *"Gandhi Mahatma ki jai!"* and other policemen come and bang them too, and the women raise such a clamour and cry that the crows and bats set up an obsequial wail, and the sparrows join them from the roofs and eaves and the cattle rise up in the byre and the creaking of their bones is heard. And then men rush from this street and that street, and the police inspector seeing this hesitates before coming down, and Rachanna barks out again, *"Mahatma Gandhi ki jai!"* And the police inspector shouts, "Arrest that swine!" and when they come to arrest him, everybody gets round him and says, "No, we'll not give him up." And the police inspector orders, "Give them a licking," and from this side and that there is the bang of the lathi and men shriek and women weep and the children begin to cry and groan, and more and more men go forward toward Moorthy, and more policemen beat them, and then Moorthy says something to the police inspector and the police inspector nods his head, and Moorthy comes along the veranda and says, "Brothers!" and there is such a silence that the Kartik lights glow brighter. "Brothers, in the name of the Mahatma, let there be peace and love and order. As long as there is a God in heaven and purity in our hearts evil cannot touch us. We hide nothing. We hurt none. And if these gentlemen want to arrest us, let them. Give yourself up to them. That is the true spirit of the satyagrahi. The Mahatma"— here the police inspector drags him back brutally, but Moorthy continues—"The Mahatma has often gone to prison . . ."—and the police inspector gets so angry at this, that he gives a slap on Moorthy's face, but Moorthy stands firm and says nothing. Then suddenly Rachanna shouts out from below, *"Mahatma Gandhi ki jai!* Come, brothers, come!"* and he rushes up the steps towards Moorthy, and suddenly, in sinister omen, all the Kartik lights seemed quenched, clay pots and candelabras and banana trunks and house after house became dark, and something so sinister kicked our backs that we all rush up behind Rachanna crying, *"Mahatma Gandhi ki jai!"* and now the police catch Rachanna and the one behind him and the one behind the one who was behind him, and they spit on them and bind them with ropes, while at the other end of the courtyard is seen Rangamma, Badè Khan beside her. Then the police inspector thinks this is the right time to come down, for the lights were all out and the leaders all arrested, and as Moorthy is being dragged down the steps Rachanna's wife and Madanna's wife and Sampanna's wife and Papamma and Sankamma and Veeramma come forward and cry out, "Oh, give us back our men and our master, our men and our master," but the police inspector says, "Give them a shoe-shower," and the policemen kick them in the back and on the head and in the stomach, and while Rachanna's wife is crying, Madanna's wife is squashed against a wall and her breasts squeezed. And Rangè Gowda, who has stood silent by the tamarind, when he sees this, rushes down and, stick in hand, gives one bang on the head of a policeman, and the policeman sinks down, and there is such a clamour again that the police inspector shouts, "Disperse the crowd!" and he slips round the byre with Moorthy before him, while policemen beat the crowd this side and that side, and groans and moans and cries and coughs and oaths and bangs and kicks are heard, and more shouts of *Mahatma Gandhi ki jai! Mahatma Gandhi ki jai!*"

And this time it was from the Brahmin quarter that the shouts came, and policemen rushed toward the Brahmins and beat them, and old Ramanna and Dorè came forward and said, "We too are Gandhi's men, beat us as much as you like," and the policemen beat them till they were flat on the ground, mud in their mouths and mist in their eyes, and as the dawn was rising over the Kenchamma hill, faces could be seen, and men became silent and women became sobless, and with ropes round their arms seventeen men were marched through the streets to the Santur police station, by the Karwar road and round the Skeffington Coffee Estate and down the Tippur valley and up the Santur mound, and as the morning cattle were going out to the fields, and the women were adorning the thresholds for a Kartik morning, Brahmins and Pariahs and Potters and Weavers were marched into the police station— seventeen men of Kanthapura were named and locked behind the bars. And the policemen twisted their arms and beat them on their knuckles, and spat into their mouths, and when they had slapped and banged and kicked, they let them out one by one, one by one they let them out, and they all marched back to Kanthapura, all but Moorthy. Him they put into a morning bus, and with one policeman on the right and one policeman on the left they carried him away to Karwar. We wept and we prayed, and we vowed and we fasted, and maybe the gods would hear our feeble voices. Who would hear us, if not they?

The gods indeed did hear our feeble voices, for this advocate and that advocate came and said, "I shall defend him," vakils and advocates and barristers came and said, "And we shall plead for him," and the students formed a defence committee and raised a huge meeting, and copper and silver flowed into the collection plate, and merchants came and said, "And here we are when money is needed." And when Moorthy heard of all this, he said, "That is not for me. Between truth and me none shall come," and Advocate Ranganna went and saw him and said, "Moorthy! The Redman's judges, they are not your uncle's grandsons," and Moorthy simply said, "If truth is one, all men are one before it," and Ranganna said, "Judges are not for truth, but for law, and the English are not for the brown skin but for the white, and the Government is not with the people but with the police." And Moorthy listened to all this and said, "If that is so, it will have to change. Truth will have to change it. I shall speak that which truth prompteth, and truth needeth no defense," and Ranganna spoke this of corruption and that about prejudice, but "truth, truth, and truth" was all that Moorthy said, and old Ranganna, who had grown grey with law on his tongue, got so wild that he banged the prison door behind him and muttered to himself, "To the mire with you!"

And then came Sadhu Narayan who had renounced hair and home and was practicing meditation on the banks of the Vedavathy, and he said, "Moorthy, you are a brave soul and a holy soul. And there is in you the hunger of God, and may He protect you always. But Ranganna comes and tells me, 'I cannot change his heart. You are a religious man, go and speak to him,' and I came to see you. I have neither hair nor home, and I have come to tell you, *this* is not just. Defend one must against evil; if not, where is renouncement, continence, austerity, and the control of breath?" To which Moorthy says, "You are a holy man, Sadhuji, and I touch your feet in reverence. But if truth needs a defence, God Himself would need one, for as the Mahatma says, truth is God, and I want no soul to come between me and truth." And Sadhu Narayan speaks about the world and its wheels and the clayey corruption of men, but Moorthy always says, "Truth, truth, and truth," and Sadhu

Narayan gets up to go and he says, "May at least my blessings be on you!" and Moorthy falls at his feet and hold them in grateful respect.

And it was only after this that Sankar, our Sankar, who was the secretary of the Karwar Congress committee, comes and says, "Well, Moorthy, if such be your decision, my whole soul is with you. Gandhiji says, a satyagrahi needs no advocates. He is his own advocate. And how many of us did go to prison in 1921 and never touched the shadow of an advocate. I am an advocate, you will say, but you know I am an advocate only for those who cannot defend themselves." And Moorthy says, "Then if you agree with me, brother, there can be nothing on my conscience," and Moorthy's lips tremble and he falls at Sankar's feet, but when Sankar lifts him up, Moorthy says, "No, brother, you are my elder and a house-holder. I need your blessings." And Sankar says, "If so it is, my blessings are always with you"; and Moorthy feels so exalted that he goes to Sankar and embraces him and says, "Brother, you are with me?" And Sankar says, "I am with you, Moorthy," and then they sit for a while holding each other by the hand, and as the warder comes and says, "Now it is time for you to go, sir," Sankar rises up and says, "But I can hold meetings for you, Moorthy?" and Moorthy says, "Of course, brother!"

And Sankar goes straight to Advocate Ranganna and Advocate Ranganna says, "Certainly." Then he sees Khadi-shop Dasappa and Dasappa says, "Oh, most certainly." And then he sees the president of the college union and this one says, "We are wherever you are," and so Sankar sends for his Volunteers and says, "A meeting in the Gandhi maidan today," and Volunteer after Volunteer goes out to the cloth bazaar and the fish bazaar and the flower bazaar and the grain bazaar, and as the noon cools down, there is a huge crowd in the Gandhi maidan, and the Volunteers are there in khadi kurta and Gandhi-cap crying out, "Order, brother, order! Please take your seats, brother, please!" and Sankar goes up to the platform, and there is a huge ovation and *"Mahatma Gandhi ki jais,"* and Dasappa comes and there is an ovation again, and Advocate Ranganna comes and there is an even greater ovation, for everybody knew he had lately thrown open his private temple to the Pariahs, and with folded hands people hymn up, "Vandè

Mataram." Then they all squat down and Sankar and Ranganna and Dasappa make speeches about the incorruptible qualities of Moorthy, and they say how the foreign Government wants to crush all self-respect, and they then speak of charka and ahimsa and Hindu-Moslem unity, and somebody cries out, "And what about the Untouchables?" and Sankar says, "Of course, we are for them —why, has not the Mahatma adopted an Untouchable?" and somebody cries out again, "Ah, our religion is going to be desecrated by you youngsters!" and Sankar says, "Brother, if you have anything to say, please come up to the platform," and the man says, "And you will allow me to speak?" and Sankar says, "We have no enemies," and the man is seen coming from the other end of the maidan, a lean, tall man in durbar turban and filigree shawl, and he wears gold-cased *rudrakshi* beads at his neck, and he goes up the platform and says:

"Brothers, you have all heard the injurious attacks against the Government and the police and many other things. I am a toothless old man and I have seen many a change pass before me, and may I say this: All this is very good, but if the white men shall leave us tomorrow it will not be Rama-rajya we shall have, but the rule of the ten-headed Ravana. What did we have, pray, before the British came—disorder, corruption, and egoism, disorder, corruption, and egoism I say"—he continued, though there were many shouts and booings against him—"and the British came and they came to protect us, our bones and our dharma. I say dharma and I mean it. For hath not the Lord said in the Gita, 'Whensoever there is ignorance and corruption I come, for I,' says Krishna, 'am the defender of dharma,' and the British came to protect our dharma. And the great Queen Victoria said it when she put the crown of our sacred country on her head and became our beloved sovereign. And when she died—may she have a serene journey through the other worlds!—and when she died—you are too young to know, but ask of your grandfathers how many a camphor was lit before the temple gods, and how many a sacrificial fire was created, and how many a voice did rise up to the heavens in incantation. For not only was she a great queen, a mother-queen, but the most courageous defender of our faith. Tell me, did she not protect it better than any Mohammedan prince had ever done? Now I am an old man.

You are all young. Things change. But what I fear for tomorrow is not the disorder in the material world, but the corruption of castes and of the great traditions our ancestors have bequeathed us. When the British rule disappears there will be neither Brahmin nor Pariah, Vaisya nor Sudra—nay, neither Mohammedan nor Christian, and our eternal dharma will be squashed like a louse in a child's hair. My young brothers, let not such confusion of castes anger our manes, and let the religion of Vasistha and Manu, Sankara and Vidyaranya go unmuddied to the Self-created One. Now I have said all I have to say. . . ."

But before he has stopped somebody says, "So you are a Swami's man?"—and the old man says, "And of course I am, and I have the honour to be."—"And the Swami has just received twelve hundred acres of wet-land from the Government. Do you know that?" says a youngster.—"Of course, and pray what else should he do if he is offered a *rajadakshina*, a royal gift?"—and the youngster says, "So the Swami is a Government man?"—and the old man says, "The Swami is neither for the Government nor against it, but he is for all who respect the ancient ways of our race, and not for all this Gandhi and Gindhi who cannot pronounce even a *gayathri*, and who say there is neither caste nor creed and we are all equal to one another, while the Swami . . ."—And somebody cries out, "Do you know the Swami has been received by the Governor?"—and Sankar rises up and says, "No interruptions, please!"—and the old man answers, "And of course, but why not? And do not the *dharma sastras* say the king is the protector of faith? And I cry out 'Long live George the Fifth, Emperor!' " and he hobbled down from the platform.

Then came youngster after youngster and said Moorthy was excommunicated by the Swami, for Moorthy was for Gandhiji and the Untouchables, and the Swami was paid by the British to do their dirty work. "I have grown in the Mutt," says one, "and I have known what they do. The Mutt, brothers, is the best place for retired high court judges, police inspectors, and God-dedicated concubines, and they are not with us, are they?" And Sankar rises up again and says, "Now it is better we talk of other things," but the young man continues, "The whole trouble has been hatched by the Mutt." Then Advocate Ranganna gets up and says, "And

I too have been excommunicated, for I have thrown open the temple to the Pariahs," and there is a violent ovation, and Ranganna continues, "And I know one thing too that few know, and it is time I said it in the open," and everyobdy began to stand up and the Volunteers cried, "Sit down, please, sit down!" And when there is silence again, Ranganna continues: "Not long ago, I received a visit of a man, and he comes to me and says, 'The Swami would like to see you,' and I say, 'If the Swami likes to see me, I am indeed most honoured!' and straight I go the next morning with fruits and flowers, and the Swami receives me with smiles and blessings and he says, 'I need your help, Ranganna,' and I say, 'Of course, everything is yours, Swamiji,' and the Swami says, 'There is much pollution going on and I want to fight against it,' and I say, 'I am for fighting against all pollution,' and the Swami says, 'For some time there has been too much of this Pariah business. We are Brahmins and not Pariahs. When the Pariahs will have worn out their karma, and will have risen in the waters of purification, nobody will prevent them from becoming Brahmins, even sages, in their next lives. But this Gandhi, who is no doubt a very fine person, is meddling with the *dharma sastras,* the writ laws of the ancient sages, and I am not for it. He said he would like to see me, and I saw him and told him what I thought of it. But he said we did not interpret the *dharma sastras* correctly, and of course it was ridiculous to say that, for who should know better, he or I? But one cannot break the legs of the ignorant. Now, what I have to say is simple: we want to fight against this anti-Untouchable campaign, and I may tell you in confidence, the powers that be, well, they are with the guardians of our trusted traditions."

" 'Swami,' I said, 'how can you accept the help of a foreign Government? Do not the *dharma sastras* themselves call the foreigners *mlechas,* Untouchables?' and the Swami said, 'Governments are sent by the divine will and we may not question it,' and he added, 'And I may say the Government has promised to help us morally and materially,' and at this I got so angry that I rose to go, but the Swami held me by the two hands and said, 'Do take your seat!' but I said, 'No, I cannot, I cannot,' and it was on that very day I took the vow to open our temple to the Pariahs, and that is why I opened it to them. . . ." There was a long ovation—"And therefore, brothers, know for sure what religion is wearing behind its saffron robes. Choose between a saint like Mahatma Gandhi who has given up land and lust and honours and comfort and has dedicated his life to the country, and these fattened Brahmins who want to frighten us with their excommunications, once the Government has paid them well."

At this the police inspector comes up and says, "I put you under arrest!" and Advocate Ranganna answers, "Well, on what authority?" and the police inspector shows him a magistrate's order, and Ranganna offers himself up to the police, and there is a huge, hoarse cry, and ovation after ovation rises—"*Gandhi Mahatma ki jai!*"—"*Vandè Mataram!*"—and processions immediately form themselves, and with Volunteers on either side they march through bazaar and street and lane, and women rush to the veranda, and children follow them still muttering the multiplication tables, and as dusk falls and lights flash from house to house, so shrill rises the cry of "*Mahatma Gandhi ki jai!*" that by the Imperial Bank buildings police cars are already waiting, and the crowd is violently dispersed.

And when the morning came the papers were full of it, and Rangamma's blue paper brought it all to us, and that is how we knew it all. And then we looked at each other and said, "So that is how it is with Bhatta," and everybody said, "And so it is!" and Rangamma said, "That is why Badè Khan was so often seen with him," and Nanjamma said, "Do you remember, sister, he was nowhere to be seen on that awful night?" and everybody said, "Yes, surely, and fools we were not to have seen it earlier," and we all felt the kernel of our hearts burn, for Bhatta had walked our streets with a copper pot in hand and we had fed him. Only Ramakrishnayya said, "There is still many a good heart in this world, else the sun would not rise as he does nor the Himavathy flow by the Kenchamma hill," and all looked at the stars and said, "Yea, the stars of the seven sages hang above us," and as a wall-lizard clucked propitiously, we all beat our knuckles upon the floor and named the holy name, and there came with it such peace into our hearts that we walked back home with the light in our souls. And somewhere beyond the Bebbur mound, somewhere beyond the Bebbur mound and the Kenchamma hill, out against the sky that

91

rises over Karwar, out over the river, there seemed to stand, as one might have said, the supple, firm figure of Moorthy, a Gandhi-cap upon his head and a northern shirt flowing down his waist to the knees. And there was something in his eyes that shone and showed that he had grown even more sorrowful and calm.

And week after week passed, and Rangamma's blue paper brought us this news and that news, and Pandit Venkateshia said, "Why should I not make it come?" and he too began to receive it every Saturday evening, and Rangè Gowda came and said, "Rangamma, Rangamma, I do not know how to read, but my little mosquito goes to school and, if he is worth the milk he has drunk, he will read it out to us," and he too began to get the paper through Postman Subbayya, and evening after evening we gathered on Rangamma's veranda, and when Ramakrishnayya had explained to us a chapter from the *Vedanta sutras,* kneading vermicelli or shaping wicks for the festivals, we began to speak about Moorthy, while our men sat at the village gate, rubbing the snuff or chewing the tobacco leaf, and it seems they said many wicked things about the Government.

Then Seenu would sometimes go to Karwar with a Friday cart and come back with a Tuesday-morning cart, and he would tell us about Sankar and Advocate Ranganna and Seetharamu; and Vasudev, too, would sometimes go in a Skeffington Estate lorry, and he would sometimes slip through the evening and tell us about Moorthy and the case, and everybody said, "The Goddess will free him. She will appear before the judges and free him." And Rangamma vowed she would offer a Kanchi sari to Kenchamma if he were released, and Ratna said she would have a thousand-and-eight-flames ceremony performed, and Nanjamma said she would give the Goddess a silver belt, and Pariah Rachanna said he would walk the holy fire, and all said, "The Goddess will never fail us— she will free him from the clutches of the Red-man." But Vasudev, who was a city boy, said, "No sister, they will give him a good six months," and we all said, "No, no, never!" and Vasudev said, "Well, think what you will, I know these people," and Rangamma then suddenly said, "Let me go to the city and see cousin Seetharamu; he is an advocate and he can tell me something about it," and Nanjamma said, "I too will come with you, sister, for I have to go to my daughter's confinement, and now or in three weeks is all the same to me," and that is why one Pushya night Kitta put the bulls to the cart, and Rangamma and Nanjamma went down to Karwar to see Moorthy.

And when they had bathed and said their prayers, Rangamma said to Seetharamu, "Seetharamu, who is looking after Moorthy's affair?" and Seetharamu said, "Why, Sankar!" and she said, "Why not go and see him?" and he said, "Of course!" and he put on the turban and the coat and they went straight to Sankar, and when Sankar saw Rangamma he said, "Aunt, it is a long time since I saw you—how are things with you?" and Rangamma answered, "Everything is safe—but I have come to speak about Moorthy," and Sankar said, "I love him like a brother, and I have found no better Gandhist," and Rangamma said, "Why, he is the saint of our village," and Sankar said, "Some day he will do holy deeds," and Rangamma said, "Is there nothing to be done to free him from prison?" and Sankar said, "We have done all we can, but the police say it is he who arranged the assault, the assault of the Pariahs on the police," and Rangamma said, "Siva! Siva! Never such a thing would our Moorthy do," and Sankar said, "Of course, of course, aunt," and Rangamma said, "Is there nothing I can do here?" and Sankar said, "Nothing for the moment. But stay and wait for the results," and Rangamma said, "So be it," and that is why she did not come back even for the harvest reapings.

And when she came back for the corn distribution Barber Venkata said, "And mother, what about Moorthappa?" and Pariah Rachanna took his two measures and said, "And, mother, what have the Red-man's Government said about Moorthappa?" and Boatman Sidda said, "If this Government's people were really sons of their father, they would have asked us to stand and bear witness before them!" and Goldsmith Nanjundia said, "Oh, let them do what they like. Our Moorthy is like gold—the more you heat it the purer it comes from the crucible," and the women said, "Oh, when you strike a cow you will fall into the hell of hells and suffer a million and eight tortures and be born an ass. And if this Government cannot tell the difference between a deer and a panther, well, it will fall into the mouth of the precipice," and Rice-pounding Rajamma, who had an evil tongue, said, "May this Government be

93

destroyed!" and she spat three times. And so, from day to day, people said this against the Government and that against the police, and when our Rangè Gowda got dismissed from his patelship, they all cried out, "Oh, this is against the ancient laws—a patel is a patel from father to son, from son to grandson, and this Government wants to eat up the food of our ancestors," and everybody, as they passed by the Kenchamma grove, cried out, "Goddess, when the demon came to eat our babes and rape our daughters, you came down to destroy him and protect us. Oh, Goddess, destroy this Government," and when the women went to cut grass for the calves, they made a song, and mowing the grass they sang:

> Goddess, Goddess, Goddess Kenchamma,
> The mother-in-law has wicked eyes,
> And the sister-in-law has a hungry stomach,
> Betel-nuts never become stone,
> And a virgin will never become pregnant,
> Red is the earth around the Goddess,
> For thou hast slain the Red-demon.

> Goddess, Goddess,
> The mother-in-law has wicked eyes,
> And betel-nuts will never become stone.

And Kanchi Narasamma, who had a long tongue, added:

> Lean is the Brahmin-priest, mother,
> And fat is he when he becomes Bhatta, mother,
> Fat is he when he becomes Bhatta, mother
> And he will take the road to Kashi,
> For gold has stuck in his stomach,
> And he will take the road to Kashi.

> And the sister-in-law has a hungry stomach,
> Betel-nuts will never become stone.

To tell you the truth, Bhatta left us after harvest on a pilgrimage to Kashi. But, don't they say, sister, the sinner may go to the ocean but the water will only touch his knees?

And when Rangamma went back after the corn distributions, she went straight to Sankar instead of staying with cousin Seetharamu, for she had seen much of Sankar and she had liked him and he had liked her, and he had said to her, "When you come to Karwar next, come and stay with me, aunt, and you will help me in my work," and Rangamma had said, "I am poor of mind and of little learning, what can I do for you, Sankaru?" and he had answered, "That does not matter, aunt—what we need is force and fervour, and I am living with my little daughter and my aged mother, and you may perhaps arrange my papers and look after the Congress correspondence," and though Rangamma was the humblest of women, she liked this, and she said, "If the gods choose me, I will not say 'Nay,'" and that's why she went to stay with Sankaru. And when Waterfall Venkamma heard of this she said, "Oh! this widow has now begun to live openly with her men," and she spat on the house and said this man had her and that man had her, and she began to say she would go to the courts and have back Rangamma's property, for land and lust and wifely loyalty go badly together, like oil and soap and hot water. But she said, "Let Bhatta come and he will do it for me." But our Rangamma was as tame as a cow and she only said, "One cannot stitch up the mouths of others. So let them say what they like." And as everybody knew, Sankar was an ascetic of a man and had refused marriage after marriage after he had lost his wife, and everybody had said, "This is not right, Sankaru. You are only twenty-six and you have just put up the Advocate's signboard, and you will soon begin to earn, and when you have a nine-pillared house you will need a Lakshmi-like goddess to adorn it," but Sankar simply forced a smile and said, "I have had a Lakshmi and I, a sinner, could not even keep her, and she has left me a child and that is enough." But his old father came and said, "But, no, Sankaru, you cannot do that. You are our eldest son, and you have to give us at least a grandson so that when we are dead our manes will be satisfied," but Sankar smiled back again and said, "If you want the marriage thread to be tied in an ocean of tears, I shall. But otherwise I will not. I have a daughter and I will bring her up. And you will come and stay with me and we shall have a household running," and the old mother wept and the old father knit his eyebrows, but Sankar smiled back and said, "I shall obey you," but they did not press him further, and they said, "His wife Usha was such a godlike woman. She would never utter a word loud, and never say 'nay' to anything. And when she

95

walked the streets, they always say what a holy wife she was and beaming with her wifehood, and never a mother-in-law had a daughter-in-law like her," and they both said, "Well, we can understand Sankaru. When one has lost Usha nothing can replace her." And they never again gave Sankar's horoscope to anyone, and they came to stay with him and look after his sanctum and his child.

And the old father, who was a retired taluk office clerk, knew how to write English, and he said he would address envelopes for Congress meetings, and sometimes he went to join Dasappa, who had opened a khadi shop in the town. And when Dasappa was ill or away on Congress duty, it was old Venkataramayya who looked after the shop, measuring out yard after yard of khadi and saying, "This is from the Badanaval centre, and that is from the Pariahs of Siddapura, and this upper cloth is almost the work of the Mahatma, for where do you think it comes from?—Sabarmati itself!" And when a young man came to buy a towel or pair of dhotis he would say, "Hè, have you read the latest *Young India?*" and if he should say "Nay," he would tell them they were a set of buffaloes fit to be driven with kick and knout, and thrusting the paper into the young man's hands, he would offer him a chair and say, "Read this, it is useful," or, "Skip through this, it is less useful," and when children came he gave them pinches and peppermints and told them stories of Tilak and Gandhi and Chittaranjan Das, and such funny stories they were, too, that they called him Gandhi-grandpa. And his wife cooked food for the family and she said, "One day Sankar will earn as much as Advocate Ranganna, and he will buy a motor car, too," but Sankar laughed and said, "Mother, you must forget your dreams. Don't you see I am not a man to make money?" At which Satamma said this about what Ramachandra had said about Sankar's reputation, and that about Professor Patwardhan's appreciation: "Your son, Sankar, he is a saint," and when he walked the main bazaar, they used to say, "Look there, there goes the ascetic advocate." People sometimes looked at his khadi coat and his rough yarn turban and laughed at this "walking advocate," and others said, "No, no, he follows the principles of the Mahatma."—"And what, pray, are the principles of the Mahatma?"—"Why, don't you know Sankar does not take a single false case, and before he takes a client he says to him, "Swear before me you are not the criminal!" and the client says this and that, but Sankar always comes back to the point and says, 'You know if you do not tell me the whole truth, well, I may be forced to withdraw in the middle of the case,'" and, indeed, as everyone knows, he withdrew in the middle of the case between Shopkeeper Rama Chetty and Contractor Seenappa over false accounts, between Borèhalli Nanjunda and Tippayya, and you know how he withdrew in the last criminal case they had in Karwar. You see, this is what really happened. One Rahman Khan was supposed to have tried to murder one Subba Chetty, for Subba Chetty had taken away his mistress Dasi. And everybody said, "Poor Subba Chetty, poor Subba Chetty!"—and everybody said, "He will win the case easily." And Subba Chetty was an old client of Sankar and so he goes to Sankar and tells him the story and swears it is all true, and Sankar says, "Now this is going to be a criminal case, and if you have hidden a thing small as a hair, you will come to grief, Subba Chetty!" And Subba Chetty sheds many a tear and says he is a good householder and he would never tell a lie and the lingam in his hand is witness to it. And Sankar takes the case and prepares the papers, and he says he will have to see Dasi, but Subba Chetty says, "Dasi is very ill, father, but her word is my word and my word is hers," and Sankar says, "Bring her before the sessions," and Subba Chetty says, "If Siva wills, so it shall be," and Sankar says, "Then you may go"; and the case is filed and summonses are sent and the day of the hearing arrives, and Subba Chetty is the last to come and says the wheels broke down and the rains, how they poured, and this and that, and when Dasi comes to the bar she is as hale as a first-calved cow, and she turns this way and she turns that way and she does her hair and wipes her eyes and stands up and sits down and bites her sari-fringe, and Subba Chetty gets angry and says, "Stop this concubine show!" And when the cross-examination begins it is Advocate Ramanna who begins to heckle her with questions, and Dasi breaks into a fit of sobs and says something and Subba Chetty cries, "Woman! Woman!" and Dasi runs up to the advocate and falls at his feet and says, "I know nothing, father! Nothing!" And when Sankar hears that, he asks the judge for permission to speak to his client, and he says to Subba Chetty, "On your mother's honour, tell me if you

97

have not concocted the story to pinch Rahman Khan's coconut garden?" And Subba Chetty trembles and says, "No, no, Sankarappa!" But Sankar has seen the game and he turns to the magistrate and says, "I beg to ask your Lordship for an adjournment," and the magistrate, who knows Sankar's ways, says, "Well, you have it." When Sankar gets back home, he asks Subba Chetty to speak the truth, and Subba Chetty tells him how he had employed Dasi to go and live with Rahman Khan and to enrage him against Subba Chetty, "with drink and smoke and lust," and with drink and smoke and lust Rahman Khan had cried out he would murder that Subba Chetty and had run out with an axe and Subba Chetty had cried out, "Murder! Murder!" in the middle of the street, and Dasi had run out innocently and tried to calm Rahman Khan, who was so weak that he had rolled upon the earth, an opium lump. And when Sankar heard this he said, "Go and confess this to the magistrate," and the next day the magistrate gave him three years' rigorous imprisonment, with one year for Dasi. And Sankar asked pardon in public of Rahman Khan, who got six months, too.

It is from that day that people said, "Take care when you go to Sankar; he will never take a false case." And he took but the lowest fee, and when the clients were poor he said to his clerk, "Make an affidavit for Suranna's Dasanna. Stamps, private account, please," and people began to come to him more and more and never was there a man in Karwar that had risen so quickly in public esteem and legal success as he. But he never bought a car and never dressed in hat and shoes and suit, and always smiled at everyone. And when the court was over he did not go like Barrister Sastri and Advocate Ramrao to the Bar Club to have whisky-and-soda and God knows what, but he went straight to the floor above the khadi shop, where the new Hindi teacher Surya Menon held classes, and when Sankar had time he divided the class into two and gave a lesson to the latecomers. He said Hindi would be the national language of India, and though Kannada is good enough for our province, Hindi must become the national tongue, and whenever he met a man in the street, he did not say "How are you?" in Kannada, but took to the northern manner and said "Ram-Ram." But what was shameful was the way he began to talk Hindi to his mother, who understood not a word of it, but he said she would learn it one day; and he spoke nothing but Hindi to his daughter, and if by chance he used an English word, as they do in the city, he had a little closed pot, with a slit in the lid, into which he dropped a coin, and every month he opened it and gave it to the Congress fund. And if any of his friends should utter an English word in his house, he would say, "Drop me a coin," and the friends got angry and called him a fanatic; but he said there must be a few fanatics to wash the wheel of law, and he would force his friends to drop the coin and if they refused he dropped one himself.

And he was a fanatic, too, in his dress, you know, sister. When he went to a marriage party he used to say, "Everyone must be in khadi or I will not go," and they said, "Oh, one must have a nice Dharmawar sari for the bride; she cannot look like a street sweeper," and he would say, "Well, have your Dharmawar saris and send your money to Italian yarn makers and German colour manufacturers and let our Pariahs and peasants starve," and when they pleaded, "Just one Dharmawar sari?" he would say, "I am not the head of the family, but if you wear anything but khadi I will not go!" And that is how nobody in their house nor in their cousin's house had any new Dharmawar saris, and when they went for any kumkum and haldi invitation, they put on their old saris and slipped out through the back door. And he also made the whole family fast—fast on this day because it is the anniversary of the day the Mahatma was imprisoned, fast on that day for the Jallianwalabagh massacre, and on another day in memory of the day of Tilak's death, and some day he would have made everyone fast for every cough and sneeze of the Mahatma. "Fasting is good for the mind," he would say, and even on the days he fasted he was in full spirits and went to court and spun his three hundred yards of yarn every morning instead of his prayers, and he said the gods would be happy when the hungry stomachs had food.

But what a good expression he had on his face, sister! He looked a veritable *Dharmaraja*. And Rangamma told us never a man smiled more and sang more at home than he, and he was always the earliest to rise and the last to go to bed, yet he was always in the best of health. "Lemon water and gymnastics, gymnastics and lemon water, can keep the plague at the doorstep," he used to say, and to tell you the truth, never had Rangamma looked so healthy and serene as she did then. She was nearing forty, but she looked hardly thirty-three, and there was not a grey hair on her head. And she would work, too, then, she could talk and write and hold classes and sometimes she even went, they said, to meetings with Sankar. And once Sankar had asked her to say a few words about Moorthy, and she had stood up and spoken of Moorthy the good, Moorthy the religious, and Moorthy the noble, and she had found no more words, and she had come down from the platform and had begun to shiver and tears had come into her eyes. But she said that was the first time, but if she had ever to speak again she would have no such fears, and of course we knew she was a tight-jawed person and she could speak like a man.

Rangamma came back from Karwar for the Magh cattle fair, and two days later we heard that the Red-man's judges had given Moorthy three months' rigorous imprisonment. The whole afternoon no man left his veranda, and not a mosquito moved in all Kanthapura.

We all fasted.

The next day the rain set in and it poured and it plundered all the fields and the woods, and Ramakrishnayya, going to spit over the railings of the veranda, stumbled against a pillar and, falling, lost consciousness, and that very night, without saying a word, without giving a sigh, he closed his eyes forever. And everybody said, "The rains have come; oh, what shall we do for the cremations? Oh, what?" And Pandit Venkateshia immediately sent for the beadles and asked them to raise a mango pandal on the banks of the Himavathy, and the good Pariahs, they worked hour after hour during the night, and when the next morning the body was washed and the corpse tied to the bamboo, the rains suddenly lifted themselves up, and behind the jack-fruit tree the sun rose like a camphor censer alit, and while the waters were still gurgling in the gutters, the procession hurried on, and they lighted the pyre in the open, and the head burst but a moment later, and we lifted our eyes to the heavens and muttered, "He goes the way of the saints." And Rangamma vowed she would take his bones to Kashi, but all of a sudden the river began to swell and when it came crawling by the pyre, people asked, "What shall we do? Oh what?" but the swell bubbled out by the pyre and Rangamma gave a sigh, and when the body was ashed down whole and only a few cinders lay blinking behind the bones, a huge swell churned round the hill and swept the bones and ashes away. And we all cried out, "Narayan! Narayan!," and that night, sister, as on no other night, no cow would give its milk, and all the night a steady rain kept pattering on the tiles, and the calves pranced about their mothers and groaned. . . . Lord, may such be the path of our out going soul!

11

WHEN RAMAKRISHNAYYA was dead we all asked, "And now who will explain to us Vedantic texts, and who will discuss philosophy with us?" And Nanjamma said, "Why, we shall ask Temple Ranganna!," but we all said, "Temple Ranganna! Well, he can hardly read the texts he repeats morning and evening, and he cannot explain to us about *Vidya* and *Avidya!*," and Rangamma said, "Why, you know he is also a Bhatta's man; after all, sisters, why should not one of us read the texts and we comment on them ourselves?" and Nanjamma said, "No, we shall have someone to read the texts, and you shall lead the commentary," and Rangamma said, "Oh yes! why, our Ratna knows how to read, and Ratna and my sister are going to come and live with me, now that my mother has gone to my brother, and their house has to be re-built," and we all looked at each other, and we were silent, for never was a girl born in Kanthapura that had less interest in philosophy than Ratna. But we all knew Rangamma was a good woman and a pious soul, and if Ratna merely read out the texts, well, her tongue would not pollute them, would it?

And so every afternoon Ratna began to read the texts to us, and when it came to discussion, Rangamma would say, "Sister, if for the thorny pit the illusioned fall into, you put the foreign Government, and for the soul that searches for liberation, you put our India, everything is clear;" and this way and that she would always bring the British Government into every page and line. And it must have been all due to her stay with Sankaru, for never had she spoken thus before, and she told us story after story from the Vedas and Puranas, and we all said, "Why, our Rangamma is becoming a learned person, and she will soon be able to discuss philosophy like Ramakrishnayya," and the more we listened the more she impressed us, and we felt there was a new strength come in Rangamma, and we said to her one day, "Rangamma, Rangamma, is it the city that gave you all this learning?" and Rangamma is silent for a moment and then says, "No, sisters, it is not only that!"—"Then what else, sister?"—and Rangamma says, "Why, there is something else"—"And what is that, Rangamma?" and Rangamma says, "Why, sisters, I saw Sadhu Narayan."—"And what did he say?" asked Nanjamma. —"Why, he said nothing. He only taught me how to meditate. He said, 'You do not know how to practice meditation, and I shall teach it to you,' and he taught me the first principles of Yoga, and I sit every morning now, and I take breath through the right nostril and the left nostril like my father did, and strength has been flowing into me." So Nanjamma said, "Why not show it to us, sister? You are not the only one who wants to grow saintly," and we all said, "Show it to us, Rangamma, show it," and Rangamma said, "Well, so be it." And on the following Thursday, after the clothes were washed and the ablutions over, we sat by the Himavathy, and Rangamma repeated the name of her guru, Sadhu Narayan, and she showed us how to control our breath, and from that day on Nose-scratching Nanjamma, and Post-office-house Satamma, and Gauramma and Vedamma and I, and even Ratna, began to feel stronger and stronger, the eyes burned brighter in the sockets and the mind deeper in the spirit.

And one day, when we had been practicing this for days and days, Rangamma said, "Now, sisters, I have seen something in the city, and I should like to see it here." We all thought she was going to show us some new exercises, but they were no new exercises; she only said we should all get together and stand and obey her, and that when the Mahatma will call us to act, we shall have to go out and fight for him, but we said, "Nay, nay, we are not men, Rangamma!" but Rangamma said, "In the city there are groups and groups of young women, girls, married women, and widows, who have joined together and have become Volunteers—Volunteers they call them—and they practice exercises like the police, and when meetings are held they all get together and maintain order." And Nose-scratching Nanjamma said, "Why, I am not a man to fight, sister!" and Rangamma said, "Why, sister, you need not be a man to fight. Do you know the story of Rani Lakshmi Bai, and do you know how she fought for India? Once upon a time when the

English were still not masters of the country, there were many, many kings, and one king could not bear the other. So the English went to this king and said, 'We shall help you to rule your people. We shall only collect taxes for you and you shall live in your palace and be a king,' and they went to another and said, 'Why, you have enemies in the south and the east and the north, and you have to defend yourself against them, and we have a strong army, and we have much power and powder and we can defend you,' and the raja said, 'Well, that is a fine thing!' and he gave them titles and land and money. And so the English would go from one maharaja to the other and one day they would be the kings of India. Now there was an imprisoned king in India called Tantia Topi, and then there was Rani Lakshmi Bai, and then there were small kings and big kings and many landless kings, and they all said, 'We shall throw the Red-man into the sea,' and they all waited for the propitious moment. And then, sister, suddenly the army rose against the Red-man, for the Red-man wanted the Hindus to eat cow's flesh and the Mohammedan to eat pig's flesh, and the army rose and fought against the Red-man—that is why they call it the Soldiers' Revolt, in their language—and this king and that king said, 'Now this is the time to strike the English,' and they gathered together, and the worthiest of them was Rani Lakshmi Bai of Jhansi. Why, she rode the horse like a Rajput, and held her army against the British, beating them on the left and on the right, and the British went back and back, but one day they defeated her and she died upon her horse fighting to the last, fighting for her enslaved Mother. This, sister, I have read in books in the city, and Sankar told me many such stories. And know, too, sisters, how the Rajput women fought with their husbands, and if their husbands were defeated and the enemy was going to enter the fortress, they prepared the pyre and all went round it in prayer and finally jumped into the flames, for never a Rajput shall be slave."

And Nanjamma said, "Why, that's the story, The Red Pyre, in . . . what's that woman? . . . Saradamma, yes, in Saradamma's novel," and Rangamma said, "Of course, of course, and we are but unworthy of all these people and of all the people who are in the Congress and who fight with the Congress—Kamaladevi and Sarojini Naidu and Annie Besant, all the heroic daughters who fight for the Mother—and we, we think of nothing but the blowpipe and the broomstick, and the milking of the many cows. We, too, should organize a Volunteer corps, and when Moorthy returns we shall go to meet him like they do in the city." And we all said, "That will be beautiful!" and each one said, "I shall wear the Dharmawar sari and the diamond hair-flower"—"And I shall wear the sari I wore at Nanjamma's daughter's marriage, that everybody liked so much, and I shall wear the gold belt too," and those who were widows said, "Well, I shall wear only the gold belt and the necklace, now that I cannot wear the bangles," and Ratna said, "I shall part my hair to the left, and wear just a tiny kumkum mark and wear the sari till it reaches the toes and it will float and flutter so well"; and Rangamma said, "We shall offer him *arathi*," and all our hearts gladdened; and we said, "That will be like a bridegroom's welcome ceremony to go and meet Moorthy on the Karwar road by the Kenchamma temple," and we said, "We shall do as you like, sister," and that is how we became Volunteers. And Rangamma said, "Let us not call ourselves Volunteers—let us call ourselves Sevika Sangha," and we were called Sevis. . . .

And when our men heard of this, they said: was there nothing left for our women but to vagabond about like soldiers? And every time the milk curdled or a dhoti was not dry, they would say, "And this is all because of this Sevi business," and Radhamma's husband beat her on that day he returned from village inspection, though she was seven months pregnant. And Post-office Satamma's husband would not talk to her: "Why, soon it will be as if the men will have to wear bangles and cook, so that you women may show yourselves off! You shall not set your feet in Rangamma's house again!" Rangamma goes to him and says, "So you are not a Gandhi's man. Because Moorthy is in prison you are no more a Gandhi's man," and Suryanarayana says, "I am a Gandhi's man, aunt. But if I cannot have my meals as before, I am not a man to starve . . ." and Rangamma says, "If you don't have your meals on time, it is not because of our Sevika Sangha. We practice only in the afternoon," and then Suryanarayana says, "I don't know, aunt, but I want my wife to look after my comforts and I go out every morning and come home in the evening through rain and dark and storm," and Rangamma says, "Of course, Satamma has to look after your

105

comforts. If we are to help others, we must begin with our husbands," and she tells Satamma, "Your husband is not against Sevika Sangha. He only wants to eat on time." Satamma grumbles and swears and says she serves him on time, and it is all false; but Rangamma tells her to be more regular in cooking, and we all say, "We should do our duty. If not, it is no use belonging to the Gandhi-group." Rangamma says, "That is right, sister," and we say, "We shall not forget our children and our husbands." But how can we be like we used to be? Now we hear this story and that story, and we say we too shall organize a foreign cloth boycott like at Sholapur, we too, shall go picketing cigarette shops and toddy shops, and we say our Kanthapura, too, shall fight for the Mother, and we always see the picture of Rani Lakshmi Bai that Rangamma has on the veranda wall, a queen, sweet and young and bejewelled, riding a white horse and looking out across the narrow river and the hills to where the English armies stand. And what do you think? —one day, Sata's Rangi came running to us and said, "Aunt, I was playing with Nanju. And I said to him, you shall be the British army, and Ramu will be the Kashi maharaj and the Oudh maharaj and the Punjab maharaj, and I will be Rani Lakshmi Bai, and he says he wants to be the Rani, and I say, 'But I am the woman,' and he says, 'That does not matter,' and I say, 'I am the woman,' and he says, 'I will not play,'" and Rangamma calls the children and says, "You will be Rani Lakshmi Bai once, and you will then put on a turban, and he will put a kumkum mark on his face and he will be Rani Lakshmi Bai," and the children were so happy at this that they went away puffy-cheeked and satisfied.

And sometimes, when we stood in Rangamma's courtyard, Rangamma would say, "Now, if the police should fall on you, you must stand without moving a hair," and we would feel a shiver run down our backs, and we would say, "No, sister, that is too difficult," and Rangamma would say, "No, sister, that is not difficult. Does not the Gita say, the sword can split asunder the body, but never the soul? And if we say, we shall not move a hair, we shall not move a hair." And one day Nanjamma came and said, "Sisters, last night I dreamt my husband was beating me and beating me, and I was crying and my bangles broke and I was saying, 'Oh, why does he beat men with a stick and not with his hands?' and then when I saw him again, it was no more my husband, it was Badé Khan, and I gave such a shriek that my husband woke me up. Sister, I cannot fight like that," and Rangamma said, "Well, you will be with us, and if the fight begins, I shall say, 'Are you ready to fight with us, sister Nanjamma? Ready to fight without moving a hair?' and if you say, 'Yes, sister,' you will come with us, and if you say, 'No,' we shall say, 'That does not matter, our Nanjamma is only afraid,'" and we say, "That is a fine thing, for we cannot say if we can face the police lathis." But Rangamma says, "When you and your daughters and your husbands walk the holy fire, does it scorch or not, sisters?" and we say, "No, no, Rangamma"—"When Madanna and Rajanna and Siddayya smite their bodies with swords, when the grace of Kenchamma has touched them, does it cut them, sister?" and we say, "No, no, Rangamma"—"When That-house Srikanta was graced by the goddess every Tuesday and fell flat on the ground in adoration, did you ever see a bruise on his skin, sisters?," and we say, "No, no, Rangamma"—"Well, we shall fight the police for Kenchamma's sake, and if the rapture of devotion is in you, the lathi will grow as soft as butter and as supple as a silken thread, and you will hymn out the name of the Mahatma." And we all grow dumb and mutter, "Yes, sister, yes," and then Venkatalakshmi says, "But, sister, there will be Moorthy, too, and he will defend us," but Rangamma merely waves her hand and says, "We shall see, we shall see. . . ."

And sometimes Seenu or Vasudev would come when we did our exercises, and they would say, "We, too, should organize such a corps, but the boys will not come," and Rangamma says, "Why in your Pariah school you must have some boys," and Seenu says, "No, Rangamma. Since the arrest of Moorthy they are all afraid. They say, 'We are not all going to sit behind the cage-bars like kraaled elephants,' and when I say, 'What does that matter, we are for the Mahatma,' they say, 'Yes, yes, learned sir, but our lands will go uncultivated, and there will be neither child nor woman to pull the weeds or direct the canal water,' and I say, 'We are fighting so that the rents may be lowered and the foreign rule vanish, and you will all live happily,' and they say, 'Oh, father, we cannot hope for Ramarajya in these days; we live in Kaliyuga, learned sir,' and I say, 'So you will not fight for the Mahatma and Moorthy?'

and they say, 'Nay, nay, we shall fight, but we don't want the prison,' and the women say, 'Oh, it's good as things are, and we haven't more holes in the mouth for more morsels,' and with this and that they are growing weaker and weaker. But Rangè Gowda says, 'Let the harvests be over, and we shall cane these idiots to follow you,' and I tell Rangè Gowda he should be with us, and he says, 'With whom am I then?' and he gets angry, and I say, 'You are with us of course, Rangè Gowda,' and some day we, too, shall organize a Volunteer corps. But, sister, you can have your eleven Volunteers in the courtyard, for you are women. But when Badè Khan sees us, he will fall on us." And Vasudev says, "In the Estate he spits and beats everyone. Already he has moved down to the hut by the main gate, and he and his dog and his woman keep guard over everyone that crosses the stile. But, sister, the fever of the country has got him, too, and he moans heavily from his bed. And his woman is not so bad, you know. When she sees me, she winks and lays her head upon her hand to say 'He is asleep,' and I slip out like a rat. After all, she is one of us. . . ."

Then Vasudev turns to Rangamma and says, "Why not start our bhajans again, sister? We shall keep it going as though Moorthy were not in prison," and Seenu says, "So we should." But Moorthy said to Sankar, "Let them prepare themselves for the fight. But no processions or bhajan lest the police fall on them!" and Vasudev says, "No, if Moorthy were here he would start the bhajans again," and Rangamma says, "So I think, too," and we all say, "That will be fine." And on the Saturday that followed, Seenu went and blew the conch from the promontory, and men rushed to the temple, men and old women and children and all, and we all said, "Now it is going to be bright again in Kanthapura," and we knew not how to hold our hearts within our breasts. Cymbal, conch, and camphor, clapping hands and droning drums, the perfume of the sandal paste, flowers in the hair, and in our eyes, Siva's eyes.

> Changing he changes not,
> Ash-smeared, he's Parvati's sire,
> Moon on his head,
> And poison in his throat,
> Chant, chant, chant the name of Eesh,
> Chant the name of Siva Lord!

12

IN VAISAKH men plough the fields of Kanthapura. The rains have
come, the fine, first-footing rains that skip over the bronze
mountains, tiptoe the crags, and leaping into the valleys, go splashing and wind-swung, a winnowed pour, and the coconuts and the
betel nuts and the cardamom plants choke with it and hiss back.
And there, there it comes over the Bebbur hill and the Kanthur
hill and begins to paw upon the tiles, and the cattle come running
home, their ears stretched back, and the drover lurches behind some
bel tree or pipal tree, and people leave their querns and rush to
the courtyard, and turning toward the Kenchamma temple, send
forth a prayer, saying, "There, there, the rains have come, Kenchamma; may our houses be white as silver," and the lightning
flashes and the thunder stirs the tiles, and children rush to the
gutter-slabs to sail paper boats down to Kashi. And Agent Nanjundia's wife, Chennamma, and Subba Chetty's Putti are already in
the street, filtering the waters for the gold dust; and Priest Rangappa
opens his book bundle and looks into the calendar and says, "Oh,
tomorrow is the *rohini* star, and people will yoke their bulls to the
plough." And, umbrella in hand, there is Rangè Gowda, a coconut
and betel leaves in his arms, and he goes to Priest Rangappa and
says, "And when, learned sir?" and Rangappa looks this side and
that, for the beadles were no more Rangè Gowda's, and the village
was no more Rangè Gowda's, but the voice it was for ever Rangè
Gowda's, and so Rangappa looks at the ground and says, "Why,
tomorrow, Rangè Gowda." And Rangè Gowda goes home and
swears at the beadles, and Beadle Chenna says, "And when is it,
Patel?"—"Why, tomorrow, you rat of a woman," and Beadle
Chenna goes home and sleeps, and when the frogs have stopped
croaking there is Chenna with his drum in his hand crying, "Oh,
Ohè, this morning the plough will be blessed," and people say, "Oh,

this morning already," and Satanna rises up and says, "Why, my right eye winks: we shall have a grand harvest," and Weaver Chennayya rushes up and washes himself, and puts oil on his hair, and his wife goes to the back yard to pick flowers in the garden, and Chandrayya puts on the velvet coat he had made in town when he won his case against Sidda, and Ramayya opens his eyes wide and looks between the tiles and says, "Oh, Sun God, give us a fine harvest this year and I'll pay up Bhatta's three hundred seventy-five rupees, and marry my last daughter and offer to Kenchamma the goat that I promised her for my woman's cure," and Pariah Timmayya says, "Oh, why must I wake? My yoke is without bulls, and my field without grain," but his wife, strong woman that she is, she says, "Go, man, the gods are not so unkind," and Timmayya grumbles and groans, and with neither flower nor caste mark he goes into the street—while men and boys drive the bulls out, ploughs on their shoulders and whips in their hands, and when they come to the river, they rub the bulls and wash them and tie flowers to their horns, and "Hè, hè," they shout as they drive them to the temple courtyard.

"Hè, hè," the rains have sunk into the earth, and Gap-tooth Siddayya drives his stick into the earth and says, "Why, she has gone four fingers deep," and they all say, "Why, it rained as though the goddess had asked for it." And then, when the day is all wide and the men and the bulls are all come, there comes Priest Rangappa with his holy jug on his head and his wet clothes in his hands, and says, "You are all here! hè?" and they answer, "Yes, learned sir," and he opens the door, pulls wide the holy curtain, bathes the goddess and adorns her, and Trumpet Lingayya and Pipe Ramayya are there, and they stand by the champak and they blow the horn to the east and the west and the north and the south, and from the east and the west and the north and the south, in the ringing rain-cleared air, there comes back the rasp and roar of the horn, and people are seen rushing with their ploughs and bulls, and the bells of the yokes go ringing through the temple grove. They are coming, Rachanna and Madanna, and even Potter Ranga and Pariah Sidda and Timmayya's son Bhima, and Mota and Tippa, who have neither bulls nor fields, they, too, come with flowers in their hair. And Priest Rangappa says with his gruff

110

voice, "And you are all ready, you sons of my woman?" and they all cry out, "Of course! Of course!"—"And where is *he?*" and they answer, "The Patel is coming, there he is!" and the Patel is seen coming on his horse, his filigree shawl thrown over his shoulders, his durbar turban on his head and his English reins in his hands, and Mada running behind him, as though collector and governor could wipe the saliva off their mouths, but never would Rangè Gowda be anything but Patel in Kanthapura. And when he reaches the Black-serpent's-anthill he gets down, throws the reins into Mada's hands and walks up unhurriedly to the courtyard. And Priest Rangappa is heard to ring the bell in the sanctum, and all eyes grow dim and the eyelids droop and everyone says, "There, there the goddess is going to show her face," and they tremble and press against each other, and when the legs itch they do not scratch, when the waters drip they do not shake, and then suddenly the curtain is drawn, and Mother Kenchamma is there straight, bright and benign, and the candelabra weave their lights around her, and they say, "Maybe, she has passed a good night!" Then Priest Rangappa lights the camphor and lifts it up to her jewelled face and takes it round her diamond hands and ruby feet, and then flowers quietly roll down her face, and they all say, "There, she has sent us her blessings. O Kenchamma, give us a fine harvest and no sickness, Kenchamma, Kenchamma, goddess," and even the bulls stand without waving their tails. And then Rangappa comes with a pot of holy water and splashes it now on this bull and now on that, and they shiver and slouch back, waving their bells to the goddess, and the camphor and the sandal are brought, and men take the camphor and the sandal, and they all look up to see if the sun is visible somewhere, and there, beyond the temple grove over the Horse-head hill, there is a ruddy streak as wide as a sari hem, and they tremble and fold their hands and whisper. And then Rangè Gowda whispers to Priest Rangappa and Priest Rangappa to Subbè Gowda, "Why, yours are the youngest bulls. You will tie them to the yoke," and he is so proud, and he comes forward to his three-year-old Amrithamahal bulls that he had bought at the Santur cattle fair, and the plough is clean and sharp, and everybody looks up again and again for the goddess' vehicle, an eagle, to show itself, and as Priest Rangappa goes on chanting the hymns and ringing the bell, there he comes from over the temple spire, there he comes, the feather of God, and turns once, twice, thrice round the temple and the men and the bulls, and the horns shout across the grove and the valley to the mountaintops. And Priest Rangappa breaks a coconut on the rock and they throw flowers and coloured rice as Subbè Gowda cries out, "Hèhè, hèhè, ho!" and the plough cuts the earth and spatters the clods, and the farther they go the lighter does it cut. And when the serpent field and the village common and the tank gardens are done, Subba lifts the plough right out, and the bulls run the faster, and they cry, "Hoyla! Hoyla!" and throwing the flowers and splashing the rice, they rush past the Skeffington Estate, and Bhatta's Devil fields, and the riverbank, and once the temple tank is reached, Subba staggers and swirls round, and going down the mound comes straight into the court-yard, and he stops—and they all stop and cough and wipe away their sweat, while Temple Rangappa breaks a coconut again and offers it to the bulls. And they all throw puffed rice at each other and they offer Rangappa a nickel coin each, and then Rangappa goes in and comes out with a silver pot of holy water, and he throws a handful in each of the eight directions, and they say, "Now, we can till the earth," and with the sacred flower behind their ears, and their hearts rich with holiness, the women rush back to their homes and men to their fields, crying, "Hoye! Hoye! Hoyeee-la!"

And Siddanna's neighbour shouts to Madanna, and Madanna's neighbour shouts to Rachanna, "Hè, the dame is soft, hè, brother?" —"Oh yes, soft as a pumpkin's kernel."—"Hè, the river is rising, brother, do you see the brownish waters?" And then there is a grunt and gurgle from over the Blue Mountains, and a fine, swish-ing rain pours down upon the earth. They stop the bulls, and seated beneath the tamarind trees, they light their bidies, and when the cows are milked, women take them their food. Today there will be sweetmeats and fresh rice. "Oh, you prostitute of a wind! She's showing her tricks again. Stop, you bitch!" There! The winds die over the river, and the rain pours on.

O Kenchamma, in a week we shall have ploughed and manured and sowed. Send us rain for three days, dry weather for two days, and rain again, a fine, soft rain, Kenchamma. And when Moorthappa comes, let the rice be fine as filigree and the mangoes yellow as gold, and we shall go out, horn and trumpet and gong before us, and break coconuts at his feet. O Moorthappa, Kenchamma will protect us all. . . .

They say he'll come, Moorthy, when the winds will have risen.

Then everybody said, "We shall do this for Moorthy's coming and that for Moorthy's coming," and Rangamma said she would offer a feast at the river, a moonlight feast, and Nanjamma said she would offer a syrup-and-banana libation at the temple, and some said they would spin more and more, and Pariah Lingayya said he would offer Moorthy a red khadi shawl, and Seenu said, "Why, I shall make the boys sing 'Oh, such were our men of 1857.'" But Vasudev said Badè Khan was looking strange lately, and that something must be in his head, but Rangamma said, "Well, so be it, what does it matter? We are so many now," and everybody said, "Well, it will be fine when Moorthy comes." And Chinnamma's mother-in-law was so happy that she said, "The rice-eating ceremony of the child, well, it will be when Moorthy is our guest." Pariah Rachanna says, "Why not build a pandal at the entrance of the village, like we do when the collector comes?" And they go to see Rangamma. "Mother Rangamma, when is he coming, our Moorthappa?" and Rangamma says, "I do not know, it must be on Saturday or Tuesday," and Lingayya says, "Then you'll tell us poor folk, mother, and we shall make it bright, and have a pandal and have the camphor lighted to the village-gate goddess," and Rangamma feels so happy that she says, "Why, it will be grand."

And that afternoon, Postman Subbayya, who had no fire in his stomach and was red with red and blue with blue, comes running with the Blue paper in his hand and says, "Rangamma, Rangamma, your Moorthy is released," and we all say, "Show us that, show us!" and Rangamma snatches the paper and reads out that Moorthy has been released from prison, and that he has said this and that, and Sankar had organized a huge meeting to receive him, and we all said, "So he's coming now, he's coming," and we left our vermicelli paste and cotton wicks and we sang, "The Blue god he comes, prancing and playing," and the Pariahs went to the mango grove and tore down young leaves and twigs, and Patel Rangè Gowda said, "Take two banana trunks from my garden," and they

113

slew two banana trunks, and when evening came there swung over the Karwar road a yellow arch of banana leaves and a green festoon of mango leaves, and the two candelabra stood like Brahma's guardians of the twin portals, and everybody said, "It will be so fine on Tuesday, it will be like the swing festival of the goddess."

But when Venkamma hears of this she says, "Oh, you polluted ones, this is what you are going to do! Well, well!" and she rushes straight to Rangappa to consult him about her daughter's nuptial date, for young Nanja had come of age a few days before, and she says, "Can it be this Tuesday, Rangappa?" and Rangappa finishes his evening prayers, and takes a pinch of snuff and, opening the calendar, he says, "Why, it could be; but they say that fellow Moorthy is coming," and she says, "It is just that, Rangappa —don't you see?" and she sends messengers to Alur to inform her gap-toothed son-in-law of the nuptial ceremony, and the next morning at the river she says, "I want my daughter to go to her husband's house soon. Tuesday will be the nuptial day, and you are all welcome, sisters, and the invitation will be sent to you," and we all say, "But that's the day Moorthy is coming," and she says, "Well, choose between a Brahminic feast and a feast for a polluted pig," and they say, "Why, of course, Moorthy was excommunicated; but how funny that we forgot all about it since he's been in prison!" and Venkamma cries out, "That's it, sister. You forgot it. But this body that has borne eight children cannot forget it. If you had a daughter to marry, you would not forget it, would you?"

In the evening the invitation rice is sent—it is Priest Rangappa's wife Lakshamma who brings it, and she says, "In Venkamma's house there will be a nuptial ceremony on Tuesday. You are all invited," and they offer kumkum to her silently in return, and everybody asks, "And now what shall we do?" and they speak of it to their husbands and their husbands speak to their aunts, and the aunts say, "Why, you cannot refuse a nuptial feast. If there's no married woman to offer kumkum water to the wife and husband, well, tomorrow you may have your own daughter's marriage, and she may go unblessed!" and they all say, "Of course! Of course!" And the next morning everyone is late at the river, and when Rangamma goes up the steps, they all whisper together, "Now we are safe. Now we are safe," but as they pass through the

Pariahs' quarter and the Weavers' quarter and the Potters' quarter, they see that a mango-leaf garland of welcome hangs at each door and the courtyards are swept and washed and decorated. And at the village gate carts are seen to come up, carts from Alur that bring Venkamma's son-in-law, and his relations and his relations' relations. And when they are at the mango grove, they see Badè Khan coming down the Bebbur mound, his dog and boots and cummerbund and all. And Nose-scratching Nanjamma turns to Satamma and whispers, "It seems Nanja gets a hundred-and-fifty rupee diamond nose ring."—"Oh, probably it's his first wife's nose ring," says Satamma sadly.

The cornets are already piping the song of welcome on Venkamma's veranda.

They said Moorthy would come by the blue bus that runs from Kallapuri to Karwar, and we all said, "That will be when the sun has passed over the courtyard," and we were at the village gate when the cattle had drunk the afternoon rice water and gone, and the Pariahs were already there, with blankets and coconuts and horns, and the weaver folk were there with silk upper-cloths, and the potters with pots and the betel-sellers with betel leaves, and even lazy Rangè Gowda was there, rubbing his eyes and waving his turban to keep away flies and perspiration—so sultry was the day. And Rangamma and Ratna were in the shade of the pipal platform, and Satamma's daughter, Ranga, and Nanjamma's daughter, Sata, were there too. "Oh, you need not come to Venkamma's dinner, children. You are still young, you can go to meet Moorthy," they had said, and given them a cold meal and a glass of watered curds. And Ranga and Sata prepared the kumkum water, and they gave us all coloured rice, and we all said, "He'll be here soon—he's coming, he's coming," and the stones beneath began to scorch us, and someone said, "Why, the bus must have met with an accident," and everyone said, "No, no, speak not of such ill omens," and the Pariahs scratched their legs and began adjusting the grapefruit here, the coconut there, and the mango leaves everywhere on the pandal, and people sat down and opened their betel bags and snuff-boxes, and some said, "Come let us remove these stones," and they removed the pebbles from the path.

And suddenly there was a screech and the sound of a horn, and

115

we said, "Why, that's the car!" and we all thought that the bus had stopped at the fingerpost. Seenu and Vasudev, who are there, will stand, with shut eyes and gaping mouths, expectant. Then he'll come down to us. First he; then his bundles. And people will say, "Who is he that people wait on him?" Oh, if only we were there. . . . And then he would take the road to Kanthapura, and we said he would be firm and soft-eyed and pilgrim-looking, and we imagined him with this look on his face and that flash in his eyes, and Pariah Lachamma said, "Maybe the goddess will send a wide rainbow and a rain of flowers to welcome him," and she stood there gaping at the skies and murmuring funny things to the goddess. And hearts began to beat, and yet we saw no Moorthy, and still no Moorthy, and still no Moorthy, and not a hair of his head was seen, and we were silent as though in the sanctum at the camphor ceremony. Still no Moorthy, and the bus had surely passed by the river, over the bridge and up the Santur valley, and Rangamma got so anxious that she sent Pariah Lingayya to run and see, and Pariah Lingayya ran and ran, and from the top of the road cried out, "No, no," and we all looked to this side and that and no Moorthy and no Seenu either was to be seen, and our hearts began to beat like drums, and Ratna said, "I'll see if he's come by the mango grove," and Ratna ran like a boy, and behind her ran young Chenna, and Chenna was followed by Cowherd Sidda; and then came a voice from the promontory, it was Sennu's, and he was calling us, and we cried out, "What is it? What?" and we rushed with the kumkum water spurting and splashing, and the flower garlands tearing in our hands and the coconuts heavy, and what should we see in the Brahmin Square but a cordon of policemen round Rangamma's house, and Rangamma says, "Oh, what are they doing?" and Seenu answers, "Why, Moorthy is here. They took him off the bus at Madur and brought him by the Elephant valley and the Bear's hill by car," and Pariah Chenna says, "And we never heard them come," and Pariah Lingayya says, "Ah, they've been up to tricks again," and they speak to one another, and then such a cry came to their tongues that they shrieked out, *"Vandè Mataram!"* and Rangè Gowda cries out, *"Mahatma Gandhi ki jai!"* and the police inspector comes out of the house and says, "No shouting please. Please disperse." Pariah Lingayya and Rachanna cry out again,

"*Mahatma Gandhi ki jai!*" and the children who wanted to sing, began "Oh, such were our men of 1857," and this boy and that boy takes it up and a shout of songs goes up the evening blaze, while a whirlwind rises and throws dust and sand into our eyes, and still the song rises and rises, and Rangamma comes up the veranda and says, "Brothers and sisters, in the name of Moorthy let us disperse," and we all stand silent as a jungle. And then Rangè Gowda says, "Let us obey the mother," and he goes toward his street, and Mada follows him, and then Mada's brat, and then the Pariah women and the Pariah men, and we slip through our back yards and we stand on our verandas and see the policemen have gathered on Rangamma's veranda, and Rangamma is listening to them, and Ratna is behind her, and by Ratna is Seenu, but Vasudev is no-where to be seen. Perhaps he has already slipped back to the Skeffington Coffee Estate. The policemen do not leave Rangamma's house till the nuptial dinner is over and the hands are washed and the betels chewed and the couple blessed. And as the guests walk back home, their glasses in their hands, they look at Rangamma's house and say, "They've come again," and Nanjamma says, "Oh, they'll bring us pain again," but there was something in the house, something in the very walls, said Nanjamma later, that seemed to shine and send out holy incense. Sister, Moorthy was back home.

At midnight the policemen walked away through the main street, and the Pariahs' street and the Weavers' street, but now a young Badè Khan had joined the bearded one, and he too came to live with us, and he too took a hut and a woman and settled down in the Skeffington Coffee Estate.

In the morning we saw Moorthy at the river. Why, sister, he was as ever—as ever. Why, when one goes to prison, one is as ever!

117

13

"Now," said moorthy, "we are out for action. A cock does not make a morning, nor a single man a revolution, but we'll build a thousand-pillared temple, a temple more firm than any that hath yet been builded, and each one of you be ye pillars in it, and when the temple is built, stone by stone, and man by man, and the bell hung to the roof and the eagle-tower shaped and planted, we shall invoke the Mother to reside with us in dream and in life. India then will live in a temple of our making. Do you know, brothers and sisters, the Mahatma has left Sabarmati on a long pilgrimage, the last pilgrimage of his life, he says, with but eighty-two of his followers, who all wear khadi and do not drink, and never tell a lie, and they go with the Mahatma to the Dandi beach to manufacture salt. Day by day we shall await the news of the Mahatma, and from day to day we shall pray for the success of his pilgrimage, and we shall pray and fast and pour strength into ourselves, so that when the real fight begins we shall follow in the wake of the master."

"Meanwhile, brothers and sisters, let us get strong. The Congress men will have to swear again to speak truth, to spin their daily one hundred yards, and put aside the idea of the holy Brahmin and the untouchable Pariah. You know, brothers and sisters, we are here in a temple, and the temple is the temple of the One, and we are one with everything that is in the One, and who shall say he is at the head of the One and another at the foot? Brothers, and this too ye shall remember, whether Brahmin or bangle-seller, Pariah or priest, we are all one, one as the mustard seed in a sack of mustard seeds, equal in shape and hue and all. Brothers, we are yoked to the same plough, and we shall have to press firm the ploughhead and the earth will open out, and we shall sow the seeds of our hearts, and the crops will rise God-high. Brothers, that is the vision of the harvests that will rise, and we shall await, clean, with the heart as clean as the threshing floor, strong as the pivot of the pressing mill, and we shall offer our first rice and our first ragi to the Goddess Supreme. Pray, brothers, pray, for the Mahatma is on the last pilgrimage of his life, and the drums are beating and the horns are twirling, and the very sea, where he's going to gather and shape and bring back his salt, seems to march forward to give him the waters of welcome. Let us be silent for a while and be united in the One."

Seenu rang the gong, and the eyes shut themselves in silence, and the Brahmin heart and the Weaver heart and Pariah heart seemed to beat the one beat of Siva dancing.

Strength flowed from the wide heavens into the hearts of all men. And we sent our strength of heaven to the eighty-two pilgrim men of the Mahatma. And we too would start our pilgrimage soon, with Moorthy before us. "Prepare yourselves for action," said Moorthy, and Siva knows how, but we forgot the blowpipe and the child's cradle and the letting-off of the morning cattle, and we would go out with him, Moorthy. What is in him, we ask, that binds our heart so? After all, we saw him as a child, sister. And yet. . . .

Moorthy told us of the pilgrim path of the Mahatma from day to day; for day after day the Congress committee sent him information, and day after day he received a white paper from the city, and day after day this boy and that young man came up with the Saturday carts or Tuesday carts, and now that there was a bus, sometimes as we sat kneading the vermicelli or cleaning the rice, we would see the tall khadi-clad Volunteers coming by the afternoon bus, and they went straight to Rangamma's house, and they were shut up with Moorthy, and when they were gone, Moorthy would ask Seenu to ring the gong for the bhajan, and there he would tell us of the hundred and seventy patels that had resigned their jobs— a hundred and seventy, mind you—and of the thirty thousand men and women and children who had gathered at the roadside, pots and beds and all, to have the supreme vision of the Mahatma, and then Rangamma says, "Oh no, the Mahatma need not go as far as the sea. Like Harischandra before he finished his vow, the gods will come down and dissolve his vow, and the Britishers will leave India, and we shall be free, and we shall pay less taxes, and there will be no policemen." But Dorè, who hears this, laughs and says, "This is all *Ramayana* and *Mahabharata*; such things never happen in our times," at which Pariah Rachanna gets angry and says, "It is not for nothing the Mahatma is a Mahatma, and he would not be Mahatma if the gods were not with him," and Dorè says, "Maybe, maybe, Rachanna, I do not know," and we say, "In five days time he will be by the sea—in three days time he will be by the sea—poor Mahatma, he must be tired out with this walk. Why should he not take a horse carriage or a motor car?" But Moorthy repeats, "No, no, sister, he will not take it. He says he likes our ancient ways, and like the ancients he will make the pilgrimage on foot," and our hearts gladdened, for no one ever goes like that to far Kashi, do they? And our Nanjamma says, "Oh, yes, when he arrives by the sea, something is surely going to happen," and everybody says, "Maybe, maybe."

And when the Monday evening came, we knew it would be the morrow, it would be at five the next morning that the Mahatma would go out to the sea and manufacture salt and bring it home, and we could not sleep and we could not wake, and all the night we heard the sea conches cry like the announcing cry of the Belur conch that goes trailing its "om" through the winkless night, and people wake and music plays, and with torch and hymn is it sought, and with torch and hymn is it brought from the river below to the temple above, and people lie many a night in fearful fervour for some pointing finger of the heavens—so did we lie all through that wakeful night, but no shadow ever flew across the stars, and no dreamer ever woke with a pointing dream. And when the morning was still on the other side of the dark we rose one by one, for we would bathe in the river like the Mahatma, at the very hour, at the very minute. Moorthy and Rangamma were at the river already, and just as the morning was colouring the hills of the Skeffington Coffee Estate, we all said—men, women, and boys, Seenu, Moorthy, Vasu, Nanju, Ramu, Subbu, Govinda—"Ganga, Jumna, Saraswathi," and rising up we dipped again and cried out, "*Mahatma Gandhi ki jai!*" And Priest Rangappa, coming up, says,

"Oh, you are all earlier than ever today, hmm?," and we say, "Today the Mahatma manufactures salt with his own hands, Rangappa, and we dip with him," and he laughs and says, "Is that so?," and we knew why he said this, for as everybody knew now, Bhatta had been writing to him, and Bhatta had asked him to gather the grains and the hay and the money, and we said, "Well, another one is lost for us!"

And when we had washed and beaten our clothes, we sat for our meditation and we walked back home, with something new within our hearts. And for the midday meal we gave our men *paysam* and *chitranna* as though it were Gauri's festival, and the men were happy. Why would they not be? And in the evening there was bhajan.

And the next day the white papers told us the Mahatma had taken a handful of salt after his ablutions, and he had brought it home, and then everybody went to the sea to prepare salt, and cartloads and cartloads of it began to be brought back and distributed from house to house with music and clapping of hands. The police do not know what to do, and suddenly they fall on a cartload and the peasants say, "Take it! Take it!" but the police say, "You have broken the law," and the men say, "But we have broken it long ago, and the Mahatma broke it first," but the police do not know what to answer, and they drag the men to prison, they drag them and spit on them and would have beaten them had not many and many a white man come to see the pilgrimage of the Mahatma. And so day after day men go out to the sea to make salt, and day after day men are beaten back and put into prison, and yet village after village sends its women and men, and village after village grows empty, for the call of the Mahatma had sung in their hearts, and they were for the Mahatma and not for the Government.

And we said to Moorthy, "And when shall we start to march like the Mahatma?" and Moorthy says, "Why, as soon as I get the orders from the Karwar Congress committee," and we say, "But ask them to send it soon, for ten heads make a herd and one head a cow," and Moorthy says, "So it is, but I am a small man in the Congress, and I wait for the orders." Then Rangamma says, "If you want to fight, sisters, let us practice the drill more often, like the men," and we say, "Of course! Of course!" and now we stand in

Rangamma's courtyard from the time the hands are washed till the time the cattle come home, and we stand straight and hold our hands against our breasts, and Rangamma says, "Now, imagine the policemen are beating you, and you shall not budge a finger's length," and we close our eyes and we imagine Badè Khan after Badè Khan, short, bearded, lip-smacking, smoking, spitting, booted Badè Khan, and as we begin to imagine them, we see them rise and become bigger and bigger in the sunshine, and we feel the lathis bang on us, and the bangles break and the hair tear and the lips split, and we say, "Nay, nay," and we cannot bear it, and Dorè's wife Sundri begins to cry out and she says she is frightened; but Ratna, who is by her, says, "Be strong, sister. When your husband beats you, you do not hit back, do you? You only grumble and weep. The policeman's beating are the like!" and we say, "So they are." And we begin to get more and more familiar with it. And we say that in a week, in ten days' time, Moorthy will say, "March!" and we shall march behind him, and we shall do this and we shall do that, and now when we meet Badè Khan our eyes seek his lathi and we find it is smaller than we had imagined, and his shoes have less nails, and his lips are less thick. Rangamma says, "Send out rays of harmony," and we send out rays of harmony, and we say, "No, it will not be so bad after all," and we say too, "And there is the Mahatma," and his eyes, benign like old Rama-krishnayya's, look down on us with strength and affection. Nan-jamma says, "No, sister, I do not imagine the Mahatma like a man or a god, but like the Sahyadri mountains, blue, high, wide, and the rock of the evening that catches the light of the setting sun," and I say to myself, "That's what he is. High and yet seeable, firm and yet blue with dusk, and as the pilgrims march up the winding path, march through prickles and boulders, thickets and streams, so shall we march up to the top, we shall thump up and up to the top, and elephants may have left their traces, and the wildfire go blazing around us, and yet we shall know on the top is the temple, and that temple is bright and immense, and when the night is slept through, the gong will sound over the pilgrim lines for the dawn procession of the Mountain God"; and so from that day we said we shall call the Mahatma "The Mountain," and we say we are the pilgrims of the Mountain, and whatever thunder may tear through the heavens or the monsoons pour over it, it is always the blue mountain at dusk.

"And what shall we call Moorthy?" said Radhamma.

"Why, the Small Mountain," said Rangamma, and we all said "That is it," and so from that day we knew there were the Small Mountain and the Big Mountain to protect us.

The Ganges, sister, is born on the snows of high Kailas.

Oh, but when will it come, the call of the Big Mountain, Siva, Siva?

14

THE CALL of the Big Mountain never came, for one morning, as we were returning from the river, Seenu comes and says the Congress committee has sent a messenger on bicycle to say the Mahatma was arrested, and we ask, "And when shall we begin, when?" and he answers, "Next week, sister," and when we are back home we see Moorthy and Rangè Gowda and Rangamma and Pariah Rachanna all gathered before the temple, and Moorthy seemed to be all speech and Rangè Gowda all gestures, and we ask ourselves, "What are they deciding, what?" And children gather round them, and one comes from this street, and one from that and there was quite a fair about, and when the kitchen fire is hardly lit, the temple bell goes ringing in the street, and we rush to the veranda and hear Seenu crying out, "The Mahatma is arrested! the Mahatma!—and next week there will be a Don't-touch-the-Government campaign. And today everyone will fast, and the Congress panchayat will meet, and in the evening bhajan."

And we said, "That is fine," and we poured water over our fires, and we drank a glass of curds and we dozed the whole afternoon, and every minute people could be heard hurrying about anxious and silent, and when Vasudev is passing by, Nanjamma says, "And the Skeffington people, are they with us?" and Vasudev says, "Of course, of course, but not many." Then there is the sound of Moorthy speaking and of Rangè Gowda shouting, and Pariah Rachanna whispering this and Rangamma saying that, and bicycle after bicycle comes from the city, bicycle after bicycle carrying the orders to the Congress panchayat, and the Volunteers go straight to Rangamma's veranda, and they talk to Moorthy. Then for a while there is silence, but Rangè Gowda starts again and then Rachanna and then Rangamma.

Thus it deliberated, the Congress panchayat, till the cattle came home, and when we had lit the lamps and had given a cold meal to the children, we took our baths and went to the temple, and there was Seenu in the sanctum and he would tell us nothing, and when he went up the promontory and blew the conch, people came—men, women, children—and the Pariahs and the Weavers and the Potters all seemed to feel they were of one caste, one breath. Then Moorthy came himself, straight as an aloe, strong and calm, and we say he looks as though something is passing through him, and when the camphor is lit and the flowers offered, he stands up and says, "Brothers and sisters, the call is come, and men, women, and children will have to begin the Don't-touch-the-Government campaign."—"But how is that to be done, Moorthappa?" asks Pariah Rachanna, and Moorthy, uplifted and sure, speaks in answer, "That's what I am going to explain, brother Rachanna," and he talks of the taxes that are not to be paid, "even if the Government attaches the lands," and of the toddy booths that are to be picketed, "for toddy trees are Government trees, and toddy booths are there to exploit the poor and the unhappy," and he continues, his voice rising higher, "And we shall establish a parallel government, and it is this government that will rule and not that, and the first act of our government is to appoint Rangè Gowda patel again," and we feel our throats warm, and we look at Rangè Gowda waving away his hand saying, "Oh, that's nothing, nothing!" but Moorthy continues, "For the Congress is the people and the patel is the people's man and Rangè Gowda is our man, and if the new patel comes and says, 'Give me the revenue dues,' you will say, 'I do not know you—you are not our man and we will offer you neither seat nor water,' but never be harsh to them nor wicked, and above all," he said, his voice becoming graver, "remember each one of you is responsible for the harm done by another, and the first time violence is done against the police or those that are not with us, we shall stop the movement and wait for six months and more in penance and in prayer that our sins may be purified. Brothers and sisters, remember we are not out to fight the white man or the white man's slaves, the police and the revenue officials, but against the demoniac corruption that has entered their hearts, and the purer we are the greater will be our victory, for the victory we seek is the victory of the heart. Send out love where there is hatred, and a smile against brute force like unto the waters of the Himavathy that spread over boulder and sand and crematorium earth. Brothers, remember, too, I am but a pebble among the pebbles of the river, and when the floods come, rock by rock may lie buried under, and yet there are some that stand out pointed and dry, and it is they that give you a hold for your slippery, seeking feet. The police will take away one after another among us, and yet sometimes they may leave the leaders out for fear of disorder and desperation. But my time too will come. And when it comes, brothers and sisters, I ask of you, be not awed by the circumstances, but rather follow on and on, follow the one who follows me, for he is your chief, and the Congress has made him your chief. For who, sisters, but the first daughter milks the cow when the mother is ill? Obey your chief and love your enemy, that is all I ask of you."

"And remember always, the path we follow is the path of the spirit, and with truth and nonviolence and love shall we add to the harmony of the world. For, brothers, we are not soldiers at arms, say I; we seek to be soldier saints." And just then Rangamma, who sat by the central pillar, unknowingly began to ring the gong, as though the curtain had fallen and the goddess beheld, and tears came to our eyes, and even our men felt there was something in the air, and they too looked unaware, and there was not a cough nor a sneeze but only the eyelashes quivered and closed, and Moorthy, in-lit and bright, says softly, "You are all with us?" and we cry out, "All! All!" and, "You shall harm no one?"—"None! None!"—"You shall go to the end fearlessly?"—"All! All!"—"And there shall be neither Brahmin nor Pariah?" and the Pariahs shout out, *"Mahatma Gandhi ki jai!"* and an uncontrollable emotion takes hold of us all, and Moorthy says, "The panchayat has decided that it shall be on Friday the seventeenth that we shall begin the fight," and Pandit Venkateshia says, "Few days could be more auspicious," and we say, "So only three days more," and Moorthy says, "Till then, pray, purify yourselves and pray," and we all cry out, "Narayan! Narayan!" And Horn Nanjappa plays the tune of blessings and the gongs ring and the drums beat, and as the last carts are creaking round the street, music floats out of the temple, and we clap our hands and sing and our eyes are filled with tears.

Why, sister, for no *Harikatha* have such tears flowed down our cheeks.

Two days later, our sari fringes tied tight to our waists, our jewels hid deep beneath the earth, with men on the right and children beside us, with drum and horn and trumpet and a cart before us all adorned with lotuses and champaks and mango twigs, in which are seated Moorthy and Rangamma and Rangè Gowda and even Pariah Rachanna, we march on and on, and when we come to the village gate Seenu sounds the conch from the top of the promontory, and Vasudev, with his twenty-three Pariahs from the Skeffington Coffee Estate, breaks a coconut before us, and when the camphor is rising before the god, we all bow down in trembling prayer, and when the conch blows again we rise, and with the horn shouting and shining over the ripe valley, we turn Bhatta's empty house and we hurry down to Boranna's toddy grove.

We were a hundred and thirty-nine in all, and we marched out to Boranna's toddy grove.

And men came from Tippur and Subbur and Kanthur, kumkum on their foreheads and flowers in their hair, to see us pass by, and chrysanthemums fell on us, and rice and Bengal gram, and thus we marched out, a hundred and thirty-nine in all, to Boranna's toddy grove, our hearts round and ripe like an April pomegranate. And Puttanna made a song, and we beat our feet and we sang,

> At least a toddy-pot sister,
> At least a toddy-leaf, sister,
> We'll go to Boranna's toddy grove,
> We'll go to Boranna's toddy growth,
> And procession back at least a toddy-leaf, sister,

and we marched on to Boranna's toddy grove.

And when we were hardly at the main road corner, we saw, beyond the mango grove, the red horse of the police inspector, and our hands began to shiver, and we held our breath beneath our breasts, and we said not a word to one another, and then when Moorthy had seen it too, he got down out of the cart, and Rangè Gowda followed him and Rangamma and Pariah Rachanna, and the cart stopped and we crossed beside it with Moorthy before us,

127

and as we neared the toddy grove we began to see by the lantana fence policeman after policeman, their lathis tight in their hands, and the police inspector going among them and bending down and whispering to this one and that, and the horse wagging its tail and brushing away the summer flies.

And when we were by the Tippur stream bridge, the police inspector comes toward us and says, "You are forbidden to march to the toddy grove," and Moorthy smiles back and says he knows that but he thanks him all the same for saying so, but that he is following the instructions of the Congress and he would follow unto death if need be. And the police inspector says, "I warn you for a third time, and I say that what you do is against law, and the Government is ready to use all the force it possesses to put you down," and Moorthy says again, "Thank you," and he moves on; and just as we are near the toddy grove, the morning carts of San-tur turn round the Kenchamma hill corner, and when they see us and the crowd behind us, they stop and come down to see what is all this procession and police about, and we say, "Well, there will be some more people with us." We begin to count our beads and say Ram-Ram, and the nearer we approach the stiffer become the policemen, and as Moorthy and Rangè Gowda try to push open the gate of the grove, the police stand before them and push them back, and Pariah Rachanna cries out, "Say *Mahatma Gandhi ki jai!*" and we all cry out too, "*Mahatma Gandhi ki jai!*" and we say we too shall enter the toddy grove.

But the men were before us and the children huddled between us, and the police surrounded our men and tried to push them back, and suddenly Pariah Rachanna slipped out and ran and we all turned to see where he was going when he jumped across the lantana fence—with one leap he had crossed the ditch and the fence—and he fell and he rose, and as he rushed to climb a toddy tree the police made toward him, but he was already halfway up the tree when the lathis banged against his legs. And the cartmen, who had gathered round us, began to shout, and we cried out, "*Vandè Mataram!*" and somebody began to clap hands and push forward, and we all clapped hands too and began to sing, and the police began to push us this way and that. When Pariah Rachanna was torn down from the toddy tree, our hearts began to beat so

128

fast that we cried out, *"Hoye-Hoye!"* and we pushed forward with the men. And the police inspector this time shouted out, "Attack!" and they lifted the lathis and bang-bang they brought them down on us, and the lathis caught our hair and rebounded from our backs, and Pariah Ningamma beat her mouth and wailed, "Oh, he's gone, he's gone, he's gone," and we say to ourselves, "Oh, how inauspicious!" and we shout out, *"Mataram Vandè!"* with all our breath, and the children are so frightened now that they take it up and shout and shout and shout, and the police break through us and, one here and one there, they catch the children by the hair and by the ear and by the jacket, and the mothers sob behind them and the cartmen cry out, "Shame, shame," and the lathis still shower down upon us. Then suddenly there is a cry, and we raise our heads and see the red horse of the police inspector charging upon the cartmen, and the cartmen spit and howl and rush for their lives to the mango grove, and there is another cry, and somebody says Pariah Lingayya has jumped over the fence, too, and the police leave us and rush at him and more and more men jump over and they tear down the lantana fence. And the police inspector gallops across the road and brings down Chandrayya and Ramayya with the knob of his cane, and they roll over and fall into the ditch, and we say, "Now, Rangamma, we'll go forward," and just then, as though in answer, Moorthy shrieks out across the fence, *"Mahatma Gandhi ki jai!"* and we see his lips split and four policemen around him, and somehow our eyes turn all to the Kenchamma hill and as we say, "goddess, goddess," we see the scattered crowd of children rushing here, rushing there, and mothers, aunts, sisters, grandmothers rushing behind them. And Rangamma cries out, "Now, sisters, forward!" and we all cry out, *"Mahatma Gandhi ki jai! Mahatma Gandhi ki jai!"* and we deafen ourselves before the onslaught, and we rush and we crawl, and swaying and bending and crouching and rising, we move on and on, and the lathis rain on us, and the cartmen have come back again and they feel so angry that they, too, cry out, *"Mahatma Gandhi ki jai!"* and they, too, rush behind us, and we feel a new force in us and we say we shall enter the toddy grove and tear out at least a toddy branch and break at least a toddy pot. And there are shrieks and shouts and cries and sobs, and the more we are beaten the more we get

129

used to it and we say, "After all it is not bad—after all it is not so bad," and our bangles break and our saris tear and yet we huddle and move on. Then once again Rangamma shouts, *"Gandhi Mahatma kai jai!"* and we all rush forward and the crowd rushes behind us and the gate creaks and breaks and we all rush toward the trees, one to this and one to that, to saplings and twisted trees and arched trees and anthills crumble beneath our feet, and the leaves tear and crunch, and the lathis break on our backs and hands and heads. And stones are thrown at the tree trunks, and pots break and spatter down, and someone cries out, *"Mahatma Gandhi ki jai!"* and we rise with it, and we see up there on the top of the toddy tree is someone, and he is cutting down branch after branch of the toddy tree and the men gather them like sanctified flowers and women slip in here and crouch along there, and policeman after policeman tries to climb the tree, and one falls and everybody laughs, and another goes up proudly but he slips down again, and the police inspector says, "Moti Khan, you'd better try," and as he is trying to go up the other policemen fall on us again, and we rush to this side and that, while somebody pulls down Moti Khan and the man on the top spits down on him, and a wave of laughter whirls up the toddy grove. But we never saw what came of it, for one by one they took us to the road, and there we stood huddled together between policemen, and we said the work of the day is done, and wives searched for their husbands and mothers for their sons, and brother searched for brother and sister-in-law for sister-in-law. And when the calm had flowed back to our hearts, we touched our bones and our knuckles and our joints, feeling the wounds fresh as burns, and when we saw all the people gathered to see us, there was something in us that said, "You've done something big," and we felt as though we had walked the holy fire at the harvest festival, and, policeman on the right and policeman on the left, we marched down to the Santur police outpost.

There they took only Pariah Rachanna and Lingayya and Potter Siddayya, and when we all thought, "Now we are free—we can go," they drove us into trucks, one truck, two trucks, three trucks, men in one and young women in another and old women in another again, and they took each in a different direction, and when the night fell, they left us on the Beda Ghats and others on the Karwar road and yet others again on the Blue Mountain road, and when we were on the highway we all began to tremble and we said, "Oh, we are in the middle of the jungle!" and our knees shook and our hair stood on end, and the whole forest seemed to rise up a wall of a thousand voices, and the road hissed this way and that, and tongued over a rill, and shot up the mountains to the seven-hooded skies and all the serpent eyes of the sky looked down bright and bitter upon us—and at last it was Rangamma who said, "Don't be afraid, sisters. Tell me, how many are you?" And we huddled together in the middle of the road and said, "We are twenty-two in all," and Rangamma said, "Form a line," and we formed a line, and she said, "Now march, singing," and we said, "Let us sing loud so that the panthers and the porcupines may be frightened away," and we sang, "Wheresoever we look, you are there, my Lord!"

And we sing it louder and louder and we march fast and fearful, until we are wet with perspiration and we forget the wounds on the thigh or the bruises on the face or the ache in the bones. And at last, when we had gone God knows how long, there on the top of the hill we see the dangling light of a cart, and the dust seems dust and the hand seems a hand and the trees, oh, nothing but trees, and after all we are not afraid, are we?—and the nearer comes the cart the louder we sing, and when it is in front of us Rangamma cries out, "From what town, brother?"— "Why, from Rachapura," says he, and then he gets down, and the bulls ring their bells and yawn. And Rangamma tells him we are women and Satyagrahis and we are hungry, and he says he had heard about us in Kanthapura and that the police are still there, and Nose-scratching Nanjamma can bear no more and she says, "We are hungry, Rangamma—we have not had a meal since morning"; and Rangamma says to the cartman, "Perhaps you've something to eat?" and he says, "Why, I have copra," and Nanjamma says, "Anything. Anything," and he lets down the yoke and he opens a sack and he gives us copra, one copra each, and Rangamma says, "Are there no more carts coming behind you?" and he says, "Yes, there are,"—"And can you not take us to Kanthapura? We shall pay you two rupees a cart," and he says, "We shall see when the other carts come." And we seat ourselves in the middle of the road, and now we can hear the jackals wail and the twitching trill of the jungle insects, and now and again the bulls shake their heads and the clanging of bells goes tearing down the mountain path and trailing up to the sturdy heights, and then the creak of the carts is heard, and cart after cart comes down the hill and the cartmen say, "All right, we'll take you to Kanthapura," and we say, "How much?" and they say, "Ask the waters of the Himavathy!" and we say, "No, no!" and one of them says, "Hè, sisters, I've been to the city, to the big city, to Bombay, and I have been a weaver there, and I have seen the Red-man and the man that fights the Red-man, the Mahatma, and I say, 'If we touch but the dirt of a coin, we'll be born in a million hells.' What do you say to that, brothers?" And the cartmen say, "As you like, Timmayya," but he spits on them and calls them sluts and says, "The Mahatma is born once and not twice, and if ye be such hang-lip hagglers, I'll go up and come down once, twice, thrice, a hundred times, taking these sisters to Kanthapura," and they all turn their carts, and they say, "You are a funny fellow—but you say there's a Mahatma, and maybe his ire will be upon us." And they say, "Hoye-Hoye," and we climb into the carts, and hardly in, head against head and arm against arm, we lean over one another, and we doze and doze and snore and snore, and we groan up the hills and we grind down them, and when we have passed over a rattling river bridge, there's the familiar noise of dogs barking and doors creaking, and people are heard washing their hands after dinner, and Rangamma says, "Stop the carts, brother," and we wake up and get down, for we are in Santhapura and Rangamma's cousin Subbayya is landholder there, and he says to the cartmen, "You can go now, I'll take them home," and they get a coconut and betel-leaf good-bye.

And we all sit in the hall, and Subbayya's wife, Satamma, says, "Oh, take only this much milk, aunt!—Oh, only this banana, aunt! —Just this handful of puffed rice!" and we are so tired that we say, "Yes, yes." And people come from the Potters' quarter and the Weavers' quarter and say, "We came to give you welcome. So it's you who fought the police!" and an old woman comes to the door and says, "Learned sir, I hear there are some pilgrims come, and I have a new calved cow, and I can offer fresh milk to the pilgrims," and this way and that, milk and syrup and puffed rice and coco-nuts are offered and we tell them each our story and they say, "Oh, poor mother—oh, poor mother," and we get courageous and say, "But that is what we should do to drive the British out!" Then, when we get up to go, lantern after lantern is seen in the court-yard, and everybody says, "We shall follow you up to Kanthapura. One never knows these days. Why, only this morning we found elephant dung at the temple corner." And they gave us new carts, and beadles walked in front of us, lanterns in their hands, and before them walked Iron-shop Imam Khan, gun in hand and fire in his eyes, and our carts clattered and creaked through the dense, droning night, by the Gold-mine hill and Siva's gorge and up the Menu crag and down again to the valleys of the Himavathy, where lies Kanthapura curled like a child on its mother's lap. And when the carts had waded through the still, purring waters of the river and the bulls crunched over the sands of the other bank, we said, "Here we are," and mother and wife and widow-godmother went up to their lighted, lizard-clucking homes. And when the wounds were washed and the bandages tied, we lay upon our beds, and it seemed as though the whole air was filled with some pouring presence, and high up, from somewhere over the Skeffington Coffee Estate and the Kenchamma hill and the Himavathy, night opened its eyes to let gods peep through the tiles of Kanthapura. Sister, when Ramakrishnayya and Satamma returned from their pilgrim-age, what did they say? They said, in Kashi, when the night fell, gods seemed to rise from the caverns of the Ganges, to rise sheer over the river, each one with his consort, and each one with his bull or peacock or flower throne, and peep into the hearts of pilgrim men. May our hearts be touched by their light! May Kenchamma protect us!

The next morning, with bell and camphor and trumpet, we planted our trophies before the temple. Five twigs of toddy trees were there, and a toddy pot. Venkamma of course said, "Look, look, a toddy god have they made of a moon-crowned god," and she spat on us and called us the toddy people. Yes, yes, sister, we are toddy people! But we don't marry our daughters to gap-toothed sons-in-law. Nor like Bhatta do we go on Kashi-pilgrimage with toddy contract money. Do we?

15

THE FOLLOWING Tuesday was market day in Kanthapura, and
we had risen early and lit the kitchen fires and had cooked
the meals early and we had finished our prayers, and when the
food was eaten and the vessels washed and the children sent with
the cattle—for this time they wouldn't come with us—we all gathered at the temple, and when Seenu had blown the conch and lit
the camphor, we all marched toward the Kenchamma grove, and
the cattle sellers stopped their cows and calves to see us, and the
oil women put down their oil jugs and asked, "Where are you
going, brothers and sisters?" and old Nanjamma who could never
hold her tongue says, "Why, to picket toddy shops," and Moorthy
cries out, "Silence! Silence!" and the cartmen pull aside the bulls
and jump out of the carts to see the procession pass by, and when
we are by the Skeffington Coffee Estate, Betel Lakshamma, who
sells flowers for the Kenchamma worship, is there and she says to
Moorthy, "And you are the soldiers of the Mahatma? And it's you
who defied the police?" and Moorthy smiles and says, "Yes,
mother," and she says, "Then you'll free us from the revenue
collector?" and Moorthy says, "What revenue collector?"—"Why,
Raghavayya, the one who takes bribes and beats his wife and sends
his servants to beat us,"—and Moorthy does not know what to
answer and he says, "We are against all tyrants," and she says,
"Why, then, come to our village, son, and free us from this childless monster," and Moorthy says, "We shall see," and she says,
"We ask you to come," and Moorthy says, "I shall write to the
Congress and if they say yes, I shall come," and then old Lakshamma, who is a very clever woman, she says, "Let us garland
you," and Moorthy cries out, "No, no," but she says this and that,
and garlands him and says, "You are my Lord, and though I saw
you like a rat on your mother's lap, I knew you'd do great deeds

and bring a good name to the Himavathy." And when old Madanna of the banana shops sees this, he stops his bulls and tears a few bananas from the banana bunch and he offers them to Moorthy and Moorthy says, "May the country bless you, Madanna."

And we march on and on, winding up the Karwar road to the Kenchamma grove, and at every step there are corn people and puffed-rice and Bengal-gram people and bangle sellers and buttermilk people and betel-leaf people, and they stop us and say, "Take this, take this, Mahatma's men!" And then suddenly a car comes hooting down the valley and they say, "Perhaps the Taluk magistrate?"—"Perhaps the collector sahib?"—"Perhaps the planter sahib?" —and they are so frightened that they jump over the gutters and slip behind the trees and the car rushes past us and we see a Redman's face and a Red-man's beard and a Red-man's hat, and people say, "Why, that's the good Solpur Padrè!" and Ratna says, "No, no," but Moorthy cries out, "Silence, please," and we grow dumb. And the nearer we come to the fair the larger is the crowd behind us, and our hearts beat hard, and when we are by the Kenchamma grove, Moorthy says, "One man or woman at every arm's length," and seventy-seven in all we stand by the Kenchamma grove and up the Skeffington Road, one man or woman at every arm's length, and Moorthy stood over the Monkey's bridge, with Ratna and Rangamma beside him, and across the rivulet, on the dry meadow crouched the toddy booth, but the police were already there.

We had never stepped upon the Coffee Estate road, and each time the cart passed by the Kenchamma grove, in secret fear we would never look toward it. And we imagined the sahib standing here, standing there, by the Buxom pipal-tree, by the Ramanna well, and we thought there he's looking for a woman, he's behind the aloes there. And the leaves would flutter and there would be a cough or sneeze, and our limbs would tremble and we would look away to the Kenchamma grove, and sometimes, when on a morning a cow or a calf strayed over the Skeffington road, we cried out, "Hey-Hey," from the main road and we waited for a Pariah to come and we sent him to drive it home. And today, as we stood on the Skeffington road, broad and bright with the margosa trees that lined it to the iron gate, where two giant banyans hovered from either side, as we looked up the hill, up the twisted road and past the trees to the porch and the stables and the bamboo nettings of the bungalow, a shiver ran down our backs, and we all wondered how Moorthy could stand so near the gate. And yet Moorthy was calm and talking away, waiting for the first coolie to come out, the first coolie who would come out with his week's earnings at his waist, and go straight to the toddy booth; and we waited and waited. Vasudev had told us it was Pariah Siddayya who would lead them out, and we looked this side and that, and we said, "They're coming! They're coming!" and we looked at the Estate trees, high and lean and protective, and the little coffee shrubs beneath, and there were birds in them and wind and darkness, and as the sky was growing cloud-covered, we said, "Now it is going to rain and the people will not come out," and yawning and perspiring we look away toward the market where people are hurriedly putting up their shops, the pegs are hammered in and the tents stretched out and the carts are emptied and the bulls wave their heads and flap their ears to drive away the flies, and then one by one they kneel and flop down for a comfortable munch —and donkeys bray and pigs snort and the Padrè's voice comes curling up the tamarind tree with pancake smoke from Puttamma's frying pan, and there is music with the Padrè's voice and it is tambourine music and band music, and the cymbals beat, and people gather and the Padrè sings on and on in *Harikatha,* while carts come round the Kenchamma hill and people come behind them, and when they see us they come near us and they talk to Moorthy, and Moorthy explains to them why we are here and they say, laughing, "Why, you will never stop a man drinking!" and others say, "Ah, you are like that Padré there talking of drink and sin." Yet others say, "You are right, learned sir, but if you put a dog on the throne, he'll jump down at the sight of dirt; thus we are," but Moorthy says, "No, no, you cannot straighten a dog's tail but you can straighten a man's heart."

But suddenly he leaves them and runs forward and we say something is the matter, and Moorthy stops on the bridge and looks toward the Skeffington Estate gate, and we all look toward it, too, and we only hear the wind whistling before the rain patters on the trees, and the cawing of a crow or two; and we say to ourselves, so there's nothing the matter, nothing. Then we hear a sputter of leaves and see dark shapes behind the leaves and we hold our breath and say, "There they are; they're coming," and when the gateway opens, there's a seesaw lightning and we hide our faces behind our saris and we are afraid; and when we look up at the gate, it's not the coolies we see but the maistri, in white, clean-washed clothes, and he stands and looks at us and drives away the flies from his pock-marked face. Then he goes in and Moorthy says, "March forward!" and trembling and thumping over the earth we move forward, and we say something is going to happen, and nothing but the wind that rises from the Coffee Estate is heard, and we look away across the streamlet to the fields that widen out into the valley and the russet crops under the clouds. Then the police inspector saunters up to the Skeffington gate, and he opens it and one coolie and two coolies and three coolies come out, their faces dark as mops and their blue skin black under the clouded heavens, and perspiration flows down their bodies and their eyes seem fixed to the earth—one coolie and two coolies and three coolies and four and five come out, eyes fixed to the earth, their stomachs black and clammy and bulging, and they march toward the toddy booth; and then suddenly more coolies come out, more and more and more like clogged bulls clattering down the byre steps they come out, and the women come behind them, their sari fringes drawn over their faces and their eyes fixed on the earth, and police-men walk beside them, they walk beside the coolies with bulging stomachs and bamboo legs, coolies of the Godaveri banks, and they are marched on to the toddy booth, to Boranna's toddy booth, to drink and to beat the drum and to clap hands and sing—they go, the coolies, their money tied to their waists and their eyes fixed on the earth, and Moorthy looks at them and we all look at them, and we, too, move toward the toddy booth; and then a drop of rain falls, more drops of rain fall, and the coolies are still marching toward the toddy booth; and we look at them and they look at us, goat-eyed and dumb and their legs shuffling over the earth, and we say, "What will Moorthy do now? What?" Then Moorthy says, "Squat down before the toddy booth," and we rush and we stumble, and we rise and we duck, and we all go squatting before the toddy booth, and the coolies are marching behind us and the policemen tighten round the booth, and then, quick and strong, the rain patters on the leaves and the thatch and the earth. Maybe that's the blessing of the gods!

With the rain came the shower of lathi blows, with the rain splashing on our hair came the bang-bang of the lathis, and we began to cry and to scream, and the policemen began to beat the coolies forward, but they would not walk over us, and they would not fall on us, and from the toddy booth came the voice of Boranna, and he shouted and he spat and he said he would give the Brahmins a toddy libation, while the crowd shouted back at him and called him a life-drag and a nail-witch and a scorpion, and the police inspector, more furious than ever, took his cane and drove at the crowd, and the crowd thinned out shrieking and moaning, and then the market people, when they heard the noise covered their heads with gunny bags and ran toward us, and the crowd clamoured all the more, and somebody shouted, *"Mahatma Gandhi ki jai!"* and the whole crowd shouted, *"Jai Mahatma!"* and they pushed on toward us—and the police became frightened and caned and caned the coolies till they pushed themselves over us; and they put their feet here and they put their hands there, but Rangamma shouted, *"Vandè Mataram!* Lie down, brothers and sisters," and we all lay down so that not a palm-width of space lay bare, and the coolies would not move, and we held to their hands and we held to their feet and we held to their saris and dhotis and all, while the rain poured on and on. And the police got nervous and they began to kick us in our backs and stomachs, and the crowd shouted, *"Mahatma Gandhi ki jai!"* and someone took a kerosene tin and began to beat it, and someone took a cattle bell and began to ring it, and they cried, "With them, brothers, with them!" and they leaped and they ducked and they came down to lie beside us, and we shouted, *"Mahatma Gandhi ki jai! Mahatma Gandhi ki jai!"*

Then the police inspector rushed at the coolies and whipped them till they began to search their way again among us, but we began to call out to them, "Oh don't go, brother!—don't go, sister!— oh, don't go, in the name of the Mahatma!—oh, don't go in the name of Kenchamma!" and our men pulled the coolies down, and one after another the coolies fell over and they too blocked the way, and the police, feeling there was no way out, caught hold of us by the hair to lift us up, and we struggled and we would not

138

rise; and when Rangamma was made to sit, the police inspector gave her such a kick in the back that she fell down unconscious, and Ratna cried out, "Oh, you dogs," and the police inspector spat in her face and gave her a slap that brought blood out of her mouth. But Moorthy said, "No swearing, please. *Mahatma Gandhi ki jai!*" and we all cried out, *"Jai Mahatma!"* and such a crowd had now gathered around us that we felt a secret exaltation growing in us, and we shouted out, *"Vandè Mataram!"*—and everybody cried, *"Vadè Mataram!"* and somebody remembered, "And at least a toddy leaf, sister," and we sang back, "And at least a toddy pot, sister," while the rain poured on and on, a thunderless rain, and the streamlets began to trickle beneath us and our hair was caught in the mire and our hands and our backs and our mouths bled, and then, when we lifted ourselves up a little, we saw one, two, three coolies entering the toddy booth. And Moorthy shouted out again, *"Mahatma Gandhi ki jai!"* and a blow gagged his mouth, and he could not shout again. And then Seetharam and old Nanjamma and all of us said, "He's fallen, Moorthy. He's dead, Moorthy. Oh, you butchers!" And we shouted, as though to defend him, *"Mahatma Gandhi ki jai!"* and old Nanjamma cried, "Narayan! Narayan!" and what with the oaths and cries and the "Narayan! Narayan!" and the thuds of the lathi and the ringings of the cattle bells and the rain on the earth and the shouts of the market people and the kerosene tin that still beat, we all felt as though the mountains had split and the earth wailed, and the goddess danced over the corpse of the Red Demon. And when the police inspector gave an order, we all pressed our heads tight to the earth to wait a lathi shower, but the police gathered together and charged on the crowd and dispersed it and we could hear the tents falling and the clash of vessels and bells and benches, and with hardly a policeman about us, the coolies rushed again toward us, and called upon us, "Sister, sister; brother, brother," and we said, "Do not drink, do not drink, in the name of the Mahatma," and they said, "By Kenchamma's name, we shall not," and when they see this, the policemen leave the market people and rush again upon us, and they drag the Pariahs by the leg and beat them, and we rise up and we say, "Beat us," and they say, "Here is one for you," and we get a kick on the stomach, and we lie flat upon the earth. Then the police inspector says, "Throw water on them," and the police go to the toddy booth and come out with pots in their hands, and they dip the pots in the side gutters and potfuls and potfuls of water are thrown at us, and they open our mouths and they pour it in and they lift up our saris and throw it at unnameable places, and the water trickles down our limbs and drips down to the earth, and with more beating and more beating and more beating we fall back one by one against the earth, one by one we fall by the coolies of the Godaveri, and the rain still pours on.

We wake up in a truck and we are put on our legs by the promontory and we march back home, sixty-seven in all, for Siddayya and my Seenu, and Vasudev and Nanjamma's husband, Subbu, and Rangè Gowda are taken to prison. But Moorthy they would not take, and God left him still with us.

The next morning we woke up to find that the Pariah street was filled with new huts and new fires and new faces and we knew that over three and thirty or more of the coolies of the Godaveri had come to live with us. And men on foot and horse and cart came from Kanthur and Subbur and Tippur and Bebbur to see Moorthy and join us. And we all said, "The army of the Mahatma is an increasing garland. May our hearts be pure as the morning flowers and may he accept them!" For, after all, sister, when one has a light on the forehead one can march a thousand leagues. Siva is poison-throated, and yet He is the three-eyed. May the three-eyed Siva protect us. . . .

16

THEN THE PEOPLE in Rampur picketed the Rampur tollgate toddy booth, and the people of Siddapur, the Siddapur tea-estate toddy booth, and the people of Maddur, the Maddur-fair toddy shop, and men and women and children would go to the toddy booths and call to the drinkers, "Brothers and sisters and friends, do not drink in the name of the Mahatma! The Mahatma is a man of God; in his name do not drink and bring sin upon yourself and upon your community!" And songs were made by the people:

> The toddy tree is a crooked tree,
> And the toddy milk a scorpion milk,
> And who is it that uses the scorpion milk, sister?
> And who uses the scorpion milk, sister?
> Why, the wandering witches of the marshes;
>
> Say, sister, say the wandering witches of the marshes,
> And the witch has a turban and a lathi stick,
> O king, O king, why won't you come?

and people sang it on the river path and behind the temple, and washing the thresholds and rinsing the vessels and plastering the walls with dung cakes did they sing, and women sang this to their men, and sons sang this to their fathers, and when somebody told how in Bombay and Lahore people gathered at dawn to go singing through the streets, women in Rampur said, "We, too, shall do it," and they, too, rose up at dawn and gathered at the temple, and they, too, went singing through the twilit streets and stood before house after house and sang:

> Our king, he was born on a wattle mat,
> He's not the king of the velvet bed,
> He's small and he's round and he's bright and he's sacred,
> O, Mahatma, Mahatma, you're our king, and we are your slaves.

141

White is the froth of the toddy, toddy,
And the Mahatma will turn poison into nectar clear,
White will become blue and black will become white,
Brothers, sisters, friends and all,
The toddy tree is a crooked tree,
And the toddy milk is scorpion milk,
O king, O king, when will you come?

And some who were intelligent, like the city boys, would say, "Oh, brothers, in the name of the Mahatma do not drink, for drinking is bad and the Government profits by your vice and the usurer profits by your debt and your wife goes unclothed and your children unfed and never again will you see a hut and hearth," and so on; and some, too, would come to fetch a Pariah or a Potter from Kanthapura to help them in their fight, and Moorthy would say, "Go, go with him," and through the night they would wade across the river by the Kenchamma hill, where no policeman could catch them, and off they would go through the cactus growth and the cardamom gardens and the tamarind groves to picket the toddy shops, and when they came back they told us this about their wounded and that about their women; and when Potter Ramayya came back from Santur he said that in house after house they had a picture of Moorthy, in house after house a picture of our Moorthy taken from city papers, and it seems they said, "Tell us something about this big man?" and Potter Ramayya would weave out story after story and they would say, "You are a happy people to have a man like that." And we were so proud that we said we would bear the lathi blows and the prisons and we would follow our great Moorthy, and day after day we said, "What next, Moorthy?" and day after day he would say, "Today fast, for Vasudev is going on hunger strike," or, "Today you will offer a feast for the liberation of Potter Chandrayya." And when the feast was ready we went, trumpet and horn before us, to receive Chandrayya, and he told us of the knuckle-beatings and back-canings. "Bend down and hold your toes," they were told, and when they bent down, a Red-man would come with canes kept in oil and—bang-bang—he would beat them on their buttocks and on their knees and on their thighs. And then he would say, "Salute," and they would say, "Salute what?" and he would say, "The Government flag"; and someone would cry out, *"Vandè Mataram!"* and everyone would take it up, and shout out, *"Mataram Vandè!"* and there would be showers of lathi blows. And he told us, too, of the city boy who, while the lathi blows fell, rushed across the courtyard, clambered up the drain-pipe or the guava tree or the roof and hoisted high the national flag, and he was dragged down and kicked and caned and given a solitary cell, and he could not speak a word, and they gave him only water as lentil soup and washed paddy as rice, and he would shout and say, "Take it away," and the jailer would bang the door behind him, and with the caning ceremony again, the food would be thrust into his mouth and pushed in with their fingers; and at every shriek came a swish of the cane, and then he would vomit all and lie in troubled sleep.

"And yet he bore it all," said Chandrayya. "And though he was a Brahmin, he ate with us and slept by us and worked with us and said, 'Brahmin or no Brahmin, the same stomach hungers in all men,' and he spoke of the hammer-and-sickle country, always and always of the hammer-and-sickle country, and so we called him the hammer-and-sickle boy. But they gave him a pair of fetters again and a solitary cell, and we never saw him again."

But it was Seetharamu who came out of prison and told us the most terrible story. He said he had the great fever three days after he had been in prison, and they ordered him to get out as usual and grind the oil seed, and though he said he was too weak, the warders cried, "Ass! Pig! Badmash!" and beat him with their canes and drove him to the yoke; and there they put him to a mill and, whip in hand, they cried, "Hoy-hoy," as though he were a bull, and made him run round and round the oil mill until he had ground three maunds of peanut oil. Then suddenly he could run no more and gasping he fell on the floor and nothing but blood came out of his mouth, blood and nothing but blood, and so they released him and he lay in Ratnamma's house for a fortnight and more. And Moorthy said, "That is how you should be. Bear all as though your Karma willed it and everything will be borne." And we said, "So be it! If Seetharamu and Pariah Lingayya and Chandrayya and Ratnamma's husband, Shamu, can bear it, why not we?" and we said, "Let it come and we shall do this for Moorthy and that for Moorthy," and day after day we went out to picket this toddy shop and that, and Boranna said, "Now I am not going to keep a shop

143

where there's no sale," and he closed it, and Satanna closed his shop and said, "I am not going to bear in this life and in all lives to come the sin of women being beaten," and Madayya said, "Why, I am but a servant of the toddy contractor, and why should I see the police beat our women and men?" and he joined us, and the blue paper said there were four-and-twenty shops closed in Kanthapura *hobli* and we said, "That is a great thing."

And then we turned to Moorthy and said, "And what now?" and Moorthy said, "Why, the June tax assessments are going to begin and there will be much trouble," and we said, "Then that's good," and we bandaged our wounds and put on our bangles and we lived on as before, and the peasants went into the ripening fields and led water here and led water there, and weeded and raked and built boundary walls, and they turned to Kenchamma and said, "O you protector of water and field, protect this!"

But day after day, revenue notices fell yellow into our hands, and we said, "Let them do what they will, we shall not pay our revenues." And the new patel came, and behind the patel came the policeman and behind the policeman the landlord's agent, and we said, "Do what you will, we shall not pay." And the policemen would shake their fists at us and say, "Take care, take care. Things are not as before. You pay or the Government will squeeze water out of stone. You will have to pay," and we would stand beside the threshold and say, "We shall see." And then we would rush through the back yard to see Rangamma or Moorthy, and they would say, "Don't worry, sister, don't worry"; and the police would go to the Pariah quarter and beat Rachanna's wife because her husband was in prison, and Madanna's old mother because she was speaking to Rachanna's wife, and Siddanna's two daughters because they squatted behind the garden wall and sang:

> There's one government, sister,
> There's one government, sister,
> And that's the government of the Mahatma.

And they beat Puttamma's father because he had spat on the false patel, and Motanna's young son, Sidda, for the policemen had

144

made eyes at his sister and he had thrown dung in their faces. And the policemen had tied him to a pillar and beat him before all, and when they went out, down came a shower of old slippers and old broomsticks and rags and dung and stone, and, swearing and threatening, the policemen left the quarter. And but for Priest Rangappa, who paid for Bhatta, and Waterfall Venkamma, who had lands wide as a loincloth, and Postmaster Suryanarayana and Shopkeeper Subba Chetty and of course Agent Nanjundia, and the terror-stricken Devaru the schoolmaster who owed only two rupees and five annas for his bel field, and Concubine Chinna, for she said she knew neither Government nor Mahatma and she paid for those who look after her lands as they paid her for what she gave them— it's only these one, two, three, four, five, six, seven families that paid the revenue dues; and Moorthy said, "That is great; we shall win. We shall win the battle and we shall defeat the Government," and day after day we woke up and said, "Today they'll come to attach our property. Today they'll take away our vessels and our sacks," and we dug the earth and hid our jewels and we dragged down the vessels and threw them into the wells and we thrust rice sacks and jaggery sacks and lentil sacks behind the bath fuel, and we said, "Well, let them find it, we shall see." But no policeman ever came again to our houses, though one heavy morning all the roads and lanes and paths and cattle tracks were barricaded, by Kenchamma hill and Devil's field and Bebbur mound and the river path and the Pariah lane and the Skeffington path— stones upon stones were piled on the road and tree upon tree was slain and laid beside them, and canal banks were dug and the water let through, and thorns were laid where cactuses grew and earth was poured over it all, and one, two, three, four, five, six policemen stood behind them, bayonets and bugles in their hands, and for chief had they a tall white man.

That afternoon there was a beating of drums and we slipped behind our doors and we peeped between the chinks and we heard a new beadle cry out, with long "aas" and long "gaas" as though he had never drunk the waters of the Himavathy, that if the revenues were not paid and the laws obeyed, every man, woman and child above six in Kanthapura would pay one rupee and three pice, one rupee and three pice as punitive tax, for new policemen

145

were there to protect us and new money had to be paid for them, and the Government would rule the country and the troublesome ones, one after another, would be sent to prison. And when the night fell, through the bathroom came a soft tap-tap like a lizard spitting, and when we went, lantern in hand and trembling, and said, "Who may that be?" a voice came and it was Moorthy's, and we opened the door and said, "Come in, come in, Moorthy," and he said, "No, no, sister, I've come to say the fight has really begun. And if the patel or policeman or agent should enter the house, take the sanctum bell and ring, and we shall know they are there and we shall be here before you have swallowed your spittle thrice," and he said, "I am going, sister," and then the footsteps died away over the back-yard gravel. So, Rangamma and Ratna and Moorthy went from house to house to speak of the sanctum bell that should ring, and we kept our lights and we thrust logs against the doors, and we kept our eyes open all through that empty night, and not even a fair cart ever passed by the streets of Kanthapura. Only the cattle chewed the cud and the rats squeaked through the granaries, and when a lizard clucked we said, "Krishna, Krishna," and with dawn came sleep.

17

THE NEXT MORNING, when the thresholds were adorned and the cows worshipped and we went to sweep the street-fronts, what should we see by the temple corner but a slow-moving procession of coolies—the blue, pot-bellied, half-naked coolies, tied hand to hand and arm to arm—boys, old men, fathers, brothers, bridegrooms, coolies of the Skeffington Coffee Estate who had come to live with us and to work with us and to fight with us—they marched over the bouldered streets, their blue bodies violet in the glittering sun, and with one policeman to every two men and one armed soldier at the back and one armed soldier at the front, they marched through the Brahmin street and the Weavers' street, and the Potters' street, and children ran shrieking into the houses and women who were drawing water went empty-handed, and now and again one could hear the flip-flap of the whip and a cry or a yelp—the coolies of the Skeffington Coffee Estate were marched bent-headed through our streets to show who our true masters were, and we knew they would be driven over the Bebbur mound and the Bear's hill and the Tippur stream, and two by two they would be pushed behind the gates, for the white master wanted them. And our hearts curdled and we cried, "Oh, what shall we do? What?" and the sanctum bell did not ring, nor the conch blow, and something in us said, "Moorthy, where is Moorthy?" and our hearts beat like the wings of bats, and we clenched our hands, and we rushed in, swirled round, and fell prostrate before the sanctum gods, and yet no call came. But out of the flapping silence suddenly there came from over the promontory a shout and a cry and shriekings and weepings and bellowings, and we rose and slipped by the cactus fence and the lantana growths, and through the plantain plantation of Nanjamma, to the temple, and from the top we saw below the Pariah women and the Pariah girls and the Pariah kids and the Pariah grand-

147

mothers, beating their mouths and shouting, tight squatting on the path to stop the march of the coolies, shouting and swaying and clapping hands and lamenting:

> He'll never come again, he'll never come again,
> He'll never come again, Moorthappa.

> The god of death has sent for him,
> Buffalo and rope and all,
> They stole him from us, they lassoed him at night,
> He's gone, he's gone, he's gone, Moorthappa,

and Rachanna's wife, indignant and dishevelled, cried out:

> Hè, leave us our men, hè, leave us our souls,
> Hè, leave us our king of the veranda seat,
> But say, sisters, he's gone, he's gone, Moorthappa,
> He's gone, he's gone, he's gone, Moorthappa,

and they clapped hands again, and they wiped the tears out of their eyes, and more and more women flowed out of the Pariah street and the Potters' street and the Weavers' street, and they beat their mouths the louder, and the children ran behind the fences and slipped into the gutters and threw stones at the police, and a soldier got a stone on his face and the police rushed this side and that and caught this girl and that. And the women stopped sobbing and when Rachanna's grandson called out, "Catch me if you can,"—they caught him and held him leg up and head down and—flap-flap-flap—they beat him on the buttocks and head and spine and knee, and they threw him on the grass edge. And the women stopped their sobbing, and one here and one there they rushed toward the child and they laid him on their laps and wiped the blood from his mouth and they said, "Rangappa, Rangappa, wake up Rangappa!" but only slobber flowed from his mouth, and all of a sudden a tearing, gasping yell came from the women again, while the coolies marched blinking and blank before them and even the voice of God seemed to have died out of their tongues.

But we who were on the promontory could bear the sight no more, what with Rachanna gone and Rachanna's grandson gone and Moorthy gone, too, and we shouted out, "Butchers, butchers, dung-eating curs!" And the police rushed at us, and we slipped away by the temple yard and the cactus growth, but they saw us, and stones flew at us and sticks, and the swing of the whip, and they whipped us and kicked up and spat on us, and when Puttamma shouted, "Cur! Cur!" a policeman flings his lathi at her legs and down she falls and, smacking his lips and holding her breasts, he says, "Take care, my dove, you know what I would do with you," and we who are trying to run away, slip round and say, "No, no, we must not run away," and we run round and round the mango tree and the lantana bushes, and we think of Puttamma and her husband and her child and her mother-in-law, and we think of God, and the yell of the Pariah women still comes rolling across the promontory, and we feel like mad elephants and we do not know where to go. And then there is a loud cry, "Ayoo-ayoo," and its Puttamma's, and we rush toward her, creeping and crawling beneath the lantana bushes, and then, when we are on the path again, we see a policeman upon her, and we feel our limbs earthlike and we want to pull him up, and Puttamma is all black in her cheek and her mouth gagged, and we cry out, "Help! Help!" but from the Main street and the Pariah street we hear nothing but shouts and lamentations, and we rush away to get help, and we see street after street filled with policemen—policemen on the veranda and by the granary and on the threshold and over the byre; and when we enter there's nothing to be seen but uniformed policemen. The shrieks of the Pariah women are still shrill in the air, and where shall we find someone, where? And we run to the back yard and the police are behind us. And Puttamma?

Seethamma goes to her neighbour Lingamma, for Lingamma is an old woman and she has done nothing, but the police are already there, and when they see Seethamma they say, "Ah, you've come, my bitch, and your husband is in prison and you need some cooling down," and she shrieks out and she rushes to find refuge somewhere—and Kanthamma and Nanjamma and Vedamma and I are there, and as we ask, "What is it, daughter?" a lathi bangs on her head and she falls down as flat as a sack, and from the byre wall comes the voice of a policeman, "Ah, you're out for a moonlight party, are you?" We rush toward the temple, and shrieks come from the Brahmin street and the Weavers' street and the cattle began to moo and moan, and the flap-flap of the whips is still heard from the mango grove beyond the promontory, for the coolies were still being marched on—and we think neither of Puttamma nor Seethamma nor Moorthy nor the Mahatma, but the whole world seems a jungle in battle, trees rumbling, lions roaring, jackals wailing, parrots piping, panthers screeching, monkeys jabbering, jeering, chatter-chattering, black monkeys and white monkeys and the long-tailed ones, and the flame of forest angry around us, and if Mother Earth had opened herself and said, "Come in, children," we should have walked down the steps and the great rock would have closed itself upon us—and yet the sun was frying-hot.

And we ran here and we ran there to seek refuge, and in Satamma's house and Post-office-house and Nine-pillared house, man after man had been taken away during the night, while we had slept the sleep of asses, and the women who had their husbands taken away were tied to the pillars and their mouths gagged, and those who said, "No, no," were asked not to leave their houses till midday, and that was why there were so few women at the promontory and no Rangamma either.

And then we said, stopping, "Oh, what has become of Puttamma and Seethamma?" and we rushed from back yard to back yard; and zinc sheets were removed and sanctum gods and pickle pots and bell-metal vessels were thrown across the streets, and the byres were empty, and bulls and buffaloes and cows and calves had rushed into the kitchen gardens and the granaries; and our hearts were burning with anger, as we turned to this side and that and we said there is but one safe place and that is the temple sanctum, and as we skirted Rajamma's house, what should we see by Rangamma's ver-anda—a crouching elephant, and a crowd around it, and the mahout poking its ears and kicking it, and it roared and it rose, and it wailed, and it dashed against the door, the crowd of policemen cheering it on and on, and we heard the door creak and crash, and a loud shout of "Well done!" arose. But a policeman had seen us. and we had seen him, and we cried, "Ayoo-ayoo," and jumped across the broken wall, and the sparrows rose like a tree from their booty of rice, and we asked ourselves, "Which way shall we go—which way?" And we hurried through the central hall, and we rushed to the veranda to see Seethamma's courtyard, where beds and bells and broomsticks lay strewn everywhere, and across the byre walls children were heard weeping; and we said, "Let's slip past Ratnamma's vegetable garden," and we jumped across the fence and from behind the jack-fruit tree, where we stand to take breath, we see the barricades of the Karwar road, with one man and two men and three men and four men around and a white officer beside them. And from the Pariah quarter there comes a yell, and we look to this side and that and we see nothing, and then suddenly on the Bebbur mound we see the coolies still marching, bent-headed coolies still marching up, and the Pariah women, tired, still yelp but with broken breath, and we say, "Oh, what about Radhamma, Ramayya's Radhamma, who is ill?" and Kanakamma, who was with us, says she passed by Radhamma's door and she heard the second child crying, and a bundle of hay lay at her door, and we say we should one of us go there, and Timmamma says she would go and she was old and nobody would notice her. But suddenly we see ten or twelve women hurrying round the temple corner, and the police whips swishing, and children following them screaming, and there's Radhamma among them and Radhamma is trying to run, too, and we say, "Shout to her to come up to this garden," but Timmamma says, "No shouting," and slips down the lantana growth and she sees Radhamma and Radhamma sees her and they all rush toward us, and we say, "This is not safe, let us run to Nanjamma's back yard," and Radhamma is behind us and Timmamma is leading her by the hand, and suddenly Radhamma gives a cry and falls and she twists her body about and screams and we gather round her, and we say, "Perhaps the moment is come," but Timmamma says, "It's only seven months, no, no, it's not that," but it was that indeed, and the child comes yelling out and Timmamma tears the navel-string with her sari fringe and the dirt is thrown into the earth, but the mother is still moaning and shrieking and crying. And then there's a cry in the Post-office-house, and we ask, "Oh, what? Oh, what?" and Timmamma says, "Go and see, sisters," and we duck down and run, and the nearer we are the surer is the voice and it is the voice of Ratna, and we enter by the bathroom, where the fire is still burning and the calf still munching the straw, and we rush to the kitchen to see Ratna fallen on the floor, her legs tied ankle to ankle and her bodice torn, and the policeman, when he sees us, slips away over the wall, and Ratna, sobbing and hugging us, told us how she had fallen on her stomach again and again and had

151

spat and had screamed and had beat him with her hands, and we were so happy we had come in time, and we bent down and loosened the strings, and as no policeman was near us, we said, "Now we shall stay here for a breath," and little Vedamma went to bring Radhamma and her child, and we all sat in the kitchen, our eyes groping.

Then when Ratna is up and washed and could speak, she says, "Now, sisters, this is no safe place; let us find a refuge," and somehow we said there's the voice of Rangamma in her speech, the voice of Moorthy, and she was no more the child we had known, nor the slip of a widow we had cursed, and Timmamma turns to her and says, "Oh, where shall we go, daughter, with this new mother and child?" and Kamalamma says, "Why, to the temple," and Ratna says, "Wait, I shall go and see if the path is safe," and when she is at the bathroom door, she comes running back shouting, "Fire, fire, Bhatta's house is on fire! Surely it is the Pariah women," and we all rush to the bathroom door and we see the eaves taking fire and the white flame rising silk-like in the sun, and the pillars creak and the byre spits out jets and jets of stifled smoke that curls over the ripening fields and the ruddy canal, and moves up the Bebbur mound, and we hear the mahout's cry "Ahè, ahè," and the heavy hurried thumps of the elephant moving up the street, and from over the promontory still comes the shriek of the Pariah women and the Pariah children.

And the shouting grows shriller, and we say, "Surely there's a new attack," and we say, "Now we must run to the temple," and Timmamma gives her hand to Radhamma, and Ratna takes the new child in her sari-fringe, and Vedamma and Satamma and Ningamma and Kanakamma and I walk through Seetharam's back yard, by the well and round the tulsi platform, and we slip beneath the lantana growth, and we say, "Now we are safe," and we crawl toward the back of the temple. And there is a sudden crash and one of Bhatta's veranda roofs smashes to the earth and the air is filled with hissing sparks, and there is a loud cry, and even from the temple we could hear the swish of water being thrown, and the banging of the police lathis on the rising fire, and Satamma says, "And my house too may catch fire," and she says she would like to go and see, but Timmamma says, "Stay, Satamma, the police are there, and what will you do but hold your head and weep?" but she speaks of the hay and the rice and the beds and the only roof she has over her head, and Ratna says, "You are a Satyagrahi, sister, be patient," and then she goes skirting the temple, while Timmamma carries the child, and holding to the wall she enters the temple veranda and she says there's no one in the temple and she rushes back and says, "Come!" and we run behind her, and Timmamma with the child in her arms and Vedamma and the new mother beside her, and we all stand trembling before the unadorned god, and we all beat our cheeks and say, "Siva, Siva, protect us! Siva, Siva, protect us!" and each one made a vow of banana libation or butterlamps or clothes or jewels for the goddess, and each one said may her husband or brother or son be safe in the prisons.

And as we turned toward the god and goddess in prayer, there is heard another crash from Bhatta's burning house, and the lathis still beat upon it and the water still swishes over it, and now that the elephant has arrived, they put buckets full of water into its trunk, and the mahout cries, "Ahè, ahè," and groaning and grunting the elephant struggles forward. But halfway it swings round and runs for the gate, while the fire rises as high as the coconut trees, and the rice granary catches alight and the popped rice splashes out flower-like into the air, and the fire flows down the cattle shed and the hayrick and we all say, "Well done, well done; it is not for nothing Bhatta lent us money at 18 per cent and 20 per cent interest, and made us bleed," and Ratna says, "Say not such things, sisters, we are all Satyagrahis," and Satamma says, "Satyagrahis or not, he has starved our stomachs and killed our children," and we all say again, "Well done, well done."

And from the foot of the Bear's hill there is a long cry again, for the coolies of the Skeffington Coffee Estate, who had not been able to join us, have raised a clamour to receive the coolies that were being dragged in, and white dhotis are squashed by khaki clothes, and shouts and cries come, and from the Tippur stream rises the sound of the horn; and we turn toward Tippur and we say, "They are coming to our rescue, they are coming to help us," and there are white figures moving forward, and from the Santur grove comes the noise of drums, and we say, "They're coming," and we look once to the god and once to the east, and once to the god and once

153

to the northeast, and we look once to the god and once to the north-
west, and we say all these men, all these men and women and
children of the Himavathy are with us, and they'll all come with
drum and trumpet and horn to free us. And then suddenly Vedamma says she has the fever and she trembles and moans, and
Ratna says she will go back to Seetharamu's house to fetch blankets,
and when we say, "No, no," Ratna says, "Oh, don't be a woman,"
but hardly is she beyond the threshold than a policeman has seen
her and begins to run up the promontory, and Ratna rushes in and
bangs the sanctum door and the bar is drawn and the latch slipped,
and he beats and beats against the door and we all stand shoulder
to breast, and breast to arm, and arm to back, pressing against the
door, and he gets so tired that he puts on the outside lock and turns
the key, and another policeman comes along and says something
about sealing, and we cry out hoarse behind the door, and we cry
and moan and beg and weep and bang and kick and lament, but
there's no answer—and at last as the afternoon drew on, and
our stomachs began to beat like drums and our tongues became dry,
at every sound we said, "The people of Tippur are coming to free
us, the people of Rampur are coming to free us." But as we put
our ears to the door we hear only the crunch of military boots, the
mooing of a calf, or the rasping creak of a palm tree, or suddenly
there would rise from the village gate the tired, hoarse sobbings
of the Pariah women, and the last crashing crackle of Bhatta's fire.
And Ratna said, "Now, we will never know when they will rescue
us from here. Let us light the sacred flame and make bhajan, so
that someone may know we are here," and we searched for the
matches and the oil lamp, and we lighted the sacred flame, and our
mouths bitter, we clapped our hands and we sang:

> Siva, Siva of the Meru mount,
> Siva, Siva of the Ganges-head,
> Siva, Siva of the crescent moon,
> Siva, Siva of the crematorium dance,
> Siva, Siva of the unillusioned heart,
> Siva, Siva, Siva. . . .

And when our breath was gone and our tongues dry, Ratna
would say, "Now, I'll tell you stories like Rangamma," and she
told us of the women of Bombay who were beaten and beaten, and

yet would not move till their brothers were freed, and the flag that they hoisted and the carts and the cars and the trains they stopped, and the wires that the white men sent to the Queen to free them, and the women of Sholapur who, hand in hand, had marched through the streets, for twenty-five of their men had been shot, and the policemen would not work and the soldiers guarded the streets, but the women said, "We are behind our men," and they cried, *"Vandè Mataram!"* and they said, "Give us back our men!" and not a tear they shed, for they worked for the Mahatma and the Mother. And so story after story she told us, of Chittagong and Lahore, of Dandi and Benares, and we each put our head against another's shoulder and some snored, too, and dozed away, and Radhamma's chill went down and the fever rose and we pressed closer and closer around her, and we put our sari-fringes and our bodice-cloths upon her, and the child lay upon Timmamma's lap, white and quiet.

And we would be roused again and again with the champak-like light shining and wavering on the dark around Siva, and with the holiness of the sanctum within our hearts we lifted our voices and sang, and we forgot the Pariahs and the policemen and Moorthy and the Mahatma, and we felt as though we were some secret brotherhood in some Himalayan cave. And one by one we put our heads against a neighbour's shoulder and tired and hungry we yawned back to sleep. But someone would be chanting away, and clapping away, and through half-wakened eyes Siva would be seen, staring and weird, and such terror would come over us that we would rub our eyes and sing again. Then the light went down and the sanctum's hooded darkness thrust itself over us, and we woke each other up, and we banged the door, we kicked and screamed and moaned and we banged the solid door. And yet no voice ever came in reply, but only the squeaks of the bats and the swish of the twisting river. We slept and we banged and we slept and we kicked, and at last with the cawing of crows came a hurried step, and we woke each other up, and when the door opened we saw Pariah Rachanna's wife Rachi at the threshold. She had heard the screamings and moanings through the sleepless night, and with dawn she had slipped to the patel's house and the women gave her a key and she had jumped over Satamma's wall and Temple Rangappa's fence, and falling on the main street, she had rushed up to the temple and unlocked it. We slowly rose up on our clayey legs, and when the morning light threw itself upon us we felt as though a corpse had smiled upon a burning pyre.

How empty looked the Karwar road with Bhatta's house burnt down!

Through the morning we ploughed back home.

That very morning we heard of Puttamma. She was in bed and ill and wailing. She had fits and fears and tearing angers. She asked for her child and pressed it to her heart and threw it over the bed, saying, "I am not your mother, the earth is your mother, your father is your father—I have sinned." The father, poor man, was ignorant of this, being in prison. But she said, "There he is, there, behind the sanctum door, and he will throw me into the well." But we said, "No, no, Puttamma, the gods will forgive you," but she broke into sobs, and her mother-in-law came and threw water over her face, and cooled her down. And when we went to the door and asked, "What happened, Nanjamma?" Nanjamma told us of Pariah Siddayya who was in the lantana growth, and he had seen Puttamma and the policeman on her, and he had fallen upon the policeman and torn his moustache and banged and banged his head against a tree, and had brought Puttamma back from back yard to back yard, and men helped him in this back yard and that, for many were there that were hid in the lantana growth, and that was what we heard and saw, and that was how, when night came, rice and pickles and pancakes went up into the lantana growths. And when the beds were laid and the eyelids wanted to shut, we said, "Let them shut," for we knew our men were not far and their eyelids did not shut.

18

THREE DAYS later, when we were just beginning to say Ram-Ram after the rice had been thrown back into the rice granary, the cradle hung back to the roof, and the cauldron put back on the bath fire, and the gods put back in their sanctum, and all the houses washed and swept and adorned and sanctified, and when one by one our men were slipping in and then hurrying back to their jungle retreats, what should we see on that Saturday—for it was a Saturday—but one, two, three cars going up the Bebbur mound, one, two, three crawling cars going up the Bebbur mound like a marriage procession, and we all said, "Why, whose marriage now, when we are beating our mouths and crying?" And we saw men in European clothes get down one by one under the dizzy sun, and soldier after soldier would go toward them and stand at a distance and salute them, and then the sahib-looking people went down the mound and by this paddy field and that, and they would lift this hand and point that way and lift that hand and point this way. Then more horns hooted from the Kenchamma hill, and this time they were open cars, open cars like those of the Skeffington Coffee Estate, and in them were Pariah-looking people, and we said, "They, too, bring their coolies." But something in us said, "Now things are going wrong," and Rachanna's wife rushed to Madamma and Madamma went to see Seethamma and Vedamma, and Vedamma and Seethamma said, "Come, we'll go and see Ratna, for she is our chief now."

Then suddenly there was a drumbeat and we all rushed behind our doors and the drummer stood at the temple square with policemen on the left and policemen on the right, and he said something about the supreme Government and the no-taxer and the rebels, and then we heard the name of this field and that, and we put our ears against the door and we heard of Rangamma's coconut field and Satanna's triangular field and Pandit Venkateshia's tank field and Bebbur field, and Seetharamu's plantation field, and then, when he came to Rangè Gowda's big field, we said, "Even the big field," and we knew there was nothing more to do; and we saw sand and water and empty stomachs, and suddenly we knew why these men had come in their cars, and why the cars were followed by open cars, and we all had tears in our eyes. And we rushed down the back yards and jumped over the hedges, and we met Satamma who was standing by her well, her bundle and children beside her; and she said the drummer was saying the village would be sacked again, and she said she had seen enough and she would go away to the town, and she said she had done nothing and she was not a Gandhi person, and it was all this Moorthy, this Moorthy who had brought all this misery upon us. And we asked, "Where will you go now? The policemen are not your uncle's sons, are they? Come, Satamma, come, we will go to Ratna; for Ratna is our chief now and she will lead us out of it." But Satamma says, "What, to that bangled widow? She will lead us all to prostitution, and I am not going to have my daughters violated," and she said this and that and then she said, "All right, I'll come," for she knew there were barricades and policemen at every footpath and cattle path. So we hurried this way and that to Sami's house where Ratna now lived (for Rangamma's house was under lock and seal), and we knock at the door and somebody comes and says, "Who is there?" and I say, "The goat has two teats at the neck and two at the stomach and the stomach teats are we, *Vandè Mataram*," and they know it is us, and they open the door, and when we enter we find Nanj-amma's daughter, Seethu, and Post-office-house Lakshmi and Pandit Venkateshia's daughter, Papamma, and Sata and Veta and Chandr-amma, and Rachanna's wife and Madanna's wife and many a Pariah woman, and Bangle-seller Ningamma is there too, and they are all looking at the hall door behind which somebody is surely speaking. And we all turn toward them and ask, "Who?" and they whisper back, "Why, *they!*"—"Who are *they?*"—"Why, the boys." —"What boys? Moorthy?"—"No no, the Mahatma's boys," and then like a flash came the idea. Yes, Moorthy had told us, hadn't he? The city boys would come to our relief. And we all said, "Well, there are all these city people to help us," and we felt our hearts beat lighter, and when we heard the drummer beat the drum we felt nothing sinister could happen to us, now these boys were there, and they would win us back our harvests.

And more and more women joined us, and children followed them, and old men followed the children, and there was a close silence, and everybody sat looking at the tight hall door, when suddenly it opened, and there was Ratna, and she said something to Seethu and Seethu said something to her neighbour and the neighbour said something to us, and we all gathered our sari-fringes and we waited, and the door opened again, and one of the boys came out, and with him was Pariah Madanna, and we said, "So, he's back, hè?" and we looked at each other and we looked at Madanna's wife and Madanna's wife smiled back at us knowingly, and we said, "So, he, too, was only in the jungles," and we said surely there are many others that have come back, and our stomachs heaved with joy. And more men came out of the hall, and there they were, Puttanna and Chandrayya and Seethanna and Borappa and Potter Sidda—and the city boys, they were like princes, fair and smiling and firm, and one of the Volunteers, the one with a square face and a shaking head, he stood by the threshold, and said, "Sisters, there is nothing to be frightened about. We knew the Government would auction the lands today, and our men are going to come from the city, hundreds and hundreds of men are going to come from the city, for we have decided to hold a *Satyanarayana Puja,* and it will be held in this house, and our men will escape from all the policemen the Government can send and all the soldiers the Government can send, and yet men will come from the city, and they will come for the *Satyanarayana Puja,* and no land will ever be sold, for the Government is afraid of us," and Nanjamma says, "No, no." But the Volunteer goes on, "Yes, sister, yes, the Government is afraid of us, for in Karwar the courts are closed and the banks closed and the collector never goes out, and there are policemen at his door and at his gate and beneath his bedroom window, and every white man in Karwar has a policeman beside him, and every white man in Siddapur and Sholapur and Matgi and Malur has a policeman beside him, and it is the same from Kailas to Kanyakumari and from Karachi to Kachar, and shops are closed and bonfires lit, and khadi is the only thing that is sold,

159

while processions and songs and flags go through the streets, picket-ings and prabhat pheris, and the police will beat and the soldiers open fire, and millions and millions of our brothers and sisters be thrown into prison, and yet go and ask them, who is our King? They will say, 'Congress, Congress, Congress and the Mahatma,' and hand in hand they go, shouting, 'Victory, victory to the Mahatma.' Brothels are picketed and toddy booths and opium booths and courts are set up and men tried and condemned, and money set in circulation, the money of the Mahatma, and the salt of the sea sold, and the money sent to whom? to the Congress; and it is the same by the Ganges and the Jumna and the Godaveri, by Indus and by Kaveri, in Agra and Ankola, Lucknow and Maun-puri, in Madras, Patna and Lahore, in Calcutta, Peshawar and Puri, in Poona and in Benares—everywhere; and millions and mil-lions of our brothers and sisters have gone to prison, and when the father comes back, the son is taken, and when the daughter is arrested, the mother comes out of prison, and yet there is but one law our people will obey, it is the law of the Congress. Listen, the Government is afraid of us. There is a big city in the north called Peshawar, and there the Government has always thousands and thousands of military men, and our brothers, the Mohammedans, one and all have conquered the city, and no white man will ever come into it. And they have conquered, sisters, without a gunshot, for all are Satyagrahis and disciples of the Mahatma. They bared their breasts and marched toward the machine guns, ten thousand in all, and bullets went through them, and a hundred and twenty-five were shot through and through, and yet they went up and conquered the city. And when our soldiers were sent to shoot them, they would not shoot them. For after all, sisters, these soldiers, too, are Indians, and men like us, and they, too, have wives and chil-dren and stomachs to fill as we."

"Monsters, monsters," Rachanna's wife cries out. And the Vol-unteer replies, "Monsters, monsters, yes, they may be, but we are out to convert them, the Mahatma says we should convert them, and we shall convert them; our hearts shall convert them. Our will and our love will convert them. And now let us be silent for a while, and in prayer send out our love that no hatred may live within our breasts. And, brothers and sisters, the battle, we will win. . . ."

And we all closed our eyes and said our prayers, but our eyes would quiver, and we saw cars go up the Bebbur mound and the bel field and the tank field and the big field, filled with these Pariah-looking coolies, and soldiers were at our doors and policemen in our sanctums, and vessels lay broken on the streets, pickle pots and gods and winnowing pales. And we say, "No, no—this will not do, this will not do," and Ratna says angrily, "Then you are not for the Mahatma!" and we say, "We are, we are!—but we have only a loincloth wide of land and that is to be sold away, and who will give us a morsel to eat—who?" and Ratna says, "Oh, don't you be frightened—the Congress will look after it. Why, the Congress is ours, and much money is there in the Congress, and many a man has sent sacks and sacks of rice, and there are camps in Seethapur and camps in Subbapur, and camps, too, across the Mysore border in Shikaripur and Somapur and Puttapur . . ." But we said, "That is not enough, Ratna, and we are not cattle to leave our homes and our fires and the sacred banks of the Himavathy."

But Ratna was already away and she was saying something to the boys inside, and we all went back home to light our fires and to put something into our stomachs; but the bath fire would not take and the sanctum clothes were not dry, and when we went to the back yard we could see the cars still shining like Brahma's gates on the Bebbur mound, and the harvest simmering with the northeast wind that came from the Himavathy bend, and rising up the Kench-amma grove and the Bear's hill went shaking the trees of the Skeffington Coffee Estate, and we felt we could tear our saris to pieces and slice our heads into a million morsels and offer them up to some ten-headed ogre. Of what use all this *Satyanarayana Puja*—and all these Moorthy's prayers—and that widowed Ratna's commands? Prayers never paid revenue dues. Nor would the rice creep back to the granaries. Nor fire consume Bhatta's promissory notes. Mad we were, daughters, mad to follow Moorthy. When did Ken-chamma ever refuse our three morsels of rice—or the Himavathy the ten handfuls of water? . . . But some strange fever rushed up from the feet, it rushed up and with it our hair stood on end and our ears grew hot and something powerful shook us from head to

161

foot, like Shamoo when the goddess had taken hold of him; and on that beating, bursting day, with the palms and the champaks and the lantana and the silent well about us, such a terror took hold of us, that we put the water jugs on our hips, and we rushed back home, trembling and gasping with the anger of the gods. . . . Moorthy forgive us! Mahatma forgive us! Kenchamma forgive us! We shall go. Oh, we shall go to the end of the pilgrimage like the two hundred and fifty thousand women of Bombay. We will go like them, we will go . . . !

Men will come from the city, after all, to protect us! We will go . . . !

We drew two carts across Sami's courtyard so that nobody could see the procession we were preparing, and flowers were brought, and sandal and banana trunks, and Ratna went and brought a picture of Satyanarayana and stuck it in the middle, and somebody put a Gandhi at his feet and set a flower upon it, and even *sajji* was being made in the kitchen, and butter and banana and syrup, and when camphor trays and kumkum trays were decorated and the wicks sharpened, Ratna says somebody will blow the conch from the promontory at dusk-fall, and the men who would be lying hidden in the jungle and by the river, and village men and city men would rush from this side and that and, with the Satyanarayana procession in front of us, we would go through the Brahmin street and the Pariah street to the village gate and across the lanes and the pastures and the canal to do field-Satyagraha.

And now and again, when we heard footsteps, we all rushed back into the byre for fear we should be seen, and then Seeth-amma, who was plucking flowers in the back yard, came and said, "Sisters, sisters, do you know more buses have come and more men have come from the city for the auctions?" and we all said, "Only a Pariah looks at the teeth of dead cows. What is lost is lost, and we shall never again look upon our fields and harvests." And then someone comes running in and says, "Why, there are women there, too," and we could not stop our fears and we rushed to see who these bitches could be, and Timmamma, who had keen eyes, says, "Why, they are our women; cannot you see? Agent Nanjundia's wife Subbamma is there, and there is Kamalamma's Kanchi sari too," and we all say, "Well, one soul lost for us." Then Timmamma says, "Why, there is Venkatalakshamma too—Venkatalakshamma who fed Moorthy. Why, sister, a woman who could have starved her stepchildren so, could never be a Gandhi woman," and Seeth-amma says, "And there is Priest Rangappa's wife Lakshamma too, I think."—"To buy off for Bhatta, surely," cried Ratna. And we sought to make out who this woman was and who that woman was, but we could hardly see, for the evening was drawing near. And then suddenly there arose the clamour of the Pariah women and the sudra women, for a white man stood there on one of those trucks, and he was turning to this side and saying something, and turning to that side and saying something, and hands were thrust up, and people pressed against one another, and voices shot across the valley as clear and near as though they came from the other side of the Brahmin quarter, and the Pariah women shrieked and shrieked, they beat their mouths and shrieked, and the children joined them, and our hearts began to give way, and Ratna said, "Now no more of this—nobody wants to see a drowning person," and we all rushed back to the Satyanarayana procession-throne.

But the clamour still rises from beneath the promontory and we can hear Timmi, Timmayya's Timmi, cry out, "Oh! The bel field! May your house be destroyed—may your wife die childless—I'll sleep with your mother!" And the lamentations begin and lathis strike and the shriekings die down; and then we turn back to see suddenly that there is a city man at the byre door, and Ratna says, "Why, that's Sankaru," and we say, "Why, the Sankaru, the Sankaru," and we feel a holy presence among us, and behind him are more men, more boys from the city, and he walks silently toward us and sees our throne ready and says, "That is good," and Ratna is trembling with joy and she says, "Why, when did you come?" and he says, "Never mind. Is everything ready, for soon must the conch be blown," and we all say, "Who will blow it? Who?"

And with the coming of the evening, we hear the last shouts from the Bebbur mound, and dogs bark and bats flap about, and then there is such a cry again from the Sudra lines and the Pariah lines that Ratna rushes to the back yard, and we all rush behind her, and from beneath the giant mango by the well we see the Pariah-

163

looking men of the Bebbur mound go down crowd by crowd, sickle and scythe in hand, crowd by crowd to the big field and the Bebbur field and Lingayya's field and Madanna's field and Rangamma's field and Satanna's triangular field, and then the cars start, and one by one the cars go down and sail away beyond the Kenchamma hill, and we say, "It's lost, it's lost, but they are not going to reap tonight, and it shall be ours one night more." But from inside the trucks they take out big, strong gaslights of the city, and like a veritable marriage procession they bring the lights down—coolie behind coolie brings them down. Dusk falls and night comes and all our fields lie glimmering under the pale yellow lights of the city. Then Sankaru rushes in and cries out, "Now, Ratna, blow the conch!"

Ratna blew the conch from the top of the promontory, and with the blowing of the conch rose the *"Satyanarayan Maharaj ki jai! Satyanarayan Maharaj ki jai!"* from Sami's courtyard, and the throne was lifted up, and we marched through the Brahmin street and the Potters' street and the Pariah street and the Weavers' street, and doors creaked and children ran down the steps, and trays were in their hands, and the camphor was lit and the coconuts broken and the fruits offered, and one by one behind the children came their mothers, and behind their mothers their grandmothers and grand-aunts, and people said, "Sister, let me hold the torch. Sister, let me hold the sacred fan." And shoulder after shoulder changed beneath the procession-throne, and the cries of *"Satyanarayan Maharaj ki jai! Satyanarayan Maharaj ki jai!"* leapt into the air. And somebody said, "Let us sing 'The Road to the City of Love'," and we said, "That's beautiful," and we clapped our hands and we sang, "The road to the City of Love is hard, brother." And hardly were we by the temple corner than policeman upon policeman was seen by the village gate, and they were coming, their lathis raised up, and when they saw it was a religious procession they stopped, and we shouted all the louder to show it was indeed a religious song we were singing, and we came nearer. "It's a religious procession, hè, take care!" says one of them, and Ratna says, "Oh yes, we'll take care," and the policemen walked beside us, twisting their moustaches

164

and swearing and spitting and blustering, and Ratna stopped every hundred steps and blew the conch three times, and camphors were lit again, and the coconuts broken, and, "Satyanarayan Maharaj ki jai!" was shouted out into the night air. And the police turned to Lingamma and said, "Where are you going?" and Lingamma said, "I do not know." And they turned to Madamma and said, "Where are you going?" and Madamma said, "The gods know, not I," and they went this side and that and tried to threaten Lakkamma and Madamma and Seethamma and Vedamma, but they shouted out, "Satyanarayan Maharaj ki jai!"

And at last the police inspector came, and this time he was on foot, and a policeman followed him, lantern in hand, and he stops the procession and Ratna blows the conch three times and says, "Stop!" and we stop, and he says to Ratna, "Where do you go?" and Ratna says, head up, "Where the gods will," and he says, "Which way do your gods will?" and he twists his face and laughs at his own joke, and Ratna says, "Where evil haunts."—"You will get a nice two years, my nice lady."—"So be it." And now, "Satyanarayan Maharaj ki jai!" and she gave three long blasts with her conch.

And as we began to march, it was not "Satyanarayan Maharaj ki jai!" that came to our throats, but "Vandè Mataram!" and we shouted out, "Vandè Mataram—Mataram Vandè!"; and then suddenly from the darkened Brahmin street and the Pariah street and the Weavers' street and the lantana growths came back the cry, "Mahatma Gandhi ki jai!" and the police were so infuriated that they rushed this side and that, and from this courtyard and that garden, from behind this door and that byre, and from the tops of champak trees and pipal trees and tamarind trees, from beneath horse carts and bullock carts, men in white jumped out, men at last from the city, boys, young men, householders, peasants, Mohammedans with dhotis to the knees, and city boys with floating skirts and Gandhi caps, and they swarmed around us like veritable mother elephants round their young. And we felt so happy that we cried out, "Vandè Mataram!" and with the groan of the boys and the cry of children under the lathi blows, from the Karwar road to the Kenchamma hill, voice upon voice rose, and from hill to hill like wildfire blared, "Mataram Vandè!" And some near us stamped the earth and cried, "Inquilab Zindabad—Inquilab Zindabad!" And

"*Inquilab, Inquilab, Inquilab,*" rapped out someone clear and fierce through the starlit air, and "*Zindabad*" we roared back, and such a roar swept through the streets and the valley that we said there are more men still, ten and tens of thousands of men, and the policemen's curses were lost in the ringing of bells and the blast of the conch. And then somebody behind us blew the long horn, and it twirled up and swung forth and clattered against the trees of the Skeffington Coffee Estate, and another and another curled up, and yet another that arched over the Kenchamma hill and the Bebbur mound and trailed away snaking up to the Blue Mountain tops. And we said more and more men will know of our fight, and more and more of them will come, and we clapped our hands and we stamped the earth and we marched on, and we shouted, "*Inquilab, Inquilab Zindabad!*" and between two shouts we asked the city boys, "Where are we going, where?" and the city boys said, "Why, to the barricades."—"And what barricades?"—"Why, the Skeffington barricades," and a neighbour would pinch us and say, "Say *Mahatma Gandhi ki jai!*" and we cried out, "*Gandhi Mahatma ki jai!*" and the city boys would say, "We'll take it, sister, we will. In Peshawar the whole city . . ." and lathi blows fell on us, but "*Inquilab Zindabad!*" was the only answer we gave.

And suddenly, across the Bebbur mound, we saw shapes crawl along and duck down and rise up, and we said, "Perhaps soldiers— soldiers," but, "In Peshawar," says the city boy, "you know they would not shoot," and we said we too are soldiers, and we are the soldiers of the Mahatma, and this country is ours, and the soldiers are ours and the English they are not ours, and we said to ourselves, a day will come, a day when hut after hut will have a light at dusk, and flowers will be put on the idols, and camphors lit, and as the last Red-man leaps into his boat, and the earth pushes him away, through our thatches will a song rise like a thread of gold, and from the lotus naval of India's earth the Mahatma will speak of love to all men.—"Say *Mahatma Gandhi ki jai!*"—"*Inquilab Zindabad, Inquilab Zindabad!*"—and the police lathis showered on us, and the procession-throne fell, and the gods fell and the flowers fell and the candelabras fell, and yet the gods were in the air, brother, and not a cry nor lamentation rose, and when we reached the village gate, suddenly from the top of a pipal someone swings down and he has a flag in hand, and he cries out:

> Lift the flag high,
> O, lift the flag high,
> Brothers, sisters, friends and mothers,
> This is the flag of the revolution.

and the police rush at him, and he slips in here and he slips out there and the boys have taken the flag, and the flag flutters and leaps from hand to hand, and with it the song is clapped out:

> O lift the flag high,
> Lift it high like in 1857 again,
> And the Lakshmi of Jhansi,
> And the Moghul of Delhi,
> Will be ours again.

and there is a long cry, "Down the hedge, here," and we rush down the aloe lane, and the police find they are too few, and they begin to throw stones at the crowd and the crowd gets angry, but the boys shut them up and sing:

> O fire, O soul,
> Give us the spark of God-eternal,
> That friend to friend and friend to foe,
> One shall we stand before Him.

And suddenly there is an opening in the hedge and the gaslights and the coolies and the barricades are seen, long barricades that lie like an elephant's carcass under the starlight, and men stand by them, and behind them the trucks, and behind the trucks the wide-eyed lantern of the Skeffington bungalow, and down below, in Satanna's triangular field men are still working, the coolies from the city are still reaping. And all of a sudden we cry out, *"Gandhi Mahatma ki jai!"* and they look at us and stop their work but they do not reply, and we shout the louder, *"Vandè Mataram! Inquilab Zindabad Mahatma Gandhi ki jai!"* and the police, seeing the crowd out of their hands, kick and twist the limbs and bang more fiercely, and Seethamma is thrown upon the cactuses and Vedamma and Kanakamma after her, and we could hear their wailings, and we run to them and pull them up, and we run down the lane and the field-bunds and we come to the canal, and the women cry out,

"We cannot go! We cannot go!" and the men drag them and the police push them in, and the pebbles slip under our feet, and saying, "Ganga, Jumna, Saraswathi!" we look up into the wide, starry sky, and there is something in the air resonant like the temple bell, and the bell rings on and on, and we wade through the canal and we sing, "That friend to friend and friend to foe," and the procession still moves on—and suddenly, by Rangamma's coco-nut-garden field, from behind the waving, brown paddy harvest, there is a cry sharp and clear, then a rasping hiss as though a thousand porcupines had suddenly bristled up, and we see rising from behind the ridge, ten, twenty, thirty, forty soldiers heads down and bayonets thrust forth. We whirl in shrieks and shouts and yells, and we leap into the harvests. And a first shot is shot into the air.

And there was a shuddered silence, like the silence of a jungle after a tiger has roared over the evening river, and then, like a jungle cry of crickets and frogs and hyenas and bison and jackals, we all groaned and shrieked and sobbed, and we rushed this side to the canal-bund and that side to the coconut garden, and this side to the sugar cane field and that side to the bel field bund, and we fell and we rose, and we crouched and we rose, and we ducked beneath the rice harvests and we rose, and we fell over stones and we rose again, over field-bunds and canal-bunds and garden-bunds did we rush, and the children held to our saris and some held to our breasts and the night-blind held to our hands; and we could hear the splash of the canal water and the trundling of the gun-carts, and from behind a tree or stone or bund, we could see before us, there, beneath the Bebbur mound, the white city boys grouped like a plantain grove, and women round them and behind them, and the flag still flying over them. And the soldiers shouted, "Disperse or we fire," but the boys answered, "Brothers, we are non-violent," and the soldiers said, "Nonviolent or not, you cannot march this side of the fields," and the boys answered, "The fields are ours," and the soldiers said, "The fields are bought, you pigs." And a peasant voice from the back says, "It's we who have put the plough to the earth and fed her with water," and the soldiers say, "Hè, stop that, you village kids," and the boys say, "Brother, the earth is ours, and you are ours too, brown like this earth is your skin and mine," and a soldier shouts out, "Oh, no more of this

168

panchayat—we ask you again, disperse, and do not force us to fire!"
Then, it is Ratna's voice that says, "Forward, brothers, in the name
of the Mahatma!" and everybody takes it up and shouts, *Mahatma
Gandhi ki jai!*" and marches forward. And a shower of shots suddenly burst into the air, and we close our eyes, and when we open
them again there is not a cry nor shout and the boys are still marching forward, and the soldiers are retreating, and we say, "So that
was false firing." But the city boys will not stop, and the crowd
moves on and on, and beneath the stars there is a veritable moving
mound of them from the Bebbur field to the canal field.

And we say, "Let us rush behind Bhatta's sugar canes, there they
cannot catch us, for if they come to one row, we will slip into another," and we stumble and rise again, and we hold to our children
and the night-blind, and we duck and we rise again, and, our eyes
fixed on the soldiers, we rush toward Bhatta's sugar cane field.
And when we are there, Satamma says, "The snakes, the snakes!"
and we say, "If our karma is that, may it be so," and we huddle
behind the sugar cane reeds and we lie along the sugar cane
ditches, and we peep across the dark, watery fields, and the children
begin to say, "I am afraid, I am afraid," and we say, "Wait a
moment, wait, and it will be over soon." And, our hearts tied up
in our sari-fringes, we gaze beyond the dead harvest growth, and
the crowd still moves forward toward the gaslights, and by the
gaslights the coolies still bend their heads and cut the harvest, and
a man is there, crying out, swearing away—their maistri. And the
nearer the crowd comes to the coolies the louder is the shout,
"Gandhi Mahatma ki jai! Inquilab Zindabad! Inquilab Zindabad!"
And suddenly we see shadows moving in the Skeffington Coffee
Estate, shadows moving like buffaloes on a harvest night, and not
a voice comes from them, and we say, "Surely, they are not our
men," and yet we say, "The Skeffington coolies will not let us
down." And then, as the pumpkin moon is just rising over the Beda
Ghats, there comes a sudden cry from the top of the Bebbur mound,
and we jump to our feet and we ask, "Oh, what can it be, what?"
and a flag is seen moving in the hands of a white-clad man, and
the police boots are crunching upon the sand, and we say somebody
is running toward the barricades—but who? And the crowd is still
by the Bebbur field, and the flag is still there, and there is a furious

169

cry coming from the Bebbur mound gate and a crash is heard, and we hear the coolies rushing at the barricades and they, too, have a flag in their hands and they blow a trumpet and shout out, *"Vandè Mataram! Mataram Vandè!"* and there is an answer from the crowd below, *"Inquilab Zindabad! Inquilab Zindabad!"* and between them is Rangè Gowda's big field and the Bebbur field and the triangular field.

And of a sudden the coolies of the city stop work and at a command the lights are all put out, and there is nothing but the rising moon and a rag of cloud here and there and all the stars of night and the shining dome of the Kenchamma temple, and the winking lantern from the Skeffington bungalow. And the Skeffington coolies, black with their white dhotis, tumble and rush down, and there is another shot in the air, and this time we see the flag of the coolies flutter as they advance toward the crouching barricades; and a white officer is there, and there is surely a horse beneath him, for he is there, he is there, he is everywhere, and one of the soldiers cries out something from the barricades, and the coolies answer one and all, *"Mahatma Gandhi ki jai!"* and then someone sets fire to a dhoti and throws it at the soldiers, and there is a long, confused cry like that of children, and we see lathis rising and falling, darting and dipping like fishes, and the coolies shout out, *"Mahatma Gandhi ki jai! To the fields! To the barricades, brothers!"* And the crowd below, wading through the harvests, shouts back, "Say, brother, *Inquilab Zindabad! Mahatma Gandhi ki jai!"* And they seem so near the Skeffington coolies that they have just to jump and they will be at the top of the mound and the Skeffington coolies have just to jump down and they will be with the crowd, and between them stand the city coolies, white and bearded and motionless. And when the Skeffington coolies shout again, *"Inquilab Zindabad! Inquilab Zindabad!* Say, brother, *Inquilab Zindabad!"* a volley spits into the air, and in the silence that follows, there is a voice that shouts out, "Stop, or we shoot."—"Shoot!" answers one of the coolies, and a shot bursts straight at him, and another and yet another, and there are cries and gasps, and people beat their mouths and lament, and the crowd below feels so furious that, shouting *"Inquilab Zindabad!"* they run forward, and the police can stop them no more, and they jump over field-bunds and tumble against gaslights and fall over rocks and sheaves, sickles, and scythes, three thousand men in all, and from the top of the mound soldiers open fire.

And there follows a long tilting silence, and then yells and moans and groans again. And we say, "No, we can see this no more, we, too, shall be with them." But Lingamma says she is feeling like doing something, and Lakshamma says her heart is fainting, and Nanjamma says, "I'll be with the children." So Vedamma and Seethamma and Lakshamma and I, we go up behind the crowd, and the bullets scream through the air, like flying snakes taken fire, they wheeze and hiss and slash against the trees, or fall hissing into the canal, and Vedamma gets a bullet in the left leg, and we put her on the field-bund, and we tear up a little paddy and we lay her on it and she says, "Rama-Rama, I'm dying—Rama-Rama, I'm dying," and we say, "No, it's only the leg," but she says, "No, no," but we know it is well, and there is such a cry, such a lamentation from the crowd, that our hearts are squeezed like a wet cloth, and we say, "Vedamma, Vedamma, stop here and we will get some help." And already in the big field men are being bandaged, and we say, "Brother, brother, there is a woman wounded," and somebody says, "Ramu, go and see her." And a Volunteer hurries torch in hand to bandage Vedamma, and we see already, two, three, four stretchers bearing away the wounded, and they say the Congress ambulance is there, that it had slipped through swamp and jungle, and the wounded would be carried to it. And we say, "How are things going, brother?" and the Volunteer says, "They are resisting," and we ask, "And women, are there some women?" and he says, "Why, there are many."—"And you are a city boy?" we ask. —"Yes, yes, sister," he says, and we say, "We'll follow you," and he says, "Come," and we run behind him, and the shots fall here and fall there, and in the darkness we can see a white group of men moving up, a white group of city boys, and behind them are women, and behind the women the crowd again, and the wounded shriek from this field and from that, voices of men and boys and old women, and above it all rises from the front ranks the song:

> And the flame of Jatin,
> And the fire of Bhagat,
> And the love of the Mahatma in all,

O, lift the flag high,
Lift the flag high,
This is the flag of the revolution.

And the Skeffington coolies cry out, *"Mahatma Gandhi ki jai"*; and the coolies of the harvest take it up and shout, *"Mahatma Gandhi ki jai!"* and we are near them and they are near us, and they say something to us and we do not understand what they mutter, and we say, *"Mahatma, Mahatma, Gandhi Mahatma!"* and they put their mouths to our ears and say, *"Gandhi Mahatma ki jai!"* and, *"Punjab, Punjab!"* But our ears are turned to the firing and we strain our eyes to see the coolies on the mound, the coolies of the Skeffington Coffee Estate, but all we hear are shouts and shrieks and yells. Then suddenly from the Himavathy bend there is such a rush of more coolies that the soldiers do not know which way to turn, for the city boys are still marching up, and women are behind them, and the crowd behind the women, and there are the coolies across the barricades; and there is such joy that a wild cry of *"Vandè! . . . Mataram! . . ."* gushes from the valley to the mountaintops and all the moonlit sky above us. And the white man shouts a command and all the soldiers open fire and all the soldiers charge—they come rushing toward us, their turbans trembling and their bayonets shining under the bright moon, and our men lie flat on the fields, the city boys and the women, and the soldiers dash upon us and trample over us, and bang their rifle butts against our heads. There are cries and shrieks and moans and groans, and men fly to the left and to the right, and they howl and they yell and they fall and they rise and we rise, too, to fly, but the soldiers have seen us, and one of them rushes toward us, and we are felled and twisted, we are felled and we are kicked, we are felled and the bayonets waved over our faces—and a long time passes before we wake and we find Satamma fainted beside us, and Madamma and I, who were soaking in a ditch, crawl past her. And then there is a shot, and a fleeing man nearby is shot in the chest and he falls over us, and the moon splashes on his moustached face, his peasant blanket soaked in blood, and he slowly lets down his head, crying "Amma, mother! Amm—Amm!" and we wipe the saliva from his mouth, and we put our mouths to his ear and say, "Narayan, Narayan," but he is already dead. There is no more charging now,

172

but a continuous firing comes down from the Bebbur mound. The moon still shines and with it the winking light of the Skeffington Coffee Estate.

There is a long silence.

We're in the big field. Where is Ratna? Where is Venkateshia's wife, Lakshamma? And Nose-scratching Nanjamma? And Seethamma and Vedamma and Chinnamma and all? "How are you, Madamma?" I ask. "Hush!" says someone in front of us, hid beneath the harvest, and as we raise our heads, we see men hid behind this ridge and that in this field and that, and their white clothes and their tufts and braids. And there is Kanthapura, too, across the canal and the aloe lane, and there's not a light, and the streets are milk-splashed under the moon. There's Rangamma's veranda and Nanjamma's mango-well, and Sami's courtyard with its cart, yokes on the earth and backs in the air; the dustbin is by the main street square, and the Corner-house coconut tree is dark and high. There seems to be not a beating pulse in all Kanthapura.

Now, there's the gruff voice of the white officer and the whispered counsels of the soldiers. Soon they'll begin the attack again.

The attack began not from their side but ours, for someone broke open the gas cylinders of the city lights, and they made such a roar that the officer thought it was a gunshot, and immediately there was a charge, and the soldiers came grunting and grovelling at us, bayonets thrust forward, and shot after shot burst through the night, and we knew this time there would be no mercy, and we rose and we ran; and someone from the Bebbur mound had run up to the barricades where there was neither soldier nor officer, and had tried to hoist the National flag, and the coolies rushed behind him, and the coolies from the Hamavathy bend rushed toward them, and there was a long "Vandè Mataram!" and the soldiers, fiercer, dashed behind us, and man after man gasped and cried and fell, and those that were tying bandages to them, they, too, got bayonet thrusts in the thighs and arms and chest, and we spread over field and bund and garden, and when we came to the canal there were so many of us to wade through, that the boys said, "Go ahead, go ahead, sisters," and they stood there, holding hand to hand and arm

173

to arm, one long aloe-hedge of city boys, their faces turned to the Bebbur mound. And the soldiers rush at them, but one goes forward and says, "Brother, we are nonviolent, do not fire on innocent men," and the white officer says, "Stop," and he says to the soldier, "What does he say?" and the soldiers laugh, "They say they're innocent," and the officer says, "Then ask them if they will be loyal to the Government," and the boys ask, "What Government?" and the officer answers, "The British Government," and the boys say, "We know only one government and that is the government of the Mahatma," and the officer says, "But ours is an Indian Government," and he says to a soldier, "Plant this flag here," and we who are on the other side of the canal, we lie behind the bund, and we look at the flag being planted just between Satamma's boundary stone and the bel tree, and the moon is still there and the fields fretful with a mountain wind. And the officer says, "Salute, and march past the flag, and you will be free," and then he says, "Come out," and the boys cry in answer, *Inquilab Zindabad! Inquilab Zindabad!*" and the boys at the back begin:

> O fire, O soul,
> Give us the spark of God-eternal,
> That friend to friend and friend to foe,
> One shall we stand before Him.
>
> And the flame of Jatin,
> And the fire of Bhagat,
> And the love of the Mahatma in all,
> O, lift the flag high,
> Lift the flag high,
> This is the flag of the revolution.

And suddenly a boy rushes to the flag and a host of bayonets are thrust at him, and another boy rushes up behind him, and at him the officer aims his pistol, and then others cry and shout and rush at the flag, and the parrots and the bats and the crows come screeching out of the bel tree; and the coolies are now running down the Bebbur mound, and there is a hand-to-hand fight, and some, frightened, fall into the canal, and others go rushing this side and that, but the city boys, they squat down, they plop on the harvests and they squat down. But someone has hit the officer and he falls, and then curses and bayonets fly, and the coolies of the Bebbur mound have arrived, and they are holding the gaslight boxes in front of them, and some carry gas cylinders on their heads, and they carry sickles and lathis in their hands. But a voice is heard saying, "No violence, in the name of the Mahatma," and we know it is Ratna's voice—but, where is she? where? And the coolies answer back, "*Mahatma Gandhi ki jai!* Say, brother, *Gandhi Mahatma ki jai!*" and the soldiers rush toward them and fall on them, and the coolies fall on the soldiers, and the city boys cry, "Stop, stop," but bayonets are thrust at them too, and there is such a confusion that men grip men and men crush men and men bite men and men tear men, and moan on moan rises and groan on groan dies out, while the ambulance men are still at work and men are bandaged, and shot after shot rings out and man after man falls like an empty sack, and the women take up the lamentation: "He's gone—he's gone—he's gone, sister!" they beat their mouths and shout, "He's gone—he's gone—he's gone, Moorthappa!" and somebody adds, "He's gone—he's gone—he's gone, Rachanna!" and over the moans and the groans rises the singsong lamentation, "Oh Ammayya, he's gone—he's gone—he's gone, Rachanna!"

And men are kicked and, legs tied to hands and hands tied to legs, they are rolled into the canal, and the waters splash and yells rise up, "Help, help, Ammayya!" And the coolies rush up and some shout, "*Mahatma Gandhi ki jai!*" and others shout back, "*Vandè Mataram!*" and a bayonet is thrust at one and he falls, and again through the night rises the lamentation, "Ammayya—he's gone—he's gone—he's gone, Moorthappa," and it whirls and laments over the canal and the sugar cane field and the Bebbur mound and Skeffington Coffee Estate and the mango grove of the Kenchamma temple —and crouching, we creep back through the village lane, behind lantana and aloe and cactus, looking at the Bebbur mound, where the Gandhi flag is still flying beneath the full-bosomed moon, and the canal-bund beyond which three thousand men are shrieking and slaying, weeping, wounding, groaning, crawling, swooning, vomiting, bellowing, moaning, raving, gasping . . . and at the village gate there's Satamma and Nanjamma and Rachamma and Madamma, and Yenki and Nanju and Pariah Tippa and old Mota and Beadle Timmayya and Bora and Venkata, and the children are there, too, and old men from the city, and the coolies of the

175

fields who said, "Punjab, Punjab." And we ask ourselves, "Who will ever set foot again in this village?" and Madanna's wife, Madi, says, "Even if you want to, the police are not your uncle's sons, are they? For every house and byre is now attached." And then more and more men crawl up, and more wounded are brought up, on shoulders and arms and stretchers are they brought up, naked, half covered, earth-covered are they brought up, with dangling legs, dangling hands and bleeding hands, and with bleeding mouths and bleeding foreheads and backs are they brought up, city boys and peasant boys are they, young and bright as banana trunks, city men and peasant men, lean-ribbed, long-toed, with cut moustaches and long whiskers—peasant women and city women are they, widows, mothers, daughters, stepdaughters—and some speak in free voices and some in breathless sputters, and some can do no more than wallow and wail. And women walk behind them, beating their mouths and singing, "Oh, he's gone—he's gone, Cartman Rudrappa; *Hè,* said he to his bulls, and *hè, hè,* said he to his cart, *hè, hè, hè,* said he to the wicked whip; he's gone—he's gone—he's gone, Rudrappa," and another woman adds, "He's gone, Potter Siddayya. . . ."

And old Rachanna's wife, Rachi, can bear the sight no more, and she says, "In the name of the goddess, I'll burn this village," and we say, "Nay, nay, Rachi," but she spits once, twice, thrice toward the Bebbur mound, and once, twice, thrice at the village gate, and she rushes toward the Pariah lines, and Lingamma and Madamma and Boramma and Siddamma follow her, crying, "To the ashes, you wretch of a village!" and they throw their bodices and their sari-fringes on the earth and they raise a bonfire beneath the tamarind tree, and they light this thatch and that thatch, and we cry out, "Our houses, our houses," and they say, "Go, ye widows, don't you see the dead and the dying?" and more and more men and women go this side and that and say, "If the rice is to be lost let it be lost in the ashes," and granary and byre and haylofts are lighted. And then, as the flames rise, there are shots again, and the soldiers rush toward us, and we run and run, with the cows and the bulls and the pigs and the hens bellowing and squawking about us, and bats and rats and crows and dogs squealing behind us, through Pariah street and Potters' street and the Weavers' street did we rush, and slipping behind Rangamma's back yard, we dodged among tamarind and pipal and lantana and cactus, and Seethamma and Madamma and Boramma and Lingamma and I waded through the Himavathy, and Rachamma and Rachamma's child, and Ningamma and her granddaughter and her two nephews joined us; and then more and more women and men joined us, wounds in stomachs and wounds in breasts and wounds in faces, with bullets in thighs, and bullets in the toes, bullets in the arms—men carried men, men carried wounded women and yelping children, and they laved them in the river, and they gave them water to drink and when we were twenty-five or thirty in all, one of the city boys said, "Now we start, and we shall reach Maddur in an hour," and we rose and woke the children, and they rose with us, and beneath the hushed arching mangoes of the road, stumbling into ruts and groping over boulders, we trudged up the Maddur mountains, and not a roar came from the jungles and the moon and stars were bright above us.

And in Maddur there were policemen, and they, too, rushed to smite us, and we said, "We have borne so much, let them," and they spat and they kicked and they crushed and they banged, and then an old woman from here and a pregnant woman from there, old men, girls and children came running, Maddur women and Maddur old men, and they took us to this veranda and that, and gave us milk and coconut and banana. And they asked this about the fight and that, and of their sons who were with us, and their fathers and their husbands, and of Mota who had a scar on the right eye, and Chenna who was this-much tall, and Betel-seller Madayya, you couldn't mistake him, he was so round, and we said what we knew and we were silent over what we knew not, and they said, "Ah, wait till our men come back, wait!" But we said the police would not leave us alone and we'd go away but we'd leave our wounded with them. And we took our children and our old women and our men and we marched up the Kola pass and the Beda hills, and, mounting over the Ghats, we slipped into the Santapur jungle path, and through the clear, rustling, jungle night we walked down to the banks of the Cauvery. Across it was Mysore State, and as dawn broke over the hissing river and the jungles and the mountains, we dipped in the holy river and rose, and men came to greet us with trumpet and bell and conch, and they marched in front of

177

us and we marched behind them, through the footpaths and the lanes and the streets. And houses came and cattle and dung-smell and coconut shops and children and temple and all. They hung garlands on our necks, and called us the pilgrims of the Mahatma.

Then we ate and we slept, and we spake and we slept, and when they said, "Stay here, sisters," we said, "We'll stay, sisters," and we settled down in Kashipura.

19

THIS DASARA will make it a year and two months since all this happened and yet things here are as in Kanthapura. Seethamma and her daughter, Nanja, now live in Malur Shanbhog Chikkanna's house, and they eat with them, and grind with them, and Chikkanna, who has no children, is already searching for a bridegroom for Nanja. "I'll find her a Mysore B.A.," he says, and day after day horoscopes come, and he says, "This one is better, but the other one I have heard about is better still." But Nanjamma, Pandit Venkateshia's wife, Nanjamma, is alone in Temple Vishveshvarayya's house, and she says, "I'm no cook, and yet that's all I do for the Mahatma!" That one was never born to follow the Mahatma, I tell you, she and her tongue and her arms, and her ever-falling sari. And Pariah Rachanna's wife, Rachi, has found a place in Kanthenahalli Patel Chandrayya's house, and she comes now and again to the Brahmin quarters with her pounded rice or her dung cakes. Her granddaughter, Mari, is working in Chenna's house, and they say she's already asked for in marriage by Kotwal Kirita's son, the second one, who works with the elephant merchants from the north. And the marriage is to take place as soon as the father is out of prison. And Timmamma and I, we live in Jodidar Seetharamiah's house, and they say always, "Are your prayers finished, aunt? Are your ablutions finished, aunt?" before every meal. "Aunt, aunt, aunt," they always call us for this and that, and the children say, "The Mahatma has sent us his relations. There is the aunt who tells such nice stories," and that is me, "and the aunt of the pancakes," and that's Timmamma, and they all laugh.

In the afternoons we all gather on the veranda pressing cotton wicks and hearing the Upanishads—it's Temple Vishwanath's son Shamu, who's at the Mysore Sanscrit College, that does us the readings. Of course, it can never be like Ramakrishnayya's. They say

Rangamma is to be released soon. And maybe my poor Seenu too, though they have sent him to a northern jail, for what with his hunger strikes and *Vandè Matarams,* he had set fire to the hearts of all around him, and they gave him another six months. But Ratna had only one year, and the other day she came to spend a month with us, and she told us of the beatings and the tortures and the "Salute the Union Jack" in the prison. That was not for long though, for the Mahatma has made a truce with the Viceroy and the peasants will pay back the revenues, the young men will not boycott the toddy shops, and everything they say, will be as before. No, sister, no, nothing can ever be the same again. You will say we have lost this, you will say we have lost that. Kenchamma forgive us, but there is something that has entered our hearts, an abundance like the Himavathy on Gauri's night, when lights come floating down the Rampur corner, lights come floating down from Rampur and Maddur and Tippur, lights lit on the betel leaves, and with flower and kumkum and song we let them go, and they will go down the Ghats to the morning of the sea, the lights on the betel leaves, and the Mahatma will gather it all, he will gather it by the sea, and he will bless us.

They have burnt our dead, too, by the Himavathy, and their ashes too have gone out to the sea.

You know, sister, Moorthy is no more with us. The other day, when Ratna was here, we asked, "When is Moorthy to be released?" and she says, "Why, aunt,"—and how deferential Ratna has become! —"he's already freed."—"Freed!" we exclaimed,—"Yes, since the pact with the Viceroy many a prisoner has been released."—"And when is he coming here, Ratna?"—"I don't know, aunt, for he says —well, I'll read to you his letter." And she read the letter. It said: "Since I am out of prison, I met this Satyagrahi and that, and we discussed many a problem, and they all say the Mahatma is a noble person, a saint, but the English will know how to cheat him, and he will let himself be cheated. Have faith in your enemy, he says, have faith in him and convert him. But the world of men is hard to move, and once in motion it is wrong to stop till the goal is reached. And yet, what is the goal? Independence? Swaraj? Is there not Swaraj in our States, and is there not misery and corruption and cruelty there? Oh no, Ratna, it is the way of the masters that is wrong. And I have come to realize bit by bit, and bit by bit, when I was in prison, that as long as there will be iron gates and barbed wires round the Skeffington Coffee Estate, and city cars that can roll up the Bebbur mound, and gaslights and coolie cars, there will always be Pariahs and poverty. Ratna, things must change. Jawaharlal will change it. You know Jawaharlal is like a Bharatha to the Mahatma, and he, too, is for nonviolence and he, too, is a Satyagrahi, but he says in Swaraj there shall be neither the rich nor the poor. And he calls himself an 'equal-distributionist,' and I am with him and his men. We shall speak of it when you are here."

Ratna left us for Bombay the week after. But Rangamma will come out of prison soon. They say Rangamma is all for the Mahatma. We are all for the Mahatma. Pariah Rachanna's wife, Rachi, and Seethamma and Timmamma are all for the Mahatma. They say there are men in Bombay and men in Punjab, and men and women in Bombay and Bengal and Punjab, who are all for the Mahatma. They say the Mahatma will go to the Red-man's country and he will get us Swaraj. He will bring us Swaraj, the Mahatma. And we shall all be happy. And Rama will come back from exile, and Sita will be with him, for Ravana will be slain and Sita freed, and he will come back with Sita on his right in a chariot of the air, and brother Bharatha will go to meet them with the worshipped sandal of the Master on his head. And as they enter Ayodhya there will be a rain of flowers.

Like Bharata, we worship the sandals of the brother saint.

There was only Rangè Gowda that ever went back to Kantha-pura. She was here, with us, his Lakshmi, and Lakshmi's second daughter—the first one was in prison—and her three grandchildren of the one, and the seven of the other. She was in Patel Chennè Gowda's house, for they had heard of Patel Rangè Gowda, and they had said, "You are one of our community, come in and stay with us all this life and all the lives to come, sister!" And she waited for Rangè Gowda. And one day he came back—and we had gone to light the evening light of the sanctum, and the children came running and said, "There's a tall man at the door, and he's frighten-ing to look at," and when we went to see him, it was Rangè Gowda, and he was now lean as an areca-nut tree, and he said he had just come back from Kanthapura. "Couldn't leave," he said, "till I had drunk three handfuls of Himavathy water," but he had gone, to tell you the truth, to dig out his jewels, and he said the Corner-house was all but fallen, except for the byre, and Rangamma's house was tileless over the veranda, and Nanjamma's house door-less and roofless and the hearthstones in every corner. "All said in a knot," he concluded, "there's neither man nor mosquito in Kanthapura, for the men from Bombay have built houses on the Bebbur mound, houses like the city, for coolies, and they own this land and that, and even Bhatta has sold all his lands, said Maddur Chennayya, has sold it all to the Bombay men, and the Bombay men paid him well, and he's now gone back to Kashi. 'In Kashi, for every hymn and hiccup you get a rupee,' he said it seems, and he and his money have gone to Kashi. Waterfall Venkamma, it appears, has gone to stay with her new son-in-law, and Concubine Chinna still remains in Kanthapura to lift her leg to her new customers. I drank three handfuls of Himavathy water and I said, 'Protect us, mother!' to Kenchamma and I said, 'Protect us, father' to the Siva of the promontory, and I spat three times to the west and three times to the south, and I threw a palmful of dust at the sunken wretch, and I turned away. But to tell you the truth, mother, my heart it beat like a drum."

NOTES

CHAPTER 1

Red-men. Standard Hindu colloquialism for the British; also, to a certain extent, for all Europeans. From their complexions. To most Indians, even today, the ordinary Teutonesque coloring seems remarkably florid, far more red than white. The term probably has no connection with *Redcoat,* as used to designate British soldiers at the time of the American Revolution; except for ceremonial purposes the red uniform had been abandoned by most British military units by the time of imperial hegemony on the Indian subcontinent.

Dal. Strictly, a yellow split pea native to northern India; more loosely, any of several peas, such as the cajan, or lentils which form a staple of the Indian diet. Together with rice, dal is the indispensable Indian food at all economic levels. It would be hardly any exaggeration to say that every Indian eats his dal every day of his life. Figuratively, the same as "bread-and-butter" in English, i.e. a man's wherewithal, his livelihood.

Bandicoot. Hindus, of course, abhor on principle the taking of life, no matter what the circumstances, and hence the problem of dealing with vermin involves a deep moral and religious dilemma. The practical consequences of this can be, in the case of the bandicoot, particularly unfortunate. The bandicoot, whose name derives from the Dravidian root-word meaning "pig-like," is a large rat, known to be a carrier of plague. Most villagers understand nothing of hygiene, however, and for them the bandicoot is simply a nuisance, a bringer of dirt, a thief. Much effort is expended in driving him out of homes and granaries, people pray that he may find happiness in the fields and forests; but he inevitably returns. A bandicoot creeping in a gutter or scurrying along a wall is a sight as common in India as that of squirrels in America.

Dharmawar sari. Dharmawar, in Mysore, is a center of the sari-making industry, noted particularly for its fine saris in the classical style, made almost always of silk. Although Dharmawar saris are used for daily wear by those who can afford it, they are considered especially important in South India for weddings and other ceremonial occasions. A common analogue for anything fine.

Dhoti. A fabric used for loincloths by Indian men; also the loin-cloth itself. The manner of tying the dhoti is a subject of considerable attention, and may vary from a simple three-cornered diaper to a complex pajama. Different styles may indicate both locality and caste or family affiliations, while other styles are associated with special occasions, such as marriages, funerals, and religious ceremonies. The cloth may be coarse or fine, cut to various lengths.

Paysam. A milk-and-vermicelli sweet eaten on special, usually holy, days.

Inter. Examinations required before one may enter the intermediate classes at the university. In order to study for the Inter, one must present a Matric, which is the pre-university diploma required for matriculation.

Khadi. Home-spun cotton cloth. The term is used specifically to designate the native product, as opposed to mill-made fabric from England. Since the forced importation of foreign manufactured goods, which undercut native handicrafts and lowered not only the general economic level but the traditional folk culture as well, was a particular grievance of the nationalists against the colonial powers, khadi became an emotion-laden word in the Gandhian vocabulary.

Brahmin. A member of the highest caste. Perhaps a general word on caste will be helpful. According to the Hindu tradition there are four castes: Brahmin (priestly); Kshatriya (kingly or warrior); Vaisya (mercantile and agricultural); Sudra (artisan). The caste of untouchables, a somewhat later development, makes a fifth. Presumably the original castes derive from the time of the Aryan invasions of India, and designate the successive waves of invaders as they established themselves in distinction to the native populations. In the course of time, however, innumerable sub-castes or communities have sprung up, often along craft or tribal lines, and every Hindu belongs to a specific sub-caste. In Kanthapura, a village of perhaps a hundred families, there may have been fifteen or twenty sub-castes, each governed by its own council of elders. The system had its advantages; each sub-caste looked after its own unfortunates, for example, with a dole for impoverished widows, dowries for brides who needed them, help for those beset by sickness and disaster. But individual freedom was greatly restricted. Members of a sub-caste could marry only within their sub-caste, could live only in the district set aside for their sub-caste, could engage only in occupations reserved for their sub-caste, etc. In general, every individual enterprise—social, commercial, conjugal, or whatever—required the approval of the elders. Today, caste is discouraged or at least de-emphasized in official Indian policy, especially with respect to the untouchables; but the system is deeply rooted in the Hindu religious tradition, and the people, particularly the villagers, are slow to relinquish it.

Thothi. An inner courtyard. Sidda's house, in other words, was built in the grand style, with an enclosed central court for private use.

Zamindar. A landlord, but with emphasis on the "lord." Sometimes the zamindar would own a whole village.

Gauri's festival. Like other religions, Hinduism sets aside particular days for the ceremonies dedicated to particular gods, goddesses, saints, wise men, etc. Gauri's festival is celebrated in Bhadon, the month which includes the last part of August and the first part of September. Gauri was one of the names of the consort of Siva and the mother of Ganesha, and her festival is observed by women. It is exceedingly important, an occasion of the greatest solemnity. The observances, conducted in the home, center upon ritual words and gestures, ritual foods, and ritual gifts, these latter consisting chiefly of black beads and earrings presented by the mother to her daughters. Gauri's festival is followed soon after by Ganesha's festival, which is a temple festival celebrated primarily by men. (Ganesha is also called Ganapati.)

Linga. Phallus; symbol of Siva. In highly stylized form, the linga is a pervasive religio-cultural symbol throughout all phases of Hindu life, especially among the Shakta sects. Its counterpart is the *yoni.*

Sankara-jayanthi. A folk entertainment of the most solemn kind, the jayanthi is, in India, a public recital by a noted Brahmin of the events associated with the life of a particular god, hero, or saint, together with moral interpolations. Usually an image of the god is present, and the jayanthi ends with ritual offerings of camphor and fruit. In this case, the subject of the jayanthi is the life, mostly legendary, of Sankara, the great Vedantic philosopher who lived in the eighth or ninth century and who was esteemed so highly for his learning and sanctity that he came to be regarded as an incarnation of Siva. He founded the sect of Smartava Brahmins, who became especially powerful in South India, and some of the monasteries which he established in Mysore still exist. With the ascendancy of Vedantic philosophy in the middle ages, Sri Sankara became the first saint of the Hindu calendar, and so he remains today. He taught a strict non-dualism. Indeed, he held that the Principle cannot even be called One, since this would imply a Two. It can be defined only as "beyond duality," *Advaita.* Later philosophers tended to modify this Vedantic austerity; see under *Ramanuja.*

Maya-vada. The philosophy of Maya, according to which all physical appearance is illusory.

Bhajan. Hymn-singing. It should be borne in mind, however, that "hymns" in India are as likely to be philosophical as strictly religious in content, though actually the distinction between the two, so important in the context of western dualistic scholasticism, can scarcely be made at all in the context of the Hindu unitary tradition. Bhajan is usually an affair of the caste or sub-caste; but there is nothing to say a whole village may not sing hymns together on great occasions.

Harikatha. Literally, story of God. Generally the Harikatha performer extemporizes a verse narrative based on one of the Indian legends, with music and dance to heighten the effect. Sometimes the music and dance stop, and the performer explains the whole thing in familiar prose.

Parvati's winning of Siva. Siva, the supreme ascetic, was locked eternally in meditation. The other gods, however, wished him to form a union with the Goddess of the Himalayas, Parvati, and they met in concert to see what could be done. Kama, the god of love and the first-born of all the gods, was persuaded to use his powers, with the result that Siva's meditations were disrupted by an awakening sense of desire for the beautiful goddess. For this offense, Siva opened his third eye, which is located in his forehead and has the power to destroy evil, and with its powerful beam he blasted Kama into nonexistence. Nevertheless, having once felt the charm of love, Siva could not forego it. He eventually married Parvati, and was so pleased with his new life that he relented and permitted Kama to be born again as Pradyumna, the son of Krishna and Maya (delusion). Kalidasa, the great classic poet of India, has described this episode in his poem *Kumarasambhava.* Representations of Siva always include the third eye, usually closed, in the middle of his forehead.

Ganapati's festival. One of the most moving of Hindu festivals, certainly the most popular. It comes at the end of the rainy season, and unlike most festivals cuts across caste lines: in the city it is celebrated by whole quarters, in the country by whole villages or even whole districts. The festivities include singing, dancing,

189

drama, and especially moral discourses and dialectical exercises. Ganapati is another name for the elephant-headed god, Ganesha, who is the leader of the minor Hindu deities; he is the god of wisdom and the remover of obstacles, and hence is invoked at the beginning of any new enterprise—for instance, on the first page of a book. Today in India the Ganapati festival, which often lasts ten days, has become a sort of national cultural festival, embracing many activities.

Wet land and dry land. Rice and sugar cane both require very extensive irrigation, and in consequence the fields reserved for their cultivation are called wet land. Dry land is for the so-called dry crops: cotton, millet, ragi, etc.

Revenue. For a long time taxes in India were collected through the so-called zamindar system. Each landlord was required to pay the government an annual "revenue" based on the extent and productivity of his estates, and he was expected to make up a certain percentage of this amount from proportionate assessments on the peasants who worked his land as shareholders. But no supervision was exercised over the zamindar's collections, with the result that the system was vastly abused. Many landlords took in far more than they paid to the government, and of course they pocketed the difference. This corruption was one of the chief grievances held by the village peasants against the British administration, and needless to say tax reform was a primary objective of the new Indian government after independence.

Ascetic's bowl. The itinerant monk is a frequent sight in India. Many Hindu men, especially Brahmins, become monks in old age, after they have discharged their obligations to their families; and whether or not they attach themselves to a particular sect or monastic order, tradition requires that they beg for their food. A begging bowl is essential. Most are made of wood, but occasionally a skull is used. The begging bowl is a powerful, pervasive symbol in all Indian art and culture, of both the past and the present; it is responsible, for instance, for the characteristic flat domes of many Indian temples—at least such is the tradition.

Sitar. A musical instrument resembling a guitar, with a varying number of strings. Though its origin was probably in North India, it has been popular throughout the country for a long time.

Swaraj. The political doctrine of self-rule.

Damayanthi. Once upon a time there was a beautiful prince, whose name was Nala. His kingdom was Nishada, and he was a master of the sixty-four arts. Above all, however, he was a famous charioteer. The horses obeyed him as they would no god or man. Now there was also a princess, the most fair of fair, and she belonged to Vidarbha, the neighboring state. One day a group of swans alighted at Nala's feet, and he sent a message through them: go and tell Damayanthi the fair, of Nala the prince of Nishada, skilled in the sixty-four arts and especially in the knowledge of horses. Damayanthi knew at once that he was her lord; and she prayed and she pined that he might become her well-wed husband. So, when the swayamvara (the bridegroom-choosing ceremony) was held in the beautiful walls of the capital of Vidarbha, the gods themselves appeared and took human shape, each with his princely necklaces and precious stones, crowns and velveteens; and each one looked handsomer than the other. Which one could Nala be? Princess Damayanthi was perplexed. But then she said: "But I love only Nala," and forthwith she could see it was indeed he who had a shadow, who perspired, whose clothes were twisted and misshapen, whereas the gods stood there each more perfect than the other, casting no shadows. Damayanthi at once put her garland around Nala's neck and won him, and to Nishada they went, duly wed, with trumpets and banners and many Brahmins to chant their hymns of welcome.

However, there was an evil god, Kali (not to be confused with Siva's consort, Kali), who could not accept the humiliation of being passed over for a mortal. He entered Nala, and made him play dice. Nala immediately lost his kingdom to his brother. Then Nala and Damayanthi wandered homeless in the jungles, sleeping on thorny beds and frightened by the wild animals. But so evil was the influence of Kali and so terrible was the sorrow

191

of Nala at seeing the fair princess in this desperate condition
(with bleeding wounds and rags around her fair form) that one
night he cut the one garment they shared for sleep in two, and
fled. Damayanthi, waking, wept and sobbed, and, wandering a
long way, came back at last after much suffering to her father's
house.

> Whither, beloved Gambler, whither art thou gone,
> Cutting off one half my veil,
> Abandoning me, thy devoted wife,
> > Asleep in the forest?
> Ever do I await thee,
> As thou wouldst desire me.

Meanwhile Nala had engaged himself as a charioteer to Rituparna, king of Benares. But the spies of Damayanthi's father discovered his disguise and told the king of Vidarbha of Nala's new
position. Damayanthi then guilefully declared that now, since
there was no trace of her husband, a second bridegroom-choosing
ceremony would take place, and to this came as usual all the
princes and the gods. But the one who astonished everyone was
Rituparna, so quickly had he arrived, as if mountains and waters
were at his command. Who then could be his charioteer? Of
course, it was only Nala. In fact, Rituparna had discovered this
himself on the way to Vidarbha, so fast and splendidly the horses
flew. Rituparna was an adept in numbers; if he saw a tree he
knew immediately all the number of leaves upon it, if he saw an
army he knew the number of infantry, cavalry, elephants and
retainers. This knowledge he gave to Nala in return for Nala's
knowledge of horses.

The moment Nala knew numbers, the evil Kali left him, and
thus Nala could beat anyone at dice. Damayanthi discovered
Nala's disguise, and when the reunited couple came back to
Nishada again, Nala's brother, Pushkara, was defeated in a dice
game for the kingdom. Nala and Damayanthi thereafter ruled
their kingdom happily for a hundred years. When it rained it
seemed as if flowers fell, when the fields sprouted crops it
seemed as if pearls grew on the stems, and when women walked

abroad they knew virtue was protected; and nobody in Nishada ever heard a child cry.

Sakunthala. Vishwamitra, the mighty sage, was so deeply immersed in penance that the great god Indra was terrified lest the world, with the three universes, be shaken into bits and no place remain safe for god or man. Thereupon he sent a celestial maiden, Menaka, to tempt the ascetic from his studies. Such were Menaka's charms that the sage's meditations were broken, with the result that the celestial maiden found herself with child. Her work done, she went to the Himalayas and there left the child with the sakuni birds, who looked after the little girl with great care, sensitivity and love, such as birds give to their young ones. The sage, Kanva, discovered the girl, and called her Sakunthala because she had been brought up by the brave Sakunis.

As years passed she grew in beauty—her eyes were like beads, her breasts were full and round, tied tight with fiber-cloth of the jungles, her waist was thin as a flame, and her limbs fell like two wings of a waterfall. With jingles at her feet and the veil all about her, she walked as if the essence of earthly sweetness had been compounded by the gods and made into this fair maiden whose name was Sakunthala. One day Dushyantha, the king, became lost while hunting in the jungle. Thirsty and disappointed at not finding the right game, he came upon the hermitage of Kanva. There he beheld Sakunthala, and like a creeper's leaves in a mountain wind his heart fluttered and he was captivated by her beauty. Love was born at once. And as she offered the king all the hospitality due to a prince, her foster father being away, the king was overpowered by his love for her and her love for him. Thus before the father had returned home, they performed a marriage-of-love, and with many sweet promises to take her with him when he returned to his capital, Dushyantha left. But because a curse had been put upon her by an angry hermit, the king forgot all about her. She was with child. And when the boy grew up, she took him and went to Dushyantha, who remembered nothing of what had taken place. Was this not some kind of blackmail?

Meanwhile Sakunthala, while bathing in the river, had lost a ring that Dushyantha had given her in the forest as a token of remembrance. A fisherman, catching a fish in his net, cut it open and found the ring in it. He wanted to make money by selling the ring, and so he went to the bazaar; but there the king's policemen caught him, for the ring was seen to be the signet ring of the king himself. The fisherman was brought before Dushyantha, and when the king recognized the ring and remembered the circumstances under which he had parted with it, he heard a voice from heaven cry out: "Indeed, it is she, and the child is your heir Bharata." Asking forgiveness of Sakunthala for his unkingly behavior and taking his son on his lap, Dushyantha declared to the world that this indeed was Bharata his son and heir. And Bharata became a great prince, the greatest of all India; it is because of him that India to this day is called Bharatavarsha, the Land of Bharata.

Kalidasa, India's greatest dramatist, who lived in the sixth century, made his famous play *Sakunthala* from the original story as found in the even earlier Sanskrit epic, the *Mahabharata*.

Mahadeva. One of the many names of Siva. It means simply the Great God.

Brahma. The supreme god, the self-existent deity, creator of gods, men, and the universe. In the long course of its development, however, Hinduism has largely displaced the active worship of Brahma by distributing his creative powers to other gods. Brahma sleeps, as it were, in the earliest region of myth.

Ganges. Not only the largest of Indian rivers, but the most holy. The story goes that the sage, Bhagirata, performed such penances to bring the Ganges down to earth, in order to revive his dead ancestors, that once she started from the heavens she flooded the whole universe, till beast and man had nowhere to hide. The sage then began praying to Siva, who forthwith appeared and took the river up and tied her into a knot in his hair. That is why Siva is also called Gangadharesha—the Lord-bearer of Ganga. Many famous hymns have been addressed to the Ganges by poets, saints and sages.

Godavery. Like every Indian river, the Godavery has its legend. The sage, Gautama, is said to have revealed to Rama, hero of the *Ramayana* epic, the great sanctity of the river, which is called the Southern Ganges. The Godavery, Gautama said, is connected with the Ganges by subterranean passages. It was on the bank of this river that, in the *Ramayana,* Rama and Sita lived with Lakshmana in exile at Panchavati, which is still one of the important places of pilgrimage for all Hindus. Today the main rail line from Bombay to Jhansi and Delhi passes by Nasik, two miles from Panchavati.

Cauvery. This river, the most famous of South Indian rivers, is noted for her elegance, her dramatic movements (creating islands here, waterfalls there) and her rich historical heritage. She is one of the most beloved of India's holy streams. Also spelled Cauveri or Kaveri: the Koeberis of Ptolemy.

"The divine origin of the river is related in the *Kaveri Mahatmya* of the Agneya and Skanda Puranas. She was first Vishnumaya, a daughter of Brahma. By his direction she became incarnate as Lopamudra, a girl formed by Agastya (with the view of her becoming his wife) of the most beautiful parts of the animals of the forest, whose distinctive beauties (mudra) as the eyes of the deer, etc., were subjected to loss (lopa) in her superior charms. Balarama gave Lopamudra as a daughter to Kaveramuni, whence she acquired the name Kaveri. In order to secure beatitude for her new father she resolved to become a river, the merit of whose waters in absolving all sin and blessing the earth should accrue to him. But when she became of age Agastya proposed to marry her. To reconcile the conflicting claims, Lopamudra, or the mortal part of her nature, became the wife of Agastya, while Kaveri, or the celestial part, flowed forth as the river." (L. Rice: *Mysore and Coorg,* Vol. II, 1875.)

And the famous Tamil poem *Silapaddikaram* sings: "Hail to thee, Cauvery! . . . Thou walkest along, listening to the songs of ploughmen, the resonance of sluices, the roar of the breaking waters, and the noise of the festive crowd celebrating the freshets. . . . All this flow of thine, along with the din of merrymaking, is expressive of the prosperity of our king. . . . Hail to thee, Cauvery!" (Translated by Dikshitar.)

The Cauvery rises in the mountainlands of Mysore, in the small but well-known province of Coorg, and passes thence across the plateau of Mysore and down into the plains, creating the famous waterfall of Sivasamudram (where today we have a powerful electric generating station); in the lowlands it crosses the rich rice fields of Madras state and enters the Bay of Bengal, forming a magnificent delta that is famous in history, poetry and commerce. Cauvery Pattanam, the City of the Cauvery, was one of the foremost ports of the ancient world.

Asoka. Few figures in world history have played so important a part in the evolution of mankind as Emperor Asoka (272-232 B.C.). Heir to the great empire of the Mauryas (with its celebrated capital of Pataliputra), he conquered all his neighbors, and within a few years was master not only of the whole of North India up to the frontier of present Afghanistan, but of South India almost to the confines of the Tamil country. But his war against the small state of Kalinga so filled him with remorse that he disbanded his army, turned his soldiers into carriers of peace, and decreed that in his state only the moral law, dharma, should govern men's lives. Thus the famous edicts of Asoka.

"The country of Kalinga," runs edict No. 13, "was conquered by King Priyadarsi, Beloved of the Gods, eight years after his coronation. In this war in Kalinga, men and animals numbering one hundred and fifty thousands were carried away captive from that country, as many as one hundred thousand were killed there in action, and many times that number perished. After that, now the country of Kalinga has been conquered, the Beloved of the Gods is devoted to an intense practice of the duties relating to dharma, to the longing for dharma, and to the inculcation of dharma among the people. This is due to the repentance of the Beloved of the Gods on having conquered the country of the Kalingas.

"Now the Beloved of the Gods thinks that, even if a person should wrong him, the offense should be forgiven if it is possible to forgive it. . . . Verily, the Beloved of the Gods desires

196

the following in respect of all creatures, viz. noninjury to them, restraint in dealing with them, and impartiality in the case of crimes committed by them.

"So what is called conquest through dharma is now considered to be the best conquest by the Beloved of the Gods. . . . In the conquest through dharma, satisfaction is derived by both parties. . . . Such conquest brings happiness to all concerned, both in this world and in the next."

Such was the message of Asoka, which he sent not only to all his subjects but also, as he says in the same edict, "as far away as the distance of six hundred yojanas where the Yavana [Greek] King named Antiyoka is ruling, and where beyond the kingdom of the said Antiyoka, four other kings named Turamaya, Antinkini, Maka, and Alikasundara are ruling also, and, towards the south, where the Cholas and the Pandyas are living, as far as Tampraparni." Antiyoka is Antiochus II (286-246 B.C.); Turamaya is Ptolemy Philadelphus (285-247 B.C.) of Egypt; Antikini is Antigonas Gonatas (277-239 B.C.) of Macedonia; and Alikasundara is perhaps Alexander of Epirus (277-255 B.C.).

It was largely through Asoka's compassion that Buddhism was carried to countries outside India—to Ceylon, China, and the West.

Asoka's name has such importance in Indian history that the insignia of the present government is the three-lion symbol taken from one of the Asokan pillars. He is constantly in the minds of politicians in India today, especially as in some ways the message of Mahatma Gandhi seems to coincide with the high moral designs of Emperor Asoka Maurya, the Beloved of the Gods.

Chandragupta. Lived 324-300 B.C. Grandfather of Asoka; called also Chandragupta Vikramaditya, founder of the Mauryan Empire. He had the celebrated sage, Kautilaya, as his chief minister—Kautilaya who laid down the principles of Indian policy, the Arthasastra. But there is also another great Chandragupta Vikramaditya, several centuries later, who reigned in Ujjain and who had the nine jewels at his court, including Kalidasa, the poet, and Varahamihira, the astronomer. The name Vikramaditya (Lord of Victory) has come to be so familiarly used that any victorious king is called Vikramaditya and all legendary figures eventually are called Vikramadityas. Apart from being a famous king, Chandragupta Vikramaditya gives his name to the Vikrama era, one of the two important historical Indian eras. The other is the Salivahana era, which has now been accepted officially as the era from which the government of India is to date its documents. This year (1963) is 2020 of the Vikrama era and 1885 of the Salivahana era.

Dharmaraya. (Also *Darmaraja.*) Raja of dharma; which is to say, king of the ultimate law, one who is totally in accord with the moral and metaphysical order of final reality. In ordinary usage, the term is given to anyone who is good, kind, compassionate, etc., but its profounder implications can be seen in the fact that Dharmaraya is the honorific of Yama, king of the dead. In this passage, however, the title refers to the eldest of the Pandava brothers, Yudhishthira, who was a wise ruler and a pacifist; his story is told in the *Mahabharata.*

Akbar. After the first Islamic invasion of India in the eleventh and twelfth centuries, toward the sixteenth century came the Moghuls, who established themselves as Emperors of India. The first was Babar, and his grandson was the great Emperor Akbar (1556-1605), one of the most beautiful figures of Indian history —in fact, of world history. "Daring and reckless," writes Pandit Nehru in describing Akbar, "an able general, and yet gentle and full of compassion, an idealist and a dreamer, but also a man of action and a leader of men who roused the passionate loyalty of his followers. As a warrior he conquered large parts of India, but his eyes were set on another and more enduring conquest, the conquest of the minds and hearts of the people." He maintained one of the most brilliant courts in the world of his time, and he surrounded himself not only with scholars, princes of the royal Rajput blood (whose friendship he sought and won), but also of religious men and philosophers of all creeds and of many Asian and European nations. He had a Hall of Debate, where Jesuit missionaries, Zoroastrians and Jains, Hindus and Mullahs, discussed philosophy and religion, and each one thought the

198

emperor was won over to his creed. But Akbar's great ambition was to found a universal religion, for he saw truths in most of the creeds and Truth in none of them. There is a touching story told of Akbar, which is perhaps not true historically, but is so widely believed as to become a part of Indian tradition. The great saint, Mira Bai, a princess of the Rajput blood, had abandoned home and husband to chant the name of the Lord, the Lord Krishna, and it was the Emperor Akbar's great desire to hear her sing. Tradition says that Akbar made himself look like a Sadhu—a monk—and sat rapt in devotion, hearing the saintly Mira Bai sing of her Lord of Brindaban, Lord Krishna:

> Mine the mountain-bearing cowherd,
> None but he, none but he—my Lord.

Ramanuja. (11th century) The foremost name in Indian philosophy after Sri Sankara. He differed from Sri Sankara in maintaining a "modified non-dualism"; that is, he believed in the existence of man and God as two separate though similar realities, whereas Sri Sankara had held that all is fundamentally one and indivisible. Sri Ramanuja's influence was very great indeed, and led to the worship of a personal deity in India and to the attitudes which dominated Indian religion from the thirteenth century until about the beginning of the nineteenth. The movement produced many famous saints—Mira Bai, Tulasi Das, Tukaram, the Alvars of the Tamils. After Ramanuja came Madhava, who taught complete dualism, and the later saints were deeply influenced by his teachings as well. This whole movement, Ramanuja and Madhava, is called the Bhakti (or Absolute Love) movement.

Kailas. The heavenly abode of Siva and Parvati, high in the Himalayas. There Siva lives with his attendants; with his chief guardian (and attribute), the bull, Nandi; and with his beloved consort, Parvati, who listens to the cries of human hearts in distress and, as the Mother of Compassion (Karunya), intercedes with Siva to help the poor folk in trouble.

Gujerat. One of the ancient provinces of India. It begins near the city of Bombay, and extends northward and northeastward, covering a large area, the center of which is Ahmedabad, the principal city of Gujerat. Gujerati is the language spoken by the people of the province. Next to Gujerat are the old provinces of Kathiawar, Cutch, Malwa, and Rajputana. The people of Gujerat have been famous merchants throughout history, but some of them have also been ministers to the Princes of Kathiawar. This was the case with the family of Mahatma Gandhi.

Kali. A female divinity. Strictly speaking, Kali ("the black") is one name of Devi, the consort of Siva. Devi, the supreme goddess, has two aspects, one benign and the other fierce; and Kali is a representation of her fierce side. Kali—goddess of destruction, goddess of terror, goddess of bad luck. But owing to the shifting meanings and myths of Hinduism, which is largely an unwritten religion so far as most of its practitioners are concerned, Kali has come with many Indians to mean the whole goddess, both terrible and compassionate. In South India, Kali is primarily the divinity of the poorer classes.

Hair ceremony. A boy's hair is first cut (among the upper classes in South India) between the ages of three and five, at what is called the chowla ceremony. The ceremony is supposed to have a great effect on the mental development of the boy. The father and mother, surrounded by friends and relatives, sit before a sacrificial fire, and then with the recitation of hymns, the father cuts a lock and gives it to the mother. "The razor with which Savithri, the knowing one, has shaved [the beard] of kings Soma and Varuna, with that, ye Brahmins, shave now his [hair], that he may be blessed with long life, and old age, etc., etc."

Pathan. People of northwestern India. They are known for their loyalty and violence.

Jamadar. A petty officer of the police force. A sergeant.

CHAPTER 2

Patwari. Hereditary tax collector. A village resident, always a Brahmin. Generally unpopular, though not necessarily because of his connection with the British. Indians, like a few others, do not care for the revenue agent.

Patel. Village executive chief; a hereditary office. The patel is responsible for maintaining order. In general, he acts as a policeman, a small-town constable, though in some villages he may also perform the functions of a minor judge. Between them, the patel and the patwari were the traditional village functionaries, often combining their forces to exert tremendous pressure on the villagers; corrupt practice was by no means unusual. By using and perpetuating this traditional Indian administrative structure, the British undoubtedly prolonged the much-praised social stability of Indian village life; but at the same time they helped to aggravate the resentments of the villagers, who became more and more disgruntled with the patel-patwari system. This was particularly true as the system shifted from its traditional place in the Hindu religio-cultural context to become a mere appendage of British colonialism.

Betel-bag. Betel is the popular masticatory of India, as common as chewing gum in America. The betel itself is a vine, a species of climbing pepper, but it has given its name to a small palm, the *Areca catechu,* upon which it frequently grows. Hence *betel* is the ordinary term for both the nut of the tree, which is astringent and pungent to taste and possesses the properties of a stimulant, and the leaf of the vine. The betel-nut is usually wrapped in a leaf which has been pasted together with chunam (chalk or lime), and the whole thing is then popped into the mouth and munched for hours. Among other results, the teeth turn black. Small bags, often highly embroidered, are used by all classes of people for carrying their chewing materials. Tobacco leaves are sometimes used instead of betel leaves by those who can get them.

Clogs. Wooden clogs, often very heavy, are tied to the necks of cattle in India to stop them from running too fast, lest they should escape and graze where they are not supposed to or slip away to the jungles and become food for wild animals. Clogs are also placed with a coconut-shell bell around the necks of cows that have newly calved, so that people may keep away from them; for usually cows are fierce during the time after they have given birth to a calf.

Lathi-ring. A ferrule. The lathi is a heavy bamboo stick, often metal tipped, carefully cut to the height of a man, and is carried by most people in India, especially in the north, to protect themselves; but they are also used in the house for various purposes— carrying heavy burdens, for instance, or to frighten away snakes. Lathis are used by all Indian police as their billy and so have become an insignia of authority.

Salt-giver. "Be faithful to your salt-giver"—that is a famous Indian expression. Salt has always been highly prized, possibly because the Aryan invaders did not know salt and discovered it for the first time upon coming into the Punjab. Sometimes friendship is sealed between people by throwing salt into water.

Pipal-tree. The sacred fig of India, known for its great size and longevity. The Bo Tree of Buddhist Scripture, under which Gautama sat meditating at the moment when he achieved heavenly enlightenment, was a pipal. Every Indian village has one, usually planted at the village center, and it serves as a gathering place, a rostrum, a courtroom. Often a platform is built under its branches.

Maistri. A word used commonly in India to mean the head of a group of workmen, a gang boss, or even sometimes a small businessman who keeps a gang of workmen for use in his business. Usually the maistris belong to a sub-caste slightly above that of the workmen. They are known, often justly, for their cruelty and their exploitation of the people under them.

Rupee. The basic Indian unit of currency; in Hindi, roupaya. The rupee was formerly divided into sixteen annas, each anna again into four pice, and each pice into three pies. At one time in backward areas a pie was divided into a dozen or so seashells. At the time of *Kanthapura,* a rupee was worth something less than fifty cents in American money. Today, since the adoption of the decimal system, a rupee is made up of one hundred naye-paise (new pice), and the official exchange is one rupee for twenty-one U.S. cents.

Congress House. The Indian nationalist movement was united in the Indian National Congress, founded in 1885 as a representative body with delegates from all sections and factions. Gandhi was elected president of the Congress in 1925, and held the office until he resigned in 1934. Thus the term *Congress* became associated with the nationalist movement in general and with the Gandhian philosophy in particular; any active worker in the movement was likely to be called a Congress man, and the local headquarters of the workers a Congress house. Today the leading political party in India, which claims direct descent from Mahatma Gandhi's leadership, is called the Congress Party.

Spinning-wheel. India since ancient times has been famous for her fabrics, to such an extent indeed that ladies of the aristocracy in Rome wore only Indian muslins. Spinning was common to all castes; even Brahmins were required to spin their own sacred threads. Mahatma Gandhi believed that the national skill in spinning had been ruined by British rule, since the colonial administration had enforced regulations favoring the Lancashire textile manufacturers which reserved the Indian market for English machine-made cloths. Little by little the crafts of hand spinning and weaving died away, leaving many Indian workers unemployed and draining large sums of money from the native economy. Gandhi made the spinning wheel, or charka, a symbol of his nonviolent revolutionary movement. "Spin your way to independence"—this was a common saying among Gandhi's followers. It proved an apt symbol. For Mahatma Gandhi, the charka signified an important spiritual truth. Just as you spin your way to independence, he insisted, you must also spin yourself into the hearts of your enemies, for it is only through love that you can reach your objective. In addition, the wheel represents dharma, the unity of moral law, and also the zero (in Sanskrit, kha), which means Sunayata or Nirvana.

Khanda. A measure used in the Mysore region; roughly 350 pounds. About eight to nine seers make a kolaga, and twenty kolagas make a khanda.

Seventh-month ceremony. Celebrated during the seventh-month of a woman's pregnancy, it is a particularly moving ritual for Indians, who regard maternity as the most sacred of earthly manifestations. The pregnant woman, seated in a decorated chair, is offered homage and gifts by the other women of the village and neighboring countryside. Temporarily she assumes a numen of divine motherhood, and becomes the intermediary through whom the principle of life-in-eternity is extolled.

Seer. The basic Indian measure, roughly two pounds in weight (almost a kilogram), and in liquids about a litre.

CHAPTER 3

My Experiments with Truth. Mahatma Gandhi's autobiography. It was first published serially in *Young India,* the Mahatma's newspaper, and became virtually a manual of practice for all Indian independence workers.

Taluk. One of the five or six subdivisions of a district. In Mysore, a taluk often contains between a hundred and a hundred and fifty villages.

Holy ashes. Worshippers of Siva smear the upper parts of their bodies with holy ashes (vibhuthi) and then draw horizontal lines across their foreheads, thus symbolizing the fact that the world, which is illusory, has been recognized as such, i.e. reduced to ashes.

Obsequial dinner. On the anniversary of a death in a Brahmin family, three or more outside Brahmins are invited to an afternoon meal and are served sumptuously, while the hosts maintain the fast which they began at daybreak. The guest Brahmins are supposed to eat to satiety, so that the "spirits" of the dead may be satisfied; and the remnants of the food left on their leaves are usually given away to crows or cows, or thrown into the river; not a bit of the food given to the dead must remain behind. The "spirits" of the dead, however, are not to be considered as the souls of the dead, but rather as the thought-forms of those who have left this body. For according to true Hindu tradition, a soul is, immediately upon death, reborn in a womb it has chosen, as the caterpillar that leaves one blade of grass finds itself immediately upon another. Nevertheless, the sraddha—ceremony for the dead—is one of the most important functions of a Hindu's religious life.

Sravan. Fifth month of the Hindu calendar, falling in August-September. A time of rejoicing and festivals; the monsoons are ending, the birds call with new cries, the heavens display swiftly changing colors, and in the pools of water the new crops emerge. It is a favorite month in poetry and folklore.

> Green like fragments of jade
> The grass rises on tiptoe,
> Stretching its blades to catch the raindrops;
> With patches of green and purple and gold,
> The good earth is decked in many-colored jewels,
> Like a woman of elegant taste
> And charm of mellowed ease.

So sang Kalidasa in *The Seasons* (translated by R. S. Pandit).

Ekadashi. The eleventh day of the moon, when in orthodox Hindu families people observe a complete, a partial, or a merely symbolic fast. In certain families one does not even drink water.

Dasara. Also called Navaratri (or Nine-nights), this is one of the great Indian festivals. It comes in September-October when the earth is dry again, the harvests are beginning, the sun is tender, and the world seems revived for a new existence. Kings then sharpen their swords and, after worshipping their horses, their elephants, and their bulls, go out on a symbolic conquest of the world, called Vijayadashami or the (twelfth) day of victory. Meanwhile, Brahmins take out their sacred texts and worship them with camphor and incense. And women exhibit and rearrange their collections of dolls, visiting in each other's homes for gossip and merrymaking.

First Brahmin. At obsequial feasts and other ceremonies, the chief officiating priest. All obsequial celebrations begin with the performer wearing grass-rings, especially made (with the chanting of sacred hymns) on the spot. Leaf-cups are made of banana leaves or banyan leaves, for holding liquids like curd or paysam. In any Indian bazaar one can see a bundle of leaves to eat from and a string of leaf-cups—both sold together. But for special ceremonies the leaf-cups must be made by the Brahmins themselves, just before the ceremony begins.

Gita. The *Bhagavad Gita*, perhaps the most famous sacred book of Hinduism. It is a self-contained dramatic poem which was probably inserted in the *Mahabharata* at a date considerably after the original writing of the epic; scholars date the *Gita* at the second or third century A.D. It is in the form of a dialogue between Sri Krishna and Arjuna as they both await the beginning of action on the field of battle. Arjuna is disturbed in his conscience by the prospect that he will be called upon to commit violence against his kinsmen. Sri Krishna, who here clearly identifies himself as the Supreme Being, asks Arjuna to fight, not for himself, but in order to preserve the moral law or Dharma. How is this to be done? In answer to this, Sri Krishna launches himself into the most abstruse aspects of the philosophy of non-duality, describing how one may fight by "seeing action in inaction and inaction in action." The language of the *Gita* far surpasses most early poetry in Sanskrit, and makes it one of the most exalted poems in any literature. Its affirmation of caste may seem unacceptable to modern minds, but its extraordinarily lucid and lofty exposition of the pantheistic doctrines of Vedanta gives it a high rank in the world's mystical literature. The tone as well as the substance of the *Gita* has molded the Indian national character for 1600 years. It is safe to say that no one may understand the Hindu mind who has not absorbed the *Gita*.

Second Brahmin. The Brahmin who assists the officiating priest, or who comes after him in the ceremonial order. A priest is not considered the highest Brahmin; in fact, a priest is never treated with the same respect as a Brahmin whose sole purpose is the cultivation of sacred learning for its own sake, the reading and exposition of philosophical texts, and the practice of spiritual exercises that lead to his own final liberation (Moksha).

Curds. No Indian meal, in the south or the north, is complete without dal or curds. Every night warm milk is set aside and a bit of curd is put into it—the same process by which yoghurt is made. There are many proverbs about curds and curd-making, and many of the songs of Krishna are about his eating of curds or buttermilk or butter. One Kannada proverb says: the eloping daughter will forget to put the curd into the night-milk.

Bengal-gram. A kind of pulse often used in Indian cookery; also eaten by horses. *Khir* is only paysam, with more milk in it.

Manes. According to certain traditions the good dead (and all dead, from the point of view of their own families, are good) go to live in the Ptruloka, or celestial region, among the gods. It is they who are believed to be propitiated when the sraddha ceremonies take place every year. Perhaps a symbolic form of speaking of the thought-forms or subtle-forms which are supposed to be left behind by the dead.

Odès. These are fried cakes of Bengal (or any other) gram, salted and spiced.

Mat. In most Indian familes people sit on the floor or on raised platforms of wood or stone, with a mat to protect them and make the seat softer. At night when the beds are to be spread (for the bedding is always folded up when not in use, and heaped, one bundle over the other, in a corner) the mat is usually laid first, and on this the bed is made. In the afternoon or when sitting at any time, men and women sit on mats, and often take their siestas on mats. Mats are made of various grasses or weeds, the cheaper ones of palmyra leaf. Some mats are beautifully worked, and are soft as silk.

Come home soon. In India a young couple's first child traditionally must be born in the house of the wife's mother. Hence a bride is said to be "coming home soon" when her first pregnancy has been announced.

Ghee. Clarified butter, an essential of all Indian meals. Since butter quickly becomes rancid in a warm climate, Indians usually melt it, often adding a betel leaf or two, and then, as it cools, draw off the liquid parts, called ghee. The ghee may be safely used for several weeks after this, though it must be carefully preserved from contamination. It is also a sacramental libation used in virtually all religious ceremonies. Much ghee is poured on the fire which bears witness at every marriage, initiation, or other Brahmin rite.

> You are the great ceremonial flame,
> Without you the immortals do not rejoice.
> (*Rig Veda*)

Pheni. A vermicelli cake, delicately made from fibrous paste, cooked in ghee. It is considered a great treat at all festivities.

Head peon. The Spanish word *péon* is used in India to mean an attendant, messenger, or other subordinate agent, though actually the usage derives from Portuguese *peão.* It is heard most commonly today in offices, where it means "office boy," and the "head peon" in a large office might be a person of considerable responsibility. There is no suggestion whatever of bondage or servility, as in the American usage.

Three-pice. The three-pice bit, formerly one of the most-used coins of India, was a large, round, bronze coin. Even in the time of *Kanthapura,* however, it had long since been debased by inflation. A three-pice thing is a useless thing: not worth a farthing or a sou.

Evening ablutions. Brahmins are supposed to bathe, pray and meditate twice a day: once just before sunrise, again at the time of sunset.

Kaliyuga. The age of Kali, the iron age according to one ancient Hindu belief. There are four ages: Krita, Treta, Dwapara, and Kali. The age of Kali is the present age and the shortest of the four; it began at 3201 B.C. and will continue for 432,000 years. Each age has become darker, more evil, and more insecure than its predecessor. Thus in the age of Krita all men had fixed life-spans of 4,000 years; they enjoyed leisure and good health, and the fruits of the earth accrued to them without labor. Religious sacrifices were practiced regularly and unstintingly, and all things were in harmony. In the present age, so far have men's affairs deteriorated, the gods are forgotten, disease and misfortune are common, and no one's life is secure. At the end of this age will come dissolution: first famine, then fire, and finally flood; until all creation has been destroyed. (See also the note on *Day of Brahma.*)

Sastra. Sacred texts of every kind are called sastras. (Pronounced shastra.)

Vaisya. A member of the caste of merchants or tradesmen, the third caste. Mahatma Gandhi came from the banya sub-caste; that is, the merchants. "Brahma, the great parent of creation," says the Vishnu Purana, "gave to the Vaisya the occupation of commerce and agriculture, and the feeding of flocks and herds, for his means of livelihood: and sacred study, sacrifice, and donation

209

are also his duties, as is the observance of fixed and occasional rites."

Swami. Generic name for a monk of any order. He may sometimes be only a householder or retired businessman who is respected for his spiritual qualities. Every group of Hindu families has a swami or spiritual preceptor, to whom men and women go for moral and spiritual guidance. Some swamis come from eminent orders like the Swamis of Sringeri, an order founded by Sri Sankara himself. In common usage, however, the people of the lower castes are likely to call any Brahmin swami or saami. Hence the term is distinct from *guru*, which applies specifically to a teacher.

Touch his feet. When you meet or call on someone who is your spiritual superior, you touch his feet or prostrate yourself at his feet. In other words, you surrender yourself totally to him. Since the surrender is made to him as the embodiment of a spiritual principle, however, and never as a person, this act of humility is never interpreted as a sign of social subservience, but rather as an exercise in self-mastery.

Tirtham. Holy water. Sacred places of pilgrimage are also called tirthams, because wherever there is a holy place there is also water—to bathe in and to carry, sometimes, for the worship of the divinity. Tirtham also means the water which comes down from an image when it is washed. This water is sacred and is drunk in small spoonfuls for purification. After worship at any temple, one is offered the flame of camphor or its ashes, the flowers from the body of the divinity, and tirtham; and again, fruits that have been presented to the god.

Day of Brahma. According to one scheme of Hindu cosmogony, the universe, after it has been created by Brahma, endures 2,160,000,000 years, which is one day in the Creator's existence. At the end of this period a great fire consumes everything except the gods, the saints, and the elements, whereupon Brahma awakens from his perfect self-contemplation and creates the uni-

210

verse again. This procedure is repeated until one hundred years of Brahma's existence have passed. Then he himself expires, together with the sages, the gods, and all the universe, and everything returns to the primordial substance.

Kabul. Capital of Afghanistan, a main stopping-off point on the route between India and Russia.

Bukhara. An important central Asian city, historically a part of Persia.

Lahore. Once capital of the Punjab in undivided India, now one of the chief cities of Pakistan.

Paddy. Unhusked rice, or rice as it comes straight from the rice fields. The husking of rice is one of the important activities of village women. Standing sometimes in groups of two or three, they sing as they pound the paddy with a wooden pestle, and these songs are among the most beloved in Indian folklore.

Lantana. A wild shrub with thorny stems and red and yellow flowers. It grows in the jungles and often invades open spaces with astonishing rapidity. In the mountainlands of Mysore, lantana is used for hedges.

Eating-leaves. Banana leaves are used most commonly as dinnerware in India, not simply because many Indians in former days could not afford anything more durable, but because the leaves are clean, convenient, and may be easily disposed of. Moreover, the custom is sacred; sanitation in India is, like everything, a matter of religion. When banana leaves are not available, the leaves of a kind of teak are sometimes used, stitched together with strands of grass. Preparing these eating-leaves is often an occupation for the women and children of a family on a rainy evening when stories are told and gossip exchanged.

Shanbhog. A name used in Mysore for the revenue officer of the village; the same as patwari in other parts of India.

211

Holy bull. Often when a rich man dies, in his name a consecrated bull is let loose in the village, and these bulls cannot be ill-treated. They go where they choose, lie where they feel like resting, and are fed by everyone from shopkeepers to children. They are commonly symbols for fierce spoiled folk.

Volunteers. Young people, both men and women—and some not so young as well—who joined Gandhi's movement. Idealists, naturally, their sacrifices were often great, not only the obvious sacrifices entailed in imprisonment, banishment and confiscation of property, but the less obvious ones of lost education, opportunities relinquished, personal lives uprooted. Yet there were many more such sacrifices than most people imagine. The use of a capital letter in *Kanthapura* is meant to indicate, not that "Volunteer" was a proper name or title, but that among the common people of South India anyone who volunteered to serve the nationalist movement actively was held in great esteem.

Gandhi Mahatma ki jai or *Mahatma Gandhi ki jai.* The most famous of Indian revolutionary cries, meaning, "Victory, victory to Mahatma Gandhi!" Jai, from the Sanskrit word jaya, also implies, "Glory to," "May success come to," "May greatness shine on," "May [he] be victorious!" The kings after their battles erected Jaya-stambas or Pillars of Victory.

Vandè Mataram. The celebrated Indian National Song, taken from a novel by Bankim-Chandra Chatterjee. Vandè Mataram means: "I bow to thee, O mother."

Like Hanuman to Rama. Hanuman, called the Monkey God, was Rama's most devoted servant and disciple, as well as his first lieutenant in the campaign against Lanka, described in the *Ramayana.* It is worth remembering that among Indians discipleship is still considered a great privilege, and that every Indian, by virtue of his membership in a sub-caste, is a disciple to the guru or sage who is the sub-caste's leader.

Happalam. A fritter made of rice paste.

Jolly good blessing ceremony. A dressing down, chewing out, chastening, etc. In India the term "blessing ceremony" and "marriage ceremony" are frequently used ironically to mean castigation.

Field-bund. Between rice fields, earthen embankments are built to keep in a certain amount of standing water for the flooding of the rice, especially during the early weeks of planting. The embankments are also used to walk on, even to drive carts on. Sometimes a channel is dug in the embankment to permit the flow of water from one field to another. Rice needs a continuous flow of water, and that is why, when the farmer does not live near a river, his rice fields are always built near the village tank or reservoir. Bund, an Anglo-Indian word derived from Hindi *band,* means an embankment of a reservoir, or, in fact, any embankment. In China the same term is used for the elaborate esplanades built along riverfronts of inland cities.

CHAPTER 4

Chillies. Red capsicum, one of the essential spices of Indian diet.

Ragi. A cereal special to Mysore; a "dryland" grain (as opposed to rice). Extremely nutritious, a little of it will keep a peasant going through a whole day's work. Its Latin name is *Eleusine coracana.*

Kumkum. A red powder with which Indian married women mark their foreheads, as an auspicious and religious sign. In most parts of India, a woman whose husband has died must abandon this practice, together with her bangles, flowers for her hair, and the sacred marriage necklace or tali.

When the yokes touch the earth. When the bullocks had been unharnessed.

Toddy. An Anglo-Indian term (from Hindi *tari*) meaning the juice of the palmyra, called the toddy palm. In short, palm wine. The

213

tree grows wild in most parts of India, and toddy is a common intoxicant among the agricultural classes. Under the British, the manufacture and sale of toddy was made a state monopoly, which meant that every toddy tree, wherever it was found, belonged automatically to the government. Vast revenues came into the state treasury from this monopoly. It was the Mahatma's aim to abolish it, for it took away much of the poor man's earnings and brought degradation to the people. Today, in most Indian states, the use of toddy as a beverage is prohibited.

Panchayat. Traditionally, every Indian village is ruled by the Five Elders, who collectively comprise the Panchayat. Moreover, each community within the village—caste, sub-caste, etc.—has its own Panchayat, invested with certain judiciary powers. The system has always worked rather well, which perhaps accounts for the stable social structure of the Indian village, even today; and probably it accounts also for the insularity of village life. At any rate, it is true that the rural Indian village over the centuries has been relatively unaffected by historical and political changes, but has kept its cultural continuity intact.

Prayaschitta. Special purificatory rites must be performed by anyone who has become defiled through either social or religious misconduct. If these rites are not performed and if prayaschitta, or purification, is not obtained, then the spiritual head of the community, the swami, may declare the offender excommunicated from his caste. No worse fate can befall a Hindu; it amounts to nothing less than a loss of identity.

Gayathri. One of the most ancient and powerful of mantras; that is, a series of syllables, full of essential meaning, uttered or created by a sage, the repetition of which is beneficial to the person who knows them. A mantra is always communicated by a preceptor or guru to his disciple. At the initiation ceremony of a Brahmin, the Gayathri mantra is communicated by the family guru to the initiate. The Gayathri mantra runs as follows: "O face of the True Sun, now hidden by a disc of gold, may we know thy Reality, and see thee face to face."

214

Sacred flame. In the sanctuary of every Hindu household, at worship time an oil or melted-butter lamp is lit, sometimes several lamps, and they go on burning for many hours, even after the worship has been completed.

CHAPTER 5

Dasara havu. A very dangerous snake.

Basket and bundle. "Bag and baggage."

Krait. A venomous and most tricky serpent, *Bungarus coeruleus,* akin to the cobra. The krait causes more deaths in India than any other snake. (Pronounced *krite.*)

Father Naga. Naga means snake, especially cobra. However, in mythology Naga refers to a semi-divine creature, having a human face and a serpent's body. The Nagas, a thousand in number, inhabit Patala, i.e. the regions below the earth, and they reign there in great splendor. Many stories and myths are associated with their exploits. In point of fact, anthropologists believe that Naga was a name of a race, perhaps Scythians, who at one time inhabited part of India and were ultimately driven out or submerged by the invading Aryans. Traces of their language remain in certain place names. Perhaps they were snake-worshippers. The extent to which Indian Naga myths may have influenced European legends of underground people, especially Teutonic dwarf mythology, is problematical; but some of the similarities are striking.

Monsoon rains. The monsoon is one of the essential touchstones of Indian existence. The monsoon rains are sudden and dramatic, good material for the imagination to work on. Before the monsoon comes, intense heat ranges the earth like a marauding army, the sea heats up in the equatorial regions; and one can see, as if with an almost sub-human awareness, the monsoon winds as they rise. Then suddenly the rain bursts down, and pours and pours day after day, month after month. India has the heaviest rainfall center in the world. All earth becomes filled with pools and lakes, and white birds stand around philosophically on their long legs. The foliage turns green, the brown dust being washed off; the canals roar with new life. In the mountainlands of Mysore the monsoons pour eight months in the year. The Southwest Monsoon, the fiercest, breaks at the end of May and continues till the end of September, and then again the Northeast, gentler, thinner, coming from the Himalayan heights and the Bay of Bengal, showering the earth quickly and in the friendliest manner, pours on till the end of January. And when the rains stop, one can see the winter sky in the village tanks, and hear the sound of gurgling in the weirs that help to cultivate the rice fields and the sugar cane fields. The monsoon rains are very important for coffee plantations, too, as humidity is necessary for coffee trees, together with a sloping contour of land to drain the waters away.

> The approaching season of rain, dear love,
> Comes like a king in pride of power,
> The rain-laden clouds are rutting like war elephants,
> The water-bearing clouds
> Bend low, wend low,
> To deluge the earth with generous showers;
> And the lisping waters of the rain
> Ring sweet to the ears of men!
>   (Kalidasa, translated by R. S. Pandit)

Sri Kenchamma. Sri, fortunate, glorious, holy, etc., is a title of respect given to gods, saints, kings, and heroes, and also commonly to people in high, though not necessarily exalted, positions. It is equally applicable in the masculine and feminine genders, and hence is quite properly used for Kenchamma, goddess of Kanthapura.

Hookah. The hubble-bubble. A tobacco pipe consisting of an earthenware or wooden bowl, a reservoir of water, and a tube for pulling in the smoke. This method of smoking—by drawing the smoke through water—is popularly thought to remove the noxious elements from tobacco. The princes and rulers of India in the old days sometimes smoked elaborate hookahs of chased silver, with long silken tubes which ran all through their palace corridors. A special retainer kept the fire burning and maintained the hookah when it was not in use.

CHAPTER 6

Brahmin lines. To a certain extent, the terminology and even the ethos of the British military services permeated all Indian life during the century and a half of British hegemony. Thus Indian villages came to be laid out somewhat on the principles of a military garrison, and the different quarters were spoken of as "lines."

Tuft. Among orthodox Hindus, especially in South India, the front part of the head was formerly shaven, almost in a semicircular pattern, and the rest of the hair, as long as a woman's, was often tied in a knot at the back. Though this practice can be seen in India even today, it is becoming more and more obsolete. However, many Hindus still leave a symbolic bit of hair jutting slightly higher than the rest on the crown of the head. The tuft of hair is so important in the lay Hindu tradition that a monk is defined as he who has abandoned his tuft and (sacred) thread.

Don't touch the government. I.e., make the government an untouchable. In practical terms this meant not using government salt, not paying taxes, etc. But the meaning is greatly sharpened by the allusion to caste—though one suspects that this was an innuendo which Mahatma Gandhi himself would have disapproved.

CHAPTER 7

Ahimsa. Literally, non-cruelty; but in the context of Gandhian philosophy it has come to mean love in the fullest impersonal sense. Mahatma Gandhi's nonviolent campaign, or Satyagraha, was based upon Ahimsa (not-hurting) and Satya (truth). Nothing can ever be satisfactorily won, Gandhi held, without love, nor can it be retained and enjoyed without the practice of truth. Hence his famous saying: "I would rather India remained a thousand years more under British rule than that a lie be used to win our independence." For Mahatma Gandhi, violence and the lie were cut from the same cloth.

"Let us now examine the root of ahimsa. It is uttermost self-lessness. Selflessness means complete freedom from a regard for one's body. If man desired to realize himself, i.e. Truth, he could do so by being completely detached from the body. . . . That is the way of ahimsa." (Mahatma Gandhi.)

Mandap. Also *mantapa.* An enclosure, attached to a temple or sanctuary, in which the divinity is left to rest during processionals. Some temples have many mandaps, supported by pillars, running around the walls like an open veranda.

Banged the bell. All Indian temples have a bell, sometimes several, generally hung from the roof. As the roof of the Indian temple is never very high, one is expected to ring the bell as soon as one comes in. Children will ring the bell while sitting on the shoulders of their parents, with considerable enthusiasm. Temple bells are often fairly big. however, and the tongue may be extremely heavy.

Touched the Bull. In every temple of Siva there is his "vehicle," Nandi the bull, placed at some distance from but straight in front of the central image. (Each Indian god has his vehicle: Indra the elephant, Ganesha the mouse, Skanda the peacock, etc.) One of the essentials of worship at a Siva temple is to look at the image of Siva through the eyes and horns of the Nandi—Nandi being the symbol of the faithful devotee.

Cat's asceticism. A lecherous cat that has through necessity become celibate in old age figures in a famous Indian fable. Hence this expression. It is commonly applied to someone who is behaving hypocritically.

Kabir. A famous Indian saint whose songs are sung throughout the country. He lived from 1440 to 1518, a Muslim weaver by birth, but became a disciple of the celebrated Hindu saint, Ramananda. Kabir dedicated his hymns to the one God—Allah or Ram, he made no distinction—and many of his songs were favorites with Mahatma Gandhi.

Sivoham. A very famous saying in Indian tradition, attributed to Sri Sankara: "I am Siva." Which is to say: "I am the Absolute." An expression of total non-dualism.

Prahlada. In the popular Indian tradition (often dramatized in folk plays, harikathas, and dance-dramas) Prahlada was the son of a king, the demon-king Hiranyakashipu, who was so lost in his own glory that he claimed equality with God Himself. Prahlada, however, was full of devotion to God, which caused his father to fall into a great wrath. The boy was thrown in front of an elephant, but the elephant knelt down in worship. The boy was hurled down a mountain, but the earth rose to receive him tenderly. The boy was given poison, but the dram turned to ambrosia in the cup. Ultimately, in a discussion, the father said, "If God be, He should be even in this pillar." And Prahlada said, "Yes, yes, Hari is even in this pillar." At this, God took the form of Narasimha, half-man and half-lion, and destroyed the demon-king. Of course, Prahlada himself was none other than Vishnu, who had incarnated as the son of Hiranyakashipu in order to destroy evil and bring peace and holiness to the world.

Candelabra. Indian temples are usually very dark, and lamps always burn, especially in the inmost sanctuary. Tiers of metal

219

lamps are fixed to wooden or metal arches, and some are also hung by chains from the roof of the sanctuary.

The Holy. At the ultimate point of spiritual exaltation, the believer recognizes that all gods are One. Hence He may be called simply God, Bhagavan, or The Holy.

Krishna on the pipal leaf. Sri Krishna is often depicted by painters as a child floating down a river on a pipal leaf, with his big toe in his mouth. Sometimes these pictures, which undoubtedly seem odd to westerners, give Sri Krishna the crown of a king and the sacred thread of an initiate, even though he is still a child. Perhaps the symbolism means that when one raises oneself to the level of the Absolute—though according to Vedanta this is already inaccurate, for the Absolute can never be relative, and therefore one can never raise oneself to its level, but merely recognize that one's self has in fact never been anything but the Absolute all along—nevertheless, in the common manner of speaking one may say that when one raises oneself to the level of the Absolute, one becomes as if a child; everything is a play in the nowhere but now.

Prostration before the gods. To fall flat before the being one reverences is the common expression of surrender to the principle in that being: a son before his father, a wife before her husband, a devotee before his god, and above all a disciple before his guru. In strict respect of language, a prostration is called asthamnga namaska, or bowing with the eight limbs.

Rama-Krishna. One can name God, as for instance either Rama or Krishna or Hari or Mahadeva. Sometimes one combines these names, as Rama-Krishna or Sambo-Sankara, and repeats them at any moment of the day or night, as if they were a mantra. The names of each of the Gods—and all have many—possess a mantric significance; that is, they have at once an outer and an inner meaning, the inner meaning giving them power to help one spiritually. No mantra, however, is a mantra unless it is given by a guru.

220

Dharma Sastras. The moral code of every Hindu is regulated (or is supposed to be regulated) by a series of rites, habits, inhibitions, taboos, and ceremonies of purification; and the Dharma Sastras are a compendium of this enormous mass of permissible and impermissible usage. "The treatises on the Dharma," says Professor Renou, the well-known French Orientalist, "form one of the major branches of Indian literature: their numbers mount to several thousands, which are divided between the Vedic period and the eighteenth century. The word Dharma means the total of norms, the regulated behavior which is imposed on a person in the social situation where he stands; that is, his function according to his caste and his mode of life. . . ."

Beat the drum and denounce. In South Indian villages, even to this day, all proclamations of government, or merely of the Panchayat, are announced by the kulawadi (or beadle, who is usually an untouchable) by the beat of a drum.

Blew the conch. The conch is one of the most important symbols of Hindu religious life. Vishnu is always shown with a conch in one of his (four) hands, which symbolize the elements. There is also a belief that the conch always says the sacred mantra OM when put against the ear. The conch is blown at all moments of worship, in temples or in houses, and on very special occasions— for example, when welcoming a bridegroom or a pilgrim.

CHAPTER 8

Neem leaves. The neem is one of the sacred trees of India. In English it is also called the margosa; botanically, *Melia aradiracta.* Its leaves are very bitter to the taste, but the effect of them on the human body and mind are believed to be so remarkable that they are often used for medicinal purposes, especially by Yogis. The twig is also used by most Indians to clean their teeth; its roughness serves as a brush, and even the little juice that is expelled in the act of brushing is thought to be beneficial. An-

221

cient Hindu books of architecture and gardening specify that every house in India should have a neem tree in the garden.

Moorthappa. Moorthi-Appa, contracted to Moorthappa. Appa means father. Thus Moorthappa is a way of addressing Moorthi with respect.

Hari-Om. One of the famous mantras. Hari is a name of Vishnu, and OM of course is the mystic syllable which occurs in many religions; in the west it is used in various Gnostic or so-called heretical rites. OM or AUM contains the whole meaning of Vedantic experience. It is the First Sound, according to tradition, which came out when Ishwara or God made His first movement away from Himself in order to create the universe. It can never be used by anyone except when given by a guru. Phonologists say that when the sacred syllable is given its full pronunciation it contains the whole range of voiced sounds.

Sacred eagle. Garuda, the "vehicle" of Vishnu. Whenever one of these eagles appears, Hindus offer a prayer: "O Vehicle of Vishnu, King of Birds, etc." Many temples in India offer food to these sacred birds, and there are many legends connected with the way they appear at festivals, as if they knew the calendar and star of the God whose feast-day is being celebrated.

Ganges water. Every Hindu, throughout the ages, has had to make his pilgrimage to Benares, then go to Rameshwaram in the south of India and back again to Benares; and then only was the pilgrimage complete. The distance from Rameshwaram to Benares is about a thousand miles. Indian tradition formerly allowed twelve years for this pilgrimage, which was usually undertaken at the end of one's active life. If after twelve years the pilgrim and his wife had not returned to their home, they were believed to be dead and obsequies were performed for them. On returning from Benares finally, one had to bring some Ganges water in a copper pot. In every Brahmin household—and in the houses of many other castes as well—this pot of Ganges water is kept in the sanctuary. Many orthodox Hindus believe that the water of the

Ganges River for some mysterious reason, never becomes stale. The lid is covered, after use, with a seal of wax. At the moment of death, and at ceremonies of purification, a little bit of Ganges water is drunk.

Anjanayya. Another name for Hanuman the Monkey God, faithful servant of Sri Rama in the *Ramayana.* Anjana was the name of his mother, and so he is called Anjanayya.

Chapter 9

Rag-wide. Often for rough measurements peasants will use a loincloth; hence a "rag-wide" is a strip of land perhaps a yard in width.

Laddu. A well-known Indian sweet, often made of Bengal-gram fried in melted sugar.

Outcaste. According to Hindu tradition, everyone is bound to the caste in which he is born, as determined by the good and bad actions of his prior existence (karma). Moreover, his spiritual progress is not expedited by his rejecting his caste, but rather by his acceptance of the station to which he is born—since the world at best is only a play of relative appearances, the high and the low are merely standards of the world and have nothing to do with spiritual life as such. The spiritual life may be lived anywhere by anyone, caste having nothing to do with it. Such at least is the strict doctrine, however difficult it has been for many of the lowly born to practice it. By not obeying the rules of one's caste—as, for instance, by eating with those who do not belong to it, by marrying outside it (though this is virtually inconceivable), or by touching untouchables, etc.—one becomes an outcaste; that is to say, one is excommunicated by the swami who rules the caste. When a Brahmin becomes an outcaste, he must perform a purificatory or prayaschitta ceremony in order to gain readmittance, and then he must go through the entire initiation ceremony again, as if he were still a boy.

Chapter 10

Kartik. The seventh month of the Hindu calendar, falling usually in October-November. It is one of the most beautiful months in India—the winter sky is almost without a cloud, the moon is golden. It is a custom in South India during the first fifteen days of Kartik to light lamps at the entrances of houses, and on the last day the whole garden, the veranda, and the terraces are brightly lighted with oil lamps. Sometimes a huge metal lamp is placed in the middle of the courtyard, with rice designs at the bottom and flowers heaped on the central cone of the lamp, and with kumkum marks all over; or clay elephants carrying lamps on their backs are lighted and placed at the doorways to let the gods have light as they pass through the street. Little Kartik-lamps are placed in tiny boats and floated on the river. In Kartik the gods like to move about, and some people of course have seen them! On the top of the famous Arunachala Hill, beloved of Siva, at Tiruvannamalai, they light the top with a neverending fire under the Kartik moon, and it can be seen for many miles around.

Vakil. A lawyer, especially a small-time lawyer. This is a case of the Hindu term being used alongside its English synonym, a not uncommon way of speaking among Anglo-Indians of the clerical and political vocations.

Vedavathy. Literally, Flow of the Vedas; the name of a river.

College Union. A student organization; generally without authority (always under the British), but formed as a convenience in arranging debates, receptions, etc.

Maidan. A flat, open space, found in many Indian towns, used for fairs, for cartmen to camp on overnight, for police drill, for military inspections and parades, and often for political meetings.

224

Kurta. An Indian shirt. With the introduction of western modes of dress, many Indians had begun to use the European shirt to replace the Indian kurta. Under the nationalist influence, the older style came back, however, the kurta being buttoned on the chest, with pockets at the sides, generally longer than the European shirt.

Gandhi-cap. A small, cheap, foldable type of cotton headgear, made of simple white cloth; as such it may be washed every day. With the wearing of khadi, the Gandhi-cap became its natural concomitant, a symbol of Indian nationalism. Sometimes a Gandhi-cap on his head cost an Indian political worker three months in prison!

Durbar turban. One could appear before the Maharaja of Mysore (or, for that matter, before any other prince) only in court dress, *durbar* meaning court. The durbar turban is a lofty structure with gold lace and starched folds, made of sixteen yards of cloth.

Rudrakshi. A wild, thick-hulled fruit, used for making prayer-beads. Sometimes Brahmins, especially of the very learned class, use necklaces of these beads encased in gold or silver.

Rama-rajya. The kingdom of Rama; the rule of Rama. Whenever Hindus speak of the perfect state, the Utopia in which everyone is happy, they speak of Ayodhya under Sri Rama, as described in the *Ramayana.* There every hearth of sacrifice was intact, the ascetics performed their rites in the peace of the forest, no child ever cried, no woman became a widow, and the throne itself would burn if an injustice were done anywhere in the whole empire. Even the deer and the tiger could drink from the same pool, from the same side of the pool! The trees bore luxuriant fruit, the floods did not wash away the fields, and children came into the world never earlier than the ninth month appointed for their arrival. All because Rama, Sri Rama, ruled in Ayodhya. Light shone in every window, and lighted was the heart of every woman. Mahatma Gandhi himself said that for India to become the India of his dreams she would have to become a Rama-rajya!

Ravana. The monster-king of Lanka (Ceylon) abductor of Queen Sita. He is believed to have had ten heads. The story goes that after many years of austere meditation upon the attributes of Siva, Ravana saw Siva Himself, and the God asked him which he would prefer: (a) to be granted ten lives, each sweeter than the other, each more resplendent than the other, each filled, not with material joys, but with the holiest bliss; or (b) to be turned into a demon and killed by Siva Himself, thus attaining the supreme liberation. Ravana was so earnest in his desire for liberation that he asked for the quickest way to reach it, and hence the ten lives became ten heads and Siva, incarnated as Sri Rama, came to destroy him. The end of Ravana, according to this version of the tale, came when he was in ecstasy, saying the holy name of Rama, Sri Rama. The main action of the *Ramayana* consists of Rama's campaign against Ravana to recover Queen Sita, a campaign in which he was assisted by the monkey-god, Hanuman.

Vasistha. The sage Vasistha was guru of Sri Rama. His teachings are embodied in the *Yoga Vasistha,* believed by some scholars to be a part of the *Ramayana;* in it Vasistha gives answers to Sri Rama's many questions on metaphysical topics. The *Yoga Vasistha* is regarded as one of the greatest books of Advaita Vedanta, and is quoted as a sacred text. Vasistha is also sometimes thought to be the same sage as Vyasa, who established the Vedas in their present order.

Vidyaranya. The most important sage of Advaita Vedanta, after Sri Sankara. He is believed to have lived in the fourteenth century and to have been the head monk of the famous sanctuary, Sringeri, founded by Sri Sankara himself. Vidyaranya wrote texts on Vedanta, the most famous of which is the *Pancha Dasi.* He was also the spiritual counsellor to the founders of the Vijayanagar dynasty, Hukka and Bukka, and Vijayanagar was first called Vidyanagar after Vidyaranya, and later came to be confounded with Vijayanagar, City of Victory. The Vijayanagar empire was one of the most splendid Hindu states. In 1565, however, the Muslim invaders defeated the Rajas of Vijayanagar and destroyed their glorious city, which in those days was larger than London, pillaging its ten thousand temples. The ruins at Hampi (present name for Vijayanagar) are one of the principal centers of historical interest in India today.

Mutt. A spiritual or religious center, seat of Kula Guru, who is usually a preceptor to a community of Hindus.

From becoming Brahmins. Karma: the moral consequence of all one's acts and thoughts, taken as a determinant of one's station in the next incarnation. Thus the proper Hindu's main concern is always the improvement of his karma. There is nothing to prevent one from changing caste in one's next life; in fact, in this light it can be seen that that is what castes are for, i.e. to mark the stages of one's spiritual progress toward final purification and liberation from the cycle of rebirths. However the doctrine of metempsychosis may strike western minds, it will be seen that the theory of karma places a man's destiny clearly within his own being, and that this is a deeply rooted conviction of the Indian folk, and has been for centuries. The consequences in terms of national character can be seen today in official Indian policy on such matters as political alignment, militarism, non-intervention, and the like.

Mlechas. All those born outside the Hindu fold are called mlechas or outsiders.

Saffron robes. The robes of a monk; yellow is the monastic color in all South Asian countries.

Blue paper. A weekly newspaper; specifically, a political weekly, as distinct from the regular newspaper. Such papers often came in blue covers.

Stars of the Seven Sages. Ursa Major is called by Hindus, sapta rishi mandala, the cluster of the seven sages. The Seven Sages are Marici, Atri, Angiras, Pulastya, Kratu, Pulaha, and Vasistha.

The Holy Name. The wall lizard in South India is associated with prophecy, and there are ancient techniques for interpreting its clucking. There are even a number of texts on the subject. Often when the lizard clucks, women beat the floor and say, "Krishna, Krishna."

Kanchi. Also *Conjeevaram.* A famous place of pilgrimage, near Madras. The Goddess Kamakshi reigns there, and her name means She-with-the-Eyes-of-Desire. She is often associated with the Meenakshi (She-with-the-Eyes-of-a-Fish) of Madura, and with Vishalakshi (She-with-Large-Eyes) of Benares. Kanchi saris are famous, especially for use in temples. They are made of silk, with red and black stripes, and, for the goddesses, are considerably abbreviated.

A thousand-and-eight flames. A thousand and eight (like a hundred and eight) is a sacred number in India. Sometimes one vows, in return for a boon granted, to offer the goddess a golden belt, a Kanchi sari, a diamond earring; sometimes one gives a feast in her honor; or sometimes one simply orders a thousand and eight lamps to be lighted (with ghee or oil, according to the formula one has adopted).

Pushya. The tenth month of the Hindu calendar, corresponding to December-January.

Corn-distribution. In traditional village life, the nonagricultural workers of the village—the barber, the boatman, the street-sweeper, etc.—were paid for their services annually by each household and were paid in kind. Each house was assessed a certain measure of grain, according to its members, and once a year this measure was distributed to the workers who came to claim their shares.

Taluk office. The taluk (county) office in former days was chiefly concerned with the collection of revenue.

Young India. A famous revolutionary weekly of Mahatma Gandhi, the principal organ of his ideas. Though its circulation was never more than a few thousands, it carried the Gandhian message to every corner of India. As a matter of principle, *Young India* printed no advertising, since a paper, Gandhi said, must live by its ideas. Later the name was changed to *Harijan* (People of God), which is also now the most common Indian term for the Untouchables.

Tilak, 1856–1920. Lokamanya Bal Gangadhar Tilak was the most important modern leader of India before the coming of Mahatma Gandhi. Tilak was a fiery revolutionary, and between him and Gandhi there was a controversy over means and ends which divided the whole of the nationalist movement. Tilak believed that all noble methods (including violence) could be used, whereas Gandhi preached nonviolence and truth as the only means for attaining India's independence. Finally the Congress sided with Gandhi, but without relinquishing any of its profound respect for Lokamanya Tilak, India's man of grandeur. Tilak spent many years in jail, and wrote two very famous books; one on the *Arctic Home of the Vedas,* and the other called *Gita Rahasya* (the essence of the *Gita*). Tilak was, in fact, not only a great revolutionary but a considerable scholar, if sometimes a little biased.

Chittaranjan Das. Always associated with Tilak and Mahatma Gandhi was Chittaranjan Das (1870-1925), though he was, as it were, a junior political figure beside these gigantic men. Das was a brilliant Calcutta lawyer, a man of deep sensitivity—he wrote verse sometimes—and toward the end of his life more of a constitutional fighter than a revolutionary, though he began as a believer in bomb-throwing.

Lingam in his hand. In South India there is an important community called the Veerasaivas or Lingayats, whose members wear suspended about their necks a small silver casket containing a lingam; because this can usually be seen dangling on their chests, the Lingayats are easily distinguishable from others. The movement began as a powerful religious revolution against Brahminic ascendancy, though it has tended to fall back (as usually happens in India) upon its own hyperorthodoxy. It has

229

produced some of the most famous spiritual and literary—and lately, political—figures in the Karnatic region. Basaveshwara was the founder of the Veerasaiva movement.

Wash the wheel of law. To clean, to purify the law. The simile of wheel-washing is a good deal more meaningful in countries of unpaved highways than it is in modern Europe or America.

Haldi. Literally, turmeric. The signs of a married woman (as opposed to a widow) were kumkum on the forehead and turmeric on the cheek and feet. Consequently, when women were invited to a female gathering, it was called a haldi-and-kumkum invitation, and both haldi and kumkum were offered to the guests, together with flowers and sandal-paste.

Jallianwalabagh. After the first World War, when soldiers returned to their normal peacetime duties as keepers of order in subject territories, it was difficult for some of the battle-hardened officers to see where caution should end and violence begin. Thus in 1921, in the Sikh city of Amritsar, an innocent meeting was held in the yard of a temple, closed in on all sides by high walls. But as all meetings were prohibited (because the government was afraid of rising nationalist feeling) a military detachment was sent to keep watch over the proceedings. The meeting was attended by about three thousand men, women and children. O'Dwyer, the regular army officer in charge, apparently lost his nerve when the people failed to respond immediately to his order to disperse, and commanded his men to open fire on the crowd, with the consequence that nearly a thousand people were killed. Many of those who saved themselves did so by crawling beneath the bodies of their dead friends, for they had nowhere to escape, all the exits being blocked by the soldiers. The massacre came as a rude shock to people everywhere who were accustomed to thinking in terms of the more civilized aspects of British rule, and it created the first widespread fierce opposition in India to foreign domination. Jallianwala became a symbol of martyrdom to the whole nation. Today Jallianwalabagh has been made a National Shrine. (Bagh means garden.)

Pandal. A simple structure of bamboo poles and coconut leaves, raised almost anywhere as shelter against rain and sun; a temporary, movable canopy. Pandals are put up at marriages, initiation ceremonies, important anniversaries (for example, the sixtieth birthday of a grandfather), civic receptions, and the like. Huge pandals, to accommodate as many as two hundred thousand persons, have been erected at the annual conferences of the Indian National Congress.

CHAPTER 11

Vidya and Avidya. Two primary elements of Vedanta, corresponding to Brahman (the Absolute) and Maya (the Illusory). Vidya comes from the Sanskrit root *vid,* which means to know, and hence Vidya means knowledge. In Vedanta there is no evil as such, no ignorance (Avidya), but only the unreal appearance of evil or ignorance, just as unreal as the son of a barren woman, the horns on the head of a hare, or the water seen in a mirage. This does not mean that you do not see the water— you do see it, of course—but when you go near it you find it is a delusion. Thus truth is not the opposite of untruth. Rather, Truth is the background of everything—it is and it is what is. Even the so-called illusion must be explained in terms of Truth. Illusion, one says, is the basis of pain, duality, etc. When we examine it more closely, however, we see that illusion is only an appearance, just as the wave is thought to be in the ocean, although the ocean is only water. We look at the wave and we call it a wave, but when we take it in our hands it is water and water alone. Vidya is the Knowledge of Reality. But at the same time Knowledge itself *is* Reality: unless you know, nothing can be. Hence all is Knowledge, all is Vidya; and there never has been and there never can be Avidya or ignorance—horns on the head of a hare.

Rani Lakshmi Bai of Jhansi. Perhaps the most famous leader of the first Indian revolt against the British, the Indian Mutiny of

1857. She was a queen by birth, a beautiful, modest, but self-willed woman, who fought so heroically against the British that even they admired her. She was killed on the battlefield, and her body was secretly hidden and then burned. Later the place where her ashes were buried became a shrine.

Rajputs. A well-known clan of warriors. Their fame in battle and martyrdom is sung to this day by the bards, and now the province which contained their most important strongholds has become the state of Rajasthan. Perhaps the oldest ruling dynasty in the world is the line of the Ranas of Udaipur, traditional monarchs of the Rajputs, whose genealogy may be traced back historically to about 15 A.D. Rajput women were known to jump into fire to avoid being taken prisoner by their enemies. And the bards will sing to you of women who cut their fingers to anoint their husbands before a battle, and who then, having raised a pyre in the castle, read the *Mahabharata* until news of the battle's outcome was received: if the enemy had won, the women leapt on the pyre, but if their husbands had been victorious, then red was the arathi-water which they placed in the bowls of silver as a welcome for the conquering heroes.

Kamaladevi and Sarojini Naidu and Annie Besant. Three famous women of the independence movement. Kamaladevi Chattopadhaya was a close associate of Mahatma Gandhi, and today is in charge of the governmental department which administers village handicrafts. Sarojini Naidu (1879-1949) was a well-known poet. Annie Besant (1847-1933) was an Englishwoman, a social reformer who went to India, adopted Indian ways of life, headed the Theosophical Society, and served as a leader in the Congress.

Blowpipe. A tube of bamboo used for kindling a fire. One end is placed among the embers of the old fire; then by blowing gently through the tube one may kindle a new flame. The blowpipe is as standard in the Indian kitchen as the broom, both being common symbols of housewifely authority.

Arathi. Flame and song, kumkum water and flowers, are offered to any divinity or important personage when the occasion requires. It is a sign of honor, an offering of love and esteem, a request for benediction. In every Hindu temple the arathi is the most important ceremony; it concludes every ritual. At a wedding the bridegroom is welcomed with a newly broken coconut, and kumkum water and flowers, and flame of worship.

Sevika Sangha. The Association of Service, or Organization of Women Workers. At first, men and women organized themselves separately into groups serving the nationalist cause, and each had its own name. Later they were brought together in one national organization.

Holy fire. At the annual festival of the local divinity—that of the goddess Kenchamma in Kanthapura—the peasants dig a trench about thirty yards long and two feet wide beside the temple, and this is filled with live coals. Then the peasants walk on it. This is not hocus-pocus. Whatever the explanation, the fire-walking ceremony may be seen every year in thousands of Indian villages, performed by the peasants in large numbers and without injury to themselves, though it is seldom if ever attempted by Brahmins. In terms of the higher theology, of course, the ceremony is considered a bit spectacular and ostentatious; but it remains a deeply ingrained part of the poor man's religion.

Kraaled elephants. Before elephants are broken they are forced into kraals (wooden enclosures), where they are systematically starved. When sufficiently weakened, they are given a little food and taken out for training by mahouts. This unfortunate practice is defended by elephant trainers on the ground that an untrained elephant in full possession of his powers is too strong to be handled safely and that afterwards the beasts are none the worse for their experience. On the other hand, elephant trainers and drivers are traditionally the cynics and "tough guys" of Indian folk culture.

Eesh. Also *Isha, Ishwara,* etc. Names for the personal god one worships; here Siva.

Chapter 12

Vaisakh. The first month of the Hindu calendar, falling in March-April.

Bel tree. A sort of wild mimosa with thorny branches, often used for fences; called also Bengal quince, golden apple, wood apple; in Latin, *Aegle marmelos.* The bel is sparsely leafed, and may be seen over much of the Indian countryside. Its fruit, hard-shelled and acid to the taste, is thought to possess medicinal qualities, and is often substituted for lemons, e.g. in drinks, etc.

Quern. A small household mill for grinding corn, usually made of stone and found, in India, on the veranda or just at the entrance of the inner hall. Women, sometimes two at a time, grind the grain or rice, keeping the beat with songs. Quern songs are among the most famous in Indian folk literature.

Kashi. Benares. According to Indian tradition, all rivers are tributaries of the Ganges, or rather sisters, and so all things naturally go toward Benares.

Book bundle. The priest in India regularly visits each household in his jurisdiction, usually every three or four days, to determine the auspicious times for performing family ceremonies and household duties. This is done by means of his sacred calendar, a complex astrological chart which he always carries with him. Usually he also carries a few sacred texts, in case he is asked to read something from scripture. The calendar and the texts are his book bundle, which is such a conspicuous part of his get-up that it is as good as an insignia of office.

Rohini. In astrological calculations, a star which indicates the coming (or the absence) of rain. Rohini is a very common girl's name in India.

Champak. One of the most famous—*the* most famous—of Indian flowering trees. Its slim yellow-gold petals adorn the heads of gods and women. It has a gentle scent, almost, as it were, remembered to itself. The champak is found in most courtyards of Indian homes and in the precincts of temples.

Hoyla. A shout of rough comradeship; something like "Come on!" or "Let's go!" *Hoye.* The same.

Dame. The earth is often referred to by peasants as if she were a familiar person—a woman, a mother. They speak of the earth, and sometimes of a river, as if they were speaking of living beings.

Bidies. Country cigarettes, rolled in dry leaves.

No fire in his stomach and red with red and blue with blue. In other words, poor Subbayya had so little will of his own that when somebody red turned up he became red too, and similarly with someone blue; he was nothing but a mirror. This is a common saying in India.

Blue-god. Sri Krishna. Actually, Krishna comes from the Sanskrit word meaning black.

Brahma's guardians. All temple deities have their guardians, called Dvarapalakas, protectors of the door.

Swing festival. A means of adoration. In Kanthapura, at the time of the annual festival of Kenchamma, the goddess would be taken from her temple and brought to a cliff outside the village. Here a wooden structure supporting a swing would have been built. The goddess would be placed in the swing and set in motion, and various rituals would be performed to accompany her. In some parts of India the swings are supported in elaborate structures of stone, intricately carved.

Invitation rice. In India when you wish to invite someone to attend a social event at your house, you go to his house carrying a silver cup filled with rice which has been colored with kumkum. If your invitation is accepted, you sprinkle a few grains of the colored rice on his doorsill as you depart.

Song of welcome. On great occasions, when the chief personages appear, they are greeted by musicians. Only certain melodies are traditionally appropriate.

CHAPTER 13

Manufacture salt. The manufacture and sale of salt was a government monopoly under the British. Gandhi consequently made salt one of his symbols of British exploitation, and when he wanted to do something illegal which at the same time would hurt no one, he walked to the seaside and constructed a little saltern on the beach in order to make a handful of salt from the sea-water. This was, of course, a wholly symbolic act, a ritual disavowal of British authority; it would have been highly impractical to suggest that everyone make his own salt. Nevertheless, the Indian people, whose art and religion are full of symbolic action, followed Mahatma Gandhi's salt pilgrimages with even more fervor than they might have accorded to acts of practical defiance, and for this reason the British administrators took an exceedingly dim view of the whole business.

The letting-off of the morning cattle. Early in the morning, soon after the cows are milked, the cattle are let off to go to the woods and graze. This is one of the familiar scenes in any village household. Krishna driving the morning cattle to graze is a subject constantly used by traditional Indian painters.

Harischandra. One of the most important figures of Indian tradition. King of Ayodhya, he was so devoted to Truth that he is still called Satya Harischandra, Harischandra of the Truth. Every child knows the story, and when grown up, sees it played over and over again in the traditional theater. Mahatma Gandhi speaks movingly of how deeply he was influenced by the story of Harischandra.

So, once upon a time, Harischandra, King of Ayodhya, ruled his bright land with his faithful and holy wife, Saivya, beside him, and his auspicious son, Rohitasva, on his lap. People wondered that so noble a king could exist on this poor earth, for Harischandra told only the truth and the world in consequence was a garden of loveliness and justice. Men never spoke a harsh word to one another, nor did a woman have her breast dry up betimes, nor did a frog need to fear the vicinity of a snake. But the gods desired to test his integrity. Therefore to King Harischandra came the sage, Vishvamitra (sent by Indra), and when the king fell at the feet of the holy visitor and said, "Welcome to you, O Fountain of Light, all that is mine is yours," the sage took him at his word and said that the kingdom now belonged to him. The king said: "Yes, of course it does." "But where, Harischandra, is the gold you give when you make a holy gift?" "I have none, O Sage," the king replied, "but in three days' time I will bring to you the appropriate gold." Thus it was that Harischandra journeyed outside his kingdom and sold himself and his wife in order to give the appropriate gift to the sage. And now Harischandra became a servant at a crematorium, which is still called Harischandra Ghat in Benares in memory of this great king. One day his wife, who worked as a charwoman in a wealthy family, brought their son Rohitasva to the crematorium, for, alas, a serpent had bitten him and he had died. But the mother had no money to pay the crematory fee. When she was on the point of wrenching off her wedding necklace, which no woman would give up except at the death of her husband (for to break the sacred wedding necklace is to shake the moral law of the universe), the gods were so astonished and gratified by this act of personal integrity that Harischandra and his queen were permitted to return to their kingdom of Ayodhya, where they ruled many a hundred years!

237

Ganga, Jumna, Saraswathi. The three sacred rivers: the Ganges and the Jumna, which meet at Prayaga (or Allahabad), where from subterranean sources they are joined by the Saraswathi. "The faithful who with joyful heart hear and understand, and with utmost devotion bathe at this Prayaga of saints assembled, win the four rewards while still alive. The effects of the bath is seen at once; crows become cuckoos and cranes become swans." (Tulasi Das, *Ramacharitamanasa.* Translated by W. D. P. Hill.) Hindus often say the names of the three sacred rivers whenever they wade in, or even touch, any water at all.

Chitranna. Literally, a picturesque rice or food. Usually it is rice marinated in lemon juice and sprinkled with many condiments and grated coconut. Served mostly on sacred occasions.

Sahyadri Mountains. Local name for some parts of the Western Ghats.

Chapter 14

First daughter milks the cow. Milking the cow at dawn is one of the sacramental functions in any household. Usually it is the lady of the house who, after various brief rituals, commences to milk the most venerable cow of the pen. When the lady is ill, however, it is the eldest daughter or daughter-in-law who must perform the first milking.

Narayan. Vishnu as the incarnation of Cosmic Man. Narayan is often represented as lying on a huge snake on the calm waters of the Ocean, in the full enjoyment and contemplation of his Self ("Ocean" being, of course, the primordial flux).

Copra. Dried coconut meat. Often eaten with a bit of sugar.

Caverns of the Ganges. Some people believe that the ancient sages who came to live on the banks of the Ganges still occupy the holy river's subterranean caves, where they live on and on, almost ageless, blessing the world and enjoying the pure spiritual radiance which emanates from the Ganges' sacred waters.

CHAPTER 15

Padrè. The Portuguese word has been retained in India as a name for all Christian priests, ministers, and missionaries. The padrè is a common figure at country fairs, where he vies with other preachers and vendors for the attention of the crowd; or at any rate this was the case not very long ago.

Margosa. The neem tree. See above.

Nail-witch. When someone finds nails planted in front of his house, he may be sure that a magician has been sent there to provoke evil against his family.

CHAPTER 16

Government Flag. The flag of the Congress, also called the National flag by adherents of independence. It was a white, green, and ochre field with a spinning wheel in the center. Since independence, the Indian nation has adopted the same flag for its national standard, but the spinning wheel has been simplified to a plain wheel, signifying the wheel of dharma, the wheel of moral law and eternal life.

Badmash. A Hindi term of abuse; a scoundrel.

Maund. An Indian measure, roughly 82 pounds.

Hobli. In Karnataka, an administrative division between the village and the taluk.

Jaggery. Molasses. In the Karnatic mountainland, molasses is poured into square wooden molds and allowed to harden; then the glasslike pieces, called jaggery, are removed and carefully packed in hay.

CHAPTER 17

Siva of the Meru Mount. Each Indian god has many names; most, in fact, have a thousand or more.

In the chant given here, the references mean: (1) Meru, the supreme mountain of creation, the pivot of the universe; (2) the river Ganges, which Siva wears tied in a knot on his head, permitting only a trickle to come down to earth and form the river seen by men; (3) the crescent moon worn by Siva in his hair, symbolizing the first sound uttered by the universe at its creation; (4) the crematorium where Siva dances joyfully with a garland of skulls, symbolizing freedom from the body and the world; (5) the destruction of illusion, the goal of spiritual life, ending in the discovery that Siva alone exists, Siva the Absolute. Siva's dance is evoked in a famous poem:

> The dancing foot, the sound of the tinkling bells,
> The songs that are sung, and the various steps,
> The forms assumed by our Master as He dances,
> Discover these in your own heart, so shall your bonds
>   be broken. . . .
>   (*Tiruvallar*, translated by Coomaraswamy.)

CHAPTER 18

Satyanarayana Puja. Adoration of the God of Truth, a movable festival in India, celebrated especially as a means of removing obstacles and to obtain success in a difficult enterprise.

Siddapur. A town in Karnataka.

Sholapur. An industrial center in the Deccan, noted especially for its cotton mills.

Kailas to Kanyakumari. That is, from Mount Kailas in the Himalayas to Kanyakumari or Cape Comorin, the southern tip of the Indian peninsula. Mount Kailas was the paradise where Siva dwelled; today it is the central peak of the Kailas Range, elevation 23,000 feet. Kanyakumari is Parvati herself, who stands on the tip of India facing the three oceans. She is a Kumari, or maiden, and she will always remain so, because, according to one story, Siva did not turn up in time for his marriage. Kanyakumari is well known as a place of pilgrimage.

Karachi. Now the capital of Pakistan. Formerly the capital of Sind and the most westerly city of India.

Kachar. In Assam; the most easterly city of India.

Prabhat pheris. Early morning religious processions of women and girls. Latterly, nationalist songs were introduced among the hymns, and the prabhat pheris became part of the Indian protest movement.

Winnowing pail. Made of bamboo and leaves, used for tossing the beaten rice grains into the wind so that the husks will be winnowed from the kernels.

Sanctum clothes. Newly washed clothing must be worn each day for worship. Generally after a bath in the river one washes one's clothes of the previous day, and they are then brought home and carefully hung to dry on bamboo poles close to the roof of the kitchen or the sanctuary. They are not touched again until one has bathed. Sometimes when it rains—or the times are evil—they do not dry easily.

Shamoo. Any person, though usually a well-known figure in the village, who, being possessed by the divinity, speaks oracularly; a speaker in tongues.

241

Sajji. Fried semolina mixed with sugar and cardamom.

Inquilab Zindabad. Long live the Revolution. One of the most important revolutionary cries of the Gandhian movement.

The Moghul of Delhi. The Moghul Emperors ruled India from the
ancient capital of Delhi; Delhi is in fact as old as the Mahabharata War, when it was called Indraprastha. The Moghuls ruled
for nearly three hundred years. Though of foreign origin, they
soon realized the riches of the native Indian civilization, and
with Akbar, one of the greatest emperors, they Indianized themselves to a remarkable degree and ruled most of the country, at
least nominally, until 1857. The last Moghul Emperor was de-
posed by the British after the Sepoy Mutiny, but he was only a
shadow of an emperor by that time. He enjoyed poetry—and
flew kites!

Jatin (Das) and Bhagat (Singh). One from Bengal and the other
from the Punjab. Both were famous young revolutionaries who
did not believe in nonviolence, and who were hanged by the
British for anti-government activities. They became heroes and
their names a part of the national pantheon. This is why the song
speaks of the flame of Jatin and the fire of Bhagat; then comes
the love of the Mahatma.

CHAPTER 19

Dasara. See above. On the last day of the festival, when the monsoon rains have stopped and the world is rich with waving fields
of harvest and clear pools of water, the king leads his soldiers
(you could have seen it anywhere in India when the rajas were in
power) to his frontiers to show his neighbor the might of his
army. At the end of the ceremony, the king returns from the
frontier seated on his royal elephant, which is adorned with
jewels at the feet, ears and forehead. As the king enters the city,

the queen and other ladies of the court welcome him with holy water, silver lamps, flowers, and fruits. In effect, this is the re-enactment of Sri Rama's battle with Ravana and the triumphant return with Queen Sita; together Sri Rama and his queen will reign over the world forever. For all kingdoms are but the one Kingdom, Rama-rajya, the Kingdom of Sri Rama.

In India the biggest Dasara festival takes place in Mysore where one can still see the Maharaja of Mysore returning through the festive city after he has worshipped at the Holy Tree (the banni) in the sacred precinct at the edge of town.

Upanishads. Famous sacred texts which contain discussions and discourse on metaphysical problems. All Indian philosophy is essentially based on the interpretation of the *Upanishads,* which are themselves primarily interpretations of the earlier parts of the *Vedas.* Most scholars agree that the principal *Upanishads* date from about the fifth century B.C.

Bharata. Younger brother of Sri Rama. He ruled in Ayodhya in Rama's stead during Rama's absence on the campaign against Ravana.

Kashi. See above. As old age comes, many orthodox Hindus like to go to Benares, and often it is thought to be good to die there. Because of the number of pilgrims who come there to live, to do penance, and to die, many priests are needed to serve them, and consequently the city contains a large colony of Brahmin priests from every part of the country. These Brahmins consider that they are exiling themselves in holiness; but the truth is that their exile is full of comforts, paid for by the pilgrims who come there to seek help and offer prayers. Lodging for pilgrims, for instance, brings in a good income; and since prayers offered by Brahmins are thought to be particularly efficacious . . . well, every prayer muttered costs solid silver.

Yet Benares is the holiest city of the land, and the holiest and greatest have come there—India's sages, kings, and poets. For Benares is ruled by Siva Himself, the Absolute. Hence the famous hymn of Sri Sankara to Benares:

The cessation of mental contextures is supreme peace.
That indeed is the eldest of holy places
Which is the Mannikarnika itself (in me)
While the full-flowing, Ganges, untainted Knowledge.
Thus "I," He of Benares, the form of Pure Consciousness.

Mannikarnika is the most holy place in Benares, for it is here that Siva dug a hole in the earth for Parvati, and the waters of the Ganges flowed into it.

New Directions Paperbooks

Vladimir Nabokov, *Nikolai Gogol.* NDP78.
P. Neruda, *The Captain's Verses.*† NDP345.
   Residence on Earth.† NDP340.
New Directions 17. (Anthology) NDP103.
New Directions 18. (Anthology) NDP163.
New Directions 19. (Anthology) NDP214.
New Directions 20. (Anthology) NDP248.
New Directions 21. (Anthology) NDP277.
New Directions 22. (Anthology) NDP291.
New Directions 23. (Anthology) NDP315.
New Directions 24. (Anthology) NDP332.
New Directions 25. (Anthology) NDP339.
New Directions 26. (Anthology) NDP353.
New Directions 27. (Anthology) NDP359.
Charles Olson, *Selected Writings.* NDP231.
George Oppen, *The Materials.* NDP122.
   Of Being Numerous. NDP245.
   This In Which. NDP201.
Wilfred Owen, *Collected Poems.* NDP210.
Nicanor Parra, *Emergency Poems.*† NDP333.
   Poems and Antipoems.† NDP242.
Boris Pasternak, *Safe Conduct.* NDP77.
Kenneth Patchen, *Aflame and Afun of
   Walking Faces.* NDP292.
   Because It Is. NDP83.
   But Even So. NDP265.
   Collected Poems. NDP284.
   Doubleheader. NDP211.
   Hallelujah Anyway. NDP219.
   In Quest of Candlelighters. NDP334.
   The Journal of Albion Moonlight. NDP99.
   Memoirs of a Shy Pornographer. NDP205.
   Selected Poems. NDP160.
   Sleepers Awake. NDP286.
   Wonderings. NDP320.
Octavio Paz, *Configurations.*† NDP303.
   Early Poems.† NDP354.
Plays for a New Theater. (Anth.) NDP216.
Ezra Pound, *ABC of Reading.* NDP89.
   Classic Noh Theatre of Japan. NDP79.
   The Confucian Odes. NDP81.
   Confucius. NDP285.
   Confucius to Cummings. (Anth.) NDP126.
   Guide to Kulchur. NDP257.
   Literary Essays. NDP250.
   Love Poems of Ancient Egypt. Gift Edition.
   NDP178.
   Pound/Joyce. NDP296.
   Selected Cantos. NDP304.
   Selected Letters 1907-1941. NDP317.
   Selected Poems. NDP66.
   The Spirit of Romance. NDP266.
   Translations.† (Enlarged Edition) NDP145.
Omar Pound, *Arabic and Persian Poems.*
   NDP305.
James Purdy, *Children Is All.* NDP327.
Raymond Queneau, *The Bark Tree.* NDP314.
   The Flight of Icarus. NDP358.
Carl Rakosi, *Amulet.* NDP234.
   Ere-Voice. NDP321.
M. Randall, *Part of the Solution.* NDP350.
John Crowe Ransom, *Beating the Bushes.*
   NDP324.
Raja Rao, *Kanthapura.* NDP224.
Herbert Read, *The Green Child.* NDP208.
P. Reverdy, *Selected Poems.*† NDP346.
Kenneth Rexroth, *Assays.* NDP113.
   An Autobiographical Novel. NDP281.
   Bird in the Bush. NDP80.
   Collected Longer Poems. NDP309.
   Collected Shorter Poems. NDP243.
   Love and the Turning Year. NDP308.
   100 Poems from the Chinese. NDP192.
   100 Poems from the Japanese.† NDP147.

Charles Reznikoff, *By the Waters of Manhattan.*
   NDP121.
   Testimony: The United States 1885-1890.
   NDP200.
Arthur Rimbaud, *Illuminations.*† NDP56.
   Season in Hell & Drunken Boat.† NDP97.
Saikaku Ihara, *The Life of an Amorous
   Woman.* NDP270.
St. John of the Cross, *Poems.*† NDP341.
Jean-Paul Sartre, *Baudelaire.* NDP233.
   Nausea. NDP82.
   The Wall (Intimacy). NDP272.
Delmore Schwartz, *Selected Poems.* NDP241.
Stevie Smith, *Selected Poems.* NDP159.
Gary Snyder, *The Back Country.* NDP249.
   Earth House Hold. NDP267.
   Regarding Wave. NDP306.
Gilbert Sorrentino, *Splendide-Hotel.* NDP364.
Enid Starkie, *Arthur Rimbaud.* NDP254.
Stendhal, *Lucien Leuwen.*
   Book II: *The Telegraph.* NDP108.
Jules Supervielle, *Selected Writings.*† NDP209.
W. Sutton, *American Free Verse.* NDP351.
Dylan Thomas, *Adventures in the Skin Trade.*
   NDP183.
   A Child's Christmas in Wales. Gift Edition.
   NDP181.
   Collected Poems 1934-1952. NDP316.
   The Doctor and the Devils. NDP297.
   Portrait of the Artist as a Young Dog.
   NDP51.
   Quite Early One Morning. NDP90.
   Under Milk Wood. NDP73.
Lionel Trilling, *E. M. Forster.* NDP189.
Martin Turnell, *Art of French Fiction.* NDP251.
   Baudelaire. NDP336.
Paul Valéry, *Selected Writings.*† NDP184.
Elio Vittorini, *Twilight of the Elephant.* NDP366.
   Women of Messina. NDP365.
Vernon Watkins, *Selected Poems.* NDP221.
Nathanael West, *Miss Lonelyhearts &
   Day of the Locust.* NDP125.
George F. Whicher, tr.,
   The Goliard Poets.† NDP206.
J. Willett, *Theatre of Bertolt Brecht.* NDP244.
J. Williams, *An Ear in Bartram's Tree.* NDP335.
Tennessee Williams, *Hard Candy.* NDP225.
   Camino Real. NDP301.
   Dragon Country. NDP287.
   The Glass Menagerie. NDP218.
   In the Winter of Cities. NDP154.
   One Arm & Other Stories. NDP237.
   Out Cry. NDP367.
   The Roman Spring of Mrs. Stone. NDP271.
   Small Craft Warnings. NDP348.
   27 Wagons Full of Cotton. NDP217.
William Carlos Williams,
   The William Carlos Williams Reader.
   NDP282.
   The Autobiography. NDP223.
   The Build-up. NDP259.
   The Farmers' Daughters. NDP106.
   Imaginations. NDP329.
   In the American Grain. NDP53.
   In the Money. NDP240.
   Many Loves. NDP191.
   Paterson. Complete. NDP152.
   Pictures from Brueghel. NDP118.
   The Selected Essays. NDP273.
   Selected Poems. NDP131.
   A Voyage to Pagany. NDP307.
   White Mule. NDP226.
Yvor Winters,
   Edwin Arlington Robinson. NDP326.

Complete descriptive catalog available free on request from
New Directions, 333 Sixth Avenue, New York 10014.   † Bilingual.